THE ROAD NARROWS AS YOU GO

THE ROAD
NARROWS
AS YOU GO

LEE HENDERSON

HAMISH HAMILTON
an imprint of Penguin Canada Books Inc., a Penguin Random House Company

Published by the Penguin Group
Penguin Canada Books Inc., 90 Eglinton Avenue East, Suite 700, Toronto, Ontario, Canada M4P 2Y3

Penguin Group (USA) LLC, 375 Hudson Street, New York, New York 10014, U.S.A.
Penguin Books Ltd, 80 Strand, London WC2R 0RL, England
Penguin Ireland, 25 St Stephen's Green, Dublin 2, Ireland (a division of Penguin Books Ltd)
Penguin Group (Australia), 707 Collins Street, Melbourne, Victoria 3008, Australia
(a division of Pearson Australia Group Pty Ltd)
Penguin Books India Pvt Ltd, 11 Community Centre, Panchsheel Park, New Delhi – 110 017, India
Penguin Group (NZ), 67 Apollo Drive, Rosedale, Auckland 0632, New Zealand
(a division of Pearson New Zealand Ltd)
Penguin Books (South Africa) (Pty) Ltd, 24 Sturdee Avenue, Rosebank, Johannesburg 2196, South Africa

Penguin Books Ltd, Registered Offices: 80 Strand, London WC2R 0RL, England

First published 2014

1 2 3 4 5 6 7 8 9 10 (RRD)

LIBRARY AND ARCHIVES CANADA CATALOGUING IN PUBLICATION

Henderson, Lee, 1974-, author
The road narrows as you go / Lee Henderson.

ISBN 978-0-670-06989-7 (bound)

I. Title.

PS8565.E56165R63 2014   C813'.6   C2014-904056-3

eBook ISBN 978-0-14-319306-7

Visit the Penguin Canada website at **www.penguin.ca**

Special and corporate bulk purchase rates available; please see
www.penguin.ca/corporatesales or call 1-800-810-3104.

FOR ANU

I don't think God wants to be worshipped.
I think the only pure worship of God is by loving one another,
and I think all other forms of worship become a substitute
for the love that we should show one another.
—Charles Schulz

Hell is an idea first born on an undigested apple-dumpling.
—Herman Melville

THE ROAD NARROWS AS YOU GO

1

1

What we remember most about living in the manor on the peak of Bernal Heights was the door buzzer going off in the days and nights after comic strip artist Hick Elmdales died. For years afterwards every time we heard that buzzer, the memory echoed in our ears and reminded us of the strange connection Hick's death had to the first days of our new life. You know that sound you hear before you fall asleep, of blood whistling past your eardrum? It was the last Friday in April eighty-one, and it was our first night at No Manors.

You might not know the name Hick Elmdales, but he drew the popular *Pan* strip launched back in seventy-five to further the adventures of J.M. Barrie's characters Peter, the Lost Boys, Hook, the Darling children, signed *Walt Disney*. Hick lived and worked far, far away from the animation sweatshops in Los Angeles; he was up on top of a great hill overlooking all of San Francisco in a packratted five-bedroom on the main floor of a post-Edwardian dubbed No Manors. He ripped his motto and creed from the pages of the Old Testament and painted it on the wall over the front door as a constant reminder: *Be not forgetful to welcome strangers, for in this way some have entertained angels unawares.*

Or devils. You never know. Hick's open door drew no shortage of either—in the form of drifters, downtrodden artists, jawclenching junkies, and many an adolescent runaway doodler like us without a stable home to go back to or clear prospects.

Of all the punk squats, hippie communes, and satanic covens in the Bay Area, we ended up here, at No Manors. Perched at the peak of Stoneman Street, No Manors was the highest in altitude of all the freestanding residencies on the north side of Bernal Heights, a five-storey art deco flophouse with accidental touches of Bosch and Gaudi sprouting from an Edwardian mansion built out of the original Victorian pioneer villa circa the Gold Rush. Before the hill gave way to a steep grass park and a forest of Jack Fogg trees around the microwave tower at the peak, the manor was a rather noticeable blemish or piece of history in the working-class neighbourhood. Built as an Edwardian villa in the early nineteen hundreds and renovated in the late forties to the idea of art deco, the manor might have been the pride of the area. Now the whole exterior had been so neglected by the absentee landlord and so dicked with by tenants over the years looking for solutions to the aging edifice's damages that even a simple thing like the front entrance was nowhere to be found.

Two paid rent at No Manors, both comic strip artists. One was dead, and the other was not home. No one knew where to find Wendy Ashbubble. The name wasn't familiar to us, and neither was her comic strip, *Strays*, but this is her story.

According to friends at The Farm, Wendy never picked up her complimentary ticket.

Where is she? asked a bearded six-foot man dressed in a fishscale-sequin halter top, tight black leather short shorts, and, way down at the bottom of her long, black legs, a pair of espadrille wedges with three-inch woven wool heels. Her alias was Biz Aziz and she was a well-known drag queen who performed regularly in the Castro and Chinatown and had been on the bill the night before at The Farm singing Toni Fisher's *The Big Hurt* and *The End of the World* by Skeeter Davis. As she stood up from a beanbag chair, she fanned herself with the palm of her hand and told us to put on a fresh pot of coffee.

We happened to land at No Manors the night Hick died because we went to this all-ages show. The stage was inside an actual barn, the barn part of a hobby farm with vegetables, flowers, and a petting zoo, all situated on stolen land that sat vacant for decades next to the Cesar Chavez freeway, and it seemed everyone in the barn that night knew Hick, so when the sad news got around during a break, the whole audience and all the performers shut down and the musicians got off the stage and continued to play their instruments as we, the whole audience and the performers, walked up Bernal Hill together. No Manors sat at the dead end of Stoneman Street, right before the park on the peak.

Biz spied out the window to see who buzzed the door, then, despite some obvious doubts this time, pressed a button to let whomever it was come on in. As per those fateful letters above the door.

Quick, hide that Ziploc, I can't peg these ones, might be narco, she said and pointed to the open bag of potent marijuana hanging out on the longtable between us, a pound less a few dozen joints.

Best we could think of on short notice was under a pile of dirty clothes at the bottom of the laundry hamper in Hick's bedroom.

In came four brushcutted men who could have been brothers, with blotchy natural tans that gave their white flesh the complexion of fried perogies—they had big ingratiating smiles full of nacre teeth, middling to no chins, and short necks. Each man was squeezed into a golf shirt he had tucked neatly under a matching lint-free V-neck sweater in an offputting colour, pea soup, bisque, sulphur, puce. Pleated khaki slacks like long, brown paper grocery bags. They entered a room full of half-slumbering cartoonists in mourning who had spent the night drunk, stoned, and grieving now using each other as pillows and taking up every available bit of space.

We represent the Walt Disney company. Disney himself asked us to come on his behalf. The four strangers each passed Biz Aziz their business cards, all with the familiar embossed Cinderella castle.

How do you do?

The men brought condolences and agreed with one another that, yes, yes, yes, and yes, there was no possible explanation for Hick's untimely death except in the Lord and to that Biz Aziz almost laughed.

Là-bas I hope you mean. So what cartoons you worked on? she asked the four representatives.

No, no, we don't do fun stuff like draw cartoons, said the heaviest-set one, whose eyes barely lifted above a squint.

How'd you meet Hick?

We never. Read his strip, though, funny and smart. We wondered if you might show us where he used to draw?

From the entrance hall you could access three of the five bedrooms and the living room, which connected to a dining room, a false study, and a kitchen with a nook, and to get from here to there you had to navigate an abundance of Victorian nooks and crannies, trick doors that led to weird void rooms, and this wall or that wall might have received a facelift or two over the years to cover up the ghosts. The walls were papered, every inch covered over by bookcases overflowing and framed drawings and paintings, original Herrimans, a personalized Gould. A hoard of cheap comics now valued in the millions, rare art folios from the turn of the century, decadent novels and poetry, histories of the occult, a favourite subject—Hick's bookmark was stuck halfway through the bestselling memoir *Michelle Remembers* when he fell sick. Maybe the book killed him. That was Biz's theory. The men from Disney danced over hundreds of shoes and weaved around stacks of leather portfolios lining the floor, while above their heads loomed dozens of bicycles that hung from the ceiling, you could grab one down any time. Sculptures hung up there, too, and found objects cluttered the windowsills. Elsewhere on the floor was, for example, a lacquered and stuffed tortoise the size of a witch's cauldron.

Ah, so it *does* exist, said one Disney man to another, his palm out. You owe me five bucks.

Running the full length of the manor was the reason for their bet: the longtable, a forty-two-foot long drawing table juryrigged from scrap wood that started in the breakfast nook in the kitchen and ended at the bay window in Hick's master bedroom. Fifty cartoonists could pack the longtable with room to spare. All kinds of drawing supplies and tools cluttered the surface. The hardwood floor underneath was scuffed bone-white and stained with ink splatter. If you had to get around to the other side of it there were hinged pieces at intervals that lifted.

Here's where he sat. Biz brought Disney's men towards the window. In that canewood chair, overlooking the whole city. Damn what a view. You can't see anything now for the fog but just imagine. And behold all his drawings, shelf after shelf of portfolio stuffed to the max. What you see is what you get. That blue exercise mat was his only bed. Poor pitiable saint. Never barely went out. Everybody came to him. I loved him like a diamond engagement ring. I guess you know Hick was just about to start work on a Christmas special when he died? There's storyboards lying around to gaze at and wonder.

We'd like to see *those*, said Disney's men, sniffing around.

We eyed that laundry hamper and its telltale reek.

Hick told me his Christmas special was going to be bigger than *acid*—going to put Peter Pan up there with Santa and Jesus, Biz Aziz told them angrily as if she was lashing out at these strangers for somehow causing the death of her friend, as if somehow Disney caused his death.—He even bought a stop-motion camera rig. He was going to get *us*, everyone at the longtable to help him. Instead of you all at Disney's studio mucking … —Hick was going to make his Christmas special *right here* at home. Well, here's *his* spot. He always got this chair by the window because check it out, this is also his bedroom. It's too foggy to see right now but you can imagine the view. Like some coffee?

Disney's men said they would. As they riffled through the sheaves of paper, Biz went to the kitchen. Busying themselves as such in Hick's bedroom, no one paid too close attention to Disney's men, for it had been a long and solemn night of boozing and everyone was at rest. It was only eight or nine in the morning.

At some point in their digging around one of the men came out holding a stack of Crowley and *Creepy* comics he seemed highly suspicious of and asked us whose collection of the devil's work was *this*. We decided on a lark to claim the offending books were ours, ha! He dropped the whole stack that instant. If they weren't Hick's, he was not required to touch them, he explained. Shouldn't read stuff like this, he told us, rots your brain, turns you into a puppet, that's all these words are doing to ya. Do you want to be the devil's puppets, is that it?

Something like that, we said.

Thanks for the coffee, Disney's men said an hour later as they came out of the master bedroom after packing the contents of Hick's life and livelihood into wood boxes, cardboard boxes, and plastic crates. Don't worry about us. We have a dolly in the van …

Say now where you going with all of Hick's stuff? Biz got up once more from her chair at the longtable where she'd been drawing, and with a joint smoking in her hand, she went over and blocked the men from getting out the door. Put that shit down right now. You can't take that. What are you, thieves? Come in here out of trust and goodwill, man's not even in the ground …

At that moment, the other roommate walked in. Wendy Ashbubble at last.

Excuse me, pardon me, she said shyly, trying to budge past. Biz, you're in my way.

Wendy Ashbubble, you are home so late it is morning, said Biz. Guess what you just stepped into. A full-on *tragedy*.

Wendy's blouse was on inside out—how could she not notice? Her hair was a flustered mess she tried to contain within a headband on top of her pale, peanut-shaped head with those big adorably squirrellike cheeks and twinkling sarcastic eyes. We fell in love with her that instant, all four of us. Was it that she stood with a rolled shoulder slouch as if about to go straight into drawing, or that instead of using a finger to lift up her comically big eyeglasses when they slid down her nose she twitched like one of the rodents she drew? We fell for her, seeing her look so frazzled and dissociated from our scene, glossy and pale from lack of sleep, lost in her own experience. That totally goggle-eyed look on her face was that of a girl badly in need of some privacy but who knew she was not going to get it.

I need to shower— Hey, what's— Why are all these … Oh my god, look at all these *cartoonists* … is that … Chester Gould? she whispered.

You got to listen to me, carefully, okay, Wendy? Listen. These are Disney's men, okay? *Walt* Disney. The hospital called. Hick, he *died* yesterday. Hick is dead.

Dead? No. What? No. No. Not possible. Wendy turned a shade of green. Oh no. She fell to her knees, then all the muscles in her face spasmed and her neck and face broke out in shiny hives. I saw him yesterday. No,

9

this can't be. I'm not prepared. *That's* why you're all here. I didn't know. I was out. I was with my editor, I was with— Oh.

It looked for a moment as though Wendy was about to vomit, so Disney's men sensed an opportunity to budge their way past her kneeling in the doorway. We're just doing the job that Mr. Disney asked of us.

Put those boxes down, Wendy said. Her colour returned. That sparkle in her eye. Let me give you my perspective. Look, just *look* at how many guests are here and not one of them would dare remove a single dirty sock from this premises without Hick's personal permission, that's how much he was loved, as you can see. People come here to give, not take. Here you submit, you don't abscond. The only stealing going on around here is of ideas, said Wendy.

Isn't that right, said Biz.

These boxes are filled with property of Disney, said one of the men. It's in his contract.

Are you in his contract, too? Wendy said and scratched a hive. How are we supposed to trust you? You could be faking the whole spiel.

You stand away from his work, sweethearts, Biz Aziz told them with a fist held out. Or I'll fuckin' *lay you out cold*, believe me.

Understand how very hard this is for us personally, said the slimmest of Disney's men, with the biggest head, though, like a breadloaf. We are just crushed to bits by this news. Disney owns *Pan*. And so you know, Disney can get pretty darn ugly legally when it comes to stuff like his property.

Biz then bent over, grabbed up and overhanded a sharp bangle of costume jewellery and hit one of Disney's men upside the eyebrow. Deep enough to draw blood. Come back with a lawyer, judge, and jury next time, you squares, she barked.

Disney's men had had enough. Biz ducked and dodged their fists, whooping and roundhousing in return. Wendy took a bop to the nose. We joined in with at least two dozen local cartoonists to overwhelm Disney's men and force them to let go of the boxes in their hands. The melee lasted all of ten seconds. Wendy, screaming Graverobber! Graverobber!, was in a tug-of-war over a portfolio with one of the men from Disney. Suddenly her grip gave out, she fell hard on her ass, and Disney's man ran out the door with the portfolio.

The other three men saw their chance and grabbed whatever they could while a hundred or more cartoonists chased them down the block to their white Cinderella van, but not fast enough to stop them. Disney's men sped off down the hill as we threw kitchen utensils and curses.

As soon as Hick pressed ink to paper—in fact whatever he touched on duty—that was Disney's property. This seemed strange to us, that someone so well off could be in our situation, i.e., own nothing.

Wendy said, I need to call the hospital and we need to collect him. His body. We need a wicker basket. A big wicker basket.

Where were you all night? Biz asked her.

I'll tell you the story, she said and stared at us. Who are these ones?

We introduced ourselves thus:

Twyla Noon. Twenty-one years old. Insomniac lapsed Catholic with a fast hand, fast memory. Oreo eater. Boy chaser. Photogenic from the left side. Rather lissome for someone with such a runny nose. Previous experience: obsession with Ivan Bilibin and Kay Nielsen, high school expulsion, Freudian doodles, a dream diary maintained since age nine.

Mark Bread. Smoker's cough. Twenty years. Incomprehensible mutterer of Looney Tunes phrases or psychologically adept poet of the nonce. Hotdog aficionado. Habitual *Psilocybe* ingestor. Drawing from that place in the mind occupied by more epithets and rabble than morality. Previous experience: house painting, caricatures of teachers, high school expulsion.

Patrick Poedouce. Sexual caterer. People pleaser. Single-minded about many things at the expense of a lot more. Jealous of everyone. Borrower who did not return or repay. Annually twenty-two years old. Snappy dresser (pinched). Bridge burner (exes *and* friends). Boston-born (Florence, AZ, juvie-raised). Previous experience: a stack of letters full of advice from Bill Blackbeard, a huge collection of his own juvenilia, correspondence art school dropout, total certainty in his own greatness.

Rachael Wertmüller. Aka Aluminum Uvula. Orphan. Twenty-four. Self-loathing as lifestyle, the grotesque expression on a beautiful face. Born in Salem, Washington, where there's still an old bylaw in effect that says you can't have sex within city limits. Previous experience: sonic assailant and audio experimenter, doodler, collagist turned airbrush painter turned silkscreen genius, high school expulsion.

2

Say goodbye to the cartoonist.

No, I won't, I won't let you go, she told him. After Disney's men left the manor with their arms full of Hick's drawings and his possessions, Wendy Ashbubble broke down and confided in us where she'd been. She talked as if it didn't matter who was there, Biz or any other friend who would listen as she recounted her last visit with Hick, and how she reached over the chrome rail of the hospital bed and held his hand, the hand with a pen and untouched pad of paper beneath it, the hand with the two red welts. His face, his whole body was ravaged by more of them, as if someone had cruelly stubbed out lit cigarettes on his skin.

Did you bring me a treat? Hick Elmdales asked under his breath because he didn't want to alert his ward mates.

She pulled a sandwich from her shoulder bag, wrapped in wax paper and tied with a string, and slipped it to him. Between the slices of his favourite white bread were two Caramilk chocolate bars side by side.

I brought more strips if you ... Wendy motioned for her bag that had his portfolio of daily and Sunday colour *Pan* comics sticking out of it, ones he'd saved over the years drawing the strip. He used to call them his retirement fund. Now they covered bills.

Leave them, Hick said. I got a new medical care plan.

How so?

Urk … Feels like a leopard's sitting on my chest feasting on my intestines, he told her as he ate the candybar sandwich. Like enough's enough. He didn't know how much more of this *being sick* he could take. In frustration he started to wheeze and cough and when his fit was over she watched him take another deep bite out of the chocolate sandwich, lean back in his bed, convulse in a rush of sugar ecstasy. He said the night nurses morphined him so heavily, he could *see* his pain. Pain was a man the size of a cow made entirely of barbed wire who used you as his bedsheet. Pain was a starved leopard. Hick knew goodbye when he saw it, and he needed to tell her something.

You're not going anywhere, Hick. You're right here.

No, I'm not.

In an unprepossessing room in ward 5D at San Francisco General Hospital, writer and cartoonist Hick Elmdales lay surrounded by portable equipment, pulse-emitting heart monitors, liver, kidney, and oxygen monitors gasping with mechanical regularity, daytime soap operas transmitted wavily through a three-channel television bolted to the wall, and the kind of central ventilation in the ceiling that comes to life in noisy cycles that begin to resemble the faint call of an air-raid siren. And all while bags of clear fluid dripped into his arm from a reticulated IV line on wheels, and the same or different fluids into the arms of two other men—an arthritic flight attendant dehydrated by Marlow syndrome and a rundown screenwriter suffering through radiation treatment—three men who until this summer had nothing much in common with one another now shared a long list of woes that included sudden onsets of shigellosis and amoebiasis, severe hepatitis A and B, the frequent flyer, the unionized screenwriter, and Disney's cartoonist each saw sudden flareups of syphilis, herpes, gonorrhea, and climatic bubo that all needed massive penicillin injections, and somehow, all three men had also contracted an impossibly foreign form of skin cancer never before seen bar not on old Mediterranean men.

Still, Hick Elmdales was not the worst off in 5D. That sadly happened to be the irradiated seventy-eight-pound screenwriter who went into a coma for an hour one day and woke up complaining of apocolocyntosis. But the cartoonist was the most recent to occupy a bed in this *room of exceptional cases* (Dr. Dritz's words), and at twenty-seven also the youngest of the three. Pale and oily curls of hair lay on his shoulders and lap, showing off the threadwork of blue and red veins that pressed up from under bare patches on his scalp, his grey-green eyes wept yellow-green mucus, his swollen nose was a florid throbbing red from a runny cold, his lips were cracked and bleeding from bruised cold sores, he trembled under his layers of blankets with a fever and flu he could not shake, the reason his voice sounded so raw. Couldn't keep a thing down last night, not that this hospital's kitchen made it easy. Thanks for candybars. Hick had lost so much weight in two weeks it made Wendy wonder what the screenwriter or the flight attendant had looked like a month ago. The Hick Wendy knew was a big bouncing fleshpot of a boy, she called him a snack-loving self-entertaining redhead. He had inkstained fingertips and a big heart, and this bedridden shrunken-down version too weak to get out of bed was an ominous image of what could be and what would never be. She saw a pale poetic child simultaneously a very old man.

Thing was, Hick was overdramatic at least once a week putting together a batch of newly inked strips to send to his syndicate. Stress made him apocalyptic. She would watch him leap out of his chair, knocking supplies astray, and run from his ongoing pages spread out on the longtable and pull at his hair and come up face to face with someone and beg, *Put me out of my misery* or *cremate me. Throw me to the curb, throw me off a cliff, throw me to the hounds!* He would send pencils and pens all over. *I don't quit, I die* was something Hick said in these moments. He was prone to pent-up purple fits, it's how he survived. Smashing his own furniture. Throwing small bills out the window. Other cartoonists thought his antics were pretty funny—after all, they were the guests and this was Hick, the leaseholder. But maybe all this time he was just hypoglycemic. He would open the fridge and see no carton of chocolate milk and collapse in a heap on the kitchen floor wailing, *I can't go on!*

If Jonjay isn't back in time he can be damned to eternal shame for not saying goodbye to me, Hick told her. He's like my man-muse. He should be here. I need bolstering. Where *is* he?

Instinct. It's forcing your friend to stay away so you won't let yourself go.

Palaver. Jonjay never shows up on time for anything, Hick said. Jonjay would show up late for his *own* funeral. How is it possible to be so selfish and so generous? I don't get it. I can't hate him for neglecting me. He's my best friend.

What about me?

You're my next of kin.

Oh. The person Hick admired most was his friend Jonjay. Wendy couldn't blame him. Hick said that sometimes when he lay here with nothing else to do but regret his choice of friendships he wished he'd kept in better touch with one or two of his foster parents, but no, not really. It didn't matter, by the way. Walt Disney had come to visit him in the hospital just the day before.

Yes, Disney. Wendy missed him by about an hour. Even though Disney was a notorious hypochondriac with a deep-seated aversion to hospitals and sick people, he flew up on a Thursday just to see Hick, whom he called his *dear boy* and his *beloved representative in the daily newspapers.* That fixed look of paternal pain on Disney when he crouched through the door of 5D looking for the right bed embarrassed Hick to the core. To see the frozen, almost *showbiz* idea of pity on the great man's sunshiny face, and then to watch that expression transform into something appalled the moment he got a good look at his cartoonist. That look was far worse than pity, these sudden, abominable misgivings, Hick could practically see the regret at having made the journey. That's how Hick knew things were bad for him. The look on Disney's face.

Disney declined the chair set out for guests. He didn't remove the ill-fitting windbreaker that must've been borrowed—nor did he take off his kid gloves. In fact Hick realized Disney never touched a thing in 5D the whole time he was there, fifteen minutes tops. As the minutes passed and conversation between them faltered, Disney started to study the other sickbeds, his face shrivelled into this ugly mask of hard judgment and contempt. At one point he promised Hick emphatically that he would cover all hospital costs, and Hick wondered if a nurse or doctor had tipped Disney off that he was trading original *Pan* strips for certain medical services. Walt Disney's eyes circled the room as if to include the other sick men in his dialogue when he asked Hick if he believed in God and if Jesus was in his heart, and Hick knew what Disney was implying: Was he like the flight attendant and the screenwriter, the same kind of San Francisco lost boy? Hick was in no mood. He did not want to lie to Walt Disney. He did not want to tell Disney he loved the occult, the collision of the fairy tale and the superstitious, secret cults, the black arts, Colin Wilson and Kenneth Anger, Aleister Crowley and Yeats, read as many horror comics as family fare. That's not what Disney wanted to hear. He told Disney, Oh, I love the Bible. I read the whole book twice.

As he was about to leave, Disney turned again for one last offended look at 5D. He said, How sad, how sad, how sad, sad, sad. Sad, sad, sad.

That is the kind of sickbed story you'll laugh about as soon as you're home, Wendy told him.

I guess I do love Disney. He said to me, *You won't be forgotten.*
Wendy stifled.

Ah, hell. I never cared about this sort of stuff before. I mean, my legacy, that's supposed to be … later. Cut short it's not the same, it's intensified, that feeling of wanting one. I love stamping my strips 'Walt Disney.' Proud to. But lying here for hours and hours like I could be drawing but I'm too exhausted to and so instead I look at the holes in the ceiling boards wondering why *didn't* I do my own thing, like *you*, you know?

You still can if you want to, said Wendy. You can do anything.

Hick took a long time to catch his breath.

I thought I had forever to, he said finally. Actually life is a fragment of a fragment. And I got less than that to work with. For my life I was given a fleck off a fragment's fragment. Everything is behind me now except the vanishing point.

Don't say that. Wendy insisted he had lots left to go on his fragment, and so far he was doing better than most people his age with the *fleck of time* he'd used up. Twenty-seven, a leaseholder, renowned in his anonymity, Hick had a syndicated strip revered by his readers, beloved among his colleagues—*Pan* sets the bar unreasonably high for art and story on the funny pages (Hart), an immense talent (Schulz), a monument against the mediocre (Breathed), an ego-destroyer (Caniff), a bodhisattva of comics (Trudeau), famous as much for the forty-two-foot-long drawing table as his open door (Gould).

Don't worry about comics, Wendy said. Right now focus mind on healing body. Forget about daily gags and adventure sequences and to Disney or to not Disney.

Wendy, don't waste a breath. Look at me. Go bigger than the biggest? I failed at that. I was too modest when I should have been greedy. You deserve big disgustingly wonderful things, Wendy. You're my favourite of all the feminine persuasion.

You're my one and only fan, man.

Almost true. Wendy's syndicated comic strip, *Strays*, was less than a year old, first appearing in a couple of suburban Bay Area dailies around the time of Ronald Reagan's nomination for presidential candidate. Set in a dumpy innercity vacant lot populated by lost pets and vermin: a cat, a dog, a rabbit, a snake, a parrot, and a raccoon single mother who meet around a flat tire for drinks, eat trash, play Ping-Pong, and try to scam each other, *Strays* was in fewer than fifty papers and none outside California. A few good laughs (Aziz), another example of funny-pages mediocrity (said Crumb on a popover), you're going to be huge (her syndicate editor, Gabrielle Scavalda). Compared to *Pan's* twenty-two hundred and twenty subscriptions, the longevity of *Strays* remained uncertain (Ashbubble).

I'm serious, Hick said. His voice was down to a wretched croak, wheezing between words. Your fragment of a fragment. What else are you doing today? Work? Are you drawing? Don't blow the afternoon and go see some dumb matinee. Do something productive.

She told Hick she did some drawing this morning, nothing so funny as this week's dumb matinee. After she left here she had a meeting up at Caffe Trieste with Gabrielle *Gabby* Scavalda, in town for a couple of nights from Manhattan.

Hick's cough lasted a minute. Then he said, That sounds good. A meeting about your comic?

I don't know. Maybe just social. Gabby's family still lives in the Bay, I guess.

Your comic strip, is that what you want to do?

Yeah, for sure, I guess that's it, like, obviously of course my strip's all I want to do, not this other stuff. Freelance beer ads and pizza coupons and cereal boxes, show posters for punks, gee whiz, it's all so disorganized and I guess you're right, it adds up to nothing much. Punk playbills pay my bills, though. I have a comp for the show at The Farm tonight but I really don't want to see people.

You should. Go. People are fun. I miss The Farm and that funny donkey covered in freeway exhaust.

Naw.

Why not? Isn't that why you ran away from Canada and became

Wendy? So you could meet interesting people and *live* and suck up the toxic American fury for the good life no matter the cost?

You named me Wendy.

That's because you *are* Wendy. You're from a different world from the rest of us, more sedate, more mature. You leap the gap. Comics are kids stuff, all about getting rich off doodles. That *is* the goal. Buster Brown, Popeye, Garfield. Same thing. Bills? See my hospital bills? Seriously, it's like—it's like—aha-*aha*! Hick was gasping for air, had to stop short, and after a few unrecuperative breaths, shut his eyes.

She tried to rouse him. You forget you're this freaky prodigy natural DNA talent like an Einstein in the funny pages or something and, unlike your Disney strip, well, you forget my *Strays* appears in like not a single paper you or I ever heard of, farm gazettes and freebie advertisers the such, goshers, these subscriptions, not exactly boding well for *my* chance at free rein. For all I know Gabby is about to shitcan me today. I'm not as good as you, Hick, I'm not half you, I'm clumsy, my hand is, my eye is, my mind is.

A wake, he said abruptly. I'm serious. I want a wake. Promise me, he croaked. Make sure everyone with a connection to No Manors gets invited. For my sake, so I can say goodbye to my friends. Not the usual sobbing routine at a rainy graveside. Not that. When I die, he said, I want laughs. Jokes, pranks, magic tricks, and cheap gags, lots of drawing games at the longtable, okay? Make sure people remember me on some high.

Wendy wasn't sure what to say. A wake was something organized after *a death.*

Cover me if you must, I don't care, just let me come home one more time. Lay out a bleak black blanket on the table, must be something black, at the place where I always draw. Some candles for ambiance. Make sure all the curtains are closed before my body arrives. No mahogany coffin. Put me in a big wicker basket on the table there where I always draw. Light the candles. I want one last party at the manor.

3

STRAYS

Wendy had to zoom straight up the 101 from visiting Hick Elmdales's bedside in 5D to the North Beach for coffee with her editor. Gabrielle was a thirty-something intellectual of independent means with an imposing forehead, a succession of husbands, therapists, and jobs, no grey hairs in her blond. Wendy checked her face in the rearview, then flicked open the ashtray—she bought her car used off a teenager in Presidio Heights for a thousand dollars in cash—and smoked the last half of a joint as she started out of the parkade. She could barely focus on the road, kept thinking back to Hick laid out in bed. Cursing as she whiplashed down Van Ness, damning to hell all the red lights to Broadway, all the other drivers were *stupid incompetent ignorant ogres* and *blind*. Trolley cars slowed her go up Columbus where for a dollar she bought a ticket to park in a valet garage.

That's it, she decided, after that teeth-grinding drive, she couldn't waste her time on a comic that wasn't working, no matter what Hick said. She couldn't stand the humiliation. It wasn't in her or whatnot. In her mind there was always Jonjay's counter-life to Hick's ambitions. She was just as attracted to that other kind of artist who thrived on failure and anonymity and for whom no amount of success was better than no success at all. There was grace in self-abnegation. She could sense that's what Gabby was here to tell her anyway, that *Strays* was a total bust. She tried and tried. Hearing Hick tell her she should keep trying just reminded her how far away she was from what *he* achieved daily. Hick didn't need to keep trying, he simply was. She was not. She was not good enough. She wasn't awful, but she *was* worse than mediocre. This meeting with Gabby was fortuitous, for now was the time to sever ties with the syndicate and figure out what to do with her life. Maybe move back to Canada—she actually considered that, the traffic was so bad.

Nevertheless, Wendy and her syndicate editor embraced and said how good it was to see each other again; so it was; then Wendy lined up at the counter to order a double espresso from the flirtatious barista and came back and sat down next to Gabby at a table next to the window.

Gabrielle Scavalda said she loved people-watching, why she chose the window seat. This is one of the best corners in town for people-watching, Gabby believed. Gabrielle was the kind of emotive charismatic person you can't take your eyes off, so that as she stared at the people passing by, the people passing by stared back at her. Big round wet eyes and full cheeks and a thick coat of lipstick as glossy and fresh as red ink. Gabby dressed the part of an artist, including multicoloured glasses frames and a funky scarf, although she would be the first to admit it had been a long time, in fact not since college, that she had touched a canvas or a mound of clay. Long cream-brown hair grown out so she could pin all those curling-iron curls above her ears, then mid-conversation, let them fall loose, twist in her hands, coiling and uncoiling as she talked, then throw the whole length over one shoulder so the curls covered her full chest made fuller by an expensive bra, finally bundling all that hair back up again into a ball on top of her head. Third marriage failed on a vacation a year ago, the divorce was not finalized. It was her captivating, melancholy, and wise, freckled and shiny quality that got her hired wherever she applied. Chauvinism aside, aerobic weight-loss regimens aside, Gabby amused men, she was sure, and it made her livid. She wanted this editorship at Shepherd Media Syndicate to last, she didn't want to leave the way she'd left the *San Francisco Chronicle*, or get phased out like the time at Third Word advertising on Madison Avenue, to name a couple. This job was a fresh start for Gabby, an autonomy she dreamed of, office with a door, an imported car, modern wardrobe.

I'm overdressed, Gabby said out of the blue. She cringed when anyone rich walked in, for she'd forgotten to switch up—her purse conspicuously matched her black-on-white Chanel knockoff department store pantsuit. Fashion in San Francisco's on another planet from Manhattan, she missed it out here, how free the North Beach still was with colours, even here in the centre of intellectual upper class, clashing still mattered. That's special, that is not New York, she said. She missed facing the Pacific, she really did. Waking up three hours after Manhattan was a luxury. Manhattan's hard. The rich tried better to blend in here and the poor all purported to be artists, homosexuals ran the city, and the hobos were considered saints. Original hippies. Original beatniks. That was not actually Ginsberg who just walked by, was it? Every face that passed the window contained in a flash a whole novel Gabby could envision writing. It was a story about the struggle to climb out of the sand and be a great American. What was it that made San Francisco such an inspiration? Gabby loved it for the pastel houses stacked up on the steepest hills, the brisk ocean air bringing fog moods, the gonzo music and art legacy, this unusually high spread of nonconformists among the common hamburger-eaters. So many cartoonists!

Twelve hundred and fifty cartoonists according to the phone numbers on my kitchen wall, Wendy said.

Gabby loved this cool and casual peninsular city without any underground network of tunnels. And sitting with *her artist* in the Trieste, shopping at City Lights and just circulating through the heart of San Francisco, staying at her favourite downtown hotel, it made her want to *make art more often.*

At last she asked Wendy how she was doing, After all, that's why I'm in town. Life? Boyfriend or not? How's Hick? You look gorge, by the way, your hair is insane, it's *iconic.* And what is that you're wearing, a blouse top and a man's blazer over it, tight black denim pants, riding boots? All those accessories for your hair, wrist, ankles? You're a self-made trend, you are San Francisco incarnate.

No reason to make a big display of disagreeing with Gabby then having to tell the editor of her comic strip how far away in her mind she was from this meeting and that on a deep, totally nauseating level, she felt like absolute shit. The first sips of the espresso hit her sideways, the right half of her abdomen folded in on itself as involuntary clenching of her colon released a thankfully odourless gas bubble. She was still shaken from seeing Hick; his face was often grossly superimposed over Gabby's. Making an effort to appear present was a task—she asked what brought Gabby to San Francisco this time, a family occasion or what?

I'm here for *you,* you, Wendy, my god. No, I didn't even tell my parents I'm in town. This is business, dear, okay? She stiffened up her posture. Where to start? Okay, first off, Wendy, I want to ask you a question, and no matter what, I need you to answer honestly. It's just that sometimes your comic strip arrives late, the syndicate gets on me, or the panels are crooked and the newspapers complain to me, I know you always have a good excuse but—but after a while I start to wonder if maybe you're maybe—distracted. I mean, you look distracted *right now*.

I am.

Because it's important I know how committed you are to *Strays*.

Is that the question?

That's the question.

The answer is no, I don't know, said Wendy and twitched her glasses up her nose.

Gabby whistled a note through her lips and brushed away a figment that was not on her blazer.

A funny thing, Wendy said without smiling, I was thinking about this exact question on the drive here. I was thinking how afraid I get about my fragment of a fragment—of time, I mean, on this planet, and if I don't put my life to some good use then—then what?

Obviously you're young, Wendy, so you don't realize this is an opportunity of a lifetime to have a syndicated strip.

I do.

Then what's the problem.

Not good enough.

Commitment is the secret. It's the key to freedom and to talent. Don't confuse this with a prison sentence or a limiting of your horizons.

No, it's my talentless existence that's limiting. I am the flake you just called me, I'm late, my crooked lines are a shame, I blame bad fingers, weird eyeballs, odd sense of humour, inconsistent, unfunny jokes. It's so true. Everything you tell me is true. I'm not at the level of unpunishable mediocrity, I make a hack laugh. I came here all set in my head to quit. My friend Hick, he's—

Oh, don't compare yourself to Hick. You should move out of that place. He's a bad influence, he's so outrageously talented. He's preternatural. He's from the mysterious deep where stars and galaxies are made. Some talent is so pure and whole it exists outside the realms of time. That's Hick. He's a fable. Your talent exists in the tumultuous now and you will be defined by the changes your genius undergoes.

Right, okay, thanks, but—

I'm serious. You're great. Why do you think I snatched you up? You deserve this. Listen. Do you have plans for dinner tonight? Gabby tossed back the dregs of her espresso and excitedly chewed the grinds. Are you free?

No, I mean, rice and ... on the side with a fishsteak (she lied) and then I've got a comp to see Thee Hangnails and Biz Aziz live at The Farm, maybe I'll go ... I designed the poster.

Heard of junk bonds? Gabby tried.

Wendy hesitated only out of politeness before saying no.

That's okay, said Gabby. You know Frank Fleecen, right? No? Really no? Uh, tall, stony stare, toupée, rug, hairpiece, no? Rings no bell?

What toupée are you talking about? Junk what? Who is this?

Strange he made no impression on you. Well, Frank says he knows *you.* Works for this century-old investment bank based back in Manhattan called Hexen Diamond Mistral, but he practically runs the place from here in the Bay. Put it this way—he's a businessman's businessman. Face on the front page of the business section and financial magazine covers? I don't suppose you read the papers you're in, do you? Or any for that matter? Headlines?

Wendy said that someone once told her if you read the entire Sunday *New York Times* front to back it's the equivalent of a degree at Harvard. Is that true?

You're crazy, Wendy, up-a-tree crazy. I don't know when to take you seriously. Frank Fleecen invited me to California. In fact you're the *first person* I've told. No one at the syndicate even knows I left Manhattan. Can you believe it? I wanted to make sure it wasn't a prank. Some of the guys at the syndicate, Farraway or Ivanov or … never know with those chauvinist jokers what's funny and what's real. A secretary of Frank's secretaries called me to set this up. I flew out on the first flight, can you believe it? My chance to meet this Wall Street mogul operating out of my old neck of the—. And I'm the one slugging away in hard Manhattan? What if he's *eligible*? Ooo, Gabby Scavalda don't you dare, I said and slapped my own hand as if I would ever date someone just for their money … I'm telling myself: not another affair, not another affair … Then, get this, a Hexen chauffeur waiting at the airport took me straight to my hotel and even gave me a bump of cocaine. I can't go to sleep. The whole night, livid with horniness, the bastard. Then yesterday morning, bright and early, we meet. And it's all business. He gives me this amazing pitch. That's it.

Wendy dropped her espresso cup with a clatter, roll, and bang; having trouble following Gabby's train of thought. He's a what you say, a banker?

You really don't know Frank Fleecen? He was emphatic that he's met you. Through Jonjay is what he told me.

Jonjay knows everybody.

Jonjay knows him or the other way around, could be through Jonjay's gallery, I'm not sure. Regardless. He and Jonjay *go way back*, something Frank said maybe with animosity. I didn't pry. Can't you recall him? Tall man, fiercely stonelike gaze. Rug on top. A black rug? A ridiculous accessory, you can't miss it. No? Strange. Yes, turns out there's a wife. His high school sweetheart of all syrupy stories. Gabby asked her cartoonist if she was still seeing that one, Jonjay?

Oh gosh, I never *dated* Jonjay.

I thought last time we met you were crying about breaking up with him.

No, I was bemoaning the fact we'd never dated.

I must meet this one, he sounds like a real treat.

So this Frank guy invited you all the way out here just to tell you he's met me?

Well, I am your editor, Wendy, not your sister. Don't worry, you worked your Ashbubble charm on him somehow and now he's obsessed with *Strays*. Says he loves your little homeless critters and their adventures in the vacant lot. Says it's the theme of his entire career. Reads them in his local paper, laughs out loud, gets the whole concept. He wants to invest in them. He's what you call a Moby-Dick, Wendy, a whale, a rainmaker with a billion-dollar Rolodex, a hustler at heart, plugged in to all sorts of businesses desperate for the exact boost you need. He lines you up with makers of toys, pretty boxes, candy, clothes, kazoos, slap your characters on all those sorts of things and would also almost certainly add something like a tenfold increase in your subscriptions overnight. Forget forty-two papers, how about four hundred and twenty-two? And no more community freebies—real national papers. You came here ready to give up? I'm asking you to give *in*. And make a go of this comic. Showtime.

Excuse me for a second? I need to use the ladies' room. Wendy left Gabby to sit alone at the table among the rest of the patrons and the hundreds of former patrons pictured on the walls while she took a moment to collect herself in front of a dirty mirror.

What's going on? Don't freak out. Be professional. This is normal, this is a routine part of a job, she told her reflection dripping with water. Normally a coincidence like Hick's serious advice coming right before an auspicious business meeting would please her, please anybody, but today when Hick told her she should commit more to her comic strip, she knew somehow he was mistaken and she should do something else. Love, not the truth, motivated him to say what he did. He gave her these encouragements from the vantage point of someone who believed he was perched at the crumbling cliff of an eternal abyss. She turned to the open toilet and coughed up her espresso.

She went back and sat down again with wet hair feeling determined but not at all refreshed. If you think this is for the best for us then I trust you, Wendy said. But I could just as easy call it a day.

You might need to finally get a bank account, my dear, Gabby said and playfully slapped her cartoonist's shoulder bag on the pouch. She leaned in conspiratorially and whispered into Wendy's ear, Would you believe me if I told you our banker Frank Fleecen is waiting for us down the block? He wants to buy dinner and seal the deal.

4

Café Niebaum-Coppola occupied a deluxe corner on the ground level of the landmark Columbus Tower, its oxidized copperplate cladding the eight floors. A dinner menu and of course a wine list, and just like the Trieste, all sorts of memorabilia on the walls, in this case devoted to behind-the-scenes of a decade of films by the owner, Francis Ford Coppola. A corner booth was cordoned off with a red velvet rope, permanently reserved for Coppola, not presently dining. All the other tables were occupied. There were two men seated alone, one in a brown corduroy blazer eating fettuccine, the other in pinstripes and an obvious toupée, talking into a plastic brick. He waved as he saw them come in. He said *Bye for now* and put aside the brick.

Cute walkie-talkie, said Wendy. Didn't know they came in beige.

He told them a local company called Motorola had taken out a five-million-dollar line of credit with his bank to invent it. It's the latest greatest prototype for a cellular phone. I carry mine everywhere. Works all over the Bay Area. It's my prediction that one day we're all going to be carrying these.

Oh great, I can see it now, said Wendy gamely, a whole society of Ignatz mice carrying bricks around to crack some kat craniums.

Frank, this is Wendy Ashbubble, our favourite cartoonist. Gabby took the canewood chair facing them and called for the wine list absent from their table.

Yes, never mind my exciting new phone, please, have a seat, tell me about yourself, Frank said and eased himself into the chair next to Wendy.

Never mind the department store suit and tie or the chunky wedding band. *Don't stare*, Wendy kept saying to herself, don't laugh, don't look at it, tell yourself there's nothing on his head but normal human hair, not that hypnotic, diabolical beetle-black rug. What were its follicles *made* of? Nylon? Might as well be a Beatles moptop from a Halloween costume he went and styled with handfuls of hair product and glued down. And don't look at his eyes either, she told herself, because he was staring back at her intensely as if trying to drill through her with his gaze. The women, the waiter in his penguin suit, no matter who Frank stared at he was never first to break eye contact, and if she took a gulp of wine, the moment she looked back he was still trained on her as though his face was made of stone with all-seeing eyes, and he talked a mile a minute to keep you paying attention to him. He's trying to bore through your brain and back out the other side of your skull, Wendy thought, he seeks to prey on your indivisible vulnerability. What made the man attractive and assertive also made him repugnant and tasteless—ambition; ambition crouched there on top of his head.

I'm such a big fan, he told her. Dogs and cats living together. Rabbits and snakes. A raccoon single mother raising three on the wages of a barmaid. Vacant lot. You're comic is *so* Californian.

Shucks, thanks.

Where are you from, here in the Bay?

No, uh, actually outside Cleveland.

At last something good's come from the mistake on the lake, said Frank.

What's that? Oh yes, of course, ha ha, yes.

Anybody who's ever tried to draw kid gloves on a rodent or a cape on a muscleman has lived here. San Francisco is a cartoonist's mecca, said Gabby as her finger sang around the rim of her wineglass.

When did you learn to draw? Frank leaned in close.

He looked genuinely curious, so she told him the story. Wendy said she'd drawn on her bassinet as a baby and by the time she was in the first grade she had started passing comics around behind Miss Reeve's back to get popular, single-panel gag strips about the lives of a warren of gophers. Frank thought that sounded cute and appropriate considering she still drew rodents. She took a Rapidograph pen from her purse and started drawing on her menu the kind of Snoopy-lookalike gopher she used to draw in elementary school. Gophers lasted her up to the sixth grade, when she switched briefly to horses and princes. Then in the ninth grade, it dawned on her that if she drew pictures of what her friends wanted to see, they would pay her for them.

Ah, business-minded, too? I love this, by the way, seeing you draw, amazing, he said. Go on. What kind of pictures did you friends buy from you?

So began Wendy's juvenile career in pornography. Oh yes you heard right. Thirteen, still a virgin, Wendy assured Frank and Gabby, she started to print her own naive concept of what went into a Tijuana bible. She stapled together little scandalous booklets of eight or more graphic Xeroxes brimming with clumsily drawn fantasies about what sex might be like, acted out by well-known cartoon characters. Tintin, Minnie, Yosemite Sam, Panacea, Cruella De Vil. She reduced the drawings to wallet-sized and sold close to a hundred in the span of a semester, plus she did a swift side business selling off originals. Wilma solo. Garfield and Odie *in flagrante delicto*. Fornicating X-Men. Spider-Man and Lois Lane entangled in a web of betrayal. Tarzan meets Wonder Woman and Vampirella for a ménage à trois. The Jetsons' maid Rosie in a drossy Hanna-Barbera gangbang. *Choquant, Wendy! Si lubrique, tellement lascif, et* gross! in the words of her grade ten French teacher, a strict young blonde who wore leather skirts and strappy heels and confiscated a stack of Wendy's porns.

Frank was grinning. Gabby's eyes dilated wider and wider. Wendy was drawing on napkins some examples from this era of her work. I'm keeping these, please, said Frank. I'll pay handsomely.

She drew on commission, indifferent as to the cast, so the perviest kids could tip her upfront to see their choices go at it. She learned to draw a lot of different characters this way in a short amount of time and it was a fair little business while it lasted, Wendy admitted. Until she got expelled. That's when things went downhill, meaning delinquency, boys, and drugs. She lived in a one-bedroom apartment with her mother who meanwhile made an intermittent living as a stage manager for small, local theatre productions. Most of those paycheques went to cigarettes, observed the child Wendy, who never knew her father, a man her mother claimed had been a television actor in town for one night on a speaking engagement at a hydroelectric dam. It was her mom's gig to organize the crew, strike the stage, hire the lighting technicians, and so on. Wendy liked this story well enough to tell it now. But she left out the important part about that actor being Ronald Reagan and instead mentioned a grandfather with a kosher butchershop.

My father was a kosher butcher's accountant, Frank told her with flirtatious pride. He admitted a lot of her origin story sounded familiar, except instead of comics, for Frank it was high-stakes poker and a ten-thousand-dollar win that got him expelled and sent to a boarding school in Pennsylvania. Best thing that ever happened to him, for living in Pennsylvania focused Frank so that he was able to turn his teenage gambling problem into a mature and responsible career.

When the food arrived, Frank ordered more wine. And as they ate, Frank tried to explain in lay terms what he did for a living. Wendy polished off the other half of the muffuletta her editor ordered but was too stuffed to contemplate, then sucked back a plate of *linguine alle vongole* all to herself. The table emptied a third bottle of the house Cabernet Sauvignon, and that did the trick. Opening up now to the situation in front of her thanks to it, the detailed visions of a grand future that sounded so definitive as Frank Fleecen described them, but purposefully vague in the overall, kept Wendy at a distance from the actual mechanics of how he would bring about their success, as if everything he said about his business was excitingly beyond their ability to grasp. Put it this way: Frank provided investment opportunities for middleclass entrepreneurs who wanted to go big.

Sounds super, said Wendy.

When Reagan gave that talk about the economy earlier this month, I remember his quote from the poet Carl Sandburg, said Frank. *The Republic is a dream. Nothing happens unless first a dream.* I guess I'm what you call an American dreamer.

Me, too, said Wendy. Plus I love President Reagan.

Me, too, said Frank and unconsciously clawed the table.

Gabby pinched her shoulders up near her ears. Isn't she the cat's meow? she said.

At this point, for no particular reason Wendy could see, Frank beckoned to the waiter and asked if the kitchen could provide him with one apple. Without a moment's hesitation, the waiter, no doubt a consummate professional, saw to the request.

Frank held the apple in one hand, took a bite, and said, Here's a typical bond rated triple A, your handsome and perfect glossy fresh orchard apple.

Wendy took it from his hand and bit into the flesh. Tastes okay to me.

Bemused, Frank continued: Over here's what a so-called junk bond is. He pointed to the bowl of *zabaglione*. Sure, now this has custard and apples and blueberries and other fruits and of course it is far more delicious, he said, but some of the fruit in this *zabaglione* started out too bruised for the grocery, some were too ripe to eat on their own, and so on. Who wants a taste?

I'll try some, I love *zabaglione*, said Gabby and took the spoon from Frank's hand and after taking a scoop nearly swallowed the entire utensil without a gag. When she pulled the spoon out she said, Hmm, cinnamon and spices. So tell me, Frank, why am I eating a junk bond?

Flavours, more flavours is one thing. A bond is an apple. You buy a good apple or a bad apple. A high-yield bond is a mix, a *zabaglione*. It's a sauce theory of investment. My bond packages come in all kinds of flavours. And how many different ways can you think to package *zabaglione*? Frank asked them. Champagne flutes, bowls, jars, cans, tubes. Applesauce has a higher profit margin than apples. Applesauce has more options. I specialize in packaging the financial equivalent of applesauce-grade bonds up to *zabaglione*. What's your pipe dream for *Strays*, Wendy? he asked, because that's what I want to promise. And he touched her fingers at an opportune time when Gabby wasn't paying attention, as if to subtly remind Wendy that she was the hands-on centre of this deal.

Biggest of my biggest dreams? Phew, let me see ... , Wendy looked back through her life to the beginning but she wasn't about to tell him she wanted to meet Ronald Reagan, and the image of Hick Elmdales kept interrupting the sequence until the two trains of thought seemed to be one. She ground her teeth. She said, Gee, you know, that's funny because my mother is Jewish, so am I, but not really, actually I'm a superstitious atheist. We never went to any synagogues or church, but Mom and I loved Christmas. Mom loved wrapping and unwrapping presents, pretending there was a Santa Claus, a Jesus, a manger, she loved the songs. In my lifetime she stage-managed three versions of *White Christmas* and four *A Christmas Carols*. Christmas was the biggest day of the year for us. My daydreams all year long were about what I might get Christmas morning. I used to get to stay up late on Christmas Eve so we could watch Christmas specials on television together. I always thought it would be fun to surprise Mom one December with my own cartoon Christmas special. I guess that Charlie Brown special made a big impression, gave me the idea to draw comic strips. So I guess what I would love someday is to make a *Strays* animated Christmas special.

Frank stared so hard at Wendy she felt ready to crack. Then he burst out in laughter. Gabrielle joined in, then took a long drink and shook her head. Her cheeks had gone red.

You want a Christmas cartoon for *Strays*, Frank said, okay, now *that* is perfect. Did you hear that, Gabrielle?

I did. I can't believe it but I did.

Now that is something I can promise you, Wendy, Frank said and snapped his fingers. You can bank on Christmas. Wall Street's favourite time of year.

I'm stunned. I couldn't have hoped for better, said Gabby.

There you go. A Christmas special, he said and laughed again. I love it. I more than love it. Christmas is big business, Wendy. My parents don't celebrate, they find it nauseating, but I do. I give presents at the office. Money, too, but actual gifts. I love it. Christmas gives me a tan. And you told me she was going to be tough to convince.

Hear this girl an hour ago, Frank, before I got her to come to dinner she was talking about quitting. *Now* she's pitching a Christmas cartoon. Gabby downed the glass of wine in front of her that was Frank's. Tell him, Wendy, how you wanted to quit and I convinced you not to.

Did you really want to quit? And do what?

I thought it was obvious. Fifty regional papers is a bust. No fans. Etcetera. Drawing skills of a savage.

I'm your fan. You're a *zabaglione*, said Frank. My favourite.

You want to add me to your applesauce, is that it?

That's right, he said, I do, except in the real world, those apples are people's dreams and their livelihoods are at stake. I find ways of connecting people who can make each other's dreams come true. First thing every morning I read *Strays* in the *Spectator*. I love Buck, that dog's such a dreamer you can learn from him. And that rabbit reminds me of myself the way he turns a dime into a dollar.

Francis is a rascal.

One thing that helps me in pitch is an origin story. I love hearing about your childhood. Where did you get the idea for *Strays*?

I took a walk around Bernal Heights, she said. I love walks. I'm prone to wander.

A stray yourself.

Yes.

No, no, said Gabby. That's no help, is it? Tell him what you mean by *go for a walk*. What a flake. She doesn't mean like in some meditative way. The Wendy I know is a materialist, aren't you? You've never had a spiritual thought your entire life, have you?

Probably not, Wendy said. I like ghost stories, though.

She lives next door to a huge park full of stray pets. The whole cast of *Strays*.

Oh. I see. Frank turned to her for confirmation. True?

You know Bernal Heights? I live on the main floor of that five-storey hodgepodge apartment at the top of the hill. Looks like a fountain from Hieronymus Bosch or that big church it's taking a hundred years to build in Barcelona. Except dilapidated to hell. The peak is a big wonderful rolling shoe-shaped park reserved for a microwave tower and the local dogwalkers. There's a little forest around the antenna. But it's mostly couch grass and wild shrubweed, thistle, a few trees. It's very steep and chilly so I rarely see more than like a few others out on a bracing stroll or throwing the dog a ball. Windy. Fog blows in like icecubes and the next minute you bake under the sun, so it's a gamble what to wear. Plus I go at odd hours. Dusk and eventide. Dawns and predawns. I go when the foragers come out. All the city's lost pets live there. As soon as I moved to the manor I started to see the dogs and cats who roamed the hill. Packs and solo. I followed them to the south face, into thickets. I found rabbits and snakes. Raccoons. Rats. Owls. Great urban wildlife sanctuary. Those parrots who roost at Telegraph Hill fly by frequently. It's because of the illegal dump spot. I'd find all these animals rooting around in the trash people leave behind at the dead-end of the gravel road on the south side of the hill. All my characters, I found them there in the trash. So now whenever I need a fresh idea I go a-walkin' on the south side of the hill and watch my critters.

That is a precious story. Frank put down his fork next to the bowl of *zabaglione* and clapped his hands. Have you seen these animals, Gabrielle? I have to.

Yes, I mean, no. I got a tour and saw the rabbit thistle and the dump but I didn't see any dogs or cats. It was midday.

Well, I can't wait to come for a predawn visit to see the real-life counterparts from your strip. The actual Buck, I can't wait. That's cute as hell. If I'm going to sell, sell, sell, I need my personal tour for my pitch. *But* a tip: you shouldn't share that location in future interviews or your *Strays* animal habitat will be trampled by all the new fans you get who come to see it on tours.

Oh, they always say popularity is a mixed blessing, Gabby mused happily and maybe without noticing, collected Frank's fork in order to taste a portion of his antipasto.

Odd time to notice the Rolex on Frank's wrist but it must have cost more than his entire suit, shoes and tie and all. What did Gabby say at coffee, a billion-dollar Rolex? No, *Rolodex*, but still, and—*don't look*—but what did that say about the synthetic wig, why didn't he spend some money on *that rug* instead? It made her wonder about this man's sense of priority, herself included.

The gist of what Wendy understood Frank Fleecen would do for her—licensing and merchandise would be folded right into the investment loans he underwrote. This add-on improved the chance that the companies issuing Hexen Diamond Mistral bonds could repay. Especially if Gabby could increase readership and Wendy could keep them laughing. The circularity of this deal made her strip's popularity almost the inevitable outcome of total market saturation. Sure, a pet store franchise ought to use her characters, sure, a gas station should do a promotional mug. He regularly underwrote enormous mergers between restaurant chains and motel chains, paper and pasta factories, all of whom desperately needed something profitable to license or manufacture to pay back the loan (average twenty-two percent interest on a loan, fourteen percent return on a bond). Don't think junk, think high yield, think *zabaglione* bonds, applesauce bonds, think investments in America's future.

Significant to all Frank's exhortations was his ongoing financial relationship with client Piper Shepherd, owner of Shepherd Media, a regional threat buying up southern television channels and city newspapers and launching his own syndicate to represent journalists, illustrators, and comic strips like *Strays* and a dozen other fledglings, each with its own editor in a similarly touch-and-go situation to Gabby Scavalda's, in so much as their careers were concerned. The ladder Gabby wanted to climb, Wendy couldn't tell if the artist was even considered *on* the ladder, a different ladder, or none at all. Another thing: it was no secret Shepherd Media was in the midst of a buying frenzy. In Piper Shepherd's bid to become the new Pulitzer or Hearst, Shepherd Media brought work to Hexen Diamond Mistral, an epic need for loans to bankroll the mergers & acquisitions, and part of what attracted Frank to Wendy's comic was the synchronicity of it already being a part of this emerging empire. Therefore he strongly agreed with Gabby's strategy that from now on he make sure all future Shepherd Media buyouts included *Strays* in the boilerplate contracts. Frank estimated that within six months she would see ten times as many newspaper subscriptions.

Why do I get the sense you're both trying very hard to convince me of something I should really want so badly anyway?

Because we are, Gabby said, we are trying to——, can't you see you're young, you're not looking at this from the same vantage point as us, and you're from this generation that doesn't give a shit about—excuse my language—about bank accounts or commitment or careers, your peers want to smack around classic taboos and rebel against a jury of your peers, they don't want to develop the patience to crank out a comic strip perfect enough to turn into a rubber stamp every time, every panel, every day, for the rest of your life. Gabby spat in Wendy's face as she spoke and stung Wendy's thigh with slaps meant to emphasize her points. I'm sure all your punk friends think you should be doing this for free, right? You're young, Wendy, and this is a serious thing we're asking, more serious than what it takes to be in forty papers.

Wendy laughed and said, Know what else I want besides a cartoon? I want my own café too, like this one, with classy waiters, and full of my own memorabilia. Look at that picture of Coppola lounging with underage Cambodian whores.

Then we have a deal? Frank stood and pressed two fingers to his temple, saluted her, and welcomed Wendy to the client list of Hexen Diamond Mistral's high-yield bonds division. As Gabby applauded, tourists around them took notice of the noise, all except for the man in the corduroy blazer eating solo, who stared out the window, and the waiter came to Frank Fleecen's side in a polite way.

Will there be anything else?

Champagne, Frank waved a hand in front of their waiter's nose. If this is a *real* celebration then do we deserve champagne or what? Are we in business? Waiter, a bottle of your bubbliest Clicquot.

And three more bowls of your *zabaglione*, please, cried Wendy.

5

Buzzing drunk, the three new business partners left Coppola's café and standing on the sidewalk under the sodium streetlights watching tourists they decided instead of splitting up so soon it would be better to escort Gabby Scavalda back to her hotel. It was not far away, fifteen minutes' walk so why take a cab. Gabby loved if they would take her back, tugging on Frank's sleeve, please.

You can't see the stars at night over a foggy San Francisco. No matter how hard Wendy tried to read her fortune in the skies, the streetlights glowing off the dark moisture veiled in a phosphorescent orange the cosmos hanging overhead. So they made their way through the thickest vapours into the bright neon briars of Chinatown, laughing, passing under the sleek flashing lights, making giddy predictions for the future, the famed noodle houses and not-so-good dim sum restaurants, imported-goods stores, tarot card readers, porno theatres, food carts, racist tourists, and incontinent slummers getting in everyone's way. By chance they passed by Justine Witlaw's second-floor art gallery near Pine Street, a loft space that was the location for some pretty pretentious stuff, Wendy thought, but what did she know. Not all bad, she hinted.

Frank said he had been inside and agreed, there was only one good artist there, in fact he'd bought some pictures from Justine.

Gabby nudged her cartoonist. Your mutual friend Jonjay. What I tell you?

That's whose pictures I bought, yes, of course, Jonjay's. What sort of a fly in the ointment is he today? Frank said with a condescending shake of his head.

He's missing in action, said Wendy. Maybe in Japan.

Jonjay, the one-eyed king, cursed kid, orphan from another world— what else did I hear the PhDs call him? Tailgater?

Not genius? said Wendy, arching a heel behind her so that her shoe hung by a toe.

Watching her, Frank said, I have two of those pictures he drew using the *I Ching*. Intriguing stuff. Not the usual blasphemous contemporary shimsham. And the one on the wall in my office I like the best because he drew it based on bets he placed on a game of roulette.

Gabby loped along behind in her effort to keep up as the two in front got to talking. At last Gabby saw her opening in the pedestrian traffic to run up beside them and repeat that she must get a chance to meet this Jonjay everyone talks so much about.

Some people never change, Frank said. They've been around forever. He's that type. You see him in paintings in the Frick. He's the hieroglyph in the graffiti. Didn't I hear he used to draw from his imagination? Frank blinked up at the neon coin laundry sign as if for confirmation. That's what I heard.

Oh, sure, he still does on occasion, said Wendy. Haven't you seen his comic book? It's amazing. I haven't seen him since Cleveland a year ago. Any idea where he might be?

Last time I saw him? Must have been … five years ago at the Stanford math labs. He was auditing advanced physics classes on stochastic processes. We met at random.

Wendy slapped her forehead. Funny, I could have sworn Jonjay was like nineteen years old, I thought he was younger than *Hick*.

Timeless asshole, said Frank and slapped his hip where the Motorola was holstered like a cowboy's pistol. He *looks* like a child, doesn't he? But I know he must be more like fifty, sixty. Older than me.

Fifty! As if! Older than you? As *if*, said Wendy, giggling uncertainly and losing her balance on a cobble. Jesus.

Watch your step, said Gabby and tried to wedge her way between the two. I wonder if Jim Davis has a similar deal to ours for *Garfield*—it's the ubiquity I hope we can achieve—

Look for Jonjay at the end of chaos, on top of a terminal horizon of chaos, Frank laughed through his nose. Chaos is where you can find Jonjay. I happen to share this obsession with him, with ways to interpret randomness. Drunk walks. Stochastics. He was toying with chaos, all kinds of chaos, and I went to visit him at the Stanford labs to find out if he or someone with an actual degree could improve upon a model of my own. Since my days as an undergraduate I'd been tinkering with an equation that modified the standard approach to random movements. But Jonjay improved mine, all right. I threw mine in the trash after I saw what he had— *well*.

So you ripped him off? Wendy kidded him, but when Frank didn't follow up with any laugh of his own she realized he probably *had* stolen Jonjay's formula. That's what a cartoonist would do anyways, she said.

The students he was hanging out with back then are all millionaire microchip engineers now, but even among them, he was a natural. One of those synesthesiacs who can see math. The PhDs did not love him hovering around.

I wonder if that's where he is right now, back at Stanford. Wendy considered investigating on Hick's and her own behalf.

They saw Gabby to the lobby of her hotel and embraced and palavered a moment longer. It's been so good to see you, Gabby, Wendy said and draped her arms around her editor.

Now hasn't this been a historic night out? We're in business. Yes, bring on the multitudes.

Awesome applesauce. Wendy kissed her editor on each cheek. Her editor gallantly shook Frank's hand and giggled. She could see Gabby gnaw over the triangle of the situation. With Wendy right there she couldn't very well dangle the hotel key from a finger and ask Frank up to her room for a drink. So after a few uncomfortable pauses in the farewells, Gabby blew them a kiss and got into the old wrought-iron elevator, leaving Frank and Wendy alone in the lobby under a candelabra chandelier, an octopus's tangle of goldenrod limbs with slender flickering bulbs at the ends.

Well, gee whiz … , said Wendy, kicking up a heel and yawning into the palm of her hand. What a doozy of a day. I got a real injection of adulthood. Like I was bit by a radioactive guru. I feel supermature. Did my hair turn white?

You look radiant. I'm parched just looking at you. What's the intelligent thing for me to do right now?

Hmm, intelligent's not my department.

I should not go home to San Jose. That's what a responsible man in my state of insobriety would do. I should book a room in this hotel.

Never occurred to me. Sounds expensive compared to a cab or walking it off.

I'm too drunk for roads, sidewalks. Can barely stand. Not even the backseat of a taxi. I can't picture myself going all the way to San Jose, not at this hour, no. Frank stared for less than a second at his Rolex. I start work at *four* in the morning on a weekday and end my day at eleven at night.

I'm the one who has a car, said Wendy. And it's parked up by the Caffe Trieste in one of those lots that closes after ten. I'll have to go back in the morning and fetch it. I should be the one getting a room.

If I got a room, what do you think, would you come up for one last celebratory nightcap?

I thought you said you were *drunk*.

Too drunk for a taxi.

STRAYS

6

Upstairs in room 707 Wendy remembered there was a joint in her shoulder bag, and as the two of them smoked it leaning out the open window looking down onto Post Street, she told Frank her theory about violence in the funny pages. The basic thesis was that violence triggered memory creation. Essential to a comic strip's longevity was the imprint of violence.

Frank never got stoned, he claimed, as he poured them each two fingers of whisky from the minibar, and so if he seemed especially interested in what she had to say on the subject, he wanted her to know it wasn't because of the joint that he kept asking her facetious questions, like, Are you talking about murder? You mean mayhem, riots? Blood and guts?

Slapstick, not the real stuff—for a comic to get lodged in the reader's memory, slapstick is key. The good old vaudeville rules still apply to strips. In the right shoes, pain is funny and memorable. Because you laugh before you recognize the moral paradox of laughing at violence, you remember. Slapstick connects at a deeper level to emotional pain, embeds itself into memory, and helps make a comic strip famous. The best strips repeat the same slapstick routines, the repetition goes to show the themes. A comic strip has to find a thing to repeat and the cartoonist must draw the same things the same way. Repetition is the secret. Repetition *is* the formula. A cartoon is the world on an infinite loop. Cartooning's circularity is its success. That's why you more often forget the strips that *don't* use violence regularly.

Hit me with an example.

Okay, so my favourite is the brick Ignatz mouse tosses at Krazy Kat's head every day. Every day for forty years, that brick to the head. Unforgettable poetical violence, a violence to suit every theme imaginable. *Krazy Kat*—every punchline's the same for hundreds and hundreds of strips, a mouse hits a cat in the head with a brick.

A brick. I'll have to look up that strip.

So good. Or think of the many ways Lucy finds to pull the football out from under Charlie Brown.

And Popeye.

Wendy, shadowboxing, said, Popeye loves a scrap. With those forearm muscles and the spinach. Popeye's themes are in his punches. Charlie Brown's themes are in his crashes.

Yes, I see, yes, yes. Frank sat down beside her on the loveseat and accepted another toke on her joint, yes, he could see the point of this violence as more than a joke, yes, a key to understanding the restless, inimitable core of a comic. He smiled meaningfully at her—she could tell the topic didn't matter one whit to him. She drank up the whisky. Woop! It was strong, pungent, heady. She didn't want more, no. But she took another round for good times and continued to expound on her theory. He put a hand on her leg. She pretended not to notice. Garfield beats up Odie. Dennis is *the* Menace after all. Dick Tracy shoot-'em-ups. Alley Oop's caveman club. *Wizard of Id*'s torture chambers. B.C.'s rolling on the wheel down a steep hill. Violence is timeless, don't you think?

What about *Doonesbury*? said Frank, gamely. Not that I'm interested in politics or satire but it *is* popular. Can we crush its popularity somehow?

Trudeau slaps few sticks, she agreed. Maybe the violence in *Doonesbury* is the satire? I kind of revere *Doonesbury*, but history will show there's lots of exceptions to my theory, because it's just a theory, but think about it, most of the strips lacking violence time has forgotten.

And so what about *Strays*? Where's its violence?

Ping-Pong. Violent games of Ping-Pong.

Of course. Frank moved in closer to her. Love the Ping-Pong.

They whack each other really hard with those little white balls.

Wendy, I feel this terrible desire to kiss you right now, said Frank as he put his tumbler down on the carpet and heaved towards her that very moment as if to.

You mean me?

Would you let me? Celebrate with me, Wendy. We're on the cusp of something. I feel—

What about your high school sweetheart?

Who?

Don't you think your wife would mind if you kissed me? Wendy touched the wedding band on his finger as his left hand travelled up her thigh.

Who told you? Was it Gabrielle?

Well?

He did not but almost touched his hair. I thought we were in San Francisco. Heart of the free love movement. My wife was raised here, she's her own woman, he said. She went to college in Berkeley. Her English profs taught her all about free love. Lately our friends think we should try swinging, like they all do. Key parties. Saunas. I never. Susan—my wife— never went for any of it either, except to witness the debauched as fodder for her creative writing assignments, and she told me if I ever did swing not to tell her. So I won't.

He set his palm on the side of her face and dragged his ring down her cheek. A siren going by outside the open window made it sound like he was ripping a police car out of her face. I've never done this before. I'm happily married. I just want to kiss you right now.

So you keep secrets?

Secrets are my job, said Frank without hesitation. He kissed her once. Don't you keep secrets, Wendy?

She pulled back to inspect her feelings. Sure, want to know one of mine? I'll tell you two. Wendy isn't even my real name (she kissed him), a friend gave it to me, a very dear friend, so I kept it. And I'm not from around here. You're going to have to get me a green card (she kissed him). Gabby's paid me in cash all this time. I told her I hate banks, don't trust them. Might be why she thought I would be so tough to convince of this deal, come to think of it ...

When she put some distance between them this time, moving her hips on the loveseat made the whole room temporarily expand.

Frank dismissed her confessions with words almost breathless with lust, and once more he closed the gap: You're not the first client I have in this situation, not a citizen, with a criminal record, these are pretty common problems in business. Never mind a work visa, taken care of. I'll have one for you in a month or two. This deal we struck tonight means a lot more to me, to my future, than tiny details like a pseudonym. And a record can be wiped clean if it makes you feel any better. I've done a lot of deals with dicier people than you, a lot dicier, but this deal makes me more excited than any other because it's going to help someone creative make a lot of money—that's *you*, Wendy. And in this moment, kissing you feels right, on such a special night for us, and honestly I find you irresistible.

Gabby said we met once before but I don't remember. Where did we meet?

One hint: Blue squares.

That opening at Justine's? Drowsy art, so much free wine. That night is a blur. I went with Hick and left alone. What did we talk about?

You told me I had the kind of face you wanted to kiss.

You *are* a salesman. She moved in closer and pressed herself hard against him.

Ow! Frank sat upright and touched the flesh over his heart where he'd been stabbed.

She pulled the Rapidograph out of her bra. Force of habit, she said and underhanded the pen across the room towards her purse.

Wendy knew this would happen the moment Gabby said his name. *Sometimes you hear sex before you see sex.* Tensions at the name, *Frank Fleecen*, pulling her towards these kisses.

Want to know something about me? she asked.

Of course he did, he said he did as he kissed her neck and chest.

I have ideas, she said.

Yes, like what? Tell me. As he fondled her.

I want more than a Christmas special, she said.

Like what?

A hot-air balloon in the Macy's Thanksgiving Day Parade.

A hot-air balloon? That is a must. Of course. Absolutely. I'll arrange for it.

Breathless undressing. More lips than fingers.

I'd love to win the Reuben Award. She shivered at his caresses.

The what? What's that?

Oh, I dunno, it's only the big award they give out for the best comic strip of the year.

I'll look into this Reuben. I will, Frank whispered to her under the drum and bass of his heartbeat. His temperature rising, face pinkening, he undid his collar, then the rest of the buttons.

I want to meet the president, Frank.

Me, too. Me, too. I must sit down with him. Business to discuss, deregulation and so on. We'll make it happen, Wendy. Together.

Really? Let's make that promise right now.

I promise.

Frank was Popeye, she was Olive Oyl, and right away it was arms and legs flying this way and that and a thick fragrant fog of perspiration in the middle where their bodies connected. It was after midnight when they moved from making out, kissing hard and feeling each other up on the loveseat to the bed, where he took off her blue blazer, pulled away her riding boots, down went her blouse and tight black denim pants—they're naked on the sheets and life stood still, timeout, as they had sex for an hour or more. At one point while on top of him she saw his cellular phone out of the corner of her eye, he left it on the bedside table next to the rotary, it was so conspicuous, the size of Ignatz mouse's brick—so she picked it up and knocked him upside the head with it.

Ow! what was that for?

Temptations, she said and hit him again. And the rug stayed on the whole time.

That unstoppable rug. Sweat and rough sexplay mussed the rug to its limits but that was not enough to break the glue and dislodge it and no, no, no, he said he wouldn't let her touch, grope, pull, tear. No matter how hard she strove to make the rug fall off on its own accord, the thing stayed put, loyal to its master. She wanted to see him balder than Daddy Warbucks. Mr. Pinstripes. Mr. Zabaglione. Sex with Frank Fleecen was abrupt at first, as if his prick was a time machine and in less than a minute she was back in high school, that's how easy he was for Wendy to please. Maybe he wasn't lying when he said this was his first betrayal. Lucky for him she was feisty, she got him up and going again in no time. He was excitable and ejaculatory and fondled her until she was numb. He went longer with each subsequent go, like high school, he wanted to go as deep as possible into her, the dear boy, he wanted a lot of time with her breasts in his hands, nipples in his mouth, stirring him much like the mystery of the rug turned her on. Her breasts were natural and responded to his touch, his toupée was unnatural and untouchable and responded indirectly to her body language. His fake hair was vain but in its way honest. The toupée meant Frank thought he had flaws. All she had to do was lean on him to make him come. His success in business didn't translate right away to the bed, and despite their difference in age and his boiling over with ambition, she had the confidence and sex appeal here. Isn't this exactly the reason a girl from a frigid city moves to San Francisco? Yes, damn it all, it was. He kept praising her figure top to bottom and said how amazed he was by her. He wanted more and more. His whole face turned bright pink and ruddy like a dog's tongue. At one point he pulled out of her to swallow a glass of water. The rug was the shape of an animal, a fictitious predator, a druid's pet, she would make it *her* pet, since it was the absurd hairy image of their betrayal. It's all mine now, she growled and she clawed the air around his head as he swatted her away from the fakery glued to his scalp. At one point when she was rolling on top of and beneath the wave of her pheromones, surfing high on the deepest undertow, the reality of this affair sank in and made her shudder from the toes up. And then with a long sigh like water on fire she collapsed breasts-first onto his face. This was wrong, so obviously wrong, however much her bruised apple of a heart needed it, the compensation that sex temporarily offered her sorrow. *I'm hooked*, he said and kissed her once more before they fell soundly asleep for a minute or two. Sounds of horns, car stereos, and sirens blowing to distraction down on Post Street, and pedestrian drunks shouting misnomers; in the distance, shots fired, sirens bouncing off concrete buildings. The sound of a late-night liquor store's metal grille slammed shut and padlocked became a prison door in a dream Wendy had of solitary confinement that, when she inspected her cell, turned out to be a life sentence at the top of a sparsely treed and uninhabited mountain of gravel; this was not a sleeping dream of the unconscious but a lucid picture of her future.

Room service.

She opened her eyes to find herself alone in 707 and a maid knocking on the door, daylight flooding in through open curtains. The last of the joint they'd smoked lay stinking like a small shit on the table beside her; she swept that into the drawer on top of the Gideon Bible. *Come back later, please.* Every last thing that happened to her in the previous twenty-four hours swam in front of her eyes: bursting out of a thick lagoon of wine-red mucus came the rotting and scaly creature of Hick Elmdales with bloated gills and webbed armpits. Then the six-eyed cannibal fish of her latest fuck swam face to face with Hick and she wanted to throw up.

I should never have left Hick's side, Wendy told us. I shouldn't have gone downtown to meet Gabby or Frank. I got a dumb-luck deal the day he died. I feel like those men from Disney. I stole my big chance out from under the mattress of a dying genius.

Last thing she saw before she left the hotel room was a note on top of the television set written with her Rapidograph.

It's five in the morning and I
know you'll understand if I
don't wake you as we return
to our regularly scheduled programming …
What a deal! & what a night!!
Someday you're going to have to
tell me all about yourself …
~FF

7

STRAYS

Come Sunday all Hick's friends had arrived at No Manors save one. No sign of Jonjay. Hick's first roommate and his best friend. Inspiration for Peter in his comic—Jonjay should be here. The wake was by now swamped. So many cartoonists that at one point we climbed out a window and sat on the lilypad of shingled rooftop to get some fresh air, burping and throwing empties into a rosebush below us as we watched newcomers wiggle and worm their way inside through the packed entranceway. A lot of big fish were here, Wendy kept reminding us. Pros. The rooms were jammed with local spot illustrators for *The Face*, *Dynamite*, *Time*, and *Life*, commercial artists with clients like Budweiser or Super 8 Motels or K-tel and local mattress stores. Assistants on *Garfield*, *Li'l Abner*, and *Spider-Man* gossiping over the warts of their bosses with lush Hanna-Barbera animators airing out gripes of their own. And so on throughout the many rooms inside the quincunx-shaped No Manors. And we wondered of ourselves, *Could these tadpoles frog?*

Buzzkaabuzzkabuzzkaa, or something. That quacking sibilant door buzzer went off again and again over the next forty-eight hours as more and more guests arrived straight from the airport or off the highway. Not all the cartoonists of California lived in California, it turned out. And it turned out to be the single most eventful weekend of our mere lives so far. Most of the people we met that weekend, we would never remember their names, but plenty of the guests, we knew their work by heart already. The instructions for a wake are clear, to stay awake overnight together with the body and to not leave before dawn. Of the hundreds who came for a night, many stayed for two. Our third night in the manor was by far the busiest so far, and the entire day Wendy spent asleep in her room with the door locked and plugs in her ears and a sore throat and so Rachael put us to work. Mark and Twyla bused dishes, Patrick ran out for more food rations and beverages, and Rachael cleaned up after messes and crashes, repaired damage, and protected the stereo from the debauched.

A hundred more cartoonists and friends were seated at the longtable drinking and drawing, smoking and talking. The mood was elastic, sentimental and brusque, as professional decorum and genuine emotion quickly sunk into fiery gossip and rude mime then climbed out of trash again for a moment of silence here and there, a toast to the genius, a pause to remember better days. The topics that weekend ranged from comics to toys to nuclear conflagration. A nuclear arms race, who can build atomic bombs faster, America or the Soviet Union, who can ready and arm atomic warheads sooner, hide missiles in more places around the globe, and point them at more strategic locations, a race in which a first strike was the best defence against total annihilation—this was discussed heatedly in the same conversation as the neofatalistic popcorn movie *Escape from New York*, Henry Kissinger's bowel movements or lack thereof, and the prescience of J.G. Ballard.

Ernie Bushmiller was present throughout the entire weekend, he sat drawing fences and sidewalks and fire hydrants for fun and listened happily to the others talk fear of Soviet willpower in Europe, fear of American arrogance in Central America. Libyan terrorists. Jewish homeland. Iranian hijackers. The draft dodgers up in Canada. The bald, rosy-cheeked, liverspotted creator of *Nancy*, still nimble with his fingers and quick-witted though he abstained from political jabber, Ernie Bushmiller was shaped like a bouncing rubber ball wearing suspenders with little hands that extended out and could draw amazingly well—and that's what he wanted to talk about, drawing. A drawing was the soul of all art. Bushmiller was drawing pictures of neighbourhood fences and passing them to us to complete the picture with figures and talk balloons. His fences weren't Berlin Walls, they were barriers between childhood and adulthood, or between the imagination and its prey, easily climbed over, spied through, vandalized, and whitewashed. Bushmiller believed in the power of the pen. Talent erodes if not used, he said as he scribbled. The imagination shrivelled if not stretched.

Another senior cartoonist stepped up—it might have been *Beetle Bailey*'s Mort Walker—and argued talent was steady, it was skill and technique that eroded if not applied. But ideas gathered ideas, patience intensified the imagination, and the force of a passion strengthened all the forces in one's life, work begat work, and only in very unusual cases, some would argue, did talent split the atom of talent. Look around, said Walker, and Ernie Bushmiller scanned the room as if waiting for that spark he believed in to make this wake a fireworks.

In the living room, the *Bloom County* artist Berkeley Breathed spat and howled at the news on the TV screen, There's scaffolding over the Statue of Liberty, for crissakes! America is one big plastic-surgery disaster. Who am I talking to?

Art Spiegelman sat on the staircase below Bill Blackbeard, the local comics historian. Spiegelman balanced an ashtray on top of a row of books that ran up the stairs and the two friends shared a pack of Parliaments and talked about Hick, death, the chances of Armageddon. It's a nightmarish game of chicken that's been looming over my entire life, said Blackbeard. My parents had a bomb shelter. And I wish I had a bomb shelter.

Spiegelman scratched at his face and neck, then lit a third cigarette. Now we know how naive we were to think there was any shelter.

Patrick Poedouce said he figured if Brezhnev dropped a bomb on this house, a cartoonist could get any job he wanted.

Biz Aziz held her hand over her mouth as she retreated from the master bedroom. She had just gone to visit him. There were tears in her eyes she had to stroke away. Trembling, she sat down next to us and said, Oh he's so small, so small, like a branch. He used to be like two-fifty. One of those guys with fat genes, or hormones, you know. He was big even when I first knew him on Geary Street, he used to sell drawings off the sidewalk, practically lived on dollar hamburgers and fifty-cent pancakes. This would be like seventy-five, seventy-four maybe. I earned next to nothing back then, Biz said, but Hick earned nothing at all. Drawing comics saved us both, that's all there is to it. I was sure with my luck I was going to be the one who goes young, man. How angry I was as a teenager getting into aimless trouble, then luck gets me drafted to Vietnam, which turns out to be Cambodia, and the army takes away my weapon and gives me a pad of paper and some pencils instead, damn. I thought it would be me laid out there.

There he was at the far end of the table, shrouded in black cloth and charcoal shadows.

The deceased lay to rest in a handwoven Peruvian basket placed on top of the longtable in his bedroom. Green candleflames shone around him emitting no discernible light. The longtable in effect ended early at the open double doors to his bedroom, with the final feet of its length dedicated to him, for private visitations. Waiting for some sign from the afterlife, a moth's dance of greeting, an intoxicating fragrance, a sequence of sentient lights, any kind of clue from beyond the pale that Hick knew his friends were here. This was where he had worked and slept and where he was going to spend his last weekend in the manor. They had made his room up for the occasion. Before his body arrived, Biz Aziz saw to it everything in the master bedroom was decorated in blacks, black candles burning green, black lace, black drapes pulled across the bay window overlooking the city, and not another word about Disney's men to spoil the atmosphere. Dark black funk music accompanied the look. Periodically we raided the laundry hamper in an attempt to keep enough joints rolled to satisfy the mourners. Getting high until their eyes barely opened and drawing until their fingers cramped up was how many of them outwardly grieved. The teetotallers couldn't blame the rest for succumbing, and anyway all of us were doodling diabolical scenes.

What did he die of? guests wanted to know, but Wendy had no definitive answer. The doctors had told her he died of a combination of pneumonia, dysentery, arthritis, inflammation, cancer, and so on. That such a young man could rack up such an extensive list of illnesses was inexplicable enough, but that in the past six months more than a dozen young men had died this same way was something of a frightening mystery.

All of Wendy's stuff was at the other end of the longtable, in the kitchen nook, in a bay window that faced south towards the suburbs. The kitchen was a bright place and Wendy worked at night.

She rubbed her eyes. I'm afraid to go near that mucilaginous sludge-pile of dirty dishes in the sink … , she said. She shook her head, pulled her bottom lip, and looked out the window. The neighbours are hardcore

Evangelicals with two children under the age of ten, they must wonder what the fuck's going on. God, I feel like I'm about to throw up out of my eyes. My gut is spazzing on me. My brain is glue. I am so broken. I can't believe he's dead.

All right enough monkey business, let's get these dishes spotless for Wendy, said Rachael and slapped Twyla on the knee, pulled Mark by the ear to the sink. We can do this, Wendy, we can help you.

Filth does not know it is filth, said Mark Bread as he cracked a tall can of beer and slurped at it, looking at the dishes submerged under an oily murk in the twin sinks. There was paintbrushes and plastic easels in there, too.

Get those hands dirty, said Rachael and snapped her fingers at Patrick.

That was one of Rachael's many talents, we soon learned; she could always organize and lead us when we felt incoherent and apathetic—she pointed us in a direction. When we finished up at the sink—and you can believe it took all four of us—we felt ready for hell itself and asked for more. Wendy laughed and said that was plenty for now, invited us to sit down again in four spare chairs at the longtable and gave us stacks of paper and aimed us at some pens and pencils and said she would join us once a few more depressing phone calls got made.

It's time to draw, she said. Go ahead.

It might have been Charles Schulz we sat down next to at the longtable, Cathy Guisewite or Dik Browne, another winner of the Reuben Award, Art Spiegelman, Gary Panter. These legendary cartoonists were seated next to the most ignoble amateurs that night, us, and career or not, we all passed the time playing drawing games. Nudged in the ribs by Spain Rodriguez. C'mon, c'mon, he said, join in. We shrugged him off the first round, saying we weren't good enough for anything but washing up.

Games are kind of a tradition with big parties at the longtable, Wendy said. You must join in.

In every round of a drawing game you had five minutes to complete your picture, the majority decided a winner and the all-out loser, who relinquished a chair to a new player. The winner invented the next challenge. One would shout out:

Draw an animal you've never drawn before.

Then another cartoonist would say: Draw a spaceship with no wings.

Draw your worst idea for a superhero.

Draw a whole fairy tale—in one minute.

Draw a barouche, a calash, or a landau.

Draw a wise man on a mountain.

Draw an emergency room situation.

Draw a ziggurat, xenodochium, or schloss.

Draw a plague doctor.

Draw weightlifting monsters.

Draw Ping, Pang, and Pong from *Turandot*.

Using your opposite hand, draw a man playing piano.

Draw a pirate in Hick's style with your eyes closed.

Draw a horse race upside down.

Draw sex from memory.

Draw soldiers from World War One versus soldiers from the Cimbrian War.

Draw a caveman and a Neanderthal and a merchant marine.

Draw a scene from the life of Aleister Crowley.

Draw a dinosaur with landscape.

Draw a family of tourists with landscape using your wrong hand.

Draw an SF boho in the style of Fontaine Fox.

Draw a scene from *Hamlet* in the style of George Herriman.

Draw the San Francisco skyline in the style of Lyonel Feininger.

Draw your panic.

Draw yourself as you will look in fifty years.

Draw a Kama Sutra position performed by Shaggy and Velma.

Draw Ronald Reagan with your eyes closed.

Games preoccupied us for hours and hours over the course of the two-night wake, and so time passed almost without an appearance. Coffee kept eyes dilated all the way until Monday morning. Coffee, hot night in a cup, making our hearts race like ink on paper, we drank it for life.

Casual interrogation was another game. Questions about process, this need to know about each other's tools, as they doodled and drank and reminisced. Not for all. Not for us. This line of questioning was intended to expose, in full, the contents of each other's toolkit. There was a collector's-fetish fascination with how others did the same thing. Lay black ink on white paper, should be simple, but only in your dreams was it ever.

What type of pen? Brush or nib? What brand of nib, what size, what shape, what brand of brush, what sizes? Of all the blacks out there to choose from, what inks were favoured, what brand of watercolour was the one, what kind of paper did you go for, was the paper coated, what was its bond weight? What size did they draw their panels, and did they use a lightbox, did they trace? Did they have assistants and what were the assistants used for?

Some had invented ways to get a certain look, say, for instance, the rays of the cosmos, snowy days, rainy nights, shadows on brick, or intricate patterns on fabric. Nobody worked with quite the same set of tools, there was so much available.

What pen do you use?

The 914 Radio Esterbrook.

Name a brand, it was here. Hick had tried them all. An armoury of pens. To complement the mason jars full of brushes and pens and pencils there were hundreds of small plastic canisters to fill with diluted ink for doing washes. There were tons of flimsy watercolour palettes caked with a rainbow of paint sediment. Kneadable rubber erasers in various states of decay. T-squares, French curves, and the rest of the drafting tool family were here and ready.

Pelikan M400 14C for lettering.

Visconti black. Parker red. Holbein blue.

Yasutomo ink, swear by it. Nothing's blacker.

Hold on, let me write that down.

And an abundance of blank paper. Reams of old yellowing paper Hicks had picked up at flea markets that smelled of vanilla. Unsealed boxes of handmade watercolour paper he mailordered for on impulse. Thousands of sheets of heavy-duty bristol boards. Arches paper. Canson brand.

Take a piece of bristol that's as smooth as glass and lay some carbon-based black inks on it: sticks to the paper and dried so perfectly it looked already like print.

Reeves watercolours. A tray a week, a month.

Grumbacher brushes. Grumbacher pastels. Grumbacher.

The infamous Falcon pen from Bink Wells & Co. So smooth.

With the right tools, the right brands, the right materials, the right table, talent had no choice but to skyrocket. The right pen or brush matched up with the ideal ink on the perfect paper could turn mediocrity into mastery overnight. Could the tricks of Alex Toth be taught? Yes. His photographic eye for detail, no. But his advice to go with fixed-width nibs for borders and for lettering, okay, that we would try to remember. Why all these dirty bristleless toothbrushes on the longtable? For scrapes, washes, and blood spatter. What's that you're doing? Trimming hairs off sable brushes with a razor. The confidences of Wally Wood, were they worth considering? Wally's eyes swam in his head. His neck was wet with sweat, soaking the collar of his shirt. He told us the best thing that ever happened to comic book artists was the Xerox machine. Three, he said. He owned three.

Alex Toth got up from his chair next to Wendy's and threw his pens down, lifted his arms and scratched the air as if fighting for oxygen. Use them all! Tools be damned! Don't be a hostage to your toolkit! To Wendy's delight, he pushed himself away from the longtable, disgusted with this all-around obsession with pens. Grab a fucking Sharpie and get to work! He marched to the kitchen, shouting out, Bullshit and you know it! A drawing starts with a pencil and scrap paper!

I can't draw *Peanuts* without my tools, said Charles Schulz. That Esterbrook works for me. I'm afraid to leave my comfort zone. I guess that's why they call it a comfort zone.

Patrick took a bicycle off the ceiling and rode down the hill and bought a half a dozen Sunday newspapers so that everyone could look over the full-colour funny pages and compare colour prints from one to the other. It happened to be a Sunday of quotes by chance. With *Peanuts* on the front page of the *USA Today* pullout, Charlie Brown quoted Proverbs to Snoopy: *How long, you loafer, will you lie there? How long until you rise from your sleep?* and Snoopy answered with a different verse, *A good man cares if his beast is hungry.* Then over in Johnny Hart's *B.C.* a charred Neanderthal recited from Luke at the mouth of a smouldering cave. Cathy was on a blind date with an actor who had memorized the lines of both characters from *The Odd Couple*—Augh!

In *Pan* (the last Sunday Hick delivered before he moved to 5D) the character Wendy Darling quoted freely from Shakespeare's *Cleopatra*— *Growing up can't free me from my mistakes but it does free me from childishness ... tell me now, will Pan die?* and Pan, about to jump off a high cliff onto a ship of pirates as a stunt to impress her, paraphrased Mark Antony right back, *My queen gives me brave instruction!*

In the case of the one paper Patrick could find that carried Wendy Ashbubble's *Strays*—the *San Jose Sentinel*—the quote was unattributed Baudelaire she read off Hick's shelf—*Science is a cheat. You know what schools don't teach?* her dog Buck wondered aloud. *The next discovery.*

That's fine, fine work, best of luck to you, Charles Schultz told Wendy with a benign smile.

Hey, maybe you could give me some advice. I got an offer for some licensing and merchandising, but I worry I'm jumping the gun.

You should always worry, said Schulz as he dipped his nib in the inkpot.

The whole point of comics is merch, to nab those big bucks, said Johnny Hart. That's why we're in this slaphappy business.

Not every comic strip is here for an eternity, they reminded her, not all strips grab kids' interest and obsess collectors and become truly timelessly popular, so remember, Wendy, beggars can't be choosers, you should be happy, this is good news.

Your future is my past, Schulz told her. I remember my old worries with fondness.

It's true, said Hart glumly, your ambition makes me nostalgic.

There's no reason why every popular comic has to exploit success and inundate the world with truckloads of useless stuff nobody needs, said Biz Aziz, rolling joints to give to the needy. More product to go in the dump, more junk for rich kids to get bored over. Extraneous junk dilutes the integrity of your characters. Don't commodify your little sweethearts, Wendy.

The requests wear you down after a while, said Schulz. And you fear going broke. So many cartoonists go broke.

Hart agreed. I know better than most cartoonists how to spend money.

Junk … , said Wendy ruminatively.

The two famous strip artists regarded Biz with a fair degree of polite skepticism. The cosmetics, the beard, the long lacquered fingernails, the mourning gown. But Biz Aziz made enough money to suit all her needs selling copies of her self-published comic book memoir, *The Mizadventurez of Mizz Biz Aziz*, that she didn't concern herself with merchandise or the respect of the lowest common denominator. She was on the fifth offset issue, completing a story cycle that depicted her experience as a teenage street performer drafted to Vietnam, enlisted in the ill-fated CAT-X artist program, drawing the Christmas Offensive from behind Cambodian lines. Everything in her comic career was organized around her predilections, very businesslike when need be but bohemian more often, and more dedicated to art than any of these syndicated commercialists (her words), drawing seven days a week, costume design, and singing disco on weekends. She was the last of a generation in the city to live by an alias for good reason: her connections weren't all clean or above board, and her income mostly went untaxed. She had no assistant to help her fill orders or keep her on deadline. What did she need merchandise for when it would only spoil her fans? This way, she told Wendy, the independent way, she was at liberty to write and draw whatever she wanted without censor, and retain the total attention of her audience. Her fans expected the character Biz Aziz to say and do whatever she wanted, for the book to stay stubbornly anti-consumerist, and nothing about the real Biz Aziz's financials would change that fact. She might rather go broke than exploit her art.

Obviously you don't listen to *this* one, said Johnny Hart. I can see for myself your comic is not part of this mad rush for the gutter that ends in total anarchy.

Typical straight whiteman floccinaucinihilipilification, spat Biz Aziz and threw a fistful of sketches at him.

Excuse me? he swatted.

Fuckin' floccinaucinihilipilification, said Biz.

Hart jumped back out of his chair and shivered when he hit the window. I'm a gag man through and through. I like jokes, that's all.

You discredit when you don't get it, said Biz. In showbiz we call that floccinaucinihilipilification.

You're one of these new punks allergic to money, Hart said.

Not money, said Biz. I'm allergic to servitude.

We saw Charles Schulz cringe away from the confrontation and began to study more closely his pens and pencils, and with great care and companionship set them up for a fresh drawing. Well, he said to Wendy, whatever you decide, good luck to you.

Thank you, Mr. Schulz.

Call me Sparky.

She turned to us. Can you believe *that*? He told me to call him Sparky. It's like a blessing. I should take this deal with Frank, shouldn't I? My problem is that it feels like I stole the watch from a dead man's wrist.

There was one sour incident around five in the morning on Sunday when Biz Aziz was flirting with Vaughn Staedtler and things were moving along well when all of a sudden Staedtler shouted a string of obscenities at his former assistants as they came into the room. His assistants were suing him for hundreds of thousands in back payment on over twenty years of work on his legacy strip, *The Mischiefs*, about a clique of delinquent teens. When the fight was over, Biz took Staedtler outside to calm down and eventually he left in a taxi and the assistants stayed. It was the same for the comic—Staedtler, now in his late sixties, was retired from *The Mischiefs* after he had lost the rights in a previous court battle to his assistants, who now carried on for the Universal Press syndicate with no decrease in subscriptions. According to them, they had done all the work for the last thirty years anyway; Staedtler hadn't touched so much as a pencil since he got back from Korea, unless it was to pick up a girl. They even forged his signature.

About six or seven on Sunday night, the front door swung open and in came Jonjay.

8

Jonjay gave off a powdered-stone smell of crushed gravel mixed with trail dust and mountain dirt and a cement quarry—sand dripped from the creases in his tattered clothes. His jacket and jeans were so frayed that it looked as if he was covered in cat hair. His own hair was long, frayed, almost white it was so blond, his tan was as black as red wine in the bottle, his mouth was cracked and dry, and his hands were so callused. Nevertheless he was gorgeous, one of the angels or demons. His blond beard hung in greasy tentacles. He wore a pair of blown-to-bits hiking boots, and his bare, blackened toes stuck out the caps as if he'd run here from Russia. He dropped a leather portfolio on the floor and big sheets of toothy watercolour paper featuring delicate drawings of gnarled little trees spilled out around him. He didn't look at anyone. He said, Where is he? Took me ten days. I'm too late, aren't I?

Ten days? He's only been— Yes, since Friday, but—. Where have you been, Jonjay? Wendy said and started to cry. He died on Friday.

Jonjay's eyes went black as they fixed on the master bedroom, and he walked straight past Wendy in a kind of zombie daze. He was suffering from sunstroke and dehydration but we didn't know that yet. He made his way down the longtable running a hand over the surface for balance, almost as though he was blind, nodding to himself and whispering until he was in front of the entrance to the bedroom, where he paused and wondered aloud about his next step before going forward.

Bonjour hello, came a girl's voice.

Jonjay hadn't arrived alone. With him was a girl of nineteen or twenty, also sunbleached blond and a deep summer tan for so early in the season. Her petite figure had big curves; she was swinging a set of keys around her finger distractedly. Her attitude and face were familiar—the disinterested pout, the glassy focus. She told us her name was Manila, she picked up Jonjay on the 395, three hours south of Yosemite. Thought he was a dead animal, she said. I pulled over and rolled down the window. He lifted an arm and groaned at me. I almost died.

Manila saved my life, Jonjay cried out from the darkness, and pointed back towards her as he proceeded closer to the body. Someone fix her a drink.

I told him he needs help, he needs a hospital, Manila said, but he told me he had to come straight here. He was raving. Visions of this. Someone get him electrolytes or he's going to die. What's the scene here?

She was not surprised to learn this was a wake. Not after Jonjay had told her about the intense field of psychic energy that told him to make his way home. She believed him because she believed psychic energy flowed through everything, especially her body. She was not surprised she saved Jonjay's life, since he was born under the hour of the dragon and she was a Taurus ascending. She came to the conclusion he was the one artist on earth who understood her soul.

Jonjay leaned over the wicker basket and saw the waxed skin and stitched-together lips of the boy and no, even he denied this emaciated dome was Hick's. But he fell to his bare knees, then stood again as fast, unaware he'd fainted or not wanting to be seen praying. These gruesome almost robotic or bestial rites of grief, no one was free of this truth, a revulsion to death. We watched Jonjay's shoulders flinch with discernment at the hollowed-out face of his dear friend, white with mortuarist chalk to conceal as much as possible. It was Wendy who had put the pen and pencil in his hands resting on his chest. Yes. But just to see him now you could tell this knight's body weighed less than a small child's. A skeleton enrobed in a thin veil of powdered silk.

Jonjay embraced the body, kissed the sewn lips, then lifted himself away with a loud exhale. Actually a dryheave. Then he turned to the curtains. He tripped on a leg of the longtable as he left the master bedroom backwards in a hurry and started to speak. Candles trembled, nothing fell. He talked to Biz and then to Wendy, that is, if his monologue was directed at anybody at all, other than himself:

This one. This one used to churn his brains to make art. Hick climbed out of the mud of the Tenderloin to flip comics on their head. You read his comics. He spoke in that argot. He was no intellectual. He drew damn good pictures. And last time I saw him feels like yesterday. It was more than a year ago. Instead of time, he passes. *Soon* is not a fair promise to a best friend, I realize that now. And now. I've learned *now* doesn't exist as time. *Now* is a muscle. You can train hard of yourself to live for longer and longer periods of time in the now. Hick must have been scared to die. To contemplate an end. He never wanted to, he told me so. He believed his dependence on comics kept him young, he would live forever. It was the two of us, we salvaged the lunchroom tables and picnic benches and YMCA cafeteria tables or should I say stole to make this forty-two-foot longtable. We built this beauty. We studied all the possible inking techniques for comics. Silkscreening for covers, and printmaking techniques, and we set up the plates in the spare bedroom for twelve-colour separation just to sell T-shirts of our own design. We learned how to take pictures with fully manual cameras and do all the steps to the darkroom process to develop our pictures in a darkroom *we* built in *this* house. I was there when he bought that stop-motion camera rig for thirteen dollars off the pawnbroker across the street from Berkeley. All the editing equipment he owns I helped him find. We self-taught each other animation. Now will someone get me some paper? Will one of you find me a pen or pencil? I feel so diabolically woozy I have to sit down and make a drawing.

The guests all raised their glasses or smokes in a toast and drank, puffed, and watched as Jonjay found a place at the longtable.

Patrick snapped up a pristine Pentel black ballpoint, Rachael found a stack of bristol board, Twyla poured a tall glass of water, and Mark wellrolled two joints. Biz massaged his shoulders.

I'm beyond the brink, Jonjay said. I saw infinite horizons out there in the mountains. I spent the last three months with thousand-year-old trees. He pulled his hair and said, It's the dead I'm afraid of. The dead who are revolting. Can anything be done with the dead? What did the tribes used to do when a guru or a shaman died? Can we at least *eat* the dead?

He downed his glass of water and begged for another. Manila was right there with lemonade.

What is this? Jonjay inspected the joint in his fingers, sniffed it up and down and thought that this wasn't just the usual, it smelled distinctly of Hick's B.O. We told him the bag was hiding in the laundry hamper with his dirties.

Promise me you'll never wash those or we'll lose the last of his spirit, Jonjay said and took a plastic lighter from the table and ignited the joint and inhaled twice. Those clothes are infused with the reek of his unreal talents and it's got deep into this grass. Damn. I feel his powers already as a I smoke, can't you?

Yes, we did in fact. Hick Elmdales's presence was an unfathomable strength in the room that no one could argue with, a cloud of weedsmoke pressuring us to impress him, or the idea of him, the thought of his body there bearing down on our shoulders as we tried to stroke beauty out of a blank page. The expiring self penetrating through scented candles almost to a rank taste.

Where have you *been*? Wendy wanted to know.

His pupils focused long enough to recognize Wendy. Was *he* angry? he asked her, and Wendy promised that no, Hick forgave him—how could you possibly know?

But I *did* know, said Jonjay, that's what's so strange. For the past three months I was trekking and bouldering alone up and down in the White Mountains drawing and painting the bristlecone pines, he said. Alone and completely lost in the dry desert mountains, contemplating the multitudes, surrounded by ancient trees. I dreamed of city streets. Some of these bristlecone pines are thousands of years old. That's why I went to see them. Then ten days ago I got a message to come back, something was the matter with Hick.

What message, from who?

From a bristlecone tree, Jonjay said, staring off into the distance of the white page in front of him as he started to draw, hand moving spontaneously over the paper, a tree, no, a crocodile with a clock in his mouth. I sat in front of this one bristlecone pine and I saw litter trapped in its lower branches, and when I reached over to grab it I saw what it was, the face of Hick's Peter Pan from the cardboard package to a toy. Something about this little fragment off one of his pictures told me he was in trouble. I came back as soon as I could.

You're not too late for this. His last wish was that you be here and you are, so there's that. Wendy dried her eyes and then cried again.

We can't let his body go to waste, it's wrong.

He asked for gags and pranks, said Wendy. Don't take his wishes too far.

Jonjay sat back and examined his crocodile, a veritable dragon. Look, that's Hick's sweat on our brains, Jonjay told her, he's improved my markmaking, and my vision, my whole perspective. This doodle is as good as any I ever drew. I can see through the illusion of the white page to the perfect drawing inside. Imagine what you could draw, said Jonjay, and what we could all draw and what we could endure if we ate his eyes and ears and arms and hands.

You're grossing me out to the max, Wendy said.

Look, if we don't eat him something else will, Jonjay said. I know better than a worm how to eat this man. If we love him shouldn't we at least eat *some* of him? His mouth. His eyes. His fingers. His ears? I'll go around like a waiter and take everyone's order.

Don't be sick, please, she said. Where's your manners? My life just got *smooked*, pancaked. A grand piano of misery just fell on my heart.

But aren't you afraid you aren't inoculated from whatever it is killed him so suddenly? said Jonjay.

That's a lousy punchline, Jonjay. You do need liquids.

Who is he? we whispered to Wendy as soon as we got the chance.

Who indeed! Boo-hoo! She collapsed her face into the palms of her hands and said, He's back! The boy came back. Now I'm sunk. I thought I'd never see him again. *He* convinced me to move here. And he's been the irreplaceable absence in my life ever since I did. I expected to reunite a year ago. And it was only to replace him why I chased surfers up and down Marin County. Gee whiz, when I first got to SF I was like plucking married mycologists out of Golden Gate Park for some of that green thumb action, and flirting with arcade game grandmasters to get close to the feeling I yearned for. I fooled around with homeless chalk artists on Haight trying to find a little bit of the lowly artist in Jonjay. There was a small piece in each of these guys that reminded me of a part of Jonjay. Pheromones in common. The same walk. That carnally innocent smile. Different flakes of what I needed to make a muddled version of Jonjay in my heart.

Well, what's the matter, then? we wondered. If you're hot for him, here he is.

I guess so, she said glumly. After all that daydreaming for the man, I'm not ready for the real again. And what if he's with that *girl* now? Ugh, I can't stand the thought of him with some tart not me. I don't know how to be his platonic friend. That would be the worst. My problem is I don't like to share and my hot crush was safe from real competition when he only existed in the loins of my memory.

It was after midnight when Ronald Reagan appeared on television. Most sets were on mute, as the evening news repeated his words, *Our government is too big and it spends too much … The answer to a government that's too big is to stop feeding its growth. Well, it's time to change the diet and to change it in the right way.*

It's strange when the man you've been told your whole life is your father becomes president, Wendy told us. He was only the host of *General Electric Theater* when Mom pointed to him on the TV and said, *Look, there's your dad.* When he almost got assassinated last month, I cried.

My dad is a rodeo clown, said Rachael. Never see him. Not a part of my life.

My dad is in for life without parole, said Patrick with a tone of acid indifference. Killed his brother.

Dad is a libertarian, Mom is a librarian, said Twyla. First time I ran away I was fifteen.

Merchant marine, said Mark Bread of his own paterfamilias.

Orphanages called me their son, said Jonjay. First met Hick in such circumstances, two foster kids neglected under the same roof.

We learned a little more about his new friend Manila and her family woes, too. She was the Mexican-Québécois heiress-in-exile to the Convénçion family fortune in iceberg lettuce. The iceberg lettuce grew on megafarms in the boot of southern Mexico. Her side of the Convénçions lived on massive reindeer ranches in rural Quebec, and all their taxes went through a black box LLC in Nevada. A year ago after a European tryst with a married cousin, she bought a VW van from a palm reader and left the Quebec reindeers behind and went driving south to visit the iceberg lettuce megafarms. Her plan: reclaim her fortune. Frozen out of her family's bank account, Manila told us she stayed in pocket by making the best of a bad reputation, rooming at five-star hotels with ineligible men who paid her for sex and to help end arranged marriages by getting caught in the suburban society pages in the lounge with whatever local twit scion, and then she would drive to another city's rich enclave and do the same thing all over again, and in between she slept in the back of her all-white VW van, stealing away tens of thousands of dollars in the process. We were astounded by these stories and the money she described. She said she often needed to wash away the minor irritation that was her celebrity. Park somewhere up the 101 like Coos Bay or Crescent Beach and suntan on the VW's rooftop and surf all afternoon and at night by campfire read Huysmans in the original French. Manila thought of herself more as a sorceress than a runaway exiled rich girl. She spoke five languages and wanted to write, perhaps poetry.

Art is an orphanage, said Biz Aziz. When you make art, you leave your parents' hopes for you at the door to the studio. My parents came on a boatload of refugees from the coast of Africa during the Second World War. When my mother was murdered in Hagerstown city, my dad moved west. Cancer ate him. I raised myself since I was ten years old right here in San Franpsycho.

It took Biz Aziz another three years to complete her depiction of this wake. The cartoonist's death would appear in local comic shops late in eighty-four. Biz Aziz narrates the story of Jonjay's arrival and how he contrived to get us all to eat of the body of the deceased. She draws the guests in her inimitable style, unrecognizable silhouettes, trembling shadow portraits of cartoonists supposedly lining up to eat the flesh of a dead man. Captions with some panels spell out the situation and name a few names. She supplies no distinction between the real and the fictitious, the magical thinking and the actual doing. Biz didn't show any hints on the page that Jonjay's ceremony was a game or a trick he played, except surely it had to be. Wendy was convinced it was a gag. Biz might have believed the flesh was real at the time, or she was blurring the truth now in her uncensored comic. Part of being uncensored was the right to shock.

We remember green light before dawn floating between a black sky and black horizon. This lingering green anomaly, it was Hick's spirit's farewell. It was an unusual chlorophyll-green glow, the same colour as the candleflames surrounding his basket, and lasted unusually long. Gave us the shivers, the ghostliness of this aurora. As some guests, entirely exhausted, found their coats and shoes, dawn dragged out its rise up over a green-drenched Oakland that Monday morning. And when a single spear of bright yellow sunlight launched over the horizon and signalled the end, the manor began to empty—single file, heads bowed, out on to Stoneman Street and down the hill into San Francisco. The sunrise left green globules of its presentiment inside the manor. Zen celadon-green orbs hovered in meditative circles and formed prayerful clusters throughout the rooms in an eerie attempt to communicate, it would seem. You could see these orbs only out of the corner of your third eye, so to speak, but they must have meant Hick was still here with us in some fashion. When finally around eight in the morning these vapours left us completely, so did warmth. Though sunlight flooded the rooms, our fingers got so cold so fast they felt numb. We could see our breath in front of our faces. Wendy cranked the heat. We put on blankets.

Some trick. Eating Jonjay's offerings horrified us. To go along with the prank even as a piece of theatre made us gag. He made us go first, the strangers in the room—he gave us the loins, of all things, that he placed on paper plates. Closer inspection revealed our own doodles from earlier in the evening under the slivers of Hick's body. Laughing at him to cover for our fear, we said, No way.

He said, Go ahead.

When it came their turn, the other guests balked and blanched, too. We heard Art Spiegelman belching with nausea near a potted fern. But no one turned him down when he presented another morbid slice off the corpse. With the table manners of an upscale waiter, he named the cut and served it to you on a plate made of paper, the drawing on it your own. It was Hick's best friend who told the cartoonists, The dead *want* to give, it's the living who are afraid to take. Jonjay was acting like a seer or warlock or fool as he foretold the occult properties of this great man's flesh and warned us to prepare for what would hit us after the digestion of this numinous portion.

Swallowing the gross slippery flesh, what was going down our throats, was it takeout sushi? Was that the thing, raw fish used to trick us? Where did he get his props at such a moment's notice? In Biz's version of events in issue nine of her comic book, Jonjay is seen taking a fresh X-Acto blade from the longtable and going alone into the ink shadows of the master bedroom—; no witnesses as he performs the rite. When he returns to the others, it is with his hands cupped around a paper plate for a small filet. Isn't your art tempted if not your gut? he tempted you. He pitched the flesh to us: Your hands want to draw the way Hick's hands could. What cartoonist wants to live without a taste of that effortlessness? The worms don't deserve him. Let's share some of the secrets that made up his greatness and inoculate ourselves from what killed him.

Okay. Okay okay okay. Wendy accepted hers. He claimed Wendy's piece was foreskin and came with a spell of forgetting—the instant she swallowed she forgot the names of who stayed and who left, if Johnny Hart stayed on or was it Dik Browne? Chester Gould and his oxygen tank? And even as she accepted her piece she denied any of the scene was real.

We remember somewhat differently. We remember the nervous, agreeable laughter from the guests that invariably followed his very morbid offering. What did we eat that night? Props, like the corpse pieces in a Halloween haunted house. That was always Wendy's belief. No one took Jonjay seriously except for in his meaning. How could you accept anything but the soul of the gag, which was so dark it seemed appropriate, given who Hick was, and why Hick had considered Jonjay his best friend—because Jonjay was the kind of friend who would think of this. Jonjay was a savage but not a maniac. So we took bites. Biz Aziz chewed a heartvalve. She ate and ate without progress, marvelling at the tenacity of the muscle. Wendy choked back a second mouthful.

Once upon a time we shared in this common misconception of there being a divide between fact and fiction, but after that night our sense of the reality of events and the certainty of objects was forever deranged. How life seemed to be made up of the kind of person who controlled perception while most other kinds of people yielded to it. Even though we snuck in and inspected the body later, after everyone had had a piece, just to see if bits were missing—and there weren't, *there were not*—in all parts of our lives thereafter, both mentally and physically, Jonjay's prank would haunt us.

9

We wanted Jonjay to tell us one way or another, was the meal real or wasn't it? Twyla was the first to put the question to him, and he would ask us in return: Why do you want to know? Would that put you at ease? What do you recall?

We remember green light, green minutes, when, after hours of threatening to do so, Jonjay appeared carrying those pieces for us to eat. This sense of humour, so closely imitating ritual and evidently an appropriate honour to the deceased, was another reason we couldn't tell if what we'd eaten was in truth a fiction, or if that limpid white flesh we thought might be raw calamari between our teeth was off his body. Then there's a blank space, an absence or gap not in the narrative but in our conviction. We remember the body was removed by gentlemen mortuarists who would cremate and bury Hick in a cemetery plot in Daly City. One day we would go visit, but not soon.

Stop thinking about it, Jonjay warned us. Move on.

And for the moment, we did. Our attention couldn't cling forever to the sides of that big wicker basket. We took care of Wendy as she spent the rest of the week bedridden with a chest cold that wouldn't quit her. She slept twenty hours at a stretch. When she didn't sleep she lay on pillows on the living room floor and read sporadically from the bestselling *Michelle Remembers*. For two reasons Wendy made herself read the entire book: because Hick never finished reading it before the hospital, and because it took place in Victoria. *Michelle Remembers* contributed to her sickness's creeps for the satanic story was *all true*. Every word. She knew this island town described in these pages, it was her hometown. She and her mom used to go on bicycle rides along the seawall and frequently passed the Ross Bay cemetery where Michelle was abused by Satanists. When Wendy was asleep we all took turns reading from it too—the unlocked memories of unimaginable satanic ritual abuse Michelle had been the victim of in her early childhood, including an intentional car crash on a highway, being buried alive in a grave, and numerous other sacrificial rites in forests and caves, culminating in visitations from none other than Jesus and Azazel, aka Satan himself. All of it Michelle repressed for two decades, until in her college years Dr. Pazder's unique style of Catholicized psychiatric hypnosis uncovered the truth in therapy sessions. Later the doctor would divorce his wife in order to marry his patient.

No, not possible—it still never occurred to Wendy that Jonjay would do something so heinous. Magic was his motive, not cruelty. The reason Jonjay thought it was a good idea to perform this sort of mad theatrical mockery of flesh after death could be found in *Michelle Remembers*—and in almost all the books on Hick's shelves. This occult sideshow was Hick's lurid fascination, as an artist, not as a practitioner. Hick wouldn't condone actual practice of superstition, but he loved the aesthetic of the decadent. You could tell just by scanning the titles and authors how interested he was in whatever tread on the meridian, and how this theme inspired his drawings and his story arcs in *Pan*. Leading a double life as an amateur demonologist stoked by the literature of this tradition gave his *Pan* its subtle subversive side. Therefore Wendy would finish the last book, benign as all the rest, and break the fake curse—petty symptoms begone! She blew her nose for the thousandth time and coughed out a pint of slime.

And her second reason to read contradicted the first. Break the fake curse while looking for the proof this memoir offered of the existence of the supernatural occult forces she felt so strongly surrounded her growing up in that small rainy city on the island. Why else would such a picturesque little city village fill her with such unimaginable dread? For as long as she could recall—crib days even, those days were rattled, too.

Wendy didn't like being Canadian. She told people she was from Cleveland. She wanted to be a fullblooded American like the rest of us; she didn't want anything so insignificant as a birthplace to hold her back. She wanted American children to read her comics, buy her toys, and watch her cartoon on American televisions, and we were going to help her.

After a week bedridden with flaring rashes, fever flashes, shivers-shakes, she said it out loud: Nope, I think I have what Hick had. That's it. I'm done for. It's that fucking memoir. You shouldn't have read it, you fools. We're all going to die. And she threw the book at the wall. I finished every last word so help me. Who's next? Wendy stumbled and pressed herself against the wall, knocking down an original Dick Tracy drawing, I have this unspeakable modern dilemma, the George Orwell disease, the gay-related plague, that's what the nurses whispered in the corridor, now we have it, too.

Rachael brought her hot lemonwater and sent her back to bed with a Valium she bought on a street corner in the Mission. Sleep, sweet friend, you'll be okay, she said and pet Wendy's hair out of her face, slicked down with a cold sweat.

Teeth grinding. Wendy developed a near-permanent jaw clench after Hick's death, and at night or when she wasn't paying attention, her molars and bicuspids would squeak and crack out of tension so loud you could hear it through the walls.

I need to see a doctor about my teeth, she told Gabby over the phone.

What about your teeth?

I grind them.

You grind. Well, yeah, sign up for our Shepherd health care plan. There's plenty of options to choose from.

Goddamn *Michelle Remembers*.

Who?

The book may be cursed, said Wendy.

No idea what you're talking about.

Sleep was no escape—it was worse. She slept heavily. When she awoke her jaw was sore. All day long she was aware of a free-floating anxiety that never left her head, a grinding like a crazy caffeine rush that made her want to shit herself from migraine pain and then go carry a sign down the street with the words *The End is Near!*

We all needed help. So one day we did the horrible and grabbed the keys to her lime-green Gremlin and drove to see Dr. Dritz in 5D, who recommended blood tests for all of us. The waiting room was full of these elderly men in their mid-twenties and thirties—hair falling out, flannel jackets a size or more too big, soiled shirts, and bodies ravaged by shigellosis, pneumonia, dead veins, burnt loins, pullulating cancer scabs. The waiting room ashtrays needed to be emptied. One of these young men leaned over to Mark and said, The plague is the new black. Mark, who rarely did, laughed. While we waited we flipped through current events magazines and national newspapers—Ronald Reagan was the cowboy president who survived assassination and everyone had an observation about that but not one of the journalists wrote a word about this new fashion for dying sweeping the boys of San Francisco.

The nurse let us know that unless we heard back within twenty-four hours then our bloodwork was negative. A gloom settled over us and we flinched at the sound of the phone every time it rang. *Michelle Remembers* was put out of view. Biz wouldn't leave her studio upstairs. Wendy began to pack her few belongings and prepared for some kind of journey. Jonjay lay on the floor beside the bejewelled tiles of the carapace of his shellacked tortoise and caressed the creature's glazed face, reminiscing. He missed the days taking Dorian, his ninety-three-year-old pet, on a slow walk through Haight-Ashbury and everyone gawking and taking pictures. That was the life, Jonjay and a ravishing tortoise. This whole manor smells like death, we need to get out of here, he said and got up from one seat and went and straddled his tortoise. Let's go, my one and only friend, giddyup. Take me back to whence I came.

When there was no doubt we were in the clear, we celebrated. Tacitly. We didn't admit how happy we were to be alive. We chalked it up to the magic Jonjay played on us, placing a spell on our palates. Patrick took a bicycle and ran a trapline from one end of the city's bars to the other, and then on to the steamrooms to burn off the alcohol and meet singles and threesomes for anonymous sex. Mark's way was to drink six cans of beer and a mickey of rye, smoke three joints, and pass out in front of the turntable for thirteen hours listening to the crackle at end of side A. Biz ate copious drugs of all rate and function and spent the weekend in the Castro village a celebrity tripping from house party to house party.

And Wendy crawled out of the fear and woke up from all that praying and sat down for the first time in a while at the longtable, and with Rachael and Twyla beside her, she got down to work on another *Strays* strip—Buck and Murphy in a round of Ping-Pong.

If all else fails, I go with Ping-Pong, she said.

We remember that one wall of the living room was dedicated to a massive collection of vinyl. Hick's bootleg funk collection alone ran up to a thousand discs. He owned all the Brill Building seven-inch singles he could get his hands on. Most of the time we spent with Biz Aziz was flipping records; she loved to listen to rare Parliament or Carole King tunes while drawing, oldies gave her ideas for stage material and heavy funk was her heart and soul. She did all her drawing at No Manors; every page of her comic memoir was completed here. It turned out Biz rented a single room on a corner of the third floor, which she used as a kind of green room and costume department—all five hundred square feet was dedicated to her live performance persona. (No room for a drawing table there.) She was something of a drag nurse to the other queens in town who needed mending or on occasion commissioned dresses from her. In fact, Biz was our main source—once a month she dropped off a pound of marijuana she got from her boy in Oakland, for which we paid a thousand dollars. Split into ounces and dimebags, it was easily turned into ten or twelve thousand a month. This never would have happened if local cartoonists hadn't stopped by No Manors so often asking to try some, heard we had some, here's some cash. (None of us had the street smarts to survive on a corner.) This was how we sold a lot of very sweaty-smelling weed without much hassle, and we split the profits among the five of us, Biz included. Our fast-paced side business put cash in our pockets at a time when being Wendy's assistants was more of an honorific or internship than a paycheque.

While all this went on Manila Convençion parked her white VW van on the street outside for a few weeks, running an extension cord and plugging into the side of No Manors, trying desperately to woo Jonjay back onto the road with her. The iceberg lettuce megafarms beckoned to her and she threatened to leave for them almost every day, but when Jonjay didn't seem upset at this prospect, she stayed longer. Wendy had ways to keep him on the premises, asking him to do favours in Hick's memory, long overdue repairs to the place, protection against more of Disney's henchmen, money to tide her over until she could take on the lease.

For the time being, Hick's master bedroom remained preserved as he had left it, laundry hamper and its contents included.

10

STRAYS

Our first job as Wendy's assistants was to pretend to be. She wanted to impress her new business partner with a bustling team, so when Frank came over at dusk one evening for his appointment to see the animals, she walked him through her *studio* and introduced us as her factotums. He had his transparent ploy to see her again and she had her ploy to impress him—and strangely, Wendy made it sound like these two motives were at odds. She'd deflect him with a small army of professionalism.

Twyla Noon was who asked impertinent questions, and in the days following the wake all she wanted to know was whether Wendy planned to sleep with Frank again. The answer was emphatically *no*, Wendy wasn't going to give up her social life to become some suburbanite's idea of a mistress. That was a one-time well-played mistake on a mutual whim. Besides, now that Jonjay had returned home, her infatuation with him didn't leave much room in her imagination for a married man. *That* was the answer Twyla didn't want to hear, gunning for Jonjay herself.

As we helped Wendy ink-panel borders in prep for a weekly *Strays* strip she told us the story of how she met Jonjay. This was only about two years ago, back in her hometown of Victoria after she got expelled from school. Left to her own devices, she ended up loitering downtown all week, selling off stock of her pornographic comics to the other delinquents—she was done with sex drawings for the moment, and now she drew beasts. He had hitchhiked into Canada to visit some famed occult artist-poet living in her neighbourhood whom she'd never heard of, and while he was at it, since it was the season, he was going to pick wild edible mushrooms, dry them, and sell them to connoisseurs overseas. She saw him wander into Horizone, the video arcade in the basement where she sat most days of the week and drew beasts like the peacock monster, Adramelch, the Scox, Count Bifron, and the Zozo. Meanwhile he reached the twenty-second level on Pong on one quarter. A crowd formed around him to watch in awe. Everyone's stunned face in his face. Nothing fazed him. The speed at which the pong flew at those upper levels was dizzying. Kids were awestruck. A legend was made. Wendy didn't get up from her table to spectate like the rest of them, instead she sat back and drew the whole scene—she drew the sequence in four pages, starting with this beautiful stranger and three local skids in sleeveless jean jackets watching on either side of the screen, to the moment when he passed level nineteen and a punk girl fainted. Level twenty-two, the pong shot out like a bullet and Jonjay kept the joystick rattling with it for another fifty seconds before the screen froze. The screen literally froze mid-pong. There it was. Nothing moved. Pong or person. Everything froze. He blew up Pong. You could see for yourself that his bar was barely about to hit the pong. Computer jammed. The arcade went totally quiet, then erupted. The owner came over, took a Polaroid with Jonjay and the frozen screen, then unplugged and plugged back in Pong.

When the hubbub died down, and he got a chance, he came straight over to see her. This was how she hoped it would play out, him coming to her. Wendy the cool. Something about his no-nonsense swagger made her loins drool (her words). He said he saw her out of the corner of his eye and could tell she was drawing. What was she drawing? She showed him. He liked the pictures. He said he didn't realize she was drawing the scene. Then she brought out the demon doodles she wanted to print together as a 'zine. Those really impressed him. He thought her style was freaky and fresh and he sat down at the table in the back of the arcade next to her and took up a pen of his own. It turned out he could draw anything. I started crushing on him like one-two-three, Wendy snapped her fingers. I forgot all about money and gave him copies of my dirty comics for free, I said, *Take them, I can't look at them another second*. He made his own comic, too, he said. He took a copy out of his rucksack of *The Artist*, it was offset printed and twenty-two pages long, in full colour. Inspired by his friend Hick Elmdales, *The Artist* was Jonjay's only attempt at a comic and much too good at that. In it, the Artist was an average citizen endowed with supernatural powers by a highly evolved being the size of a cosmos, enabling him to create art out of thin air. Jonjay's drawing style was indelible, enviable, totally his own, confident, fast lines pushing and pulling the eye across the page, panels filled with bold shadows, the art was kinetic and unglued. She asked if she could keep it. He said it was his last copy of a hundred, but okay. They got to talking. She told Jonjay she was in the mood to run away—where did that come from?—she never voiced this thought until now, but listening to herself she believed it, sincerely. He told her all about all the cartoonists living in San Francisco, and about the situation at his home, No Manors, where Disney's ghostwriter-ghostartist for *Pan* lived and everybody hung out. That sounded like the place for her.

She said those words to him, What happens if I kiss you?

He said, Here in the arcade?

Yeah for sure here or anywhere. As soon as possible. Like our lives depend on it.

Okay, he said and kissed her. He tasted of seasalt, like a caramel you'd dropped in the ocean. Can we go back to your place? he asked. Quickly she processed this: she wasn't a virgin but she'd never brought a boy back to her apartment before. That would break a lot of her mom's house rules.

Isn't there somewhere else? My mother sleeps on the living room hide-a-bed. Screw it, let's go to my place. I don't care. I can lock my door. She'll have to break it down.

The lights were off in the apartment and her mother wasn't home, but in the morning when the two of them awoke they discovered she had done the laundry, cleaned all their clothes, and Jonjay's were folded neatly and laid out at the door, including socks and underwear. Cheap coffee was percolating aromatically and the first round of toast just popped out of the toaster with a cheap jolt. She whispered to Jonjay her mother never made breakfast—this was her embarrassing display of benevolence to prove Mom was *cool* with the presence of a naked boy in Wendy's bed and finding their clothes all over the apartment as if the two teenagers had exploded. The moment she left the bedroom to say good morning to her mother, Jonjay opened the window and climbed out. (She was mistaken about more than his age, she would someday learn.)

When they discovered Jonjay was gone her mother leaned out the third-floor window and looked down into the alleyway, laughed and said, You remind me so much of myself sometimes it hurts.

That was the sort of thing her mother said to make Wendy cringe. She didn't want to resemble her mother or be close to her mother, she wanted to run away. But how does one leave behind something that's within?

How to go and say goodbye, as if to life itself? Leaving brought her closer to her unknown self, that American aspect, her father. Now her mother could see she was stewing and wanted to show Wendy something she'd found in that boy's pocket when she put his pants through the laundry last night. It was a chequebook. Look at the number. The last amount credited was for over a million dollars.

So what if he's rich? Wendy said and staggered back in shock though doing as best she could to make it look natural. Her mother didn't always have money for rent at the end of the month. Wendy put the chequebook in her pocket. You shouldn't snoop through other people's stuff, Mom.

Alls I'm saying is, that's men for you. Her mother shot her a look, stood up from the kitchen table, and went to light a cigarette off the stove. Sometimes it hurts, she said.

Her mother was dead wrong. Jonjay didn't vanish from her life after one night like Ronald Reagan did with her mother. He was still loafing around in town. He wanted to see her, otherwise why would he go back to Horizon? She wasn't so catatonic with passion that she forgot to ask him about the chequebook. So you're a millionaire? she asked point-blank. He blushed and chewed his lip, asked her if she had the chequebook and if so could he have it back? Can you keep a huge secret? he asked her and she said that she could. I'm not that rich, he said.

It didn't matter to Wendy either way. What mattered was him. Once more he spent the night in Wendy's bed and her mother had to deal with it. His ideas about sex were novel but not gimmicky. His gestures were fun, brave, he smelled better than a forest, and he could flatter and spoil her. When he left town the next day Wendy grieved as though he had died. It never occurred to her she could go with him and it never figured into his plans to invite her. His next stop was not home to No Manors but to Japan to sell the coastal matsutakes he'd picked on the island. And to climb Osorezan. In her bed he'd described his plans. There was a mountain in Japan called Fear that was supposed to hide the entrance to the afterlife. On that mountain he was going to pick and eat the legendary skull mushroom, a hallucinatory fungus only found there. And so with thoughts of Fear Mountain clutched to her breast, the following day Wendy stole the money she knew her mother kept hidden in a Hungry Hungry Hippos game box in the closet, left a note with a doodle that said she was leaving the city, leaving the island the city was on, leaving the country, and she'd call from America next chance she got.

11

Just how old are you anyway? she asked Jonjay that afternoon before Frank arrived for his tour of Bernal Heights park and its community of lost pets.

Retirement age, he said and smiled with a childlike mendacity. His feet were kicked up in front of a television showing clips of hostage negotiations. This is terribly suspenseful TV, he said by the way. It's just an airplane on tarmac, and it's a repeat, but I'm hooked. Masked men waving Kalashnikovs once a day. The hijacking is a Cold War in miniature where the less that happens the better.

My editor thinks I'm twenty-five, but I turned *eighteen* this year, Wendy said and sat down beside him and stared at the TV screen. Am I in trouble? What's going on?

Men from Iran loaded with guns took the passengers on that plane hostage, Jonjay explained, and I'm not *that* old looking, am I? You wouldn't actually in a court of law mistake me for a senior citizen, would you? It's that White Mountain sunburn, gave me a lizard tan. I'm twenty-eight yesterday.

Happy birthday. As a present, take me here, now, do it. Plunge, splash, come. Here's my plan, she said without batting an eyelash and took an erasable blue pencil out of her tray and began to rough out the basic composition of each of the four frames in a weekday *Strays*. As she spoke, she drew. Tell me what you think: I'll show Frank up the hill and around the bend and find him a rabid cat and a mangy dog or two. Walk around the dump site and see him to his vehicle. Good night, no kisses. If he expects to go up my skirt I'm going to tell him that's out of the question. From now on, it's business, that's all.

Good idea. Sex is for dummies, said Jonjay, slapping his beltloops. What if you got the nastiest herpes ever from sex?

Twyla said Wendy shouldn't repress her emotions, that would be too demon-friendly. That's why a sensible woman is easily possessed by evil, because she so promptly represses the bad shit. Fuck Frank *again*, Twyla advised.

Rachael Wertmüller was skeptical of Wendy's willpower. Who are you resisting *for*? she wanted to know. Surely not yourself. Spouse? A woman you've never met?

No, for my own sanity. He can go ahead and picture me on a bed of silk for all I care. I don't want him to see my *Rockford Files* pillowcases. I'm all for the separation of businessmen and pleasure. What if he's told his wife he's gone out of town or some bullshit story because he expects to spend the night—the weekend? I don't know why I'm so scared about him coming over, but I really wish I could call this off. This was a mistake from the start. I don't like it when people have extra expectations they aren't being honest about. Secrets are bad. But if I cancel, my editor will decapitate me.

We told Wendy not to cancel. To cancel would be overthinking a good thing. She needed the business Frank promised to drum up and this was ostensibly a friendly business meeting, nothing more. If he crossed a line she could demand he retreat out of respect. If he didn't accept then we'd kill him, clearly.

A phony, Jonjay said. I remember him. Got me kicked out of Stanford. Problem is, everyone in that lab is there for one reason, pure math. Math for math's sake. It's a very clean system. There's professors and students and it's all academic, nothing ideological in the room to spoil the atmosphere of pure math. A guy like Frank spoils the atmosphere. Pure math becomes ulterior-motive math. When you know there's a stooge in the room with ulterior motives it changes the outcome of an experiment, every scientist knows that and does everything they can to avoid that. He tainted labs. Everyone felt it. Then they pointed at me. I was even worse. I tainted everything. I was auditing. I was the impurity they'd failed to notice. The impurity they were too blind to see. They hated me. So the graduates got up a petition to have me removed.

You know what he sort of told me, that he stole your formula so he could get rich off stocks and bonds.

He stole my model? Is that what he told you? Well, he did, then. Jonjay stood up from the couch and paced the living room and absently picked up the clutter on the floor. As he spoke he found gaps to wedge these toys and novels into shelves, toss a watercolour set across the room onto the longtable. His free-throw rate at the wastebin was unrivalled. He talked at a steady clip, a bit faster than usual and with a lot more sarcasm, spitting out his words. If he's using that model then he went to the labs looking to pinch something and use it for profit. Those eggheads were right all along. He didn't want people, he wanted code. But you can't steal *my* formula, said Jonjay and walked the other direction, then back again. I didn't invent this equation and I can't own it, I just discovered it exists. I hit on a model for the ages. I don't own anything. He has no idea what I use that for.

What sort of formula is it? Wendy asked.

It's more of a model, Jonjay said. When you get obsessed down to the integer with how much of life is pinballs knocking around in the universe's unending game of total randomness, there's only one ground

THE ROAD NARROWS AS YOU GO

zero for chaos theory. Not MIT, but right here in the Bay, the Stanford scene. I got fascinated with nature's architecture somehow formed up in this boiling chaos. Like conch shells, and fiddleheads, you know Fibonacci spirals, those repeated sequences in nature and so on. That blooms big in my mind. The fact there's a million squillion years of randomness flickering under those perfect forms nature designs, human life, any matter and all existence, pretty amazing.

I thought maybe you went to art school, said Wendy.

Pure math is ahead of pure art around here. Not many cities can say that. There's a lot going on in math right now, big stuff. Those physics classes I considered my art school. Like, just wrap your mind around the idea that reality itself is a random zap. I learned there are universes that *aren't real*. So I wanted to figure out for the sake of my life what can change what's random. I was like, maybe my amazement does, probably panic does. Maybe there's a mathematical model that measures fear or courage as it affects random processes. If the universe is a game of Ping-Pong, I wanted to model the whaps we make with the paddles.

Pong theory, said Wendy.

God, I love Pong. Playing Pong changed my life. When I fuck up Pong, or when I nail Pong, I want to measure precisely why, I want to create a data field to model my emotional reaction. That bouldercrashing frantic mistake-riddled emotional trip-ups that video games tap into and feed off of, for sure. I love that. My model is for deeply associative, emotional, triggerhappy free-floating human volatility. I tightened my math a hair here, a hair there to get the actions to align. A mathematical model is my kind of art. I start up from a sketch and get the lines tighter and tighter as I ink in the details, and then it's an experiment with shadows and fine lines until I think I have it. Life in all its manifold illogical conjecture, quantified.

Yikes.

Nature's data. I wanted to input natural events into my formula, and check out what I got—the meaning of life. But if you crunch the data, someone like Frank might think he's seeing the results for a stock market crash *in advance*. But he isn't, that's his imagination.

That's what Frank thinks, that he stole a crystal ball. He's my editor's idea of a whale of a client, so listen. I don't want to go broke before I get to be rich, so maybe you should tell him when he comes over that the formula he stole doesn't work the way he thinks it does. Plus I'd like to see if that news made his wig pop off.

He can do what he wants with it, said Jonjay. I'm not going to stop him. I didn't show anyone the formula. I kept it to myself. I never told him how it works. Like you said, he stole it.

Frank owns some of your pictures, too, did you know that? You should pay Justine Witlaw a visit and collect your half, said Wendy.

I make what I make to make it, he said and snorted with indifference It was clear from his expression that money and possessions repulsed him on the same basic level as rotting vegetables, but at the same time entrepreneurialism was, if anything, his art form. Because of this pompous disrespect he had for economic wellbeing, if it weren't for Justine Witlaw being savvy enough to steal up every scrap of art she saw Jonjay made, his oeuvre might be lost forever.

Compare that attitude to when around seven that evening Frank arrived for his special tour of Bernal Hill—from the moment he stepped up to the manor door he took on this persona of a thumbsucking shy teen suitor, and his bouquet and bottle of red wine tied with a pink ribbon distracted from the brick-sized Motorola cellphone hanging from his hip. He confessed right away how excited he was to see her again as if it wasn't obvious. She took the bottle and flowers and tossed them to Mark, asked if he'd like to see the manor first.

Sure, he said and stepped gingerly through the entrance of what appeared at first glance to be a slob's house, a disorganized mess of things no sane adult kept around. The range floored him if not the functionality. The longtable shall remain the centre of the legend of No Manors but guests, especially ones from other, tamer milieus, never forget seeing the dozens of pedal bicycles that hung from the ceiling in the main hall entrance, the clever solution Hick thought of to deal with all the unclaimed bikes left behind after some of the more outlandish parties in the heyday. For these bikes tipped the iceberg of hoard in No Manors. Rather than go out much, it had been Hick's preference to suck as much of the world as possible into his orbit. Hick and Wendy's favourite outings were for art supplies, to record stores, flea markets, and pawn shops. We got the impression Frank was glad to meet her assistants, if only to reassure himself that Wendy didn't live alone in this dump. No, there was Patrick in front of a video game, and Rachael over a sewing machine prepping a costume for her next live performance as Aluminum Uvula. Twyla and Mark acted on duty at the lightboxes tracing images from old *Strays* for future panels. So that was us. There might have been others. Biz or someone else from upstairs down to use the Xerox machine or a camera.

The inevitable meeting between Frank and Jonjay took place in the living room with Reagan muted on the television and one interruption from Manila Convençion who walked through after a shower with a towel around her body and another in a turban around her head. Don't mind me, she said, kicking her little wet toes up behind her.

Frank turned to Jonjay. When I saw Wendy a few weeks ago she said you were missing in action. Where have you been?

Yes, and back in the nick of time, too, said Jonjay. From what I hear you owe me one, *big*.

Frank nodded but didn't break a sweat. I do, he said. I think I owe you anything you ask for. Just say the word.

Jonjay stood and shook his hand. I'll hold you to that. I have some ideas.

No doubt you do. Are you staying here?

So far as I can see. Jonjay fell back on the sofa and lifted his legs up onto the coffee table and used the remote control to flip channels.

I like this longtable, said Frank. Reminds me of my office. It's designed in a giant X shape with my desk smack in the middle of the X and my staff spread out along the arms. Isn't your roommate the young man behind *Pan*? Frank asked.

Let's go, Wendy said. I'll explain on our walk.

She brought flashlights with her, and climbed Bernal Hill. Ice hung in the air. The only other person on the hill was a man in a brown corduroy blazer out for a walk. Within a few minutes they heard a cat mewl, then tracked its tail bounce through the brush. Further along they caught a ribby dog slavering over the residue left in some Chinese takeout boxes. And nearby a family of raccoons was sitting in a flat tire in the tall weeds, waiting a turn.

You can see why I like living here, she said.

He said this was the most fun he'd had in years.

You're not kidding, said Wendy, and he put his hands on her shoulders in preparation for an embrace. He wasn't kidding. Look, she said, this can't happen again.

Why not?

We're in business together. You're married. My roommate and best friend and total mentor died two weeks ago.

I know, this isn't rational, but I can't stop thinking about you.

Our whole relationship is supposed to be about licensing and merchandising. I don't want the start of my career to be the beginning of your betrayal. Everything will fall apart. Plus I'm not mistress material. There's too much stress in *mistress*. Plus your wife sounds cool, smarter than me, she's your high school sweetheart, wow, and you said she writes? Prose, now that is college smart, Frank. All I do is doodle humdingers and kneeslappers. The most challenging part of my day is cutting out the zipatone screens. I'm good for a product. So sell it. You get my drift? We had our one-night fling. Flings are my thing.

I met someone this month who I feel like I've known since before I was born. Like you have been waiting for me since my gene pool took off in the cosmic soup. I wish you'd told me about your friend dying so I could share in your sadness.

Okay, that's enough. All this romance. I believed your note, what you wrote that we were back to the normal world. *Regularly scheduled programming.*

I regret I wrote that. I thought it was clever of me. I meant for the moment, the time being. Until we could see each other again. What about the last line?

Something about getting to know me? I don't believe that. I think you went home and your glands got swollen up and you wanted more so you called me. Well it's still the *time being* for me. Our night together was loony-tunes, don't spoil it. We celebrated with crazy abandon, but let's remember we're professionals with obligations. Regularly scheduled programming, Frank.

The night turned cold on him. He looked away from her. The dogs on the hill barked. Cats mewled and hissed. The lights of San Francisco danced in front of them like fire on a screen at a drive-in movie and from this altitude the moon seemed ironic. He started to tremble in his cheap suit. His hair fought to keep its form. He said, You know my honest feelings, Wendy. Do you really mean what you're telling me, or are you putting up some kind of a front? Because what happened with Jonjay, that's—

You know what? Jonjay told me the math equation you stole from him doesn't work the way you think it does. How's that for you? It's not intended for the stock market, it's for other purposes. Ask him if you want to, but I guess he decided to leave you hanging. I shouldn't have said anything but I don't want you to put my comic strip at risk.

I'm in the bond market, not stocks.

See there you go. Stocks and bonds. I didn't even know there was a difference, said Wendy. I can talk about a nib or a brush. And what about kids?

What about kids?

Do you have them?

No. Why do you ask?

Because I want to know who you are. You have this entire life you suppose I can ignore. And I have a life, too, that you would discard most of, I think, just so we can fuck.

Don't say that. I want the same things you do.

Don't forget, you make this kind of deal every day, but for me, what you're giving me is this *one* shot, and it's all I get, so I have to focus on making a great comic now, not pleasing you in hotel rooms. Please, Frank, go home. San Jose needs you. No more private pitches.

And what about Friday night? Is that the kind of deal *you* make every day?

Whoever you think I am, I'm not. I'm nobody's delicacy. In the *Lady and the Tramp*. I'm a rat. There must be a dozen foxes in your typing pool you could woo if you need some wild on the side. You saw my animals with your very own eyes. They're real. They're frightened. Every last one of them. Aren't they adorable, fleas and all? I wish their lives weren't so tragic. I guess that's why I find their story funny. Now please, I say, I fondly beg you, just let me draw them. It's what I love to do.

Before he let her go back inside he grabbed her face and kissed her, held on to her face with urgency and a fiendishness that was fondness, and then instead of waiting to get slapped, slipped into the back of a limousine idling at the curb.

See you soon, he said and vanished behind a tinted window.

He was one of five people in northern California with a cellular phone. Within seconds of her walking in the door he called. Why? To say in a businesslike manner, Listen, I loved our tour of your inspiration. I hope you'll come down to San Jose soon and visit the offices. The staff is going to want to meet you.

Not likely, Wendy said.

I'll get a secretary to make the appointment.

In the meantime we made sure to record onto a blank Beta cassette the ABC documentary that night about the assassination attempt on Reagan from a month ago. And talk about full circle, get this—the president's Secret Service bodyguard dreamed of one day becoming a Secret Service bodyguard to the president after watching Reagan play the role of a cocky-lipped Secret Service bodyguard to the president in an old black-and-white action-adventure propaganda film.

Check out how serene he is in the face of absolute mortal danger, said Jonjay. He was not talking about Frank Fleecen but President Reagan after being shot near the heart. Wendy came home and collapsed on the chesterfield with her head on a pillow across from Jonjay so he could massage the soles of her feet. Listen to your father figure as he cracks pitch-perfect jokes with the surgeons before they put him under anaesthetic to remove a bullet from his chest, Jonjay said and aimed the remote control at the TV. He doesn't know if a madman or Soviets or his own government shot him. But he's still got the confidence of a bad stage actor. I don't get him. There's no depth to his psychology. He's always that good-humoured action figure, nothing upsets his good mood. It makes no sense. Unless Reagan believes he's trapped in an episode of *The Twilight Zone*. Someone convinced him—maybe it's the CIA, they gaslight him, convince him that our world is all a soundstage, and the *real* America is behind a brick wall he dare not visit.

That sounds like your own delusion, said Patrick.

Well, he can *have* his world, said Wendy, but she wasn't thinking about Reagan and his delusions, or Jonjay's, she was talking about Frank and his offices in San Jose and more importantly the wife and suburban home that loomed large and shadowy in her imagination. Of the whole affair with Fleecen, Wendy had this to say: Nobody on earth who gets to know me imagines I'm better than what they already have. Even if I wanted to be with Frank, that doesn't mean I would want to spend time with him. What I do is draw. Flings are my thing. There's no time in my life for anything but professional commitments. I'm not girlfriend, mistress, or any other kind of material. I'm this night owl with a pen in her hand. Don't touch me, I'm not yours.

The glory's the stories, said Jonjay and clasped his hands together. Comics are your gusto. History rarely hails the mistress. Except Cleopatra, all the legends surround creators. Frank's a user. Use him back. Use up the use of the user, then throw him out.

2

12

Hick Elmdales used to say that in order to pay their dues the average artist with a comic strip in the newspaper had painted at least twenty-five houses inside and out, another dozen store signs, price lists, and chalk displays, sixteen homejob tattoos, designed ninety-nine advertisements, a hundred and eleven rock concert posters, fifty-six political gags, a half-inch stack of bad art, milkcrates full of sketchbooks, and at least two dozen weeks' worth of strips before a syndicate gave you a shot at the funny pages.

She should count herself lucky, then, was what Hick implied, since it took Wendy a third of the work of an average talent to get her strip syndicated.

In her mind that meant she still owed two-thirds of her credibility, it meant her luck was in arrears. She must work off that mental debt doing extra hours. Debt was a painful sort of negative reinforcement she used as daily motivation for the next three years. For it wasn't until around eighty-four that she felt she had paid her dues to the history of comic artists slaving, and that this membership into the pantheon demanded more of her than she knew how to give. So Wendy would become a business, and in so doing she employed us.

For three years we took care of all that client work she got handed. Every toy you saw, the package the toy was in, the display for the toy store, the advertisement for the magazine, we handled that, from the sketch on up to the final *final* blueprint for manufacture, that was us. Hundreds of toys and calendars. Lots of clients. But the first contract Frank signed, that will always be the most significant. It was significant because it was the first deal. And because this deal made almost all the rest of the deals possible. That's why Gabby called so early. The phone rang before ten in the morning. Wendy was asleep. Rachael took the call. Wake her up, Gabby said. She has to hear this herself. This is big.

Gabby called because Frank had signed exclusive manufacturing rights to Lupercal Plastics, of El Segundo.

Plastic company. Okay. Good stuff. Frank didn't call *me*.

I'm the business end of your stick, Wendy. You focus on your silly doodles.

Wendy picked the hard tail of a dried teardrop out of the corner of her bloodshot eye. Why wasn't she more excited? Cream bloomed and erupted as it mixed with her coffee, and sunlight through the bay window turned the kitchen nook into a greenhouse full of dead plants and hangovers. Sorry, Gabby, you woke me up. I was dreaming I was a bat hanging upside down in a cave and flying around with thousands of other bats. I ate a centipede.

Well, it's midday in Manhattan, Wendy. Real life just ate a centipede. Frank said Lupercal is just the beginning and a long list of licences will come from this. Happy?

Yes, indeedy, said Wendy. Consider that in the month of March of eighty-one Wendy had earned a hundred and fourteen dollars and eleven cents from her comic strip. A ten-thousand-dollar signing bonus in May was a significant uptick.

Her editor ran through a list of to-dos that included a complete set of eight-by-tens of each character in three-sixty rotation. Can do?

Can do.

Gabby hung up to take another call, then a moment later called back breathless. Wendy, you are not going to believe this. Frank says Mattel wants to license *Strays* toys.

Frank called you again?

Yes. Mattel. What did I say about a whale? Wendy, I'm vibrating. Do you know how much was at stake here? Our careers, our futures. Every paper that's turned down your strip is going to think again, those dumb bastards. We're going to see a flood of subscriptions come in when word gets around Mattel is behind you. All Shepherd Media's newspapers will fall in line. I'm giddy. There's going to be kids who get Buck for their birthday.

Is Frank going to call me?

He said he would like to call you, that is, if you want him to call you. Because this is great news, but he said he respects the privacy of the artist, is what he said. Those were his words.

Oh. I see. Okay. Tell him *not* to call me. I'll call him, Wendy said. Rachael! Wendy shouted, then jumped up on the seat of the kitchen nook and pointed to us all. Twyla! Mark! Patrick! You're all hired. Then she leaped down and out of the kitchen in two strides, spilling art supplies as

she went whooping into the living room. She fell on top of Jonjay who was until a moment ago asleep on the chesterfield. Let's go for drinks, on me.

Wha— It's ten in the morning.

Celebration breakfast.

Drinks this early makes me an alcoholic but okay, said Jonjay as he scratched his chest under his shirt and picked up the tail end of a joint rolled the night before and tried to light it with a Bic out of fluid. Let's go somewhere with greasy food and a view, he said, flicking, and eventually threw the lighter across the room. Who's going to tell me what we're celebrating?

Frank got me a deal with Mattel toys.

Wow, said Jonjay, slapping his cheeks. That is the weirdest wakeup call.

Twyla thought she should get in touch with Frank right away. And be like, wow, you just turned my characters into toys, wow, that's so amazing, *thank you*, Twyla said as she put on her high purple boots and took down a bicycle to ride. This is exciting, right? You're about to get your own fucking toys.

What's Frank doing in the toy business? said Jonjay. He's making some kind of a play, isn't he? What's his deal with all these moves? Why is he all of a sudden so interested in your comic?

Let's talk about it over eggs and beer, said Wendy and followed Jonjay as far as the bathroom door, which slammed in her face. I'll call him later, she said. Let's go out and spend some of my jackpot.

That was the one time we all went out for breakfast and got hammered. Now we remember running upstairs and inviting Biz to come along and Manila being there, too, but we could be mistaken, it's hard to imagine there was ever a day when Manila could go out in public without a throng of men closing in around her. We ate dozens of eggs that morning to celebrate, eggs in every style, heaps of hashbrowns, platefuls of bacon, stacks of pancakes and waffles, along with eleven pitchers of beer.

Wendy got excited talking about her ideas for a Christmas special. No one has done a Christmas cartoon that's meant to air in the summertime, but why not, the season is wide open and the Christmas spirit is supposed to be all year round. Imagine this: Buck overhears some kids talking about the meaning of Christmas, and he gets the idea to host a Christmas party of his own for the rest of the stray animals in the vacant lot. But he doesn't know Christmas is on December twenty-fifth, and it's summertime. So there's scenes of the animals all going and finding presents for each other, making presents, wrapping them up with ribbon and bows, and they meet up for Buck's party on the night of. He's trimmed the tree and the fence, set the flat tire up, and is dressed like Santa. Francis pins the star on the top of the Christmas tree. Everything is ready. But that sourpuss Murphy comes and breaks the bad news. Christmas is in December. Not for another six months. This is when Buck gets to give a speech about the true meaning of Christmas. Then fireworks go off. It's not Christmas, but by chance it is the Fourth of July.

It's ultra-American, said Jonjay, and swallowed half a pancake.

What the hell, forget cartoons, said Biz angrily, that's a damn crass distraction from your real focus. Do that shit in your comic strip instead. Biz Aziz shook her head. You're obsessed with expansion.

She thought Wendy paid a secret price every time she cashed a cheque that wasn't directly for work she produced with her own hands, her integrity—and integrity was not easy to buy back once it was sold. Everything for Biz was about integrity or corruption, and very little in the world could stand up to her lofty ideals. She lived by them. George Clinton, Pedro Bell, and Cal Schenkel did, too. Jonjay lived by her ideals. And so should all of us, including Wendy. Biz also knew the perfect funk record to go with this moment of decision, Hick owned it, she was going to find it when we got back to the manor. The blues might know the sorrows of humanity, but funk knew its paradoxes. Because what Biz wanted to say to Wendy was that she didn't think she should sign either deal. She didn't

need plastic validation for her art. Toys are a form of exploitation—you wake up one day and realize you're not in charge of your own ideas. You turned into a factory, your characters are commodities, your readers are consumers, and fans are fetishists.

I know, Biz, but what am I supposed to do? This is my autobiography, Wendy said, my whole life is wrapped up in cartoons and comics. Thing is, when I was a kid I wanted a Snoopy toy so badly I stole one from the Kmart. I slept next to that Snoopy in my bed even after I dropped out of high school. In high school I updated my Barbie with a new stolen wardrobe every season. It's too late now for me to take up principles, said Wendy. I never thought about that stuff you California punks take for granted, hating capitalism and supply and demand. When I heard the news my first thought was of the stolen Snoopy in my bed, not Jello's lyrics or any underground. Before I could read I knew who all the *Peanuts* characters were from the toys.

There's a way to earn what Frank just waved in your face and not give anyone a cut.

Watch out, said Jonjay, taking some of the bacon off Manila's plate. Frank thinks only of himself.

What's wrong with a cut? My syndicate takes a cut.

Yeah, said Biz, a big cut. They own your comic.

The way of Biz is a hard ethos to live by, said Wendy.

Shit, said Biz and sat back in her booth and stretched out with pride.

Mere mortals surrender, said Wendy and bowed her head to Biz.

Don't listen to Biz, said Twyla, looking around at us. None of us want to look for other jobs.

Wendy sucked back the gargly remains of eggs scrambled. Excuse me while I kiss the sky. She stood up from the booth and made for the ladies' room.

Frank's cellular number was on the back of a card in her purse and instead of needing the ladies' room, she called him from a payphone next to the bathrooms, across from the cigarette vending machine and a claw game full of stuffed animals.

It's me, mister, guess what? I'm looking at winning myself a Smurf, she said and bumped her head against the phonebox a couple of times. Her finger danced next to the plastic tongue that would hang up the call. What are you doing? she asked him.

See? What did I say? He recognized her voice. I *told* you I want the same things as you, Frank purred. Allow me to invite you down to my offices, meet my raunchy but well-intentioned staff of salesmen, and sign these two very exciting inaugural contracts in person? I know everyone wants to meet you as much as I'd like to see you. Gabby told me to wait for your call. Not easy for me, since I love phones so much.

Too lazy to come to San Jose. Too shy to meet your freaks. Too wise to your ways, buddy. Just courier. I prefer UPS brown vans. The vans look so good, that earthy brown, those classic headlamps.

I'll talk to them about a licence if you like them so much. Come to the office. My staff are about to get rich thanks to your strip, so you should meet them, meet the army that sees your adorable comic as the tip of the sword in our economic revolution.

You're an hour minimum if there's smooth traffic. I'm too squirrelly for congestion. The farthest south I drive is Daly City.

F-f-f-f-funn-ee gir-rl.

Are you talking to me on your super-shoe again? The echoes sound underwater cavernous.

Yes, I'm on my Motorola. I'm seated at my desk in front of three computer screens, he said. My all-black X-shaped longtable. My generals surround me on all sides. And you must visit just to see how I decorate an office. Nothing like the stuffy banks back east or the Hexen home office.

I can't hear you. Too bubbly.

This gizmo's the breakthrough of our day, Wendy. Forget the imperfect signal. You want your own?

No nukes for me. You look crazy carrying that microwave brick next to your face. Much too cumbersome for a single lady.

If you don't want a free space-age telephone, that's fine, but all this money of yours *will* need a bank account pronto. Make up a clever company name for yourself that isn't obvious, not *Strays*, and I'll help you open a limited liability for your basic transactions with Hexen Diamond Mistral. For now I recommend you bank with my friend Douglas Chimney at Solus First National Savings & Loans. Solus have branches all over the Bay Area and are part of a network of S&Ls I work with who honour each other's clients, ideal for travel.

Look, you whale, I gotta go, she said and hung up on him.

Back at our booth another pitcher of beer had arrived as Wendy returned to her seat, and Twyla was curious to know, even if no one else was, what Frank had said.

Oh, you jerks, you saw me call him? Shit. He said congratulations and you better go open a bank account.

Wendy downed her beer in a gulp, there was only a gulp left, slammed the empty pint glass back on the table, and declared this the best day of her life.

There was another time on that drunken breakfast Wendy got up from the table to use the payphone. The call only took a couple of minutes. This time we overheard her say, Hello, hi, Mom? It's me.

Melmoth LLC was the name she chose after she gnawed over the possibilities for a few days, flipped open half the books on the shelves in the manor, waiting for a word or a phrase to jump out at her. Melmoth did, because in the story this Jewish character had no home, was a traveller, like her characters. Like her mind, a wanderer, Melmoth had no beginning or end. Frank thought Melmoth was just fine and he didn't ask her how she chose it. He set the whole thing up. His pleasure. All in a day's work, he said. He helped open this kind of company all the time to protect his clients' assets and save them taxes. Fair to say his division opened dozens of LLCs a day doing business. An LLC was also a fast and easy way for Frank to move money between shareholders and keep separate a single investor's various income streams. The paperwork took him three days and she had to sign a few documents he sent over by UPS before she could open her bank account. He asked that she keep his name out of any contracts and gave her the wire number of another unnamed LLC to use instead. In the meantime Frank fast-tracked her green card so by the end of summer she would be American, friend to the IRS.

A few days later she took the papers for Melmoth LLC down to the main branch of Solus First National S&L, located on a commercial strip in the North Beach and across from the Clown Alley all-night hamburger diner. Wendy felt hungry after a cheeseburger so she ordered a second. And onion rings, a milkshake, and a slice of blueberry pie à la mode. She loved a good burger shack. Burgers might be one of those perfect foods, and played a central role in Wendy's diet; she ate on par with the American average of five burgers a week. Her booth at Clown Alley faced the entrance to Solus First National. It was an imposing limestone structure with solid oak front doors recessed into the shadows of three-storey stone columns of the Doric order. She took the last of her chocolate milkshake and waddled over.

The interior was well appointed with a massive crystal chandelier above the tellers, middle-aged guards in black suits, English oak panelling on all the walls, and in a vitrine was a bronze statue of a horse from the age of Pliny.

The handsome manager, Douglas Chimney, wore his thick, well-oiled hair parted from the nape up, gold cufflinks sparkled at the cuffs of his white silk shirt under a three-piece banker's suit in a lint-free navy blue, and a solid gold chain attached to a pocketwatch stretched across the grainsack of his stomach. He greeted his new client with a warm obedience that showed his good grooming, opened the gate for her and led

her through. For she was no ordinary new client but one whose business came highly recommended to him by Frank Fleecen. And with a brief but imperious glance at his row of tellers and the line waiting to be served by them, asked Wendy to come and sit in his corner office where they could talk in private.

The bank manager decorated his expansive office with leather uphol-stery and more dark wood walls, balanced by stained glass windows, a decorative collection of gold-edged hardcovers, brass fittings on all the lights, alligator-skin accessories on his desk, and what must have been a fortune in rare antiquities: a bronze helmet, a chiselled stone fragment, and other exquisite objects lined the rest of the shelves, encased in glass boxes and jars.

Douglas stretched out of his chair and let the belly press against the edge of his massive wood desk as he listened with pleasure while Wendy introduced herself and told him Frank recommended this bank above all the others.

A friend of Frank Fleecen's is a friend of mine. So what can Solus First National do for you, young lady?

Well, sir … a bank account.

But call me Doug. He offered to decant her a drink from his extensive wetbar. And congratulations, I see … When are you due?

Any minute, Wendy told him without flinching. She took the watered-down rye he offered in a cut-crystal tumbler in the hand not holding a milkshake.

I must tell you it's been a real pleasure doing business with Hexen Diamond Mistral's high-yield department. Chimney sat back down at his desk with a drink and stitched his hands together in front of him and looked penetratingly into Wendy's eyes. She had recently dyed three candyfloss streaks of pink, blue, and green through the tight curls of her dark brown hair, to match her wardrobe. Her blouse was more of an artist's smock cinched with a wide leather belt to give it shape, and her pink skirt with vegetal print didn't match her diamond-pattern purple tights, green legwarmers, or the orange cowboy boots. Add a whisky and a milkshake to that look and you had Wendy at her first bank meeting.

Miss … Ashbubble, I read your file. It says you're a cartoonist. That's terrific. I'll make sure to look for you the next time I open the papers.

Watch for me in the *San Jose Sentinel*, the *Palo Alto Weekly*, and in San Francisco, I'm in *The Tenderloin Times*.

Well, the future is full of opportunities, then. Quite remarkable. I'm beginning to see why Hexen has made an investment in your career. You're obviously funny. I mean, you *are* funny. Art is so fascinating, isn't it? said Douglas Chimney, manager. Kind of like a lottery, would you say?

Not so much. My job's more like backbreaking lonely work.

Financial growth is inevitable.

Since I have nothing, I hope so.

We value business like yours. In some ways, I'm not sure, but you're the ideal client, miss.

All I want is a chequing and savings account. The milkshake gargled as she sucked up the froth at the bottom of the wax cup. Do you have a garbage can?

No.

She held on to the empty cup and switched over to drinking the whisky.

It's about your outlook, said Chimney as he made circles in the air with his hands. You are part of the Solus First National family now. And as we embark on this account, I see before me a self-starter with her sights set on the big picture, and the horizon is a long ways away, but I wonder what we'll say to each other in ten years. So, best of luck to you on this voyage, dear, and I'm pleased to provide a safe place to invest your American dream. You have our full support at Solus First National from now on, day or night.

Day or night, wow. So I have a money emergency at four in the morning …

Chimney handed her his business card; it was embossed there in script under his name: *Day or night*. That's our policy, he said. And listen, you could not ask for a better partner for your investments than Hexen Diamond Mistral. You're still young, this might seem unreal. But be mature. Don't blow it all on drugs. You'll look back on these days proud of yourself for the steps you took. All I know is what I see, and the investments Hexen makes, that Frank Fleecen makes, these change businesses. If Fleecen has designs for your comic strip then before you know it you'll be collecting antiquities someday soon too, ha ha. That's my passion, so you can see. Do you speak with Frank Fleecen on a regular basis?

Occasionally he calls to frighten me with grand promises.

Believe him. He can deliver. You be sure and tell him next time you speak that he played a significant role in the development of our investment portfolio here at Solus First National.

Will do. So you don't know Frank?

Well, we've spoken once or twice. Usually when I call or they call I speak with a top salesman of Frank's, Ed Bulabasna, whom I like very much. Frank could cold-call a dead man and make a sale. Sell water to a whale. Our bank got in early—incredible. Started buying his bonds in seventy-seven and three years later, we're sitting on a small fortune. Paid for this building's erection and then some.

Sheesh. She shot back the whisky and had to suppress a fiery reflux of milkshake and burgers as if her body was a science fair volcano, then up through a throat full of acidic prevomit came the needs of a big gassy belch. It was almost too much.

His bonds are ingenious instruments. He can spin a debt obligation so many different directions, his salesmen are loaded with an arsenal of options to suit every kind of investor.

No idea what you're talking about, she said.

Hexen bonds provide the best returns of any product on the financial market, no question. That's all you need to know. That, and he mitigates risk with the blending of his derivatives, and that risk is usually our jobs at the S&Ls to take, we take all the risk. And I must admit his sales team host some outrageous Super 8 hotel parties.

Oh hey by the way. Wendy remembered to tell Doug that Frank needed access to her account for withdrawal, deposit, and transfer purposes.

Of course, I'll add his name to your file. The bank manager raised his fingertips off his desk in a delicate but clumsy search for a pen on his desk. He took a drink of rye first.

No, if it's possible, I'd rather his name didn't appear anywhere in the paperwork, Wendy said and handed him the bank wire number Frank had told her to use instead.

Chimney's head jerked to the side and he slapped his neck as if she nicked him while shaving his Adam's apple, then he put on a small and unimpressive smile. I see, that's fine. A wire number is not a problem. Chimney added the number to this page of the files and that one. His hands feathered the paperwork one more time as if looking for any reason to inquire further. Miss Ashbubble, everything is in order then. Please sign here and here.

That night Wendy piled us into her lime-green Gremlin and took us down to Chinatown for wontons and bought us tickets to see Biz Aziz perform in her two-queen show at Valencia Tool & Tie. *JR & The Minotaur* was her loose adaptation of the TV show *Dallas* combined with the Greek myth, featuring the beloved Castro queen Lil Morphine Annie in the role of the minotaur. We bumped into old Vaughn Staedtler at the wonton house. He was eating a large bowl alone at a table near the kitchen, reading an issue of Biz's comic memoir, and also on his way to her performance later. He, too, had to make a stop for some of these incredible wontons, he said, and offered to have us join him at his open table. The restaurant was full, so we accepted his invitation. Vaughn had another small bowl of four wontons as well, he loved the wontons as much as we did. The place was a classic hangout for cartoonists. Looking around the room, we could see as many as half the tables were going to the show later. Vaughn Staedtler had seen Biz perform four or five times before and was shocked every time and seduced again and again by her beautiful voice and extravagantly costumed alien presence eating up the stage, hypnotizing her audience. With those fiery eyes and doublejointed swagger. Handmade sculptural headpieces worthy of exhibition. Doing seductively off-kilter renditions of lesser-known masterpieces from the history of pop music. All wrapped in a story concept adapted from literature and her vivid, provocative imagination. Vaughn knew he was at least twice the age of the average Biz fan, maybe the only one in the audience with grandchildren, but he didn't care, and the surrealism of youth fashion was not going to intimidate the creator of *The Mischiefs*, one of the most enduring comic icons of teen rebellion. Few men Vaughn's age could pull off wearing a black leather jacket and be so unself-conscious about it. He still wore steel-toed boots and jeans and combed his long, white hair straight back despite his hairline, it was receding at a rather handsome pace anyway. He was reading a copy of issue number five. He showed us—it was part three of three in the Vietnam issues, where Biz Aziz gets enlisted into the ill-fated and fully redacted CAT-X program as an artist-soldier to depict in charcoal the days and nights after her combat group crossed the border into Cambodia. Vaughn Staedtler showed us one page of panels featuring the silhouetted remains of a village after napalm. Each panel featured part of a poem. One caption read: *and she would rather be frozen alone on the moon.*

Remarkable individual, said Vaughn. She puts herself in harm's way and survives, she gets thrown into all the worst situations and climbs out unscathed. Like the snail who can inch along the edge of a razor blade, she's blessed with a scary kind of indestructibility that I fear could expire at any moment.

The waiter came and took our order. Not what, but size. There was an entire menu, many items, but no one in the restaurant's hundred-and-one-year history had ordered anything other than the daily special, wonton soup. The only reason we were here was for the wontons. Why anyone came here. Wontons were why Vaughn was here. Why the restaurant was completely full and a line was forming out the door. A wonton of such poetic flavours, a heartwarming, energizing, life-sustaining wonton. Our eyes wept, our noses watered, we drooled when we ate a bowlful. Six wontons was a significant meal. More than a meal, it was a rejuvenating body purifier. Over this handpressed noodle, we broke out in a sweat. Over this fresh wonton, we restored our inner vigour. What was in those wontons, what kind of meat had such a juicy texture and taste? Unicorn? Gryphon? Kooloomooloomavlock? A little bit of salvation? Its pastry was almost translucent and yet in chewing, the wonton's casing was a substantial protection for the deliciousness inside, and against plenty of chews kept its form as a flavourful packaging around the pale, wrinkly meatball bursting with its savoury juices. All submerged in a wholesome hot broth, steaming and spiced and oily that only the gauche and misinformed drink as a soup.

We got the distinct picture from all his complaining that Vaughn was not impressed that his lawyers weren't having any luck negotiating with his former assistants to lower their ask—half a million in back pay for twenty years' work. The next stop in this hellish journey of reprisal was court. His former assistants were greedy pirates, vultures, brats, and know-nothings, he said. How does it feel, Wendy, to be starting out a career in such a decrepit, devalued industry, with venal competition and vampire lawyers, comics shrinking on the page *and* in the brain, less and less attention from readers, editors, and a big zip from the critics? I'm glad I retired with my wits. I believe in resurrection. Now there's so many better options for a talented artist to make a living. Computers, Wendy, that's where you should focus. Computer art. Imagine that. What false hopes and blinkered view of the world inspired your retrograde insanity?

The comics are what I love, Wendy shrugged. I know what you mean. You find a pretty seashell and turn it over and discover a lot of creepy legs wiggling underneath. Give me a few more years and maybe I'll be as grossed out.

Promise not to say a word, said Staedtler with a conspiratorial growl, but I'm painting clowns. I swear these damn paintings are so good, fuck *The Mischiefs*, these clowns are going to put me in the history books. I'll be next to Andy Warhol. Vaughn invited us to come visit his studio any time. *Make sure to bring pot.*

Biz Aziz's drag shows had gained legendary status in the five years since her first performance in seventy-five, after returning from Cambodia and the war. For there was always the chance the cast or more likely the audience might go berserk and the night would end up in an upcoming issue of her comic memoir. This night it started with a drunk who drove his Datsun B210 up on the sidewalk right in front of the Tool & Die and mowed down five people standing in line at the door, sending three to the hospital with broken bones while the other two got away with minor bruises and concussions—tonight was a good enough example of how that legend was formed. Wendy ran to a payphone in the lobby and called for ambulances to handle four mouth-frothing, nose-bleeding ODs after a crazy-pure batch of booger sugar kicked in. So much coke had hit the streets recently, prices were down, and a rumour was going around that someone was flying shipments of uncut directly into the Bay from an outpost of Nicaragua. Before the show and during the intermission, the drag queen Taj Mahal Delusion worked the merchandise table dressed in a gold-lamé sari, erotic henna tattoos, and a foot-tall frightwig decorated with figurines playing croquet. Taj Mahal was surrounded by Biz Aziz's young fans buying back issues of *The Mizadventurez* comics. If you knew to ask, Taj Mahal Delusion also sold five-dollar tabs from a page of blotter printed with Reagan's face. This too was incredibly pure Delysid Sandoz LSD 25. Combined with the booger sugar and the equally easy access to 'ludes, everyone in the crowd was on a manic kaleidoscope high when Biz Aziz took the stage at around one in the morning.

She wore a silver fishscale cocktail dress, a massive flower corsage on her wrist and another pinned to her breast, and an upside-down chandelier balanced on her head, cut-glass teardrops twinkling under the Klieg lights. She sang like a dream, our collective dream, and her dress sparkled and shone with its million sequins. Her presence was not at all what we expected—back at the manor she was a prickly, moody perfectionist who spoke little and worked hard. But here, in front of an audience, she was a radiant exhibit, a fountain of a person who showered us with light, she embraced the stage, embraced the light, embraced every line she sang, embraced her audience, she was this all-enveloping power, and her sensuality was that of a goddess—no sooner had she stepped into the spotlight, fans started screaming, the front row lost their pants, went hysterical, and the highest threw themselves at the stage with loose-limbed fishlike abandon, almost fainting, heaving with emotions, a slobbering mob. The maze projected intermittently on a screen behind Biz was so convincing that after encountering too many dead ends it triggered an anxiety attack in someone, who ran for the corner to hide and quiver like a baby. When not a maze, images on the screen showed edits of *Dallas* episodes featuring J.R., the evil J.R., the cunning J.R., the horny J.R. Speaking from the point of view of the Ewing mansion, Biz recited lines from a short rhyming poem about J.R.'s battle with the minotaur. Her song choices added to the disorienting mood; she did a slowed-down, dragged-out, woozier version of *The Big Hurt* and a faster, rock version of *The End of the World.* Young men stormed the stage to lavish Biz with kisses and bask at her feet, and the show was halted more than once to sweep the stage of glass and due to the general rowdiness. When it came time for duets, the moment Lil Morphine Annie entered stage left to the sounds of Funkadelic's *Biological Speculation* dressed as a glitzy pink funfur minotaur, a riot broke out. A riot of giddy gay college students, stripping off their fashions—that's what too much Nicaraguan import plus acid plus a methaqualone will do to you—the stage was all of a sudden filled with mad dancing nudists. The screen behind them got torn down and parts of the PA system toppled off the stage, killing the sound.

For a moment the room fell totally silent, then erupted into unabashed mayhem. The entire room was up for grabs. Everything was being vandalized. Anything not bolted down got thrashed. Bits and pieces of the set flew through the air. A fusebox exploded and showered sparks over screaming fans. Vaughn Staedtler pointed to the exit and we grabbed Wendy and made it out in time to watch three cop cars and the paddywagon pull up out front, the cops brandishing clubs and storming the front doors of the Tool & Die.

Three hours later we had to go pick up Biz and Morphine Annie from the drunktank down at the Mission police station on Seventeenth; potential charges would follow, but for now the queens were free to go.

Thanks for the grand tour! Biz spat at the cops on the way out of the precinct, holding her high heels in her hands.

On the drive back to No Manors, Wendy parked at the coffee shop without a name where we drank strong Peruvian espresso as the sun came up and tried to make sense of what all had happened. Vaughn met us there— he drove some sleek black European two-seater with the steering wheel on the right-hand side—and despite his advanced age seemed the most alert of all of us. We were bagged. Felt like we'd been up forever. Meanwhile he talked and talked, he went on some more about his doublecrossing assistants, about his avant-garde clowns, about drawing comics for the army newspaper in Korea for three years in a mobile newspaper office under a tent. Vaughn drew dozens and dozens of G.I. gags for an editor-slash-commanding officer who had no ear for humour and rejected anything he sketched that wasn't Sinophobic or a direct insult to the Communists. Using a felt marker he pinched off the barista, Vaughn scribbled charming portraits of us in *The Mischiefs* style, and one of Biz Aziz on stage from his point of view down in the audience.

You never needed no assistants anyway, Biz told him as she sipped her espresso. She plucked the drawing of her off the table and pushed it down the neckline of her dress. She winked at the old man. You're supertalented, Vee. You should get back in the funny pages.

Nah, he said and scratched the nape of his neck. I got my sights on the MoMA now.

Yeah and thanks again for picking us up, said Lil Morphine Annie, shivering and pale in her evening gown, clutching her broken wig on the floor between her ankles. Her voice was rawer than usual, she was coming down from an anxiety attack. I sure fucking hope SFPD got enough of a look to last them a while, because I for one don't plan on visiting *that* party again soon.

Vaughn's eyes were fixed on Biz. You ravished us from up there, under the spotlights, he told her. That's why the crowd went mad. It was a collective simultaneous orgasm.

That's my art, you see, to drive men mad.

That morning instead of driving home to feed his cats and sleep, or paint more clowns, Vaughn Staedtler stayed with Biz in her room on the third floor of No Manors and so began another of his wild affairs, and one of Biz Aziz's few intimacies.

STRAYS

13

Between the summer of eighty-one and the winter of eighty-two, Frank Fleecen's office underwrote Shepherd Media's purchase of more than thirty local and regional newspapers, and in the next few years, with the aid of still more junk bonds, Shepherd Media amassed a practical monopoly on cable affiliates and local papers south of the Mason-Dixon line. Most papers had an unspoken liberal-intellectual bias when Shepherd Media bought them, but that would soon be reversed to an openly conservative, tabloid slant. Through massive layoffs and minimal rehires, staffs were reshaped to suit the new agenda. Shepherd Media snapped up firesale presses on the brink of disaster, underwriting new business plans for small potatoes like the *Carbondale Gazette* and *Boonville Herald*; Macon, Marietta, and Alpharetta, Odessa and Fort Worth all had newspapers for sale, Gainesville and Enid etcetera. Shepherd Media's original loan was to the tune of fifteen million dollars, issued as part of Hexen's high-yield bonds, those *zabagliones* he'd bragged about. Then the loan doubled and tripled, it grew until Shepherd Media had borrowed up to a hundred million in bonds. Shepherd Media and its sole owner, the middle-aged entrepreneur Piper Shepherd, had found a position as titan of industry.

Impressive, except it was on a line of credit in an industry many experts considered moribund. Every year the number of regional newspapers was shrinking. Local cable affiliates were shutting down one after another, too, went the story, as capital amalgamated and interests merged. Money was like beads of mercury in that way, money joined with money, money wanted to accumulate in one place, in the hands of one. Money was accumulating in Hexen Diamond Mistral to the tune of a two hundred million American dollars in eighty-one. The entire premise behind Shepherd Media's business plan was mocked by wiser competitors who saw smoke and mirrors. Piper Shepherd was derided on TV, portrayed as a southern gentleman of wealthy lineage with a charm school smile, the intellect of a shoe, family connections going back to the Civil War, and considering he was in his mid-fifties, the temper of a spoiled brat baby. More often than Shepherd Media, though, the journalists in New York preyed on Frank Fleecen and Hexen Diamond Mistral's high-yield bonds division, their strategies were openly criticized in op-eds invariably written by retired high-level employees of Hexen's competitors.

You can slap lipstick on a pig, went the line in the op-ed in the financial section of the *Washington Post*, but it's still Shepherd Media.

The unbuyable *New York Times* financial analyst wrote: Far from leading the sheep, Shepherd Media is clearly one of Frank Fleecen's most docile lambs, hypnotized by the Hexen Diamond Mistral chant—junk junk junk junk—following all his orders without question, even willing to stretch out on the chopping block, first to the slaughter come winter.

Meanwhile, down on the ground floor of this burgeoning empire, Gabrielle Scavalda's office had a window that looked out at pedestrians who used its reflective outer surface as a casual mirror to fix their hair and check their teeth and nose as they walked by, invariably while she was in a meeting. Once a man stuffed his hand down his pants and adjusted himself while she tried to hold a conversation with a rival editor. It was in this office in upper Manhattan where she pushed her syndicate's travelling salesmen to make *Strays* their number one priority in meetings with local editors. A lot of her days were spent fielding calls and making calls. Not unlike Frank, her business was in her contacts, and at night she locked her Rolodex in a safe under her desk.

We heard Gabby's pitch so often we could recite it verbatim. She beat the greatness of *Strays* into us until we were convinced, not that we needed convincing. We were a sounding board. Quite often when she called the manor it wasn't just to share good news or ask for an update on a revision, she used us to complain about the indolence of her travelling salesmen. Now's the time to strongarm those editors to slot in *Strays*, she would tell them,—don't let them renew another syndicate's strip ... Yeah, I'm serious, Gabby would shout at So-and-so calling from a payphone in Dottie's Diner. What's the nearest newspaper? You're where? On Kilgore Road outside Toone? Okay, I know Toone. Listen, you go tell that rat Chuck Emerald at the *Toone Tribune* to bump *Sally Forth*. Save that stuff for *The New Yorker*, right? Okay I'm looking at my map ... , Gabby would say. Tell them you finally found a note from the underground that isn't reprehensibly perverse. Say *Strays* is new wave but it's closer to *Peanuts* than to *Amy & Jordan*—say that. Same goes for a paper like Paducah's *Examiner*. They don't need headscratchers either. Dump *Levy's Law* and subscribe to *Strays* and watch sales rise. Tell them the adventure strips are done. *Judge Parker* is dead weight. No one is reading sequentials anymore. A burg like Pinckneyville needs straight laughs and *Strays* delivers gags.

These were Gabby's words.

What we gleaned from Wendy and Gabrielle: The common newspaper comic strip salesman was a dark soul with wheels under him for a reason. So far no woman had been foolish enough to apply for this unprepossessing job. The travelling strip salesman worked for a syndicate on a meagre salary plus decent commission plus maybe monthly and annual bonuses in the case of some outstanding sales. Each salesman was given a portfolio of strips to pitch and a map of America. Gas and car repairs were reimbursed, all other travel expenses including hotel were covered by a straight fifty-five-dollar per diem. Carrying a wagonload of demons and a surfeit of charm, they squandered their skills delivering hackwork to idol-less editors, these men who could sell anything and chose to make a living off comics, who lived on the blacktop and raced against their own despair. These were strange, solemn, almost always solitary men with a string of cowardly divorces behind them or just as often actively polygamists. Comic strip salesmen were known to harbour multiple families across many states, some lived multiple lives, they were all a lurid, improbable secret the salesman was able to juggle. A gun in the glove compartment of course. For all intents and purposes living out of Fords and Chryslers, the salesmen drove for hours and hours every day across their patch of America and slept in motels off the highway. The hole opening up in front of them on the highway kept getting wider. Slowly going into debt. They only came to life on the job—after a shave and a shower, cup of coffee, and squared away inside a quality suit, tie knotted, the smile came out of hiding—now he was ready to sell a strip. Suddenly gregarious, outgoing, confident, and socially adept, the best comic strip salesman was the one who seemed completely indifferent to landing a new subscription but loved the chance to get to know a new friend or catch up with an old one. Friendships were key. The friendship was what counted, being pals, going for drinks, shooting the shit, bullshitting, and other shit; the business— after all, we're just talking comic strips here—was an afterthought, more gossip than art, more of an excuse to hang out than a business. Speaking of strips, listen, Emerald, I got a deuce burning a hole in my pocket, so if you don't mind looking at dancing girls, let's go have a beer.

Aided by Shepherd Media's near monopoly of newspapers in the southern states, and Frank Fleecen's diligent work selling *Strays* to businesses, we watched Wendy's subscriptions double, triple, then a

hundredfold increase in the span of a little more than twenty-four months. Every time she ripped open a paycheque it was for an even larger sum. An incredible list of cities and towns we had never heard of before, obscure place names whose locations confounded us even when searching across an open map. Yazoo City, Mississippi; Eggnog, Utah; Coin, Iowa. A subscription to *Strays* now cost a newspaper four dollars for every daily strip and seven twenty-five for a Sunday oversized colour—fifty cents above the going rate for strips like *Drabble, Broom-Hilda*, and *Geech*. After the split with syndicate and Hexen, Wendy's cut was down to a dollar and a quarter for a daily and about two-fifty for a Sunday, for every subscription, so do the math and at her peak from eighty-two to eighty-seven, when *Strays* was in more than a thousand newspapers across America and the rest of the world, that still adds up to a couple million dollars a year to play with. And that's before the cheques that came from Frank Fleecen's licences and merchandising.

Wendy found that in the months after Hick's death, she often woke up with a stiff jaw and sore teeth, and this persisted all summer. Her top and bottom molars felt locked together. Her temples pounded. Cold liquids gave her piercing pains throughout her entire mouth and sinuses, made her brain throb. In the fall she couldn't stand it anymore and went and saw Dr. Spencer, the dentist on Mission Street Biz went to, who told her her masseters were in knots, she was going to crack a crown if she didn't get some therapy. Therapy? Spencer also made an appointment for her to be fitted for a silicone mouthguard to wear at night for the rest of her life if she didn't seek deeper help, and recommended a Jungian hypnotist named Samantha Collins in Twin Peaks and wrote down the number.

Therapy. She shivered from toes to scalp at the tantalizing thought.

She opened additional bank accounts with Solus First National Savings & Loans as time went on, to divide up her income streams and distribute money from each into investment pools elsewhere, and placing a tiny percent of her income every month into an account set aside just for emergencies. But in fact these accounts were all opened at the suggestion of Frank Fleecen, who used Gabby as an intermediary to give advice of this kind. All these accounts were accessible to Frank through his numbered wire transfer account, and the ostensible reason was that he was her financial manager. Doug Chimney never blinked an eye after the first time. When the account set aside for Shepherd Media's paycheques cracked a million in November of eighty-two, Doug Chimney handled the deposit himself, rang a bell, all the tellers and the other clients in line applauded her fortunes, and back in his office he poured her a generous glass of Louis XIII to celebrate. According to the evidence from investigations by the Securities and Exchange Commission, between 1981 and 1987, Wendy opened at least sixteen separate bank accounts at Solus First National, and Doug Chimney was fully aware of the extent to which her accounts were being used as operational funds for Frank Fleecen's most complicated deals. Whenever he saw Wendy come to make a deposit, in fact, Chimney was eager to open a few private safes in his office, let her try on the Roman Empire jewels and flip through the yellowed crinkled pages of his nearly priceless, certainly irreplaceable first edition of Hans Grimmelshausen's novel *Simplicius Simplicissimus* published in the year 1669. Then when she was drunk and pliable and floating on the vapours of brandy and the ego boost of all this wealth, he tried for more.

I'm so pleased to meet someone with an appreciation for an artifact like this.

Oh I can get into this stuff, she said. Your very own private museum, I suppose you could call it. I think it's cool you collect antiques and rare books. I love to read.

Do you?

Yes, why not? My childhood babysitter was the library, you know what I mean?

Would you like to take home an auction catalogue and see what's coming up, perhaps something in there will catch your eye? Doug handed her a thick Sotheby's magazine and, seeing his gold wedding band flash at her before she could say no, politely put the catalogue in her sidebag. He added that he thought she would enjoy the atmosphere of an auction. During a round, a hypersensitivity to motion slows down everything, so what looks frantic to the outsider is actually happening at a beautifully slow and exciting pace to the players, like in a sport, for those of us who have something at stake. Once in a while an object's make and provenance combined with its rarity and beauty tells me, it speaks to me, says I must become its protector. That's how Doug Chimney described it as he returned the three-hundred-year-old novel to its vitrine.

After her heavy deposit and surreal conversation, Wendy ran straight across the street to Clown Alley and ordered two bacon cheeseburgers and sat and stared at the front doors of Solus First National Savings & Loans and considered the insane idea of going back in there and ravishing the manager of the bank. She was a millionaire. Inside those walls lay her fortune. She wanted to make a bed on the carpet in Douglas Chimney's office out of hundreds of thousands of dollars and fuck him on that money mattress. What was her problem? Why didn't she just go home? She was already halfway through the second burger when she realized she'd eaten the first. Obviously Doug Chimney was hitting on her—he asked her to join him for Sotheby's auctions. She wasn't attracted to Doug Chimney or his position of power so much as she was attracted to the idea that he wanted to risk the troubles of infidelity for an hour with her. This propensity for illicit flings kept her single and perhaps if not lonely—after all she had us—then miserable anyway. At night her teeth grinding was louder than the creak of the old floorboards, we thought she was sleepwalking in her room until the dentist alerted her—the jaw pain and sensitive molars were why she had an appointment later that day with Dr. Samantha Collins, who clarified right away that she was a *post*-Jungian talk-based therapist who specialized in patients suffering from bruxism, vestibulodynia, and dystonia.

Dr. Collins had a private practice out of her home on Palo Alto Avenue near the water reservoir, an eggshell-white set of Modernist cubes unevenly balanced on top of one another, offset by sheets of tempered green glass. She charged a hundred and twenty dollars for fifty minutes on a warm cracked leather couch facing a view of Golden Gate Park. For that price, Wendy did more than talk about the nocturnal dreams she had while grinding her teeth. She told her doctor about daydreams, random agonies, and even her sex fantasies.

If Jonjay won't, then I imagine having lots of flings and affairs because then, you know, that's easy. I'd rather go to one of these orgy rooms downtown. Steamrooms. I'm too busy for a steady man, I've got drawing comics to think about. So that rules out the mistress role for me, too. I don't want guys to think I show up twice. Is that crazy? Sometimes I think the aura of free love brought me here. Teeth grinding aside, what I want you to tell me, Dr. Collins, is if you think I'm crazy.

So *did* you return to see the bank manager? Dr. Collins inquired politely, with a medical persistence, her legs crossing and recrossing inside her skirt, a Bic pen poised over a fresh page on a yellow legal pad.

I told him I wanted one more look at his *Simplicius Simplicissimus*.

She saw Dr. Collins for four more sessions and then moved on to a new type of treatment when it didn't stop her teeth grinding, or clenching the mouthguard when she remembered to put it in. Once she was given this go-ahead to seek out therapy, even from a dentist, Wendy let herself indulge in all of its forms, sampling from therapy's many options, and meeting eccentric and well-to-do practitioners one after the other. She seemed to derive some kind of entertainment value from these expensive visits. This, and her dream of an animated cartoon, were what she spent most of her money on. Not clothes or furniture or expensive vacations. The rest of her income got socked away. Even with the expense of therapy, she didn't burn through her escalating income half as fast as she made it.

She shopped for therapy with the same open mind and restless curiosity to try on all trends that she took to the malls, the salons, the music she listened to. In therapy she paid for the deeper attention sex in San Francisco couldn't provide her. In the Yellow Pages under *Therapy* and related searches she found enough names and promising leads in the Bay Area to entertain her for months if not years. Instead of seeing therapy as something to commit to with one doctor, her plan was to commit to seeking therapy from all kinds of different doctors and mentalists, to find out which of these practices and practitioners worked for her, and this way slowly, over the years, winnow down her auditions to a select cast of rotating geniuses who together might unravel her problem.

By way of introduction to her new doctors she would ask, What is your usual approach with the average everyday commonplace upwardly-mobile middleclass single art-type woman with psychothenia, homebody tendencies, neurastheniac at the best of times, teeth-grinding sex-addicted insomniac such as myself, with a half-Jewish theatre mother, half-mystery father of rosy complexion and fine sense of humour.

Dr. Blair's office walls were decorated with framed photos of mountainviews. She gazed at these snowcapped rockies and then at the sharp peak of the doctor's head and its white tufts of hair blowing under the air-conditioning vent in the ceiling. Dr. Blair referred with gravitas to her psychic avalanche, and to periods in life, usually at the age of thirteen, twenty-one, thirty, and then again at forty-two, and so on, when the searing cataclysm of some tragedy, a trauma buried a generation or two ago, combined with the steeper and steeper responsibilities of one's life to melt and thaw giant continents of icefrozen emotion and send them hurtling towards our bowels—fear, anger, resentment, shame, regret, loneliness all come shitting down the mountain of self. That cost Wendy seventy-five dollars.

Another eminent specialist of nervous diseases, with an office in a large private rehabilitation clinic in West Menlo near the Stanford campus, offered Wendy a seat and asked her some questions with the bright-eyed, ditzy demeanour of a third-generation hair salonist about to shampoo her hair. When the doctor rose from his chair behind his oak desk to touch his reflection in a mirror, it was revealed he was no taller standing than sitting. You were once a fetus, he said, and a womb was your first home. His cute, tanned face was the result of deep cosmetic effort to resemble saddle leather. His powdery-Valium blue eyes matched nothing about his dyed brown hair or to-the-neck sideburns.

Sometimes a person must return to their first home to find the answers. Yes, yes, he said and pressed his hands to Wendy's forehead, then her neck, then her chest, then her stomach (her chest!). Like a faith healer, godless, but totally convinced of his powers. Then he returned to his black leather upholstered swivel chair. All very common, my dear. The usual symptoms. See if you can picture this, Wendy, the central nervous system is like cable television with a hundred thousand channels, but sometimes the body won't pay the bill and some choices get shut off, and the longer you don't pay, the fewer channels you get, until one channel's left to watch. Now your teeth can't stop from chattering. And previous to this you say your best friend and roommate died. No doubt related. But let's try to find out what your friend's death triggered. I want to put you inside some blankets and I want you to imagine you are back in the womb and that you are struggling to be born, and while you are struggling I want you to think of who is being born. I want you to lie down on the floor, Wendy, on top of that blanket, I'm going to roll you up in the blanket, Wendy, then I'm going to put another blanket on top of you, Wendy, and I want you to roll up into that blanket, Wendy.

And because he was an eminent specialist and this was an hour-long session she followed the doctor's orders and rolled up inside the blankets. Then he rolled another blanket on top of that.

Wendy said the claustrophobia inside the doctor's wrapped-up rebirthing blankets was so intense, wrapped as tightly as a burrito inside a burrito, the absolute worst horror of her life, she started to suffocate. It was pitch-black. There was no air. She kept sucking woolly fabric that tasted of nicotine into her mouth. She couldn't move. When she screamed, nothing happened. She could not tell up from down. She lost feeling in her toes. Her nose ran with a torrent of mucus. She screamed and she could not breathe. It was the worst kind of dark. She couldn't move her arms or legs at all. She couldn't move anything. Her hands were pressed tightly to the sides of her chest. She was about to faint, die in these blankets. And the doctor was sitting on her. Muffled, she could just make out the doctor's voice yelling, Tell me how you feel! Tell me your feelings, Wendy!

I'm going to die, she cried. I'm dying. I can't breathe. I can't breathe. Let me out. Let me out!

That's good, she heard the doctor's muffled voice say, that's excellent. You're almost there, Wendy, push push push. You're being born, Wendy, fight to be born, fight, Wendy, fight your way free of the past.

She started to scrabble on the ground, not thinking anything other than how much she wanted to murder the doctor who was pressing his knees against the top of the blankets to pin her in place. She screamed and howled and the sweat poured off her and she shit herself, a whole damn avalanche of shit, and then she passed out for real.

When she awoke she was in the emergency ward hooked up to an oxygen mask and a brain monitor. Apparently she'd gone into a coma for more than fifteen minutes and remained unconscious for another hour. The nurse told her she should sue.

She never saw the doctor again but his bill arrived. The fee in this case was four hundred dollars.

There were other doctors.

Hopi therapy in a teepee. Dr. Paulson dressed as an Indian witch-doctor or shaman. All people share one thing in common regardless of culture or race regardless of religious dogma, the desire to reach as close to a permanent state of euphoria as possible.

Finally she heard about a fellow all the way in Berkeley who sounded almost exactly like the last thing you'd want to try. His whole theory was to do nothing other than listen to you talk. He would spend an entire session without saying a word except hello and goodbye. On her second meeting with him he asked a question: What's the worst that could happen? Then in the weeks to come the occasional question was peppered with an observation. This specialist was employed through the Nervous Disorders Department of the university and had an office on campus. He was tall and wore his hair and beard the very same length, about half an inch. Wendy said she liked that he maintained an even smile, a smile with perfect equilibrium that only ever got wider when you told him something shocking and true about yourself and only ever disappeared completely when he knew you were avoiding something on purpose. His questions sounded rhetorical, except for they weren't. The first question he asked Wendy was not to tell him about her mother and father. Instead he asked her, What's so bad about that?

She told the quiet doctor she never knew her father and that her mother died a few years ago and honestly, she didn't remember much about her, except that her mother had an old credo of her own: Don't say no to a good opportunity.

If somebody gives you an opportunity, take it, her mom said. Wendy remembered being about six or seven years old and the two of them were snug together on the squishy chesterfield watching early-early-morning cartoons on black-and-white TV (both mother and daughter had difficulties with bedtime). If there isn't any work then I volunteer. That was her mom's explanation for why she was so busy working as a stage manager and also broke. But she didn't tell the quiet therapist about Reagan. That fact, she thought, seemed too absurd in the context of this therapist's domesticated quiet, and might make her look certifiable.

133

14

It's not that it didn't occur to Wendy that most cartoons were pitched as scripts to television networks. Network producers ordered projects, they didn't buy one premade. Normally the producer would buy a script, then give it to a cohort of professional animators toiling under the rubric of a large brandname studio, who would revise the script under the guidance of the network producer to complete the project in a palatable fashion, below budget, and on deadline. And so we kept asking her why she wanted us to make this cartoon, when nobody made a cartoon like this, not to mention we didn't know the first thing about animation.

Not true, she said. This is the way the *Peanuts* Christmas special was made, Wendy told us. Charles Schulz went to the bank for a loan, made his cartoon independent of network support, then sold the final product. That's what I want to do. I want my creative control.

Twyla said, That's all fine and dandy but did Schulz's animators at least know what they were doing? I never animated anything in my life. I still don't know if I can draw.

Wendy said she would learn. We would all learn. She reminded us, all animation is a picture of one drawing after another.

That pressure is kind of heavy to put on us, though, don't you think? Twyla said. She was flattered, but outside Wendy, her drawings had been rejected. There was an event held in a local comic store to launch an issue of *Black Goliath* where she showed her portfolio to Vince Colletta, an artist at Marvel, who rejected her at a glance—proportions were fine, adequate muscles, but he wanted to see how she put panels together before he offered her some fill-in work, and gave her his card. She called and left a message and had not heard back. After a few months of this kind of rejection, living on next to nothing, she picked up a hundred bucks drawing fishing rods, various brands of camping gear and lacrosse sticks, football shoulder pads and hockey sticks, and all kinds of balls for a sporting goods store brochure. As soon as she got paid, she wanted to give Wendy eighty dollars to pay her back some of what she thought she owed her for the room and food and the rest.

I'm just a freeloader, Twyla said with tears welling up in her eyes. I've been here nine months and everyone I show my portfolio to rejects me.

You know what Hick said when I showed up on his doorstep with all my belongings in a Samsonite hardshell? said Wendy. Nothing, he didn't say a word, because he didn't even notice me for three days. That's how many others were here when I arrived. Talk about a commune. Hick never asked for a dime. All he wanted was for us to keep him company at the longtable. This cartoon is something I've always dreamed of. I don't care if this ever gets bought by a network. Okay, I do care. For sure I want to sell it to a network, of course I do. I want us to make a really amazing cartoon that will get picked up and become a classic. I don't want to sell an idea to strangers and have them make it without my input. This is my chance to do a big project all on my own.

So in our off-hours we gravitated to Rachael's room to tinker with

flip-it drawings, or painting onto transparent cells. We began to learn the difference between keyframes and the in-betweens. If we felt especially confident maybe we'd shoot a few seconds of Buck walking through the stop-motion rig. A sixteen-frame walk was the most basic principle of animation, and if we couldn't get that right, we couldn't move forward with the rest. And we couldn't get that right. Our early attempts resembled nothing like realistic locomotion, even for a bipedal dog it was more of a juddering levitation across the patch of desiccated scenery. But over time and with practice our walk started to look natural. Buck's feet landed on solid ground, he had a consistent bounce that we later developed into more of a swagger, then used the bounce as our starting point for when we moved on to making the rabbit Francis walk. We started drawing eight frames of motion a second and that was a mistake so we moved up to sixteen frames. Sixteen separate drawings for every second meant more than twenty-one thousand drawings were needed for the entire cartoon. Hundreds and hundreds of prep sketches and full-colour concept art and failed test runs and revisions to storyline went into every picture that made the final cut. The amount of work was intimidating. Not only were we drawing, we also washed the 35 mm film in our own developing baths in the darkroom Hick had set up in a cavity, and spooled the results through a film projector to critique the results of our efforts with Wendy present as our producer, director, artist, landlord, roommate.

Televisions distracted us. Plugged into all kinds of extension cords and power bars were television sets spanning decades of technological progress in cathode ray tube resolution, size, display. Jonjay found a lot of them on his scavenger hunts through the city's alleys. Not one television encased in its own wood-veneer credenza with shelves, but three. Wendy had a problem—whenever she saw an abandoned TV on the sidewalk she had to bring it home with her like a stray. We arrived at No Manors after Hick—when Wendy, Biz Aziz, and a rotating league of underage and worndown cartoonists held down the fort. Televisions, lots of televisions all going simultaneously on different channels or in choirs—this furnace of sitcoms and dramas, game shows and sports. Mental agents of the new microphone. Personalities ruled. Networks shunted faces across the screen. The TV had no other story except the microphone. The story was *you talk. Welcome to Sally Jessy Raphael—today: Satanism in America. Our guests are from San Francisco. Tell the world our millions of viewers what you think!* Repressed memories of genitals being touched? Ask Anton LaVey. Apparently there were Satanists in our preschools perverting our children out of their senses. Children and teenagers were coming to police with extraordinary memories. Unless you asked the Satanists in San Francisco who said it was against their beliefs to force anyone to do anything without permission. Satanists were for self-discovery and against child exploitation. *But that's not what the courts were seeing.* Everybody at the manor read *Michelle Remembers*—Hick's hexed hospital copy was on the longtable in front of us opened to page six—*What had been revealed in the Saturday session ... not distressing enough to explain why these memories had been so thoroughly blocked—they had been totally buried.* The doctor co-author, who discovered that memories hide inside us, helped put in jail the McCuans and the Kniffens, parents in Kern County accused of satanically abusing toddlers, thanks to his unique therapeutic techniques on the child victims. The California raisin talking about faith and forti-tude and the zero option. Reaganomics. The Iron Curtain. Nuclear Armageddon. AIDS. AIDS and Reaganomics, Reaganomics and AIDS. AIDS life, AIDS social life, AIDS parties, AIDS funerals, AIDS coffee, AIDS nights, AIDS days. Reaganomics news about the deregulation of the financial market and the privatization of the prison-industrial complex. In the spring, the president went before the National Rifle Association and said, *Well, it is a nasty truth, but those who seek to inflict harm are not fazed by gun-control laws. I happen to know this from personal experience ... Hardcore criminals use guns. And locking them up, the hardcore crimi-nals up, and throwing away the key is the best gun-control law we could ever*

have. It was hard to argue with the only president to ever live through an assassination attempt.

Hundreds of thousands of guns on the streets of San Francisco. Guns were poems to crazy people. Whatever the murder rate was, it was always never higher. Heat. Rounds going off in the night without echo, hemming-hawing police sirens and whirring ambulances on the streets of San Francisco, helicopters overhead. On Bernal Hill we could literally point to the familiar unmarked grey CIA Gulfstreams flying overhead— Looky, said Jonjay, it's the CIA's daily drop—the only airplanes landing and taking off regularly from the docks on the SF Bay, with what Jonjay suspected were shipments of untraceable cash and guns, and coming back delivering bricks of white cocaine straight from the rebel Contras who stole it out of Nicaragua. Unloaded at Hunter's Point and Protrero Hill docks by stevedores who knew the score. Tons of untrammelled Central American coke got shipped all points north, south, and east, as well as mixed right here in SF apartments. Uncut Nicaraguan cocaine was being percolated into a soul-destroyingly potent crack rock sold to basehead junkies in Protrero and Hunter's Point, the Tenderloin and Mission District.

Most of the time Wendy didn't pay attention to the news of Contras, the assassination of Ninoy Aquino Jr., or the crack murders and Lebanese terrorists, she didn't care to notice who was killing more people in El Salvador, the right or the left, as much as she wanted to stay abreast of daily news and current events, she preferred for inspiration to skip straight to the funny pages in the paper, or to watch *Dallas*, *Charlie Brown* specials, and other primetime programs. Now that they were available on VHS, she told the rental stores she wanted to own her favourite movies by Charlie Chaplin and Buster Keaton and Harold Lloyd, cassettes that cost her eighty or ninety dollars a pop. She had thousands of dollars' worth of old movies, a whole bookshelf in the manor of movies in big plastic VHS boxes she watched to get ideas for jokes.

After the break, the *Hart Files*. And today's trivia, can you name these three celebrities, born today? The answers, when *Entertainment Tonight* returns.

That is easy, said Smooth Patrick, who was drawing sketches for sequences in the animation.

Jonjay tested the manor with trivia games. Best original comic strip by a former assistant.

The Mischiefs by Vaughn Staedtler, said Biz Aziz, he was former assistant of Al Andriola on *Kerry Drake*.

First comic strips by the creators of classic comic strips.

Mark: *Charlie Chaplin* by Elzie Segar of *Thimble Theatre,* Popeye's creator.

Comic strip artists who also work in superhero comics.

Patrick: Frank Frazetta, ghosting for Al Capp on *Li'l Abner*.

Comic strip writers who are also novelists.

Rachael: Dashiell Hammett, *Agent X-9*.

Comedians who also write gags for comic strips.

Patrick: Woody Allen.

Comedians who have comic strips.

Mark: Woody Allen.

What's that clicking sound?

My teeth, my damn teeth grind unbeknownst to their owner, said Wendy and stretched her mouth open wide.

If you don't see a dentist, we said, they might all fall out.

My hell is the dentist's office, said Wendy.

You want your teeth to fall out? Jonjay said. Falsies? Your jaw caves in and you lose your chin when you wear dentures.

We got used to Hick's body odour. Those of us who had never met him knew him. We smoked him. The weed simply reeked of harsh sweat. Biz stamped her joint out in the ashtray on the coffee table, picked up one of the joints we rolled freshly for her and lit it.

You need to book a three-hour appointment at Gilligan's dentist office, said Patrick.

It feels like there's little Gilligans trying to burrow their way out of my temples, Wendy told us.

Gilligan's cult, said Jonjay.

Gilligan's Vatican, said Biz.

Wendy took a big pull on the joint Biz passed her and then she passed it to one of us and we pulled, saw stars, and laughed about it. One sure way to unlock the persistent grinding at the gate of her jaw was *men*, she confessed.

She wrote a letter to Dr. Pazder, eminent psychologist in the burgeoning study of repressed-memory syndrome, that she had us proofread.

Dear Dr. Pazder, M.D.,

Hello, my name is Wendy Ashbubble, and I am a young woman in my twenties also born in Victoria, the same city as you and Michelle Smith, your most famous patient and now your love-mate. Presently I reside in San Francisco where I am a professional illustrator and cartoonist with a degree of financial success that affords me a lifetime of security and some luxury. And like Miss Smith, I too have suffered from strange vivid and constantly recurring dreams ever since my childhood. That's why I hope to make an appointment with you at your earliest convenience. It was only after reading your memoir of what Miss Smith discovered about her past under hypnosis that I have come to believe these strange things about my life might possibly true.

And so on. In this and subsequent letters to Pazder, she alluded to a father figure of some renown, but didn't out and out say Reagan, said nothing of Hick Elmdales's wake either, because she was so certain that the strange ceremonial aspects Pazder might like to hear about weren't real. Pazder never wrote her back.

What should I do about my teeth grinding? she asked her business manager when he called from his Motorola. Frank would call from his Hexen office in San Jose about once a season, with a gentlemanly report on what was what. She could always hear more phones going off in the background and men screaming *shitbag* at each other and frantic demands.

Your teeth? What's the matter with your teeth? I know world-class dentists right here in the Bay who can take care of you.

Sounds like you're calling from a war.

I am. One big civil war fought over the phone, Frank said. Hey listen, I just got off the phone with my guy at this national real estate company. I work with them on securitized mortgages, and anyway, they can use your characters for promotions and advertising, what do you think? Worth about fifteen thousand to you.

Sure, sure, okay, sounds like a deal, she said and did a quick mental tally of what he'd accomplished for her. Toiletries, knick-knacks, patties, cakes, creams, ices, plastics, clothes—all within the span of three years, Frank got her characters plastered everywhere. Every laundromat franchise and hotel chain in America that showed off her characters in brochures and signage paid Frank for the privilege. In the early eighties *Strays* was so popular, Wendy opened parades in towns she'd never heard of whose populace were so devoted to her strip there was a statue of Buck erected in a local park. Cleveland's free weekly entertainment newspaper ran her picture on the cover surrounded by her characters and the headline *Cleveland's Own Stray Wows America.*

Wendy took up the kitchen nook at the opposite end of the longtable from Hick's bedroom, and we spread out around on either side of her. Over a matter of minutes she pencilled Buck's head on a piece of scrap paper. That started her workday. Then came a body, and a shovel, so for something to do he dug a pit, actually it turned out to be a grave. She listened to funk records Mark flipped on the turntable and the murmur of Biz Aziz singing along in the dining room as she sketched and laid out pages for an issue of her memoir. Patrick Poedouce all of a sudden with his latest idea for a strip—set in a gold rush town—practically inspired by Wendy's drawing. Letting Buck take life in her hands. This was her method of distracted idea generation. She could be on the phone with Gabby or anyone and doing this. Now Buck was digging a grave in a cemetery. She drew another Buck beside the first, this time lower in the grave and with more earth piled next to him. She drew a bat who bore a striking resemblance to Ignatz, the mouse in *Krazy Kat*, flapping his black wings over Buck's head. As she started to ink the sketch, she lost her pencil (in her hair). She still didn't know what the joke was going to be. She found a new pen, a Pentel nib. She liked the idea that Buck might get a job as a gravedigger. That suited a dog who could always be counted on to see the good side. But she didn't know the punchline yet. So she made a few more sketches of a panel with a priest and mourners. This one panel took at least five sketches, and each sketch improved on one or two things—first she brought the priest into detail, a kind of Jim Rockford in a frock, so then she had to work out the mourners, they all had to become individuals, a widower, a louche fashion-conscious daughter and her husband, an old frumpy friend, and as soon as she found characters, the next sketch retained their essence but pulled back on the rest of the detail so your eye would focus on Buck, seated at the bottom right corner with the shovel over his shoulder. And she still didn't know what the punchline was going to be.

Never mind, she began to ink the frames for three panels onto a fresh page of bristol. There was still time to come up with a joke. The first two panels would show Buck digging and set up the joke. The mourners would take up the final two panels, meaning it would have to be the unknown punchline.

In an hour she inked everything outside the last panel, which was left in pencil until she thought of a gag.

Not all strips came easy but most of them did. She could bang off two or three on a good day. This one nagged her. This first grave-digger comic sat around for weeks and weeks as she tried punchlines, but nothing quite satisfied her. She drew lots of other gravedigger comic strips though. There was one with the Ignatz bat beaning Buck in the back of the head with a skull on the last panel in homage to Herriman. Gabby called and asked for a revision on that one—she wanted to know why it wasn't just a brick like the original. Wendy was sure there was nothing offensive about the skull she had drawn, and look, there was even a skull in today's *Wizard of Id*. But her editor's issue wasn't with the potential for a skull to offend, but wasn't it funnier with a brick? So she UPS'd this bristol board back to the manor and Wendy whited out the skull and replaced it with a brick. Whereas on the same day as she had gotten her first paycheque made out to Wendy Ashbubble for the amount of fifteen thousand dollars, she also wrote, sketched, and inked another whole strip. Some cats hate Mondays, says Murphy dryly, but I don't discriminate—I hate every day of the week equally.

Gabby called from Manhattan twice a day on average. Around noon the phone would ring and Wendy would look up from her coffee and agree to accept the call, to hear out her editor's reasons to improve some joke or just to gossip about the comics business or some contract Frank Fleecen had landed recently. The latest rumour was that Garry Trudeau's threats about a sabbatical from *Doonesbury* were serious, citing creative exhaustion and a diminished motivation with the shrinking size of comic strips. Apparently Charles Schulz was heard on the golf course to say he found the idea of a sabbatical decadent and weak.

I don't blame Garry, said Wendy. I'm tired and I just got going in this racket.

I'm sure you heard, Gabby said, how Berkeley Breathed protested to his editors about the reduction in size over the past year and it got us nowhere. I have to go. Another call.

And then she called again around nine at night to sugarcoat some feedback from a newspaper. Her strip didn't *read* well—meaning that in some papers the readership complained *Strays* wasn't legible.

Okay, okay. I get it. Less detail, Wendy said. Less and less detail.

To keep apace with all the new deadlines piling up on top of her daily strip, she split up her worklist among us. To-dos stacked up for designs for toys, packaging, clothing and accessories, business logos, brand identifications, and other jobs, we got assigned to the task. Every job went through multiple drafts in the studio before it got sent to the client for approval, whether it was a picture of Buck waving his hand or the whole cast hamming it up in front of a fence, and then might go through another round of iterations before going to the manufacturer. We picked up slack.

It took Mark a couple days of work to come up with an original drawing of Buck and Murphy in a two-door coupe for a coffee mug six-month tie-in advertising campaign with Exxon to launch in the first quarter of eighty-two. Francis the rabbit and Sam the snake got salt and pepper shakers out of a ceramics company, a T-shirt design needed Raquel's whole raccoon family and a slogan (*Mama needs more sleep*), and Lupercal wanted plastic bath toys, packaging for bath sponges, one of each character.

Patrick was fast with his hands and accurate, but his sketches and ideas lacked originality, so he picked up projects that were near to running late and finished them on time. Patrick never turned down work on *Strays*; the money Wendy paid meant he could avoid any other kind of job that might take him away from the longtable, which was where he developed his own strips to pitch to the syndicates. Could Wendy introduce Patrick to her editor? Sure, Wendy said, she could introduce them next time Gabby was in town. Patrick's method was to draw in forty-hour binges, finish two or three weeks' worth of strips, fourteen or seventeen gags establishing the characters and themes and sense of humour, then sleep for an entire day, then get up and repeat the process on a whole new idea. Still, even with that, Patrick never hit the mark. The syndicates he submitted to, including Shepherd Media, rejected his strips—*Feels forced*—*Thanks but we already distribute a comic like this*—*Your art lacks universal appeal and your humour is not family-oriented.*

For inspired ideas we turned to Mark, for he could sketch something brilliant and his sense of humour was similar enough to Wendy's, but the problem was his hands shook. Too much coffee and mushrooms and the dope from Hick's laundry hamper, too much everything, so he was no good at a finished drawing, not one of Wendy's at least. His style needed room to express. Mark's own drawings resembled *Strays* in no way whatsoever except for the use of panels. He copied the layout from the pages of superhero comics and inside the panels drew big slashing ink abstracts.

The one true draftsman among us we all acknowledged was Twyla Noon, a natural with a brush and a nib who could draw better versions of the *Strays* characters than even Wendy, so she assisted on almost every project, even so far as inking the daily strip when deadlines got tight. Twyla often filled in backgrounds and inked letters. Rachael was a competent and focused illustrator who could do almost any job, but her real strengths lay in organization: she created the pipeline to track all work as it came in, developed, and moved towards deadline. This left Wendy free to do what she loved and was good at. Wendy daydreamed, she read literature, took all day to answer fan mail, doodled for hours and hours. She hunted down, stole, and modified obscure jokes. Night owl, she would stay up late and draw, pull her hair, smoke our dope, listen to old records all night, and half the day grind her teeth in her sleep.

The lesson of *Strays* was hard for us to accept, that it took a ghoulish amount of daily work to put out a daily comic strip. She listened to Shepherd Media's local radio station for cranks and reactionaries, who were good for jokes. Wired up on cups, she would set to work at the longtable scrubbing her hands together in caffeinated agitation, thinking would she rather doodle strips? Finish ongoing strips? Improve punchlines? Redraw smears? Resketch new characters? Rewrite dialogue? Read the papers for ideas? to stay current? Go out for a walk and get ideas? Look at boys? Maybe buy pens? a dress? or a pair of underwear? or toothpaste? foot lotion? Got any jokes about foot lotion?

The one time she was interviewed for *The Comics Journal* was in issue eighty-nine, published in early eighty-four. Asking the questions was a freelance comics critic named Chris Quiltain who wrote her a long letter asking to know her opinion on all sorts of tough questions such as poverty issues, the influence of junk bonds on the American economy, eighties fashion, the commercialization of the comics, merchandising deals with Lupercal, and Reagan's budget for the military-industrial complex. With all due diligence, Wendy set the typewriter out on the table and rolled a blank sheet of paper into it and we took turns typing as she dictated a reply. *The greatest president since Merkin Muffley*, she quipped. But only the obvious exchanges made the cut and the best thing about the interview was the full-colour repros of the Sunday strips Wendy watercoloured. A variation on: Where do you get your ideas? How would you describe your characters? Which character do you most identify with?

Yeah, I'm thrilled to bits the strip is a commercial success, Wendy is quoted saying, *but I'm equally proud that I'm still doing it all in-house. I live in my studio with my assistants, who are all artists in their own right, and the design for every toy, every image or representation you see out there in the world, every project goes through us. Nothing is farmed out. If I could make the toys here, I would. We've even been working for the past couple of years on a top-secret animated cartoon of* Strays *I hope to sell to a TV network.*

She didn't mention the part about letting us live here rent-free.

Q: *What was it like growing up in Cleveland?*

WA: *Oy, you mean the mistake on the lake? [laughs] A city of quiet, polite people and ugly streets. Boring. Cleveland might as well be in Canada, it's so provincial. But I guess provincial is good for raising a cartoonist. My nanny was the library. I pored through leatherbound volumes of ancient Cleveland newspapers for their funny pages … The Gumps, Baron Bean, Bringing Up Father, all that goodness. Krazy Kat is still my favourite.*

Walking up Bernal Hill through the tall wheatgrass to the acacia forest surrounding the Sutrito Tower, she let her mind wander as well, studying the ground, the flowers, the sky, the city. She loved to run through the trees and hide somewhere until she got bored. She circled the entire hill, shaped like a little California, and meandered back down the south side to watch the strays. When she came back she started to draw tires, big tires with fat treads, lying on their side. She imagined a place where her animals might meet for a drink, sit down and talk for a while in the way that characters did in *Doonesbury* or the brick wall in *Peanuts*, a recurring location.

In the early months of eighty-four, when *Doonesbury* was still safely on sabbatical, Wendy still had to open papers to see her *Strays* up against the satirical penguin Opus, whose beak seemed to grow by the month, this neurotic motherless penguin who regularly broke the so-called fourth wall and talked to the readers of *Bloom County*. Even Schulz was breaking the fourth wall, having Snoopy pick a fight with the cat next door, *Next time try to be more quiet … Or I may just have to punch your nose!* Wendy was positive Schulz must be ribbing the comic strip next door—*Garfield*—because of what Snoopy admitted to his friend Woodstock, seated beside him on the doghouse roof, *Well, if he were awake, I suppose I'd leave out that last part.* Because nobody on the planet could bop *Garfield* on the nose, in eighty-four nobody outside a swamp didn't know *Garfield*, what a powerhouse, what a juggernaut of merchandising and popularity *Garfield* was, even Snoopy knew he was being outdone by the latest laziest, most cynical cat ever to live next door.

By its third year, *Strays* earned respectable receipts. But compared to six-year-old *Garfield* in its prime, it was a shameful mess, according to Wendy, who spent the morning under a dark fuzz if a particular comic strip on the funny pages was especially strong or cleanly drawn. *Garfield* scared Snoopy, it scared Wendy, too. *Garfield* was lovably stupid, and beautiful, immaculate as a synthetic flower. The early treasuries reassured her—*Garfield* started sloppy, and even early *Doonesbury* started way more muddled than it looked today. What did it matter if every year she changed how Murphy her cat looked? There was something funny about it. She was offended by the letters and her editor's comments that consistency was key, when her drawing skills kept outgrowing her characters.

Apparently what kids liked about *Strays*, apart from the jokes, was how much easier her characters were to copy compared to *Garfield*'s, whose technical perfection was nearly impossible for little hands to accurately match. Buck was only a matter of a few strokes. Murphy and Francis, too. It took a team of cartoonists to create the modern *Garfield*. *Garfield* was so clearly a money machine. That was fine by Wendy. She preferred the simple strips, anyway, and like Schulz she liked to draw hers with a noticeably handmade line. As assistants on the strip, we did mostly grub work up until a certain point, and then after about eighty-four, Wendy started to lean on us, and we retained her loose style through careful tracings of her originals. But in those heady years as sales ramped up, the syndicate used to pitch *Strays* as a voice from *the new youth movement*, whatever that meant—a way to avoid the words *punk* or *new wave* and other tags the South and Midwest editors of audience-advertiser-pleasing newspapers considered synonymous with *homosexual* and *satanic*. *The new youth* was euphemism for all the chunky lines in *Strays*, the puckish sense of humour, and the admirably self-taught style. She held on to that style even after the toys and licences. That quality of handmade inconsistency that *Garfield* eventually gave up, *Strays* never did. *Strays* always looked handmade by one person even when seven of us worked on a single strip.

Wendy found the comics and tossed aside the rest of the newspaper.

She was vocal about her tastes, her likes and dislikes, as she moved from strip to strip.

She preferred *Tiger* to *Dennis the Menace*—pored over *Tiger* and its almost Japanese woodblock style, the perfect flow of black and white in a panel. So many strips had lasted ages, the page itself looked like a message in a bottle from another era. For decades Mort Walker, Johnny Hart, and Dik Browne had had a virtual monopoly in most papers, with two strips each. How did they get it? Most new strips that lasted hobbled along earning decent money imitating another more popular strip, so *Marvin* imitated the look of *Garfield, Captain Vincible* was a sci-fi *Nancy, Sam and Ellie* looked a lot like *Hi and Lois*. Wendy ignored most of them creatively but eyed them all for technique, even the dramatic strips like *Steve Canyon* and *Rex Morgan, M.D.*, they took up space, sometimes space was limited to nine scrunched-up shrunken strips.

She considered a threat a strip that was too similar to hers, in style, content, character types, and how recently it was launched, and so on— there were only so many spots in the newspaper. If an editor had one spot come open and it was going to a cute animal comic to shore up the *Peanuts* fans who wanted more, then Wendy had to make sure *Strays* was funnier, had more interesting drawings, and captured the times better than the rest.

Gordo posed no threat, there was no threat from *Wright Angles* or *Ben Swift*—well-drawn family strips in the mode of *For Better or Worse* weren't going for all the merchandising she was. *Inside Woody Allen*—a strip that looked like a Johnny Hart comic but was almost entirely about sex, had limited, college-wide appeal. *Eek & Meek* was a funny animal-people strip about loafers that had lasted close to two decades. It was more accessible than *Bloom County*, less mechanical than *Garfield*, not as anachronistic or offensive as so many other legacy strips; it cleaved the same path as Wendy's, acting subversive using animals, and not exactly derivative of Schulz but still well within the shadow of *Peanuts*. There weren't the cute kids, but slacker hippies and beatnik mice instead. But it was unlikely that *Eek & Meek* would become a sensation with the kids again after fifteen years. Howie Schneider was someone to learn from. Not a threat.

So for the time being, she had no major threats beyond *Bloom County*, which received critical acclaim and sold millions of treasuries however few actual newspapers subscribed to it. *Strays* was in hundreds more papers, but Opus the penguin plush stuffed toys sold in comparable numbers to her dog Buck or rabbit Francis toys (Murphy the cat toys were her third best selling). Snoopy and Garfield outsold them all.

Garfield was constantly on her mind. The omnipotent cat. She read it second after *Peanuts*. The antithesis of *Peanuts* in spirit. The two strips couldn't be more different in their sense of humour or appear together in more papers. *Garfield* was in some ways the vain mirror of *Peanuts*, an image of *Peanuts* stripped of its pretense. *Garfield* was greedy. *Peanuts* seemed to accept collaborations with business, whereas *Garfield* clearly was a business. The cat was a machine, a die-cut machine of its own likeness, stamped out every day, repeated endlessly, producing timeless, cynical jokes about the ego. A tribute to laziness of the Roman variety, with slaves. Laziness was an ironic theme for a strip that was maniacally perfect in every detail, that required so much work to make right. And in light of the mass-production of *Garfield* merchandise, there was no lack of industry behind the scenes. The cat was self-centred and lazy, and *Garfield* the strip was self-centred and tireless. Garfield hated everything Snoopy stood for. Snoopy was outgoing and a charmer, a lover, a hero, a dancer, a poet, friend to small things, considerate of his family, respectful of Charlie Brown. Garfield had none of that. Side to side with *Peanuts*, *Garfield* was its inferior. The drawings were better in *Peanuts*, but drawings aside, *Peanuts* was the unrivalled behemoth in commercial ubiquity. Not only was *Peanuts* in the most papers of any strip, but the little folks were everywhere on everything. Snoopy was up there next to Mickey, Bugs, and Popeye in the upper pantheon of product placement. And in less than a decade, so was *Garfield*. That's what fascinated her—how quickly Garfield found his place as a legacy strip. She hoped Buck and/or Murphy might one day be added to that list of legacy strips clogging newspapers and thrift stores far and wide. Not art, product—*Garfield* was the anthropomorphized fatcat company president or CEO with a self-entitled air of indifference to those he subjugates. *Garfield* was a metaphor, the strip was America.

Wendy sometimes felt that *Garfield* exposed all cartoonists as frauds after a fast buck and nothing else. Even the absurd world of *Garfield* was more patently mechanical, a wind-up toy world like a cuckoo clock. The drawings were rigorously consistent, panel to panel, strip after strip, the lines were flawless. The stoned eggs of Garfield's eyes with the lids mostly shut, his face-to-body proportions, the cat was drawn with the architectural accuracy of a cathedral, with every sign of human touch polished out. The dishes of Garfield's forward-tilted ears were shaded with the same number of black forks every time, three. The shoulders and back arches followed the draftsman's golden mean. The three stripes on the tip of the tail echoed the ears.

I'm not good enough, I'm in fact quite awful, the opposite of *Garfield*. *Garfield* scares Snoopy. The anti-Snoopy. There is a beautifulness to Garfield's plastic, immaculate, and synthetic permanence. The fakeness of the whole project of *Garfield*. I kind of love it.

Garfield appeared in well over a thousand papers worldwide, and the anthologies were monster bestsellers in the millions. In the winter of eighty-two, Wendy's comic strip had three hundred and seventy-eight North American papers and counting. By the same time in eighty-four, she was in almost a thousand. The kids got keen on her strip, teens thought it was subversive, college kids collected her treasuries, and parents enjoyed the pangs of guilt Wendy's lost pets struck in their hearts. Buck reminded the elderly readers of Charlie Chaplin's tramp and Murphy of Buster Keaton's stoneface. The rabbit reminded them of W.C. Fields.

When I die I hope this doesn't flash before my eyes, says Buck the dog as he bites dirt after drinking too much tonic at the flat tire.

Francis the rabbit comes hopping up to Sam the snake in one strip and says, *Lend me ten bucks, willya, it's Father's Day tomorrow.*

I only have seven, hisses Sam.

No problem! You can owe me two bucks.

Home is the smell I inhale for, says Buck in another strip. *If I can just smell home one more time …*

We remember the day Gabby woke her up early one morning from a deep, grinding sleep to scold her over the phone for the punchline *Up your nose*. Need she remind Wendy she was already behind schedule and now this? It's a simple two-panel daily, and in the first panel Buck and Murphy are on a fence and Buck asks Murphy, *Where would you go in a time machine?* And Murphy answers, *Up your nose*. Explain how that makes any sense?

Wendy even laughed again to hear her own joke.

Editors won't accept *Up your nose*, Wendy. Readers in the Bible belt will complain it's too euphemistic for the funny pages.

Is that a word?

So she rewrote the joke to read, *I'd go back in time to before you asked that question and kick you off the fence.*

Don't worry, I love your style, but you give printers a headache. Remember, this has to be shrunk down to the size of a bookspine. Just so I can defend it to the guys upstairs, what's funny about *today's* strip? How many trips to the hamper did you make before you drew *this* one?

Francis says, *I'm a bunny from the land of bilk and money?*

Yeah, what's funny about that? Listen, Wendy, editors are looking for new strips to tide them over while *Doonesbury's* on repeats. Come out with some sensational stuff this year and you'll be set for life. Just think about it.

She would rip open fan mail forwarded to her from her syndicate.

Another smalltown American child's favourite strip was *Strays*, there was no bigger fan in the universe, and willing to adopt Buck into a good home. She flung the letter in our direction and asked one of us to write the kid back a doodle-filled letter for her to autograph. Aren't there any letters from a Dr. Pazder today? she would ask.

On bad days, if Wendy was tapped for *Strays* jokes, she drew what came naturally to her outside comics: watercolours and gouaches of backdrops for *Oklahoma!*, *Miss Liberty*, *Dracula*, *White Christmas*, and other plays. Growing up she had watched her mother work as a stage manager for dozens of productions. Wendy could sketch these set designs from muscle memory. After losing a day of work distracted by painting, she occasionally fooled herself into thinking she was on to something and considered showing them to Justine Witlaw as a *body of work*, see what she had to say. But she never got up the nerve.

Oh, I get art all right, says Murphy in one strip. *But I don't think art gets me.*

Looking out upon the corrugated city with all the homes laid out like pastry cakes in a dessert tray up and down the hills and valleys of our great peninsula. Lit by store signs and neon advertisements and billboard commercials, skies flush with plastic lemon, lime, orange, watermelon regularly washed in the thick suds of a Pacific fog.

STRAYS

15

You found Justine Witlaw's art gallery off Pine Street west of Chinatown, up a flight of stairs over a tailor's shop open seven days a week that did full suits and gowns and alterations within the hour. Justine's well-lighted white plaster cube was open to the public Thursdays to Sundays, noon until four and otherwise for appointments. She represented eleven artists, including Jonjay. The focus was the Bay Area's contribution to the avant-garde, which Justine Witlaw sold to major American institutions. Twenty-seven-year-old Ferzetti's anti-objects were meant to attract the interests of the Guggenheim and MoMA. Nobody in San Francisco would buy O'Connell's blue squares until they heard Witlaw had sold ten to hang in the lobby of Bank of America's head office. The National Portrait Gallery in D.C. borrowed one of Klein-Regge's feminist videos for an exhibition with catalogue. Justine lent two Monelles to the San Francisco Museum of Modern Art and a commission from the Seattle Art Gallery for a permanent installation in the mezzanine. Jonjay's work was in the collection of the Austin University Library and the investment bank Hexen Diamond Mistral.

It was a Friday afternoon and the space was empty except for us and the art. *This May Be My Last Path*—the title of the current show was labelled in black vinyl letters on a pimply white wall above the name in bigger letters: David Lelio Ferzetti.

Ferzetti made plinths. A dozen of his most recent four- and five-foot rectangular white plinths carved in ivory took up the gallery floor. The surface of each plinth was a cavity filled in with silver and gold, to the effect of making tall teeth of his plinths. The fillings were the sculptures. The walls were empty. There wasn't much else to see except a price book with numbers in the low four figures, red dots stuck to half the titles.

It was Wendy who had the idea to bring Mark Bread and his portfolio along with them when they went to pick up what Jonjay was owed. Jonjay went behind the counter to fetch Justine. Moments later she came out into the gallery as if it were a ballroom. Arms spread wide, she flung herself across the hardwood to embrace Wendy in a cold, indifferent hug, and how wonderful it was to see her. The two hardly knew each other. Met once or twice. She was hamming for Jonjay. Justine never smiled. More to the point, nothing was funny. Her tastes ran to the Mandarin. She was taller than Wendy and possessed of a natural and enviable atrabilious elegance, weighed not more than a hundred pounds all dressed, even if she kept on the costume jewellery, the charm bracelets, the scarab bead Egyptian goddess bib necklace spread across the bare ribs of her décolletage, and the chunky gold-plated interlocking C's of her Chanel beltbuckle displayed in the bowl of her pelvis. The sharp blades of her hips jut out at her sides but there seemed to be no legs inside the flowing pleated pants of her peacock one-piece Kaisik Wong jumper. Justine Witlaw, wispy as she was, could fill a room.

She was most pleased to meet Mark Bread, another artist. She muted a yawn. And do you draw cutie animals, too? Justine laughed mirthlessly and took Wendy by the arm and told them all to follow her into the back room, sit, have an aperitif and catch up. A bottle of champagne popped open on her by accident moments ago and we might as well share it with her. Did someone bring pot by any chance? You're your hair, Wendy. Where had Jonjay *been* all this time? Had to cancel your solo show last year, you flake. When should they reschedule? Soon, Justine hoped. He'd need to make new work since she sold the four pieces from the flat files in the back room. No matter, last year was great for Republicans but terrible for the art market.

Mark had two joints. He lit the first and handed it to Justine. She smoked and flipped through the pages of sfumato in the portfolio Mark had laid on the glass coffee table in front of her.

Take this before it murders me, thank you, she said and waved the joint at Jonjay. Coughing brought out the hircine qualities in her. Justine quenched her throat with a fluteful of bubbly, and, blinking through bloodshots, remarked with her usual contempt that it was wonderful to see Mark hadn't been sucked into the vortex of cliché lowbrow cartoony *oompa loompa*; that lack of maturity might impress Haight-Ashbury, but it doesn't play in her gallery. My god is it this pot that reeks of superstrong B.O.?

That's Hick Elmdales's. Give her a pen, said Jonjay. Watch what she can do.

Wendy slipped the Rapidograph from her bra and gave it to Justine. She started to draw, her hand moved with dynamism beyond her ken, haunted, the hand moved of its own free will. The result—Bugs Bunny paddling a canoe through a marsh.

Zoink, said Mark.

I drew that? she said and took a deep breath.

Wendy leaned sideways in her Mies van der Rohe leather clam chair and watched Jonjay tour the room, pulling artworks off the shelves lining the walls, silently appraising his peers. If you showed comics, you'd probably sell a lot. There's so many fans in town.

My field is contemporary art, Justine sniffed. Autonomous radical ideas pushing the envelope, etcetera. The artists I represent make demands. Conceptual. Found objects. Minimal. Postmodern. Don't you, Jonjay?

Watch me run backwards at top speed through the shopping mall, was his answer.

I love how much you hate comics, Justine, said Wendy and poured herself another glass of champagne and opened a coffee-table book about soft sculpture from the seventies. I know exactly what you mean. Mostly comics are such dumb shit. But what about *Doonesbury*?

I don't *hate* comics, but I don't see what they have to do with my gallery. Mark lit the second joint. No, oh god no—, Justine waved him away, —I can't have more. I'm high as American Airlines already. Why do I smoke the stuff? I get so freaked out I think the world is caving in on itself and my next step is through an invisible curtain into a new reality.

Fear is the price of an active imagination, Wendy said. That's what my mom used to tell her actors.

Justine finished the last of the first joint in a single haul, gave the roach to Mark to keep.

Take a good look at Mark's drawings, he's a natural—and you can't say they're commercialistic or cartoonism. He's his own movement's ism.

Justine squinted down at the paper. These *are* quite provocative. Okay, one more toke. She took the second joint. Your mark-making is rigorous, agile, and uncompromising. Tell me, besides this crazy weed giving me vertigo, what is your creative process?

Mark gripped his champagne glass like a microphone at a spelling bee and said: I made these while reading *The Origin of Consciousness in the Breakdown of the Bicameral Mind.*

Julian Jaynes. Interesting. That book has been on my reading list forever. Groundbreaking study, I read the reviews. Justine passed the joint eventually. Oh fuck now I'm really high. Nothing in her posture or voice gave away she was.

LEE HENDERSON

My other inspiration is *glass*, Mark said. It was on Wendy's advice that he had practised some lines in advance. If he spoke from his heart it would invariably come out as Saturday morning Scooby-Doo blabber.

Glass is very in, reminds people of Duchamp, said Justine. Dan Graham is working in glass. I'm impressed. I make a point not to represent lovely pictures or pretty things. I represent *ideas*. Your pictures *are* lovely ideas, she said. However I prefer not to represent two artists working in the same medium, and Jonjay already subverts traditional drawings on paper, so. But perhaps there's a space. I would like to think of you for my winter group show. I'll nick some strong pieces from your portfolio if you don't mind so I can treat a few blue chippers to a sneak peek in the meantime.

Shazam, said Mark and drank deeply from his glass flute.

What do you call this series?

Wiggles, said Mark through pursed lips.

Hmm, we might want to think of another title. Or not. What are some of your other influences, in visual art?

Kirby krackles, Kirby squiggles. Biz Aziz.

Hmm. Justine nodded as though she understood when it was plain to all of us she didn't. Where are you from, here in the Bay?

Ba-deep-ba-deep, said Mark. Sweesh! Shimmysham! Slamjam! Boobie doobie blammo!

Wendy flagged the gallerist's attention. Please, won't you pass that joint, please. Jonjay, hey, Jonjay, Wendy snapped her fingers, ... didn't you have something you wanted to ask Justine?

I did? Oh yeah of course, duh. Hey, Justine, that reminds me, I heard through the ole gravepine you sold some of my drawings.

Yes, oh god, she slapped her palm to her forehead. I forgot to tell you, that's right, yes, to the collection of Hexen Diamond Mistral, a Wall Street *banking institution* that's been operating for over a *hundred* years. Good news.

Listen, if it's cool I could use my cut, said Jonjay. I'm kinda strapped.

Of course now that you're home we can settle up. Justine said her accountant was in next Friday and she would have him write a cheque for the full amount. Like all the galleries with any reputation, Justine Witlaw split sales with her artists fifty-fifty. Four large-scale drawings meant she owed Jonjay to the tune of sixteen hundred dollars.

I could use it in my pocket right now, he said and lifted a silkscreened blue square out of a flat file.

Careful with that. She jumped for her starry gold-lamé purse—it looked like a motorcycle helmet. What can I give you? Here's *fifty*. I'll peel it off what I owe. In fact, just take it.

Jonjay pocketed the fifty. You're a peach with no pit, Justine.

When I was out for dinner with Frank from that bank Hexen, said Wendy as she pushed a flute of champagne to her nose, he told me he was at that show with the blue squares.

O'Connell, said Justine. You *know* Frank Fleecen?

Yes sort of … Just signed a contract with him for my strip. What do you think of him anyway, is Frank on the level?

Justine said she wouldn't know. He bought Jonjay's pieces over the *phone*. She never spoke more than a few words to him in the times he followed his wife to the gallery for openings and then Justine was always too busy with regular clients to single him out. She presumed his wife was in charge of the art collection.

The wife. Wendy slid down a bit in her chair and lowered the lids of her eyes as she fixed her stare on Justine. What's the wife like?

An intellectual, I guess. Of the two, she seemed to make the decisions in the gallery. One afternoon she came here on her own after O'Connell's opening and I gave her the tour. Struck me as smart and down-to-earth, dressed in a sandy-blue pantsuit or something I took to mean she was ready to do business. Told me she wrote and had published a short story. Wives are often the ones who study art and decide the direction of the husband's collection, for these overworked, overpaid, guilt-ridden millionaires who want to appreciate culture but don't have the time to do the legwork. So the wife appreciates for them both. She was polite and curious the whole of my tour and I thought I had made a sale and then she said, *Why does art make me feel so stupid?* I offered to take her to the back room, and she looked through the files. All she was interested in seeing when we got here was Jonjay's pictures.

Ladies love cool Jonjay, said Jonjay, looking up from some pictures in a flat file.

That reminds me, said Wendy, swinging her Gremlin's keys around her finger. I gotta go. Need to get back to No Manors and help Rachael and Twyla put my package together for UPS by five, and there's still entire panels that need inking. Guys? Ready to go?

Justine tiptoed back to her chair, fell into a catlike position with legs crossed at the knee, wagged her ballet flat at the end of her toe, and said, Well, don't collect your money, drink my champagne, and take off, that's rude. I mean, really, stick around. Blow off UPS. Do you at least have ideas for your show, Jonjay?

Oh sure. Watercolours and drawings of bristlecone pines from the White Mountains. Dried skull mushrooms from Japan. Documentation of an event. Traces of a geological formation. That's what I have so far. And a bottle of what I call Ruthvah, Jonjay said, grinning idiotically.

Justine swooned with a contemporary art fever when he said Ruthvah was the name for a *scent*.

The watercolours and drawings of the bristlecone pines were done. The dried skull mushrooms from Fear Mountain were glazed for preservation. These and the beautiful pictures from his time lost in the White Mountains were more than enough. Why clutter the space? What he had was beautiful on its own. But Jonjay was impartial to beauty, he wanted more material, he wanted clutter.

Justine Witlaw wanted a show *this year* but he told her he wasn't ready.

In fact she had him down for a solo in September. Postpone, he said. And she said, You've got more than enough for two shows. Compared to Abrams. And she's had three shows in three years. Look, we're even, aren't we? I paid you back.

Yeah, thanks, said Jonjay. But it's still my decision when I'm ready to have a show.

Wendy shook her keys again and pointed to her wrist as if there was a timepiece there and said, UPS waits for no woman.

But as if conversation was a cliff and she was clinging to it for dear life, Justine began to digress into a portrait of her gallery. Listening to Justine talk about herself, we saw this skittish, frail woman in a designer wardrobe who was either very dismissive or making big demands of people, and you thought better of getting too close. We knew from gossip back at the manor that in the early seventies, when she started out, Justine Witlaw's wealthy father bought half the work in almost every show, so she would have the red dots needed to attract interest. The strategy might have taken seven or eight years but it worked eventually, for now Witlaw dealt exclusively with a blue-chip clientele, most of them based on the West Coast, collectors who—in her words—lived in three homes, owned two yachts, and piloted a floatplane to an island getaway. A few of her artists were in the permanent collections of minor American and European museums—but at her own admission there were years she sold everything she exhibited and years she sold nothing, the white walls were cursed, the concrete floor was hexed. Some months she sold nothing but made more money than sellout shows, by doing backroom deals on the secondary market, matching buyers for sellers, acting as an intermediary who was quieter than an auction. Not selling *her* roster of artists. She told us that she sold little Picassos her clients owned and needed urgently to sell, Renoirs and Thiebauds that surfaced after deaths, divorces, job changes, and sordid so ons. A frequent problem for shifty art collectors was the unstable value, because according to Justine unless you had exactly the right buyer, most of what you bought was impossible to resell, worthless in the short term. Justine Witlaw had an exceptional eye for hot new art, but most collectors knew her better for her intrepid nose. Matchmaking in the secondary market was an art of its own. She could see how to shape an artist's trajectory; whether she was capable of making that happen was unclear. Her Rolodex was filled by her ability to find a buyer for a little Teraoka watercolour, or one of Nengudi's squiddy pantyhose-filled-with-sand sculptures, sometimes in under twenty-four hours. Snap her fingers it was done, she claimed. Justine was a lot of times a safer bet for a collector living on Russian Hill than an auction house based out East. Sotheby's rebuffed a local collector of Tanaami and Yokoo who hoped to sell for at least a third more than paid. Justine put the owner on hold, sold the prints to a collector on the other line for double. For these services her cut was fourteen percent.

This was a city in thrall to rock memorabilia they thought was fine art, Robert Crumb, Cal Schenkel, and Keiichi Tanaami were taken very seriously. Former park-dwelling hippie turned Silicon Valley nerd turned drug kingpin turned defence lawyer. Money to burn on their nostalgia for the time they used to waste. You could sell a silkscreen of a Tadanori Yokoo for the same price as a Clyfford Still canvas out West; in California a Chris Burden went for as much as a signed Doors concert poster silkscreen; Justine sold an autographed painted cell of the Evil Queen from the Disney film *Snow White* faster than an exquisite piece of Marcel Duchamp paraphernalia—eventually to the same buyer, an Oscar-nominated character actor.

That a curator from the Guggenheim had even visited a commercial gallery in San Francisco was enough to perk up heads in the culture circles, gossip rippled out as far as the comic shops in Berkeley. Justine was *certain* the turning point would be a major solo show with Jonjay, in the way that only his mercurial standoffishness could crack the East Coast, his work, his style was bound to attract the kind of media attention her gallery deserved, notices from critics and calls from curators, museums, other galleries in SoHo, and magazine editors. Considering it's been a decade in the business, *he* would establish Justine Witlaw's gallery as the real centre of contemporary American art, since no one represented the true avant-garde of the eighties better than Jonjay. If Jonjay would only agree to a show. He had more than enough work.

He said, Naw, don't have enough stuff. All I got so far is decoration for the main event. I need to create a certain mood of, I don't know, ambivalence.

You mean imbalance? said Justine.

No, I mean ambiv*alance*. I'll come next Friday and pick up the rest, okay? Ready to burn rubber, Wendy?

As he drove us home, Wendy asked him why he didn't take Justine up on the solo show, and all he said was, Not until I get my money.

What about Mark, should he give Justine some of his pictures?

She doesn't owe you money, so … , Jonjay said. He looked out the side window as he drove, left arm dangling out in the wind while the right hand steered her Gremlin through the usual insane traffic. No, my dealings with Justine are like a cautionary tale. See, if I was a kid living in San Francisco who made a lot of abstract paintbrush squiggles on small sheets of paper, the first thing I'd do is print a comic book. Small run. Drop it in the right shops. Get the heads talking. Send some copies to the Guggenheim so you can say you're in their permanent collection. Then show some pictures with Justine Witlaw.

Wendy wasn't sure if Mark heard, his eyes were closed but maybe his mind was open. The Gremlin carried us up the steep hill of Stoneman Street to the dead end where the white van was still parked. We drove over the extension cord.

Does she have a TV in there or something? Wendy asked.

Yeah, said Jonjay.

What does she watch?

Soaps. *Solid Gold*.

Wendy scowled. She got out and opened the garage door, and Jonjay parked inside the carport.

He got out of the car and, leaving Mark passed out in the backseat, closed the door of the garage. He said he thought the door needed something to spruce it up. It was corrugated aluminum that lifted up and slid into a shelf near the ceiling, and it was painted black. What else did he want?

Wendy said she couldn't handle it, she had to know if Jonjay was going out with that damned surf pixie, she obviously wasn't just some new friend from the desert highway, was she? Was he sleeping *in* her van with her or was he sleeping *with* her in the van? Because it seemed to Wendy like the *latter*.

He didn't make eye contact with her as he said, Sort of but not really. Manila is serious about *me*, and she saved my life, so. But I'm not with her. I'm with *nobody*, he told her. I don't *date*, Wendy. That's not me. My lifestyle is unpredictable. Plus she's just a girl.

Oh, yes, you're much too old for her. Wendy combed her fingers through his hair. You're ancient, aren't you? Like a mountain.

Eternity is a tough gig, baby. And sexual solitude is essential to my meditation regimen, he said in all earnestness.

Fine then, fine, have it your way. Wendy walked away into the manor ahead of him. I'm determined to live life to the fullest, she said, even if all you want to do is sneak sex with a kewpie doll and stare vacantly at a wall. Some men find me very attractive. She winced. Then she turned around and came back and asked him for help with rent. At least you can do *that*.

I'll come up with some dough, don't worry.

Whatever. Just go to your secret bank account.

He looked around. No one else within earshot. (We would not learn until much later about the secret bank account with supposedly over a million dollars in it.) You and your misnomers, he said. Hey, you want this? He pulled the fifty from his pocket and snapped it open so

Ulysses S. Grant's portrait faced her. That's the only tune I can play and that's no lie.

Wendy struck on an idea. Let me kiss you once or twice and I'll let you keep the fifty.

16

Who were we supposed to believe, Jonjay or Wendy, or our own skin? Twyla Noon tried to woo him, too. Little did she know about the kooloomooloomavlock.

Put some time between her moves and Wendy's attempts at rekindling whatever it was happened between them up in Canada—so at the tail end of the summer of eighty-one, when Manila Convençion was back on the road and the leaves on the trees turned yellow and red, and hormones, instinct, and brute physical attraction take over like a suicide mission, Twyla caught Jonjay in the living room smoking through a bag of weed and watching reruns of *Twilight Zone* on late-night TV while Mark, in the fetal, snored on the chesterfield surrounded by empty cans of Old Milwaukee. Kittenish, quietly on her hands and knees, she pawed her way up to where Jonjay was lying on the other sofa, meowed, and threw her hair back.

He startled. Didn't see you there. What are you doing, Twyla?

She tiptoed her fingers up his chest and whispered in his ear, *Lord, I think I want you.*

Say what?

Without meaning to she called him lord. She meant it as an exclamation but it came out sounding more like how she really felt at the
moment, like a servant crawling at the feet of her desire, a vassal at his
beck and call. Behind his back, we competed to describe Jonjay. Viking.
Druid. Centurion. Prince. Olympian. Mephistopheles. Bacchus with
biceps. Romanesque. Hypnotizer. Pulchritudinist. He didn't just pay
attention; we felt his eyes locked so hard it felt as though while you spoke
he was listening not to your words but to your soul. Most of all he was a
heartbreaker.

That boy's on a higher plane of existence, Biz would say. You're all just
fuckin' floccinaucinihilipilification (and in a word dismiss our dreams).
This was the night Twyla found out the literal truth of Biz's comment.

Lord, I think I want you. Already unbuttoning the fly of his Levi's.
Come on, I brought a condom. Now's the time, she whispered. Let's do
it. Right here.

Dang, timeout, Twyla. Wow, hey, this is cool but what about Mark?

Twyla was sleeping with Mark at this time. She looked at her on-again-
off-again and said, He's dead to the world.

Look, wow, I'm sure we'd be a phenomenon in the sack and all, but I'm
on the natch. No more fucking until I capture the kooloomooloomavlock.

You can't be serious, said Twyla. It's been months.

This was the name for a mental animal more desirable than the elusive
simultaneous orgasm. Instead of sex, Jonjay would sit lotus on Hick's
exercise mat, balance lit candles in the palms of his hands, and go into an
hour-long hypnogogic trance he called *Hunting the kooloomooloomavlock.*
He'd sit there in his crawlspace or in Hick's old bedroom go into a deep state
of being. Staring into space, flying through the blue skies of pure thought
into the smog of opinion over the valley of ignorance, and through the
caves of suspicion. Glasseyed in the manner of a vampire in the dormancy
of his daily coffin. His meditation was catatonic, his eyes stopped blinking

and white droolcicles hung from his chin. The Kooloomooloomavlock was a precosmic wraith who stole from mankind the key that unlocks the gates of all-knowing. To hunt the Kooloomooloomavlock was as close as a mortal could get to the gardens of enlightenment. It was how Jonjay said he spent all his pineal energy.

He was a trained climber in a trance and on foot, and was the leader of two ascents on the Paro Chu, plus the solo he did the year Hick died of the Osorezan, the Kanchenjunga a decade before, and he was a teammate on many other expeditions, some of which he alone survived. As for astral projections, his experiences were more vast. He knew many of the world's mountains through deep meditation. The deeper he went into himself, the higher he could climb in astral projection. One day he turned the insides of No Manors into a practice mountain, to keep his skills fresh, and attempted an ascent from the basement to the attic without touching floors *or furniture*. Only the walls and ceiling. He carried chalk powder on him, to dust his hands with periodically, and a few bagels in case he got hungry as he crimped the edges of Victorian finishings, under-clinging from Edwardian doors. He rested in the pockets of high art deco cartouches, and pinched, palmed, and pulled himself steadily up the maze of five storeys, not just the main floor, to the flat-top peak. The tendons in his forearms and neck stretched at the skin as he frogged from high corner to baseboard and back up, making good time. He ate the bagels in a cubbyhole on the third floor's front hallway and arrived at the attic's summit by dark. No one took pictures, so he repeated the climb a week later for the sake of documentation.

In the attic at the top of No Manors there's a little window that opens onto the tiny flat roof, it's about the size of a tabletop. There you can see an almost three-sixty view of the Bay, Jonjay said of his view at the peak. All the traffic. Gosh. All the freeways. Lanes and lanes of cars speeding back and forth, in and out of the city, hundreds every minute. Exits. On ramps. And you should see how houses blanket the hills, houses and apartments and buildings seriously cover everything. From up there, Golden Gate looks like a park with a swing set. All these cars. It's a beautiful view, it helps you remember that it doesn't matter what direction you go, someone is always going the other way.

Jonjay was slightly dangerous, in that he had no impulse control when it came to acting on an idea, no matter what whim. He woke us up this one time, it was three in the morning, the middle of summer and a Thursday, probably this was in eighty-two or eighty-three. He still hadn't had a show at Justine Witlaw's and at this point she had only paid him back half what she owed him (cash he had to remove himself from her purse while she drank sangria). C'mon, Jonjay said, help me set this up.

Set this up. We didn't know what *this* was when we hopped in Wendy's lime-green Gremlin—she was fast asleep for this one. Jonjay had the trunk weighed down with at least a dozen eighty-pound sacks of Checkers icing sugar and he wouldn't tell us what for. He took us through town to the Golden Gate Bridge. The bridge was amazing to see at that hour, when the sun was moments away from the horizon and the bridge's long red body was totally silent like a sleeping dragon stretched out on a bed of lowlying fog, a fog full of glittering multicoloured metallic particles, and not a single car before or after us rode its great outstretched back. It was just us and the road eventually joining the horizon.

Jonjay stopped the Gremlin—*skrrch!*—in the middle of the bridge. Good, perfect, we're alone. Okay, someone stay behind the wheel and leave the car idling, watch for traffic, especially the fuckin' cops. He popped the trunk and got out.

What are you doing? Patrick said. Oh hell no, he's not going to jump, is he?

He'd live anyway, said Rachael. She scooted from shotgun to the driver's seat and eyed Jonjay through the rearview as he took a sack of Checkers from the trunk and used a knife to rip the sack open and dumped the white powder on the bridge. We watched in silence as he tore open all the sacks and caked both lanes with a pile of icing sugar. Then as soon as *that* was done he jumped back in the Gremlin with the empty bags, squealing, *Go, go, go!* and so Rachael pumped the gas and away we went. Twyla slapped his shoulder and said, What the fuck was that about? You're out of your gourd.

Sugar dump, Mark Bread repeated in an escalating falsetto. Sugar dump, sugar dump *sugar dump*.

Did you forget to take a picture of this *again*? For your documentation? Patrick asked in a contemptuous tone, rubbing the bags under his eyes. He said, I can't tell what's art for you and what's a joke. Is how tired I am a part of your art?

Relax your false tribulations, Jonjay said. He giggled. He stuck his arm out the window to feel the breeze as Rachael got us off the bridge, the Pacific Ocean rippling under us, the dark skies above sparkling, and maybe the icing sugar was like a clod of moon dust fallen to Earth. A dream that we didn't wake up from. As soon as we got home Jonjay turned on the local morning news and there was a helicopter hovering over the sugar on the bridge.

Multiple VCRs got set to record. We tuned in to different stations on different TVs as news coverage of the icing sugar expanded to other networks and Jonjay wanted to capture it all on tape. Soon every station in America was broadcasting footage of the icing sugar. It was on one channel or another all day long. CNN did a segment. But nobody knew what the sugar was, it was this *mystery white powder on the Golden Gate Bridge backing up traffic for miles in both directions.* By noon the bridge was on complete military lockdown. Nobody was allowed on or off without clearance. The ocean was being patrolled by the navy in black Zodiacs and wearing frog suits. And the whole nation's attention was turned to the bridge as the situation made us a nervous wreck. The Pentagon's scientists—the *Pentagon*, Jonjay—microsampled the powder, they tested it for everything from anthrax to bananadine. Jonjay laughed for hours watching anchormen and anchorwomen make paranoid assumptions about the mystery powder *thought to be the work of Russian agents*, sweating over the mysterious white powder *being analyzed as we speak … this act of terrorism* had the Golden Gate out of commission for *eight hours* while hazardous-materials specialists ran parallel rounds of tests in CIA labs—*CIA* labs, Jonjay!—to identify anything that might lead to a culprit. *Culprit*, Jonjay! We watched as the story made headlines all over the world when the labs came back with Checkers brand icing sugar. The news repeated the confirmation that evening, Checkers brand icing sugar, the bridge was once again open, and it was on to current events without a punchline. Jonjay considered the piece a success—he had seven VHS cassettes loaded with six hours of footage each, including hours' worth of the aerial shots of the icing sugar pile from a helicopter and an hour-long panel discussion with SFPD toxicologists who labelled this *a level one*, and a perceptive criminal psychologist who guessed either a shipping truck mishap or an adolescent prank.

I'm glad you didn't bring me along on this little excursion, said Wendy as she watched the story unravel. But thanks for stealing my car, you jerk. You owe me a back massage for that, at least.

Jonjay kept this documentation in a box labelled *A Game of Checkers* that he was going to use in his solo show at Justine Witlaw's. There was no reason for us to be afraid that someday this prank might become evidence in our trial, *as if* the CIA and the Pentagon are going to investigate a pile of icing sugar. He was never going to cop to the prank, just to recording a news cycle that fascinated him, as an artist—the documentation *was* his art. Never breathe a word of it to anybody, he told us and sliced a finger across his neck, or we'll all go to prison.

Frank happened to call the manor that day. And it wasn't like him to call—his routine of seduction-slash-business was to deliver good news through Gabrielle Scavalda, working in a whole different time zone on the whole other coastline.

Something the matter? Wendy asked.

No, nothing, he said cagily. How's things there at No Manors? She said they were fun as always. That's good, he said. I just needed to hear your voice, he said. She asked if he was on his Motorola and he laughed, yes, he was.

You know they would be glad to get you a freebie.

Who would get me a freebie of what? Wendy put down her pen and listened to him.

Guess who wants to ink a lucrative licensing deal with *Strays*?

Last time it was gas stations in Wichita, so I'm stumped. Wait. Hold the line. No way. That's the limit. I draw the line at your silly cordless wonderbrick. My animals selling cellular phone boxes? That's ridiculous. I can see it now: *When you ain't got a home and you still want a phone.*

Strays will provide the images and Motorola's slogan's up to a copywriter, Frank said humourlessly but with a laugh. But I'll pass that along. Should I have to go through Gabby as per, or do I have your blessings to get back to Motorola with an offer?

Since when do you ask for blessings? I never blessed Wichita's gas stations, I just got a work order.

This is deal is on a magnitude of ten thousand Wichitas, Frank said. Think of it as a pinnacle, Wendy. The first commercially available cellular phone. I've been waiting to ink this deal since we first met. You, me, and Motorola are about to make history. You have to be in on this. I wanted to be the one to tell you myself.

Fine then, fine, you did, thank you, she growled at him and hung up. Argh, why am I so upset at him over this? She spent another ten minutes struggling to unwind the knots in the phone cord before she got too exasperated and slumped down on the kitchen floor covered in sweat and gave up.

It's just another deal, another contract to sign, pictures to draw, not a calamity, we said as we crouched over her and undid the hogtie she'd put herself in. We'll help, don't worry.

It *is* what I want, she said. Just painful. It's like sex without touching.

In the time he lived at the manor, we noticed Jonjay's fingernails and toenails were square-edged.

He was an incorrigible nonvoter with contradictory principles and no faith aside from a Liquid Papered pentacle on the back of a sleeveless denim jacket.

He had us go hunt down cans of black and white latex house paint for an idea. He painted the garage door a matte black, and once it was dry, he brought out the can of white and painted a freehand circle and an inverted star inside it, his and Hick's favourite antisocial hex. Jonjay claimed his freehand circles were Rembrandt good, to the ninth decimal of pi.

Pure No Manors, he said as he admired his handiwork.

Wendy came out to take a look at what he'd done and we took some Polaroids to document the pentagram. He seemed rather proud of this one for some reason.

That's ridiculous, she told Jonjay. This is your idea? What are you doing? I hope your plan is to paint over it now that there's pictures.

Say what? That's there to *protect* your car. One sigil like that wards off a lot of evil, trust me. That's good for at least five years. Now look, watch see … Jonjay opened the garage door and then shut it again, to show off the effect of the pentagram. You park your Gremlin behind a wall of cool confusion. Looks cool and thieves, arsonists, rapists all respect the dark slayer of the black arts. They won't touch the house. The Lord of Chaos's amulet says to a rat stranger, *Don't fuck with me, I'm a friend of the outlaw lifestyle.*

Fine. Okay. The satanic star can stay. Only because it reminds me of Hick and *Michelle Remembers* and heavy funk music, and because you can draw such an amazingly perfect circle. You punk, thanks for your silly anti-gift.

You are welcome, he said.

However, the next day Wendy went on a joyride through town taking pictures of the city with two of us in the Gremlin with her, Rachael driving and Twyla in the backseat, and we came home to find the neighbours' kid out in front of her garage defacing the symbol on the door. In fact that afternoon we had been invited to the home studio of retired cartoonist Vaughn Staedtler, who was still being sued for back payment by his former assistants on *The Mischiefs*. The comic lived on in thousands of papers and Staedtler retired to the south side of a sprawling adobe-style duplex the colour of pink marzipan way out in Golden Gate Heights. Now his home studio was full of canvases on which he'd painted lurid portraits of clowns in thick buttery oil paint. A small college-age kid in overalls who Staedtler said was his grandson sat in a corner facing a television that played old Max Fleischer Superman cartoons. Other than that, it was the clowns. Some of the clown paintings were life-sized, others were bigger. The treatment in oils was sloppy, with colours straight out of the tube, and garish half-melted expressions on the grinning, smeary faces. Vaughn thought he'd captured some kind of metaphysical pun, *painting portraits of clowns in painted face makeup*. Scaring his audience to the point of skincrawling repulsion did not seem to be the purpose at all, so we tried our best to be positive for him. But the clowns, terrifying on their own, when added up to this army, were madness. A circus would not accept these, let alone an art gallery. So maybe they were so ghastly that he *was* on to something. There was nothing to say about them, not aloud anyway, and Vaughn Staedtler was absolutely one hundred percent certain that New York should prepare, he said, for a cannon blast across the bows of contemporary American art. He listed off galleries who would beg for his work. Gagosian, Vaughn growled.

The main reason for our visit was to sell him eight ounces of pot and we left soon thereafter. We might have had a couple other stops along the way there and back to the homes of other, better cartoonists, such was our life in those days, we the keepers of Hick's spirit.

We replenished our supply through Biz Aziz upstairs, who sold it to us in pounds, and she got it from someone in the Twomps, South Oakland. That's all we knew. That's all you *want* to know, Biz Aziz told us. You don't even want to know *that*, she said. It wasn't her habit to deal, it wasn't *ours* either, it was Jonjay who set us up with the arrangement and we all convinced ourselves it was to honour the legacy of Hick Elmdales. And fear, fear that we would go broke otherwise, and fear we would remember the substance of that night we met Jonjay if we stopped and thought about it.

And when we got home from our rounds, the Evangelical neighbours' boy was on the last strokes covering Jonjay's sigil with his own can of white housepaint.

What on earth gave you this idea? Wendy demanded to know.

The kid looked up at her, a little nervous, but without a shred of guile, knowing his fate was not in his hands. He said, My parents told me to come paint over this.

Shouldn't paint over another person's symbols, that's bad juju, kiddo. Wendy tsk-tsked him and wagged a finger. When the white paint dried she wanted the neighbour boy to come back and repaint the inverted pentagram.

That was an evil symbol, the kid said.

That was there to *ward off* evil, you li'l Tom Sawyer. She took the kid's ear and carried him back to his parents.

Along with an Evangelical wreath on the front door, the doormat said *Luke 10:5*, on the lawn was a white cross on a chopping block pedestal, and in the driveway there was a woodgrain station wagon with a giant *Vote Reagan* sticker that took up half the bumper. Wendy told the boy to wait behind her.

Did you tell your son to trespass and vandalize my property?

We saw a devil worshippers' symbol vandalized on your garage yesterday. The mother was in her apron and the father stood behind her and he scratched her neck as she spoke, which was weird. We *asked* our son to paint over this offensive graffiti.

My friend painted that pentagram for me yesterday as a gesture. It's to ward off evil.

It *represents* evil.

I live in that house and that's my garage. I think in America I'm allowed my own definition of evil.

We can see your garage door from our kitchen table, the father said. Son. Get in here. Don't hold that *lady's* hand.

Wendy told the Evangelical parents their son should come over tomorrow at the crack of noon and repaint the pentacle to teach him it's not correct to trespass or paint over other people's property just because something offends you.

They put up a heartfelt argument, but she had a point, and in the end their sense of responsibility to a loving God forced them to force their son to repaint the satanic symbol. So the Evangelical neighbours' kid came over the next day with a bucket of black paint and a brush and Wendy broke out a lawn chair and supervised. His parents could be seen at the kitchen window.

Are you a devil worshipper? the kid asked. He was painting the bottom point of the star.

Is that what your parents told you?

I don't know, he said.

Only thing *I* worship is Charlie Brown. What about you?

The boy's circle was more of a wobbly lasso and his star was more of a lopsided spider's web, but we all agreed this was far better than Jonjay's creepily perfect rendition.

Dear Dr. Pazder,

Get a load of what just happened to me. So I've got a few roommates and one of them, actually he's more of an ex-boyfriend, but anyway … he decides to …

Ruthvah ~ For Men.

Once many years ago while hunting Kooloomooloomavlock in a zoned-out meditative trance, Jonjay claimed he had met the astral projections of Aleister Crowley and his mistress. They, too, were out tracking the beast across the Himalayan Kingdom of Bhutan, those cliffs populated by mountain goats, wildcats, and monasteries. Over steaming cups of buttered tea, the three disembodied travellers became fast friends, and it was Crowley who told Jonjay the secret ingredients to the mythic love potion, a cologne so powerful no woman could resist its wearer. A brothy smell and, most important, loaded with pheromones.

What was it about Jonjay that made us join him when he took a bicycle off the ceiling and asked us to ride with him against the sun, up and down the sinewaves of San Francisco's hills, on the hunt for supplies. Racing our shadows in and out of milky fog. Trolling the flea markets and second-hand stores with him until we found the half-ounce amber cut-glass bottles Jonjay was looking for. A dusty crate filled with what must have been two hundred of these little bottles, used for laudanum in the nineteenth century. He put them in the milkcrate tied to the back of his bike and off we went to the next spot. Ingleside, Sunset, up into Richmond and the Haight, through the Tenderloin and the Seven Hills as he gathered together from Trader Joe's and whole foods outlets, aromatherapists and Wiccan spice dealers the essential oils and seeds for his recipe. The Haight's underground anarchist grocery network put him in touch with a spermaceti dealer. We biked home and that evening he went to work. He set a big round brass pot on the stove at a low heat and began to measure ingredients one or two at a time: a drop of pheromone extracted from the pineal gland of a female civet, essence of stag musk, oil of monkeyflower, wild celery called Holy Ghost, okra seeds. Added to this potent, eye-watering blend of olfactive extremes—more glandular and disagreeable than the smell of Hick's laundry—was extract of tuberose and ylang ylang for their rowdy properties, blended with base notes of powdered oud, ambrette oil, then came the biggest base note of all, a pint of whale ambergris stirred for a few minutes until the pot's fumes made you dizzy, your heart pounded, eyes dilating asynchronously. Then he let this glutinous protean jelly simmer with the lid on for three days, stirring once an hour for a minute until what remained in the pot was a clear water with rainbows of oil on its surface; it evaporated on contact and gave off a heady aroma full of imperceptibles that made your eyes flutter back as though you'd come face to face with the onion of desire.

As he waited for all the pungent ingredients of his stovetop concoction to ready, he prepped a logo to make into a tinplate etching for the bottle label. His line art resembled the work of Ivan Bilibin or Jack Kirby, this bold image of a robotized dragon with serpentine body and tail coiling to frame the name *Ruthvah - scent of Crowley - for Men*, and in the centre of the label, his portrait of Aleister Crowley as a young magician wearing the Eye of Horus as a headpiece, his face savage with insight, a tuft of hair flying out of the third eye. The stewpot of cologne, reduced to this essence, made enough to fill a hundred bottles. So he ran off a hundred labels on the printing press Hick had bought and kept in the basement next to the carport. Then he carefully glued each label onto every one-half-ounce bottle. He corked them, sealed the corks in decorative blood-red paraffin stamped with the Crowley Eye, and went out to sell his scent wholesale fifty per. He brought the girls along with him, Twyla and Rachael, Wendy, too—we volunteered as living proof. We rode our bikes like groupies for Ruthvah, pumping our legs downwind of Jonjay doused in the cologne as he led the way.

Even the women's libbers go nuts for Ruthvah. That was his unwholesome pitch to the needle-artists in the North Beach tattoo parlours. Artists whose canvas was the flesh of Hells Angels and merchant marines never thought to sell a bottle of perfume to that clientele, until *now*. Damn, this shit smells like a strip club on uncle's night. I'll buy a couple bottles, why not.

This is a highly volatile fragrance, Jonjay told the clerk at the Jupiter headshop in Haight-Ashbury, who wore leather aviator goggles and braids in his hair down to his shoulders and wondered why the scent wasn't still there on his wrist. It's strong and doesn't last long, just long enough to whet the appetite. A drop on your neck and another on your wrists and you're laid.

After one whiff, the owner's head kicked back, he stamped and whinnied and had to pull the goggles off, they'd steamed up. That is pow-er-ful stuff, he said. He bought ten bottles, cash.

Take in those heart notes, Jonjay said. You catch hints of sambac and ylang ylang as they pitterpatter across the waves of the fragrance. I'm showing this product to you *first*, was all Jonjay had to say to Isola delle Femmine, the swooning Sicilian mother who owned Dahlinks, the chic men's and women's boutique south of Market catering to the opera crowd.

Put a drop from the tester bottle on a wrist, and say no more, sales were final. No consignment. Fifty per.

What was it about Ruthvah? Definitely not the first eye-watering impression of cat litter and a man's armpit, cherry cola and dirty snow. It was the headrush from the after-effect of those heavy base notes that knocked you out, this vapour hit like a brick in the back of the head. Followed often by immediate and singular arousal. The smell of having sex mixed with the smell of wanting sex. Inhaling Ruthvah gave men the appetite, like a bull growing his first horns, it made his chest puff up, his legs bow in stride, his chin shoot up, jaw thrust forward, eyes flickering like bonfires. On women the effect was biological: you caught a good lungful of Ruthvah and it made the mouth water, nostrils and pupils dilate, nipples harden, thighs open, toes curl, the brain swooned, the tongue purred. You couldn't slap yourself out of it, the fragrance lasted on your conscience or libido long after it had evaporated from the air and your skin.

Justine Witlaw wanted twenty-five bottles but didn't have the money, and his policy of no consignments vexed her, but she relented, dug deep and bought three. She swore she would have the rest, *and* what she owed for those old sales to Frank Fleecen, which she still hadn't paid him, by end of day. Not doubting her desire one bit, Jonjay ignored her vow anyway, and we never rode back to Chinatown to collect. If she wants art, she needs to pay what she owes, was Jonjay's idea of gallery representation. He wondered if she owed O'Connell money for blue squares, or Ferzetti for his pedestals and plinths, or was he the only one she stiffed?

Instead we ended the day riding to Little Russia where we visited Anton LaVey at his Black House commune. The Black House was on California Street down from the Rumble Fish diner, on a hill that could see, on a clear day, the Transamerica Pyramid downtown, like looking at a dollar bill on the horizon. The Church of Satan's home base was a hundred-year-old Victorian house painted matte black including the windows, with high-gloss purple accents. It stood in an otherwise altogether bright, friendly family neighbourhood near Golden Gate Bridge. LaVey was another Californian like Hick Elmdales who collected an enormous and vast library of old 78 rpm shellac records. This wall of fast-spinning, crackly good ditties, and prehistoric organs and synthesizers, was the focus of an entire room dedicated to listening parties. LaVey was also nuts for Hammer horror films and liked to dress himself after Bela Lugosi or maybe a character played by Christopher Plummer. He plucked his eyebrows into angry circumflexes and wore a Vandyke beard. He wanted us to come in, hang out in his *home theatre* and watch the lost reels from Hammer's incomplete 1976 adaptation of *Vampirella*, featuring Valerie Leon.

I need to *meet* this chick, LaVey said with his inverted grin, a trademark expression he honed back in his days pumping out musical oddities at the Wurlitzer in a Los Angeles tiki bar.

Jonjay told him about Ruthvah—Crowley's own recipe, Jonjay said, and LaVey was clearly intrigued when Jonjay told him the story of meeting the man. LaVey wanted to know where in the Bhutan, and Jonjay described a trek he took across seventeen days (all in astral projection, a nine-hour meditation), climbing the giant steps of broken rock in the cliffs of the Paro region. While he listened to the story, LaVey uncorked the tester and tipped a drop onto the underside of his wrist. He bought three bottles.

Hey, man, I haven't seen you for at least thirteen months, LaVey said. Hey I heard a while back. I'm sorry about your friend Hick. He dropped a lot of Thelemic subliminals in his comic. I liked him. A great talent. A force for libertinism. I've had a few friends die recently. Terrible deaths. It's these cancer sores. They get them on their face, everywhere. One friend of mine, we called him the Turk, he turned blue before he died. Have you seen how overcrowded the hospital is? And you see how many gays it's hitting? Strange shit, wouldn't you say? Is that how Hick died?

Yeah, it is.

It's a modern-day plague I heard the CIA invented.

No one is trying to stop it, that's for sure, said Jonjay.

Give Crowley my regards, LaVey said at the door to the Black House, giving us the devil's horns and bidding us a day of total fulfillment.

And on we rode to yet another prospective buyer, and another, until he was sold out of his tiny bottles and we were all swooning, aroused to the ears from inhaling those intense fumes all day, halfway to an orgasm. It was at least as lucrative as the weed in the laundry basket. Jonjay earned five thousand plus tips from a pot on the stove. From this, he broke off twenty-five hundred and gave it to Wendy.

That's to cover the rent I owe you, he said as he hung his bicycle back

LEE HENDERSON

up on the ceiling, then stripped naked in the hallway on the walk to the
shower. I'm not rich like you think. But I am entrepreneurial.

Thanks, but that's okay, she said, and chasing after his bare ass tried to
return the cash but he wouldn't let her into the bathroom. He turned on
the shower. She shouted, I needed to borrow this back in *May* when I was
broke and none of my cheques were here yet but I scraped it together, so
don't worry. Keep it. Money is a-rolling now.

Well, gee, Jonjay shouted over the water running, I wish you'd keep
some money from my profits anyway. After all, I made this scent to pay
you back, Wendy.

I don't need money. I need—

Hey, is that you pounding on the door?

Yes! Let me in!

I'm in the shower, leave me alone!

Sliding to the floor in a crumpled ball. No, no, no, not again.

STRAYS

17

One warm blue-sky day in the mid-eighties—we want to say it was in eighty-four but it might have been as early as eighty-three—Wendy took a bicycle off the ceiling and rode down Stoneman Street to take in some fresh air, clear her head, get some exercise, and be away from the constant crushing pain of seeing Jonjay in the room. Some afternoons he was out selling batches of Ruthvah. Other times he would draw or read. In no hurry to manifest himself. He was going to spend days on end indoors in front of a television or three televisions recording shows onto VHS tapes and drawing the odd picture or two, a monk or an artist, stage actress or bodhisattva in his signature style. Then Wendy would reach a hormonal breaking point and need for him to be out of her sightline for a while. She would say, I'm losing my mind, I need to get out of here. If it was a weekend she might ride down the hill to The Farm under the freeway and dance to live folk music or hear a poetry reading by young men who wanted to exude whatever it was they thought made Leonard Cohen so charismatic. If nothing was happening at The Farm then she'd go see the opening night of an art show at Justine Witlaw's—Jonjay would never go there, in case she pinned him to a date for a solo show. In fact it took three years for Justine to pay back what she owed him from the sales in eighty-one to Frank Fleecen. Or she would go to the museum and sit on a chair and sketch the reactions visitors had to the perplexing features of modern art. She agreed to autograph signings at bookstores and comic shops for something to get her out of the manor. She took a bike and rode it as far as Broadway and then pushed on west to the public library where she sometimes liked to draw for a change, especially if she was in the mood to look at boys. When she got back from the library that evening, boy she had a story to tell us.

She came busting into the manor in a cold sweat, shivering and huffing for air, pale as cucumber flesh and belching. She flopped down at the table and with her face in her arms said, I just got approached by a *spy*.

Her routine when she visited the library was to browse the Fine Arts section for comics treasuries and random art history volumes, then go sit in a carrel with a good view of the other visitors, read her books, and sketch gag ideas to develop later back at the longtable. On this day, however, the Fine Arts section reeked to high hell of soiled pants and something more pungent than any body odour, coming from two bearded men hunched over across from each other at a table, flipping through the latest issues of *Art Monthly* and *Creative Review*. Others did the same about-face at the top of the stairs that she did and hooted at the stink. One level down on Business and Science the air was fresh, the floor unstained, and the tables were neat and tidy. The carrels were occupied by gentlemen with textbooks and notepapers, and handsome men were scanning the card catalogues on the search for esoteric subjects. She caught the eye of one man in a brown corduroy suit who looked familiar, but he didn't smile back as he went and found a carrel. He opened a slim Stefan Zweig novel, oddly not a library copy. Maybe it wasn't so odd. She decided to sit near him in case she could get him to flirt. Now she planned to always sit on this floor instead of Fine Arts where the homeless were indistinguishable from the art students and art teachers. On Business and Science there were real prospects for her to goggle. There were professionals here, or at least men inclined towards a career. A slim six-foot man with bright red hair cut in the military style walked by her carrying a leatherbound copy of *The Complete History of Plastic Surgery*. He went up to the librarian at the front desk.

Can you pull for me all the material you have on Mentor Worldwide LLC, the breast implant manufacturer?

Certainly, said the librarian, making a note on a piece of paper. I'll have that brought to your carrel.

Wendy had no idea it was possible to ask a librarian to complete such a task. As she sat in her carrel admiring the men and women for how they comported themselves and studying their clothes, she toyed with ideas of Buck as mad-dog scientist in a junkyard lab, made a sketch of Francis as a trigonometry professor at a blackboard in front of hundreds of rabbit ears; another doodle showed a patient on the operating table with her cat Murphy as head surgeon. She had never read Stefan Zweig but even the name was familiar for some reason.

She went to the librarian and asked for any information they had on the company Lupercal.

Lupercal Plastics? Give me ten minutes. Why don't I find you in your carrel, the librarian said and stood from her chair without a hint of being hard done by.

Remarkable service. She sat in a carrel with a view of city hall's domed roof and read through what the librarian brought her. Lupercal Plastics LLC was a private holding company with plastic products across several industries. Originally a manufacturer based in Long Island specializing in plastic and rubber synthetics, eventually their factories ran up and down the Eastern Seaboard. Then, at the behest of toy manufacturers in California, the company moved their head office to El Segundo. With Frank Fleecen's help, they were stripping down their East Coast operations. The most

185

recent newspaper clipping in the pile the librarian provided noted their expansion into El Salvador and Nicaragua to meet the demands of contracts for the military-industrial complex, from bootsoles to flak jackets to weather balloons. And for the civilian population, Lupercal provided the fabric for hot-air balloons and, what interested Wendy the most, Macy's Thanksgiving Day Parade balloons. The *Pennsylvania Senator* wrote about how Lupercal designed and fabricated the big Superman, Peter Pan, and Mickey Mouse balloons, and all the other floating ambassadors of commerce ringing in the Christmas season every November. It mentioned Lupercal's announcement of a sale of bonds to finance the expansion of their fabric factories, to make bigger, more elaborate balloons.

She read the name Frank Fleecen as the chief negotiator in deal after deal, including the debt financing for Lupercal's expansion into Central America—worth twenty-five million dollars in 1980.

She went back to the librarian and asked what they had on Frank Fleecen.

The financier? Now let me see, the librarian said and stretched in her chair.

It took the librarian about half an hour, during which Wendy sketched the man in the corduroy suit and a woman with a phrasebook whispering English to herself. Then the librarian brought Wendy a file folder full of newspaper and magazine clippings and two textbooks that had Fleecen's name in the acknowledgments.

Want me to get started on another subject or are you okay? the librarian asked.

Thank you, said Wendy. What an amazing service librarians provide.

Yeah well, beats the coal mines.

On top of the pile was a *New York Times* article from September seventy-seven, about the emerging financial market in debt. A picture of Frank answering the phone was surrounded by a gloss of high-yield bonds. An innovative financial instrument underwritten by a bank in

Manhattan called Hexen Diamond Mistral, a retail brokerage institution old as the hills that, until these new special kinds of bonds, was considered by its banking peers to be a backwater of corporate finance. When Hexen opened its doors on 42 Wall Street back in the eighties—the 1880s—it was known as the bank that treated Jews and blacks like respectable business-people. Backing that same old principle of equality a hundred years later, the cuddly *Times* reporter went on to write, Hexen was able to use Frank's high-yield bonds to leverage small businesses in major takeovers of goliath companies—the first banking instrument in history that was actually able to give the lower middle class a leg up to compete against the goliaths of American capitalism. She flipped open a copy of *Time* from February of the year before to an article devoted to comparing the success of things like *The Cosby Show* and Reagan's philosophies of America to the boom in high-yield bonds. Frank Fleecen's work in American finance helped regular people's businesses grow franchisally, buy up competitors, expand their real estate, rise beyond the regional, and so on. There was a slim clipping of a book review from the *Sun Jose Spectator* for a nonfiction title, *Jack in the Black*, by a local business student and former Vegas casino card counter named Jerome F. Fleecen.

Three years after the *Times* article about Fleecen's rise in the ranks of Hexen, the *San Francisco Chronicle* covered his move to San Jose in an article headlined *The Prodigal Junk Bond King Returns* and a lead that heralded his arrival: *Welcome to Wall Street West.* Apparently the banker in charge of the high-yield bond division at Hexen Diamond Mistral had swapped the bank's Seven World Trade Center offices for new digs in sunny California. *The new center of gravity in the financial universe is an unlikely building in a lowrise neighborhood of San Jose. There's no flashy name on the side to tell you Frank Fleecen, the master of the universe, has come home.* The reason for the move? Frank wanted to be close to where his parents lived and where he and his wife, Sue, grew up. Joel Diamond, Michael Hexen, and James Mistral all agreed Frank could move his office

187

to Canada if that's what he demanded, according to a clipping she came across from the *Wall Street Journal*, dated August of eighty-two. More than nine-tenths of the entire bank's profits came from the high-yield division out in California, one clipping claimed. From San Jose, where Frank reportedly sat at the very centre of an all-glass office at a giant table in the shape of an X, with traders and salesmen around the wings in a big-budget version of Hick's longtable. So, it was true, all Frank's boasts—he ruled the *Wall Street Journal* reporter's idea of the world. He was lauded by his colleagues and clients as a young prodigy of investment-grade corporate financing, capable of turning a Brooklyn kid's favourite summer treat, for example, a sugar water called Snapple, into a national competitor with Coke. Without the sale of high-yield bonds, the inventors of Rubik's Cube would never have been able to raise the money to build their prototypes to take to market.

Then she came to the articles related to her part in this story. Most of these clippings were from newspapers she'd never read, not the kind of press her syndicate picked up and forwarded to her. These were business stories that mentioned her as part of a piece on new finance. She read about the unparalleled licensing bonanza of her comic strip. One Duke University professor of business called *Strays* a junk bond–branded confection, and said her series of toys and wide line of merchandise were intended to convince bond investors and corporate shareholders that debt-financed restructuring can work. In the view of the experts and professionals interviewed by business journalists across the country, Wendy's cast of comic characters was endemic to the funny pages, they acted funny on the page but their ulterior motive was as door-to-door solicitors. *Strays* came in a broad range of new products for old revamped companies, and they introduced a fledgling business to customers using a familiar face. As mascots they improved traffic to a few privatized social services. One American automobile and a European airline used them in advertising. Here was an article from *Life* magazine that estimated Frank Fleecen made Hexen close to half a billion dollars through contracts for *Strays* negotiated using high-yield bonds. Wendy Ashbubble saw a few dimes, too, according to the reports she read of herself, her heart pounding behind her ears as each word burst in her ears. Of the hundreds of small businesses that hitched themselves to the popularity of *Strays* manufactured by the Svengali Frank Fleecen simply by slapping one of her drawings on the side of a package, the one to benefit the most was Lupercal. In a *Washington Post* piece, a former Hexen bonds salesman who asked not to be named said Frank called the *Strays* deal with Lupercal the single biggest boondoggle he'd ever conceived. The same source also said Frank wore a miner's lamp on the morning commute to work in the back of his limo so he could read K-1 financial statements before he got to the office.

Another of Frank's colleagues told the *Houston Daily Derrick* he once saw him, years after he'd made his millions for Hexen, busking at a subway stop in Keyport, New Jersey, playing classical guitar for spare change. The *Derrick* quoted Fleecen's own wife saying, *Success is not about the money for Frank. Most of his personal earnings go to charities.* A 1980 article in the *San Jose Sentinel* welcoming home their new venture capitalist asked why fewer American banks weren't brave enough to take the risks that made Frank a success—*You know what most banks are like, an old boys' club, so finally here's a man on Wall Street fighting for the little guy*, a Las Vegas casino entrepreneur told the reporter. Never drinks. Doesn't smoke. Married the girl he asked to high school graduation prom. Sue told the reporter, *We don't live extravagantly, we were not brought up to value materialism over friends and family.* Wendy tried to picture Sue: she might have a ponytail and wear pink golf shirts and worn-in jeans; she wrote short stories. Fleecen was scooped straight out of college after his graduate thesis in martingale theory for the Wharton School of Finance and Commerce in Pennsylvania made it onto the desk of Joel Diamond, the grandson of the founding partner of Hexen Diamond Mistral.

The articles Wendy read that day in the library made it sound like Frank's whole ethos was unlike other financiers'. Most Wharton alumni fought hard to keep their desks at blue-chip respectable firms like Goldman Sachs or Merrill Lynch. Firms like J.P. Morgan were the offices they competed to work for. They wanted to fight point for point on the stock market against a briar patch of Ivy League freshmen and world-class traders buying and selling bits of this pork commodity and that barrel business. But bonds? Bonds were different. Bonds weren't the jerks in penny stocks, but the market didn't have any cachet. Bonds were Frank Fleecen's secret weapon, off the Dow Jones, off the NYSE, bonds were a back door to gain access to any business, Frank saw it that way. The mirror image of a stock was a bond. In the right economy, debt was more powerful than capital. Bonds were an unregulated ocean of potential capital, in Frank's own words to the *Derrick* reporter.

Wendy went to thank the librarian again for helping her, but it was a new librarian, so she left the public library, it was around nine in the evening, and, overcome with emotion, she sat down on the bench outside. She was approached by the man in the corduroy suit who'd taken a seat at a carrel near hers and begun reading a novel by Stefan Zweig. And she remembered finding it strange that it was not a library copy but his own. As she unlocked her bicycle from a fence and wiped the tears from her eyes, he put a hand on her shoulder and startled her. Excuse me, miss, may I speak to you for a moment, please?

She straightened up and stared at him crossly. Spooked the daylights out of me, holy crap, man. Who are you? He took his hand off her and averted his eyes. She almost recognized him. He was not at all handsome up close, a chinless, mousy face with sleek, narrow features, dark eyelids like batwings pulled over his big bloodshot eyes, nostrils brimming with hair, and a smile straight out of a Munch painting. Right away she picked up the sly, practised friendliness of a cynic. Making a play. She saw a lot of that at No Manors and didn't much care for the style.

I … I saw you in the library, the headlines of your … and well, I just wondered why you were reading all those articles about Lupercal and Frank Fleecen … You don't dress for business. Are you a student?

What business is it of yours what I'm reading? She tipped her head over one shoulder and blinked at him.

He blurted out, Never mind, forget it. I … I know who you are. You're Wendy Ashbubble. I tailed you here, to the library. I'm an investigator for the Securities and Exchange Commission.

What's your commission?

The SEC. The SEC is an independent … we're a kind of police squad who oversee the stock market and the bond market. My name is Quiltain. I mean Chris Quiltain. I'm investigating the financial activities of Hexen Diamond Mistral's high-yield bonds department for evidence of insider trading. You know, gaming the pension funds, overreaching lines of credit, bullying the S&Ls, cheating the system for personal gain and whatnot. I hope we might be able to talk, Wendy.

A spy! Wendy was at a loss for breath. A spy. Watching *me*. Tailing me? I remember his face. Christ, maybe our phone is tapped. Maybe there's bugs all over the manor. She massaged her jaw and thought for a second.

So what did you *do*? we asked her. Did you talk to him?

Hell no, I freaked out. I lost my voice. Instinct kicked in, pure instinct. Flashback to my last day of high school. I got on my bike and pedalled away as fast as my legs could push until I was sure the spy wasn't chasing me any longer. He ran after me, though, begging me to stop, and he was pretty fast for a guy in loafers and corduroy pants. He threw a business card at me but I lost him in the tourist shuffle on Market Street. Chris Quiltain, from the SEC.

My idea, said Jonjay and blew out a cloud of smoke as thick as a San Francisco fog.

Tell me, please, what is it? Wendy's fingers trembled as she reached for the joint in his mouth. What do you think is going on?

No, my math, my algo-*rhythm*. The SEC guy is investigating Frank because Frank is getting rich off *my formula*.

18

Dear Dr. Pazder,

I wish I could tell you all my secrets in these letters ... Life is going OK, I guess, except there's a man who keeps following me around saying he's with the government ...

A fog of amnesia, a fog of secrets, a cold fog, a creeping fog, a laughing fog enveloped No Manors. A cold fog rolled in that pranked tourists dressed for a warm one. Locals got used to wearing layers on sunny days to protect from surprise fogs. One minute you're sucking on a perspiring upper lip, soles of your shoes sticking to the sidewalk, and the next you're clenched up, every muscle from your toes to your nostrils is seized with shivers. You're blanketed in a fog of Alaskan winter. The fog concealed the city from itself. Fog came in waves, droves, like gangs of kids. Meanwhile steady outpourings of steam rose through vents in the potholes and from the sewer drains, from all the city's underground saunas. Hiding below the cold bright fog, the secret city socialized in the high-temperature steamrooms that were everywhere, our version of corner stores. They were hot antidotes to the cold fog outside. Under the neon signs. Some steams came as cheap as fifty cents for a public bath, or a dollar for your own room. At the front desk, staff served you stiff white towels that smelled of Clorox and then you went down, down, down, lower and lower into the humid basements beneath the city where dimly lit hallways led to numbered rooms like in a hotel, where no bed other than a cedar bench, just private baths and showers were installed. A secret network of tunnels below the city streets opened into underground pool parties, with club lighting and brand-new music pumped in through speakers embedded in the walls. Dark disco caves for naked fornicators in squalid pools of piping-hot chlorinated water churning with what looked like strands of eggwhite. Down the hall and a flight of stairs you came to the second pool, in complete darkness. Here it was easy to get a blowjob or give. With a nod of acceptance, someone penetrated you. Mostly men. Men of all shapes and sizes. Steamrooms of all shade of sanitary. Usually we could afford squalid conditions. Graffiti on the walls of our private room depicted scenes from the Marquis de Sade or the latter pages of the Kama Sutra. Grime as thick as chocolate cake gathered in every corner and coated the grout on the tiles beneath our bare feet. Filth catering to lurid-ness and happy depravity—the squeamish need not apply. Deep down where it counted the most, San Francisco was perverse, everyone from the policeman who arrested drunk drivers every Friday night to the philoso-pher Michel Foucault and the cartoonists at No Manors, we all went to the steamrooms. Here was the real San Francisco, or at least the side of the city you never saw anywhere else, where a side of its true self expressed uninhibited sensuality. The steamrooms were a social network in the dark.

Jonjay was dismissive. You know what Frank's going to tell you to do if you ask him. Don't talk to anybody from the SEC. He's going to tell you to keep quiet about everything. Every detail is kept secret. That's modern corporate business. Hide and seek. When the enemy strikes, every shield must go up or the whole army may fall.

She told Gabby what happened with the spy at the library. Her editor seemed unfazed. You did the right thing ditching the creep, good for you, she said. The next thing I would do is call the police. Who knows if he's on the level. He could be some pervert or a brazen private investigator with a fake business card for every occasion. You never know for sure who you're talking to at a public library. Somebody says they're tailing you, says they're SEC. That's a creep, is who that is. You did the right thing. What if he was a fan gone psycho, right? See, this is why I never set foot in the public library. Scares me to hear this. I'll call Frank. He'll tell you the same thing I just did. Good for you. And never talk to the SEC without a lawyer present, that's what he's going to say.

And that's what he did say. Gabby called back to say she spoke to Frank and that Frank was also glad she pedalled away and said nothing. He agreed, *never* talk to the SEC. Always have a lawyer present if you do. These are not cops, he told Gabby. At least Gabby thought she should be reassured the spy was on the level. Frank knew of a Quiltain in the SEC. So he *was* an investigator, not a creep, pervert, letch.

Wendy wondered how that should reassure her.

Then Frank called her. Gabby told me everything, Wendy. I can't believe this happened. What a bastard. Can we meet and talk?

No, no need to, she said, just tell me what the fuck this is about. Spies tailing me to the library. Giving me heart palpitations. Are you in some serious trouble, mister? Because if you are, cut me loose. I don't want any part of it.

Consider spies the price of fame. I live with them on a daily basis. A scavenger like Quiltain is after you because your name rings bells in his ears, and as one of the many parasitical humans crawling on this earth who subsist on trying to rip apart the success of others, you have to endure his existence, said Frank. Quiltain thinks he can smooth-talk you into spitting up information about how I conduct my business. But our work is strictly confidential and he knows it is, and you are not required by law to answer any of his questions, nor should you. Believe me, when I hear an agent of the SEC has been watching you, I want to punch through a wall. I want to rip his stomach out and feed his half-digested shit back to him. Watching the movements of one of my clients—that is going *too* far. The SEC *will* hear about this, I assure you. I will sic my lawyer on this man for violating your privacy. Those obnoxious rats can bite the asses of my salesmen and my traders all they want, we're used to it. SEC agents come sniffing around our building all the time chewing out young salesmen and my assistants, demanding answers. Part of being in my line of work is negotiating with threats like the SEC—like keeping lice out of your children's hair. But a client is out of bounds. You don't know the rules of the game.

Oh, I do. No, I know the rules. I know the rules better than you do, said Wendy. Don't worry, I won't snitch to the SEC what I know about you and your business.

That's good, and don't remind me what you *do* know over the phone in case it's bugged, Frank said.

Gah. That's the same freaky thought I had. Oh my god. How do I find out if my phone is bugged or not?

It's somewhere inside the phone, either the handset or the base. Listen, I *want* to see you—

Wendy hammered the handset against the base screwed into the wall enough times for the phone to shatter into many flying pieces and the wall was left significantly dented. That's how bad a case of the paranoid crawlies she had. The spy Quiltain made her skin itch and the rims of her ears burn, he made her question her relationship to America. She cried, Get me out of this crazy country! as she rooted around on the kitchen floor through the gutted parts of the phone, making no sense of the broken circuitry and bells, capacitors and transmitters, which seemed old and new at the same time. If there had been a bug it was of no use now. We needed a new phone.

Be not forgetful to welcome strangers, for in this way some have entertained angels unawares.

Names names names. No Manors was a mess of names. You dropped one and picked up another. No Manors was a highly productive place to live, but it was brimming with distractions, and yet the distractions fed back into the productivity. Toys, games, books, music. But most of all people. We saw a lot of our neighbour Spain Rodriguez. At one point he even lived upstairs in a room one floor above Biz, with a shared bathroom at the end of the hall, and then he moved to his own house nearby in Bernal when some gigs started to pay off. Art Spiegelman agonized over sketches of mice for *Maus* at the manor. Robert Crumb did a portrait of Wendy in the Basil Wolverton style that was framed and for years hung over the toilet, and Aline Kominsky published a small but thick reprint of Wendy's high school Tijuana bibles under a pseudonym, Annie Hour, that happened to be a flip on her real name. Trina Robbins and Patricia Moodian came over with stacks of underground comix to pore over, Joyce Farmer doodled lots, and Gary Panter hitched up from L.A., they dropped in for an hour, a week, a month to socialize and doodle at the longtable, talking everything from political scandals to candy aisles. With so many cartoonists in the Bay Area and California, we were hardly ever alone, there were never fewer than ten people kicking around, and someone was always sidetracking us from our ostensible job as animators of a *Strays* Christmas special.

Not everyone visited. Charles Schulz lived just a couple hours north of San Francisco but Sparky, as Wendy called him, never visited again after the wake. Down-to-earth Dik Browne came around often enough. Scandals were his specialty. The porn he drew at the longtable could knock the habit off a nun, as he liked to say. At least once a year, Dik came for what he called a lost weekend. Once he lit a mattress on fire and screaming, threw it out an open window onto the street. By the time cops, fire truck, and ambulances appeared he was long gone. A young Bill

Watterson made an impression on Wendy the day he showed up at the table and started to draw. He didn't join the debate over the stuffed animal versus the plastic doll and which one sold more however. An hour later when he hadn't so much as made a sound aside from the sharpening of his pencil, she had to introduce herself, Wendy. She found herself mesmerized by his drawings. She saw all the hallmarks of genius: he was fast, every line he put down was loose but controlled—the line weight in the curve of a nose or fingers was just perfect—, and he knew his anatomy well enough to yank his characters around on the page. Even a doodle of a hotdog vendor in hell deserved to be framed. But the next morning as dawn showered light on the hungover guests, Watterson was gone. Wendy made an unrequited impression on Wayne White, who would not crumble to her many pickup lines. She liked his comebacks so much she later used them for gags in *Strays*. Name after name would drop by to draw. We tried to stay apace with the artists in our midst. Oh, our unpublishable clunkers, duds, dog shits. Oh god we were *bad*. We had a long way to go before our hands could yield what our good taste and critical eye demanded. But with someone like Art Spiegelman at the longtable, he would put down his cigarette and pick up one of our drawings that we thought deserved matches and the toilet, and say, *Hold on a second, lemme show you a trick* … , add a few more strokes here and there with his marker and hand it back to us transformed. And that was how we learned to hate ourselves and still be patient enough and forgiving enough to complete a picture.

Wendy made an unrequited impression on *Tumbleweeds'* T.K. Ryan, who dodged her advances with country & western lines she stole and used as gags in *Strays*, like *I can't, darlin', I just can't. My girl back home is a bloodhound.*

One day in the foggy summer months of eighty-three, H.R. Giger showed up with Ralph Steadman and Hunter S. Thompson at around four in the morning reeking of American whisky and asking to sit and draw with Hick and Biz. Where is Hick? Is this *the* place? They didn't even know for sure.

Sure, come on, here's the table, said Twyla Noon.

What's that screaming? Hunter S. Thompson asked as he covered his ears.

The three men stayed for two days drawing awful sick porn to compete with Dik Browne's, smoking an entire pound from Hick's laundry hamper, and drinking every bottle and can in the house. Giger sort of seduced Wendy or the other way around and that was part of the fun of No Manors for her, not knowing how she got into bed. The three men took off again in their dented white Cadillac immediately after Thompson suffered a possible concussion when he tripped into one of Hick's bookshelves and a vintage plaster statue of Popeye fell on his head. Popeye remained undamaged but the last we saw of him, Hunter S. Thompson was bleeding from his hairline and reciting in a zombie monotone chapter three of *The Sun Also Rises*.

Wendy carried on full monologues as she drew panels or pencilled new ideas, talked and talked even when it came time to ink the important lines, fill in the dialogue bubbles, and she could hold on to a train of thought longer than our attention spans, it didn't matter where she was in the process, she could make art with half of her brain while the other half socialized. Privacy and solitude were the hardest part of cartooning, and likely a place to sit and work—and talk to a constant rotation of company—saved her.

In the year *Doonesbury* was in repeats while Garry Trudeau took a sabbatical, Wendy invented a whole set of new places on her imaginary map of Bernal Heights, where her cartoon animals lived, and new gags to return to year after year. Like Murphy's imaginary alter ego, Tom Clues, a rugged detective in the style of *Magnum, P.I.* with more guns and Buck as a sidekick who gets no love. This year she named the Laid-Back Bar, a flat tire in the empty lot where Molly, the single-mother raccoon, serves drinks to the strays. The crossroads where Francis the rabbit meets Sam the snake. During the month of Reagan's campaign for re-election in eighty-four, many strips played on the theme of the campaign trail, and *Strays* was no exception. It was back in June or July that Wendy began to sketch and script the sequence to run in October and November. Sam the snake ran against Francis for mayor of the rabbit warren on a promise to protect from predators and control the population. She did jokes on the breathless news coverage of the campaign, using Nicki the parrot to recite back the speeches verbatim from inside a broken television set. Wendy stretched the election over fifteen strips, her longest sequential, and after much light satire was had, gave the results fairly to Francis.

I can't not give the election to the incumbent, Wendy said as she finished up the plotline. No matter how persuasive or sneaky Sam gets.

There are no such things as limits to growth, because there are no limits on the human capacity for intelligence, imagination, and wonder, said Ronald Reagan in front of an audience at the University of South Carolina that summer. This past year we'd seen the president on television as much as Bugs Bunny and Jim Rockford—Wendy's two other preferences for background—as the news showed him stumping the country for re-election. *We hear so much about the greed of business. Well frankly, I'd like to hear a little more about the courage, generosity, and creativity of business*, he told the National Federation of Independent Business as television cameras rolled. And to the same audience, Reagan said, *Communism works only in heaven, where they don't need it, and in hell, where they've already got it.*

She slapped her forehead when she heard that—for every time she groaned at her own bad gags, Reagan's jokes had the reassuring effect of confirming she must have a sense of humour. Funny ran in her blood.

There is a bear in the woods ... a Reagan radio commercial intoned every fifteen minutes on Shepherd Media's local FM talk channel—it played four times an hour at least. *For some people, the bear is easy to see.*

Others don't see it at all. Some people say the bear is tame. Others say it's vicious and dangerous. Since no one can really be sure who's right, isn't it smart to be as strong as the bear? If there is a bear.

Everyone at Shepherd Media sure is a *big* fan of Reagan, Jonjay observed indifferently. He was too stoned, almost drooling. On the brink of a deep meditation even though he was at the table drawing hyenas, Megaloceros, and aurochs with charcoal. He and Mark Bread had been smoking all day as they perused Hick's books on prehistoric cave paintings, thirty thousand years old, beautiful picture-narratives on the walls—a paleolithic graphic novel. Mark wondered, *They just pulled this off? Where's the prep sketches?* and the two of them fell heads over heels into a wormhole.

In the sand, said Jonjay eventually, as if he'd found his way back there. Ash on the ground in front of the walls. Feet swept it away.

Wendy liked to start president drawing competitions in a surreptitious effort to amass a personal collection of his portraits, of which she had several hundred. Not every cartoonist loved Reagan, so not all of his portraits were flattering. A lot of cartoonists loathed the man, and the caricatures they drew were not flattering in the least—in fact, they were more often morbid. The president's features inspired a lot of ruthless treatments, a lot of Basil Wolvertonized effects to flesh out the absolute ugly and downplay any decency. The age wrinkles, neck waddle, clownish apple-red cheeks, and red-lipped, half-insane smile-for-everything were all exploited for gruesome laughs. Not everyone was cruel, of course. Gary Panter loved the president more like Wendy did, as an avatar for American opportunism, and his treatment was less derisive mutant, more chiselled cowboy.

Gary Panter was a young blond-haired cartoonist with a cube-shaped head who looked like a boxer turned punk moonlighting as a set designer on *Pee-wee's Playhouse*. He had a primitive style that was highly practised, and he got along well at No Manors with his contrarian doomsday optimism. Throughout the seventies and eighties, he would thumb a ride up from Los Angeles to kick around the Bay for a week or two, hang out with pals and draw Jimbos and scribble outtakes for the *Rozz Tox Manifesto—dump the divine and conquer the consumer—be your own Trojan horse*. Rather than fork out for a hotel, he used to crash in the room with the stop-motion rig (before Rachael took it over) and later, Wendy's bedroom. Panter was an energetic and tenacious doodler who laid down ink in chunky blocks fastened together to make hieroglyphic cowboys, postnuclear punks, recursive mice, and all of a sudden a horse drawn in perfect proportion or a World War Two Browning air-cooled machine gun shredding soldiers.

Murder in the Air! hollered Gary Panter as he drew Reagan, guns ablaze on the lawn of the White House. A two-bit actor, now the president, amazing, said Gary. Leaping straight off the silver screen into the real world to save us all from the Reds. *Halle-lujah!* The president is pure Rozz Tox. Jokes for a third world war. He's got material for before, during, and after the riot police. *A hippie,* man, I remember when Reagan said a hippie *looks like Tarzan, walks like Jane, and smells like Cheetah*. Man, he gets it! That's a solid joke.

Rod Serling predicted Ronald Reagan, said Jonjay as he switched to drawing Reagan as astronaut fighting red-skinned aliens on the surface of Mars.

Hippies might be Tarzan hybrids, but Reagan is pure Muppet, said another cartoonist. I'd rather vote for Jim Henson for president than this evil Muppet.

No way, hosers, said Wendy, I love the president. He's a protector. The lifeguard watching over the public beach of the free world.

Liberals are all complaining about this and that, Gary Panter would say, but look past the Republican Party and consider the possibility this is the closest thing to Frank Zappa in the Oval Office. Ronald Reagan is using a Rozz Tox tactic to beat the Soviets.

I want to meet him one day, that's my plan, Wendy said. She didn't need to go into the details of her paternity narrative with Panter, who knew her beliefs but was not surprised to learn Reagan was the inspiration for most of what the dog Buck says and does in her comic strip.

We all agreed Reagan was more than a president and proving to be some kind of a bionic televisual superman, a puppet to his own image, an actor playing himself who simply disappears when the spotlight's off.

Wendy not only liked Reagan; she made it clear she also liked Panter. Want to take advantage of me, Gary?

I'm kinda married. Panter giggled when she tickled him on the ribs.

A nickel for every time, she said. Can a capitalistic cartoonist take such stifling traditions as monogamous marriage seriously? Wendy pet his hand and scratched the nape of his neck.

Saul Steinberg got Mark Bread's chesterfield whenever he visited the manor from New York and Mark slept with Twyla in the spare room with *Pan* merchandise. For a few nights at a time, a long weekend for a convention or to meet with friends, Steinberg was such a gentlemen—he had the charms of a Charlie Chaplin, he taught us to cook classic downtown knishes and how Warhol made his blotter drawings, and he was playful and flirtatious, too: he painted a nude in our bathtub and another nude on the ceiling of the dining room copulating with the chandelier. He even took Wendy to the movies on a few occasions, always to see the latest fantasy or science-fiction, what he called utter trash and loved to make sketches of while squirming and laughing through. Wendy called him the Picasso of cartooning and meant it, he was doing things with a pencil she could not believe possible—that his imagination existed was a gift. And once, after an all-night drawing game at the longtable, he put his face on her neck.

Ever since your comic went big, you've matured into such a beautiful woman, he said. Steinberg said he was a loyal, neurotic husband, and always kept what he called a platonic distance from what he described as Wendy's adolescent magnetism. But that morning he took her to bed.

Dear Dr. Pazder,
    I know how busy you must be but I do hope you'll find the time to write me a reply. I ask for your help because I know you are the one doctor in the world who can uncover my repressed memories and find the truth that's in me even I don't know about …

For years, Wendy wrote letters to Dr. Pazder. She told him about her life and her career, that *Strays* was in all the papers, local, regional, and Canadian ones, too, including the *Times Colonist* in his and, she confessed, *her* hometown, Victoria, Canada. Not Cleveland. She couldn't add the *New York Times* to the list, but this year, Gabby and Frank vowed to break her strip into the country's most esteemed paper.

When the postman reached the top of Stoneman Street at his usual time in the early afternoon, humping his thick stack of letters and multiple packages addressed to Wendy, one of us would invariably set to work sorting through the mail to separate bills from cheques, solicitations from swag, fan mail from private personal correspondence. Hundreds of pieces of mail came to the manor every week. Not to mention all the envelopes with the names of long-gone tenants; even if it was addressed to Hick we stamped *Return to sender* on it. Dealing with mail took up more and more time as the years went on and *Strays* went from popular to litigious. But the one letter Wendy kept watching out for, that reply from Dr. Pazder, despite all her hopes, never arrived.

What about your other psychiatrists, no luck? we wondered from time to time.

I can't be honest with a doctor when they put their own gimmick before me, she said. I end up playing along with their shtick instead of opening up.

It got so that at least once a day we could expect a secretary in the office of Dr. So-and-so to call asking for Wendy to make a follow-up appointment after missing her last.

You're honest with us. You tell us everything, we said more than once. Why aren't we enough?

But Pazder is a professional. Hypnosis is a real thing, Wendy said. People don't dispute the ability to be put under hypnosis. I'm looking for professional treatment.

She said Pazder's hypnotic spell would make it impossible for her to bullshit him. These other doctors weren't for her—she was choosy and easily bored. Sometimes her treatment would start out promising, she would come home feeling a hundred times better about herself, but then she sensed how easy it was to please the doctor, easy to trick, too, and easy for her to manipulate the therapy, and in the end, easy to ditch. She wanted someone who could dig so deep into her that Ronald Reagan would pop out of her nostrils and mouth inside the smoke of a thought bubble fully fledged. A thought bubble long repressed down in her gut, causing all this gas and bruxism, of a memory she didn't know she had, of once meeting her father when she was just a child. That strange half dream is what she wanted a doctor to uncover.

The reason I seek help, said Wendy, rubbing her temples and jawline, is because sometimes I'm so weak, I'm limper than a shoelace, more boiled than a spaghetti noodle. I can't stand up to Paddington Bear. Winnie the Pooh could take me down. My head wants to crack open.

Ah, no sweat. You're just tired, Jonjay told her. Rest. You're way ahead of the gaggle, Wendy Ashbubble. You ran away from home to become famous in America and it worked. How many people can claim *that*? Most people this day and age don't go near the shores of liberation even with a canoe and paddle, a life preserver and a Marine at their side. A crib, a swaddle, and a soother is what most people want from life. Most people can't decide what to spray in their hair. You're street smart, Wendy. You have your eye on art, and the dollar. A lot of cartoonists don't get a cut from merch, that's big. Frank's deal is pretty good for you. Look at Kirby, he doesn't get a red cent from all the Cap and Fantastic Four and X-Men toys. Think about that.

Yeah, but I looked again and Gabby negotiated so all my royalties are in Hexen's paper bonds. I'm not seeing all that much actual cash. A few thousand a week.

Forget money. What money you get, it's yours. What you lose, let go. Keep drawing and draw for the rest of your life. Drawing's your dream, not money. Draw every day all day until your fingers crack open like piñatas. You're not afraid of success, are you?

Of course I'm afraid of success. Success is the worst. Because what if now that I've got it, I flop? Every success is kind of the same, but every failure is unique in its own terrible way. Wendy spoke as she made the hatching texture of an asphalt road on a Wednesday strip with Buck's punchline—*Favourite day of the week? Payday!* That's part of what makes comic strips so popular, their fascination with failure, she said. Failure's funny. Unrequited success. We're sympathetic *and* we enjoy the suffering of a comic character. Disasters console. A comic strip has to pick a tragedy to repeat and the cartoonist draws the same tragedy every day the same way but twists it, repeatedly twists the same tragic situation, as the character makes the same mistake over and over. Repetition of a core tragedy is the secret to a strip's success, she said. What makes it classic instead of a toss, what makes it memorable, is repetition. Repetition repeats to repeat repetition. *Krazy Kat*—every joke was the same, a mouse hits a cat in the head with a brick every day for thirty years, repetition made George Herriman the James Joyce of the funny pages—this world seldom produces writing like his, hidden inside these animal hieroglyphs. Cartooning's circularity is its formula. But look: it's not pure art, it's the sort of robotic work America celebrates. Formula *is* the American formula for success. Readers demand economy, they love it, simplicity, functionality, and consistency are all praised. Mechanical repetition for the age of mechanical reproduction— think about Bushmiller's hand in *Nancy*, there's no trace of it, panel after panel he's reproducing by hand a flawless, mechanical look so exact it's intimidating. You're so absorbed by the cartoon you feel totally separated from the world. But at the same time a comic strip is *about* the world. Nothing can hold you back from representing the world in your comic strip. Even *if* in every sense of the world you are separate from the world, even if you are isolated from the world in mind and body, your comic strip must be fingers-deep in the world. Even Linus feared the snow falling was a nuclear winter. A cartoon *is* the world, a world on an infinite loop. The loop reflects on our world and its suspicious road going flat out to the end. For most comics hit the button every New Year's and start again, a single year goes by over and over so that Charlie Brown is not thirty years older now but the same eternal age. These characters, and mine, too, are designed like machines, to last beyond my lifetime.

For reasons we're about to lay out, we called Patrick Poedouce Smoothie. Smooth Patrick. More often than any of the rest of us, Smoothie went for the direct approach. Smoothie at a bakery sees a fetching stranger bend to consider her options. *These pastries look so delicious, don't they?* says Smoothie and then adds: *Aren't* you *supposed to be behind that glass?* She laughs and brushes her hair behind her ear. *Are you free Thursday? How about Friday, Saturday, or Sunday?* At a bus stop, a lovely young commuter sits down and removes a heel to massage her foot. Smoothie says, *I thought I was here to catch a bus, but I've been waiting my whole life for you.* But when he put a move on Wendy she rebuffed him.

At the longtable in the middle of the night after a long drawing session, Patrick said, Sometimes you're so amazing, Wendy, I want to kiss you.

Well you can't. I don't do roommates with the exception of.

And Smoothie wasn't used to rejection. It took a couple days of long walks and competitive Ping-Pong to get his head back on straight. He started to take on habits only Mark was known for, like drinking a beer with his morning shower, and drawing with his eyes closed. Steamrooms distracted him in his spare hours, where he spent entire nights, insomniac shifts in almost complete darkness in shared baths, doing drugs and having sex under the city. He began again, this time the long game. In his Smooth-mindedness the only thing he saw in this complex ball of frazzled nerves and clenched teeth was a greater-than-average challenge. A girl with a phobia for guys like her, guys who avoided commitment. Wendy was a curious type—she squeezed every apple or orange before buying one, opened every curtain for the views, gazed at the spines of unread books on the shelves, and had to test for herself to find out what a wife saw in her husband. If she was apathetic to his good looks and repelled by his angelic, impoverished bachelordom, he would engage her with his intellect and ambition. He dropped cute anecdotes. He went as the kite-eating tree from *Peanuts* for Halloween at the age of eight and then went as the kite-eating tree again at the age of eighteen. When it came to drawing, Smoothie's best work was imitations, reproductions, impeccable memory, he could do Popeye, Pogo, Nancy and Sluggo, Buck and Murphy without hesitation, three decades of Archie iterations, Batman and so on etcetera. A natural who treated his talent too casually until recently. Now he was ambitious. When it came to wisdom, Smoothie would drop the line, *Only you die, not who you are.* He applied that line to conversations about art, comics, history, death, so many topics. And when it came to connections, he dropped names like a trail of glamorous breadcrumbs. Crumb, obviously, Kirby, Kominsky, Robbins, Barry ... She wanted to know more when Smoothie told her he was good friends with one of the lead assistants to Jim Davis on *Garfield*. And having the same barber as Art Spiegelman was cool, but cutting your own hair was cooler in her opinion.

One afternoon sometime in there, maybe eighty-two or eighty-three, when Gary Panter or Saul Steinberg and another married visitor were pounding the streets with Jonjay shopping for comics, records, art supplies, we remember confronting Wendy about her predilections. It was probably Patrick who floated the bold idea that she preferred married men because they offered a lack of accountability, easy exit strategy, and emotional detachment. So for example she could pick up and drop a guy like Frank or Doug and go along, a night here a night there, whenever she pleased and with as many more of this kind as she desired, turning a blind eye to what a single guy might offer, for instance the kind of guy who wasn't afraid to be seen in public with her.

Rachael didn't agree. No reason to put yourself at risk of landing in the girlfriend box, she said. That's not the life for you. Every day having to look at the same man, no. Think about it—now you are free. You don't have a man, someone to betray you, cheat on you, take your money. Why commit to a man when you've got No Manors? My advice is never let a man spend more than two consecutive nights in your bed.

Gee, Twyla said. Mighty rough on love, don't you think?

No, said Rachael. Not when it comes to Wendy. And anyway, didn't San Francisco rewrite the rules on love?

Twyla snorted. Love is thicker than latex, she said. Not to mention you're being cynical about people in general, and plus don't you think doing art is a really selfish and pretentious reason to avoid sustained human contact? She was dabbing Wite-Out over Wendy's little mistakes here and there on an ambitious Sunday strip; one of Twyla's (many) jobs was corrections. She added, People always make a phony division between career and relationships as if the two are incompatible. That simplifies things to the point of intellectual absurdity.

It's not very *Strays* for her to settle down, is it? Rachael said.

Sex is not the same old hippie rock festival you can jump the fence and see for free anymore, Twyla cried out. Don't you see the hospitals are stuffed with kids dying of the incurable AIDS from fucking? We're in a plague-riddled San Francisco.

Yeah, Cheez Whiz, for love she has us, said Mark Bread and drooped his head on her shoulder so she could scratch his cheek. See, aren't I sweet?

Patrick pressed his palms to his chest and said, Hey look, hey, alls I'm talking about is single men like to have a good time, too, okay? It's not just the guys with girlfriends and wives and all that baggage who are looking for a fast hookup. Wendy's missing out on a lot of fun because she's hung up on the idea that any semblance of eligible means automatic commitment.

Twyla threw a pen at him. I'm serious, he said.

I know you are, she said.

For a while Wendy sat back and listened with amusement as we discussed her love life. A rosy blush coloured her cheeks and neck, her eyes lit up, and she stopped drawing and listened to us analyze her. She was flattered that we paid enough attention to her comings and goings to form an opinion, and fascinated by what others saw in her that she could not see. This was more information about the blind spot she sought out in rounds of therapy. She leaned forward onto the table, put her chin in the cup of her hands, and batted her eyelashes. Forbidden fruit, she said. I don't know why but I've always wanted a bite. What is to become of me?

Nothing, except you stay you, said Rachael. You're a cartoonist. Why be anything else? Why be anything but Wendy?

Funny Jonjay not being home when you decide to have this conversation, Wendy observed, perhaps too ruefully.

Patrick pushed his chair back and brushed the pencil shavings off his lap, stood and said, Well never mind then okay anyway. Hey, Wendy, I wondered if I could borrow your car. I need to get to the Sunset. I'm hanging with Bill Blackbeard this afternoon. He asked me if I wanted to check out his archive and I was like, fuck yeah. Or if you'd like to, Wendy, obviously you could come with me.

You can borrow the car, Wendy said and uncapped a Rapidograph. I'm going to seize the page.

Cool, thanks. Yeah, Blackbeard's got plans for a tenth-anniversary reprint of the Smithsonian collection, so he's going to publish some newly discovered strips.

A new edition?

I get to take a look at the archive. Can't wait.

You know what? Wendy said. That *does* sound like fun. I *will* come with you. Hold on. I should draw something especially for Blackbeard.

Smooth, very smooth, whispered Twyla to Rachael.

Wendy drew a quick doodle and amassed a basket full of *Strays* toys, bubble gum, a pint glass, and a copy of her bestselling debut *Strays* treasury, *Go, Buck, Go!*—collecting the best of her strips from the past three years, published by Bantam and Scholastic.

Patrick drove so she could take pictures of the city with a Brownie for future source material. Not that she drew a lot of backgrounds but she liked to fill binders with street scenes just in case. She used b&w 400 ASA film that when developed came out grainy, washed-out greys that made for aesthetically unappealing pictures but worked for her needs.

Does his reprint plan to go right up to the present day? Wendy asked as she snapped shots of nondescript street corners.

So far's I know, said Patrick.

Gee … that's interesting, I wonder who he'll pick. She looked at the little drawing in the top of her basket of Buck and Francis that she'd made as a gift for Blackbeard and sighed.

Patrick shot her a look. Sheesh, Wendy.

Well, I'm allowed to hope … She turned her camera to another city skyline out the side window.

Bill Blackbeard was waiting at the door of the Spanish-style split-level he had rented with his wife on the corner of one of the numbered avenues off Taraval Street in the Sunset District. Not only did he live here, this was where he maintained an enormous archive called the San Francisco Academy of Comic Art. In the early years of microfilm, Blackbeard saw how this format treated daily comics and filed to become a 501 (c) 3 organization so libraries could send him their bound archives of original crusty old papers, otherwise going to the dump now that decades' worth had been reduced to single pocket-sized sheets of migraine-inducing x-ray microfiche. Then the Smithsonian endowed his collection, and in seventy-seven, Blackbeard published a definitive history of newspaper comics—and now with the ten-year anniversary nearing, a revised paperback was in the early planning. Since then his comics collection might have doubled or tripled in size. He possessed over two million black-and-white and full-colour comic strips, by far the biggest collection in the world. And he lived right here in the city.

Patrick introduced Wendy, which was unnecessary since Blackbeard had been over to No Manors on plenty of occasions before the wake; the two knew each other at least peripherally and sometimes nodded to each other on the street. She assumed he knew her strip was a roaring success. Blackbeard was a tall, no longer slender man with inquisitive hands and a boneless handshake, neck popping out of an unpressed gingham shirt, a freckled face half covered by a set of big square glasses with wire frames; behind them his eyes were squinted, surrounded with the laughlines of a man who smiled for a living. What little hair was left on his head was snow white, cut short and neat and respectable. For a man of his advanced age, maybe he was sixty, he spoke in the likable drawl of a Bay Area gonzo, as if playing the peaceful alien meeting Captain Kirk and Spock for the first time, welcoming his beamed-down visitors to the sacred crypt and to sleep with his princesses no problem.

Did you bring the *stuff?* Hot dog. Okay, then, let's go *inside*, Bill said, rubbing his hands together with a conspiratorial flourish. He shut the door to the main floor where he said his wife was watching *Donahue*.

Wendy gave him the drawing she'd made and said how much of a treat this was for her to finally see the archive after hearing so much about it all these years. He scanned her doodle admiringly, thanked her and said it was wonderful, then carefully carried the picture down to his office.

He's like the Bela Lugosi of comics, Wendy whispered as Blackbeard led the way down two flights of narrow stairs. Blackbeard said this used to be a four-car garage until he had it converted to his archive and office. First he gave a tour of the archive. The overpowering scent of decomposing paper knocked you down before you saw what a precarious place it was, a room overstuffed with thousands upon thousands of newspapers stacked nine or ten feet high. A pair of bare ceiling bulbs lit the musty former carport and made it feel more like a catacomb, as if Blackbeard's destiny was to protect a rarely seen chamber in the new library of Babel. Much of his collection of newspapers was unboxed, just giant stacks of folded papers. Some papers were stored in crates or cabinets. Only a few pillars were made of leatherbound library collections, yet most of it was labelled. Blackbeard was the first to concede it was a rather haphazard affair. All of it tottered on the brink of what felt like imminent collapse. One serious seismic tremor and the entire archive would be levelled. There were not enough shelves for all the papers still uncatalogued and not enough room for his recent acquisitions, there was almost not enough space on the concrete floor between the towering stacks to take a safe step. One wrong move along the fault line and a high pile of Hearst papers would crumble over our heads.

Patrick opened his sidebag and removed a Ziploc with a hundred dollars' worth. It's super sticky, you might let it dry out a bit, he advised.

My wife doesn't like me to *smoke* but I *love* the shit, Bill said and toggled his head happily laughing as he made the exchange. Can you roll me one or two? I want to see how you do it. I'm somewhat terrible at it. We can't smoke in here. Let's go to my office.

There he opened a window at grass level to let out the fumes and kept what he called the stuff in best condition. Patrick used the surface of a brushed-steel fireproof cabinet to crumble up a joint under Blackbeard's connoisseurial nose; eight of these cabinets filled the room, flat files loaded with pristine examples of newspaper strips and originals. Portfolios were filled. UPS boxes yet to be opened. Manila envelopes yet to be sent. Traces of an aroma she was distinctly fond of, reminded her of childhood days in the basement of the downtown public library, that vanilla scent given off by old paper disintegrating, plus stains from cigarettes and joints and body odour. Preserved behind frames on the walls were favourite strips, original artworks, rare sketches. Cabinet and tabletops were decorated with *Annie* Beetleware shaker mugs and *Krazy Kat* tin plates and various wood figures. Every square inch of wall was dedicated to some framed piece of comic strip memorabilia.

Hey, she said and pointed to a *Strays* Sunday she'd handpainted and donated to an auction. I had no idea you bought that.

Of course I know your strip. He eyed Wendy over his glasses. Number one, your sense of humour is positively gothic. Two, you like to use four panels and that makes me happy, in an age squeezing most cartoonists down to two or three.

Well, shucks, said Wendy. I was thinking of going down to three more often.

Don't, Blackbeard said. He told her to fight the trend. Comics used to be king. I like the level of detail you deliver. Your roommate would be proud.

I miss him. I'm drawing in his shadow all day long.

Bill Blackbeard gave them a hearty tour through his many shelves of comics, stacks containing ex-library leatherbound newspapers some seventy years and older, proudly uncovering examples of *Yellow Kid* and *Buster Brown* to impress them, and as with so many other famous titles, he possessed the entire run of *Mutt & Jeff.* He hoped to get the Smithsonian to reproduce his originals at full size in his upcoming history, for he had many sketches worth sharing with readers. In these old newspapers he showed us the comics were privileged with full pages and reproduced almost to scale; some papers even had two entire pages of daily comics, near the front. And in some weekend editions each strip was given an entire page of a special section, and not only were the comics what made papers popular back then, Blackbeard said, but the size of a newspaper back then was twice what some were today. There were so many repetitively epic adventure strips and all sorts of derivative gag strips and tie-in strips that came and went, and what struck Wendy was that she didn't recognize a single one, and yet it was clear that at one time or another each of these forgotten strips had fans who felt the way we did about *Strays*, and now that all these titles had gone by the wayside in favour of a select few whose names stood out in memory, the only thing saving them from complete oblivion was this man, Bill Blackbeard.

Make sure you check out these early *Gasoline Alleys* to understand why it's the legacy strip it is today, Blackbeard said and spread out a set. How well each frame is executed, the poetry of his line, and the sublime honesty in his treatment of his subject matter.

I'm gobsmacked, said Wendy. I gotta admit I never saw any of the old *Gasoline Alleys* until your book. She let her eyes roam over each panel of this consummate Sunday strip.

Hey, that's okay, Blackbeard said. I know the feeling—that's the whole point, to keep the history fresh. He poured her a tonic water from a beer fridge and passed a can of Old Milwaukee for Smooth Patrick.

This is place is terrific, said Wendy, pushing her glasses up her nose. She quickly exchanged her tonic for Patrick's can of beer. You saved all these characters from the brink of oblivion, she said. You're practically the patron saint of newspaper comics. I want to spend a week here reading my face off. Comics are the entirety of my existence. Without comics I don't know my name. I always hoped my comic might someday grace your archives, she said and nodded to the auctioned comic.

The only collection of its kind in existence, said Patrick.

Just because I spend my time protecting the past doesn't mean I'm not plugged into what's happening now. I told you I read your strip and I do. You're an excellent candidate for inclusion in the modern section of my Smithsonian reprint.

Wow, wow, wow, said Wendy and swooned.

My eyeballs are licking their lips, said Patrick, his nose to a picture frame. Is this original handpainted *Krazy Kat* actually signed best wishes to you?

When I was a young boy I wrote Herriman a fan letter and that's what he wrote me back.

So cool, said Patrick. How much more do you need?

I want all the dailies, all the Sundays, for *every* comic ever. That is *the dream*, Bill said, and towards that goal he said he already had most, including many of the critical works like *Nemo*, *Popeye*, *Mickey Mouse*, *Prince Valiant*, *Gasoline Alley*, *Dick Tracy*, and *Krazy Kat*. I keep a master list and strike them off one by one. But *Annie*, Bill Blackbeard said and tapped his nose. I want to claim I have all of Harold Gray's run on *Orphan Annie* but the truth is I'm missing a few damn weeks of one storyline, this continuity featuring this fantastic villain by the name of Mr. Chizzler, a shady conman who pretends to be a music manager to exploit Annie's singing talents.

I read that story. It must have been at the Victoria public library when I was a kid, Wendy chewed her lip. I mean, this was when I was on *vacation* there … from where I *am* from, Cleveland. It's in their old newspaper collection. I used to read all the old newspapers for their funnies. That's what I did, even when I was on vacation … go to the library.

The *whole* story? Are you sure?

No, but I *think* so. Dozens and dozens and dozens of strips.

I'm going to give them a call. I will, I will, said Bill wagging his head so excitedly his glasses slid down the bridge of his nose. I will *right now*. I'm serious. This would be the end to a very lengthy search, Wendy.

He asked if he could leave them alone for a moment while he looked up the number and made the call

What did I tell you? Patrick said. Blackbeard loves comics.

No kidding. What an a-*ma*-zing collection. Wendy touched an original George McManus Blackbeard kept inside acid-free cardboard-backed plastic. Do you think I could take it out of the plastic for a second and *feel* it?

Go ahead, Smooth Patrick told her. Your hands are clean, aren't they?

No, she said and pulled the bristol from its protective casing.

Sixty years later, the artist's lines of ink stood up as though the paper were a thin sheet of glass. In his *Bringing Up Father*, McManus brought that classical illustration style to the funny pages, a graceful fairy tale line that was simply beautiful.

My lineage is pure vaudeville puppetry, Wendy said. Mickey, Krazy Kat, Dot and Dash, Snoopy and Woodstock, and a lot of Mutt and Jeff, Popeye, and so on. Hundreds and hundreds of loafy Shmoos in between.

She didn't care what he said next, she kissed him on the mouth. You're so stupid you're beautiful, she said and kissed him again. You're stupiful, she said, kissing him more. Patrick's eyes rolled white. You know you taste like oranges, like Tang, she said. As soon as she got Patrick hard, she straddled him, snaked off his belt, unzipped his pants, and went down on him. She did not hold back. Oh good gosh, he shuddered and instead of coming, pulled his cock out of her mouth and swung it around erect in the air, bobbling around as if a small blind man lost his cane, or the cane lost the blind man.

Where, where? she whispered. She didn't take her legwarmers off.

The floor, the floor the fucking floor, Patrick said and she stared trans-fixedly at his cock swaggering around pink and glistening.

There's not enough time! she giggled. Once her back was flat on the floor of the San Francisco Academy of Comic Art's archives and her legs were up and spread as far as they could go apart, Smoothie Smooth Patrick plunged. His prick pressed so deep into her she could feel his balls clapping her ass. Meanwhile her head kept knocking the bottom of the *Thimble Theatre* flat file so the drawers kept jerking out, an inch here, an inch there. And as much as she enjoyed what he was doing—kissing her neck and ably gliding in and out of her—the drawers of the flat file really started to worry her.

Smoothie, she whispered and tapped him on the shoulder. Smoothie.

Fuck, Wendy, you're so awesome, Wendy. You don't know how long I wanted this.

Hot damn, you're a genius! she heard Bill Blackbeard shout from the top of the staircase. You were right, you were right, hoo-wee! How did you know? They can *give* me the papers, too. My god, girl, you just completed my *Little Orphan*— Hello? Where did you both go? Now what in the fuck— Holy shit, *you two*, what in the fuck are you doing fucking—? Oh no! Watch out!

In the lurch, a flat file tipped. Bill Blackbeard felt he must trip over Wendy and Smooth Patrick in his dive to stop the steel drawers containing irreplaceable Popeye strips from crushing them.

Goddamn, I wish I could say this was the first time I'd caught kids fucking in my office, but it ain't. Blackbeard turned to face the other direction.

Patrick pulled his pants on as fast as possible, then stuffed his underwear into his pocket. Still doing up his fly, he hobbled over to Blackbeard's side and whispered in his ear, Look, man, thanks for being cool. Sorry about this but I've been trying to get with Wendy for like three years. You gotta understand I had to take this opportunity. *She* kissed *me*.

Blackbeard clapped him on the face. Haven't you kids heard? Sex carries this plague. I hope you're …

Wendy was still on her hands and knees behind a six-foot stack of bound newspapers, looking for her left legwarmer after it had somehow gotten shucked off in the action. She peeked around the newspapers, then stood up suddenly as if she'd tripped. She used her shirtsleeve to wipe spittle off the sides of her mouth. So uh … oh my god, shimminy bop, funny thing to ask now, but hey, just wondering what the chances are of *Strays* getting in your Smithsonian reprint?

Dear Dr. Pazder,
Where do I begin?

3

19

I can't go to the desert. I got this mailout to do, said Biz Aziz. Someone can take my spot.

She split the tape sealing the top of the Purolator box. Inside were two hundred copies of the latest issue of *The Mizadventurez of Mizz Biz Aziz*, straight from the printer. She thought the full-colour cover looked good—the livid, blood-orange sunset cast over her minimalist drawing of No Manors popped off the page in front of the giant apparition of Hick Elmdales clouding the San Francisco skyline behind it, as if the smokehaze from a thousand bags of pot seeped out an open window and clung to the air over the manor in a perpetual fog. A sentient fog, funny and agoraphobic. Biz turned over the copy to inspect the back cover and then flipped open the pages to check that all the corrections she'd made on the proof had stayed corrected. At two dollars, the price per issue was no doubt steep for the kiddies, but she was no big house like Marvel or DC, she couldn't sell her comics for eighty cents, she was an artist who self-financed her work with an American Express credit card in her real name. Go on, she said, have a look. Number nine was set to hit the shelves of comic shops on

Halloween of eighty-four. She was distributed through Last Gasp, a local shop that specialized in underground comix and books full of potentially harmful matter, which copies of *Mizz Biz Aziz* invariably were. Her comics weren't always easy to ship out of the country, in fact Biz had to mail some orders herself from a PO box to avoid detection from the authorities— otherwise Canadian border guards confiscated packages going to comic shops in cities farflung as Toronto, Vancouver, and Saskatoon as often as shipments to Mogadishu or Jeddah, that's how squeamish some democratic countries' border guards were about *harmful material*.

Number nine was the second issue in a two-part story dealing with the death of Hick Elmdales. The eighth issue opens with a scene in which Biz accompanies Hick to the doctor the day he learns he's got the sarcoma skin cancer and tracks the six weeks up until Biz heard the news of his death during her performance at The Farm. Issue nine opens with the wake. The hundreds of mourners are represented by her trademark chips and fragments, cracked pieces, shards of figurative black against the white page, masklike faces and perversely rudimentary figures further dissembled by the intrusive background drawn in the same manner. The comic was riveting and dizzying, and to learn Biz's interpretation of the wake made the ends of our fingers tingle. As we flipped the pages, the sometimes inscrutable images, always beautiful and complex and perfectly executed, were eased along by the diary entries broken up into the captions at the tops and bottoms of each panel. Sometimes poetic, sometimes raw, always honest, Biz's prose was not in the exact voice Biz spoke in—her writing amplified and filled in what her body language supplied in conversation. The entire genius was present in these pages, that shapeshifting free spirit roamed these pages, these pages made our mouths go dry and our cheeks hot. The middle of the comic gave us shivers, a breathtaking splash page across the staples featuring Jonjay's return to No Manors. *The dead communicate through the living*, wrote Biz in the only caption to appear on that two-page spread. Black on white, the drawing looked like a massive tableau in stained glass, nonexistent colours vibrating in front of our eyes in optical illusion. As we read these scenes, the same insecurities came hurtling back to us in waves of nausea. It wasn't so long ago that that feeling of homelessness, and it hit us hard a second time, of belonging temporarily, it made our stomachs sink like heavy sacks of lead into our bowels, thinking back to that night. We held our breath for minutes on end as we stared into every panel, then inhaled like swimmers about to go deepsea diving as we let ourselves be taken into her version of the wake.

At some point one of us, Patrick or Twyla, said, This issue is going to make you famous, Biz.

Biz shot us a look. I am already famous.

Wendy and Jonjay read, too. Jonjay read it once in a flash, gasping, and then he flipped back to the start and spent minutes studying each page. Slowly, carefully, Wendy absorbed the panels up and down, turning each page delicately as if it was the manual for a nuclear warhead, and shivered from time to time. She always wanted to see herself in Biz's comic, not that she ever asked to be, but hoped so and hinted it would be an honour, but we could tell she was having difficulty deciding how to feel now that it had happened.

Wendy finished reading and handed back her copy. You make us look like a pack of hungry cannibals, she said. Like California's cartoonist cult.

There's a letters section at the back for comments, Biz sniffed.

I didn't say I didn't *like* it. Gee whiz, Biz, it's amazing. But I'm weirded out to see myself eating Hick's human flesh. Makes me gag a little to see it. I like that you don't reveal it as a trick. That's disturbing.

Oh, Wendy, said Biz.

Every page is a hellacious piece of art. You're a sublime heretic, Biz. You deserve a stat holiday in your honour.

I already have one, darling. It's called Christmas.

So when readers ask you if this is what really happened at Hick's wake,

223

if we all ate a piece of him, what are you going to answer? That we did? When the critics come asking, are you going to say we ate him?

I don't *do* interviews, Biz said. What's the point of interviews? All I want to say on the subject I put right there in the ish, that's it, there ain't no more. If I wanted to say more, I'd put it in the book. She crossed her legs in Jonjay's direction and flashed a wide smile at him and turned her eyelids down. He was almost on the last page again. Tell me what you think, Jonjay. You see anything missing? Did I mess up a beautiful night depicting it?

There were tears in his eyes. He wiped them away and said, You should be in the museum, Biz, you're this city's greatest artist. Cripes, this is your best issue yet. What a tribute to our friend. You *were* closer to him than I ever was. I know that.

He was referring to text in the comic that exposed some of the unspoken feelings Biz had during the wake: *He's my closest friend, mine ... I burn with jealousy ... Hick's darling Wendy wants to know where Jonjay's at ... ,* a series of captions reads on the early pages depicting the silhouetted guests arriving in droves, indistinguishable except for our narrator in the bottom right corner. We searched for ourselves in these panels showing clusters of cartoonists, even the shadows behind those shadows might be based on us. *Everyone wants to know where Jonjay's at. Everyone wants to console Wendy. Poor Wendy. But I'm the desperate one. I'm in pieces. Hick was MY best friend ... None of you pretenders comes close to knowing him how I did.*

In the final pages' panels, every character is more clearly defined, it's obvious (especially to us) who is who, the edges of our profiles are unobstructed, our postures traced from photographs on the lightbox, there's no background except the casket, the action surrounding the casket is clear and unambiguous. We take our turns, we accept Jonjay's offering and eat a piece of Hick, our own special piece of this great cartoonist. The last panels of the penultimate page rise above the scene and out the windows of the manor to look down at the city. The ending is a full-page image of a radiant light surrendering to a greater cosmos. *Love made the universe* … , the caption reads.

Issue nine of *The Mizadventurez of Mizz Biz Aziz* would sell out its first printing within a week and run through another ten printings before it was reprinted in her hardcover graphic novel published by Pantheon in ninety-one. In the absence of the artist's availability for interviews—Biz refused these requests as a matter of principle—comic critics devoted lengthy Lester Bangsy essays to praising the issue, and joined in the ongoing debate over the truth of the events. Did we eat the artist or not? Was it a metaphor and if so for what? Was it a trick? Whose trick was it, Biz's on her readers or Jonjay's on the guests? When an interview Wendy did with *The Comics Journal* turned to the subject of issue nine, she said, *Biz is the Francis Bacon of comix, a terror to the common cartoonist*, and left it at that. One piece of fan mail she received from Kathy Acker, reprinted in the back of issue ten, described Biz's style as *the play of light through the leaves of a tree shaking violently in the wind*. Yes, that's how it felt, we were those leaves. It was like the entire building shook when Biz published issue nine, from the cellar to the attic, and one by one we all fell out. The issue's popularity triggered a sequence of events that forever changed Biz Aziz's life. It tucked her into a spot in the eternal canon of comic history, it stirred endless controversy and debate among comic readers that continues to the present, she lit a fire of wild speculation that created rivalrous encampments, comic gossips who believed different versions of the same event. And the issue would have unintended consequences for Wendy as well, not all for the good.

And for us. Issue nine would act as a turning point in our lives. After its release, everything change. We were in the comic—we appear in those fateful last scenes, those cannibal panels—and those unnamed silhouettes would come to define our future.

Well then, so sounds like Biz is out, said Jonjay, rolling a joint on the coffee table. Who wants to come to the desert?

Mark wanted to. As a representative of her animation studio per se, Mark was the least suited to the role of spokesman, but the daytrip appealed to his need for constant extrasensory stimulation. And besides, Rachael was coming, too, and her specialty was coming across to strangers as colder than a dead fish and incapable of listening to you prattle on about trifling petty nonsense when there was work to be done. Twyla was afraid of flying, didn't want to go, would rather draw in-betweens. Patrick had taken a part-time freelance gig as an in-betweener for *He-Man and the Masters of the Universe*, for some extra cash and the experience. Lately the newspapers were calling Frank the He-Man of Wall Street, making Patrick feel the diminutiveness of his existence all the more. When it came to the practical business of operating *Strays*, Rachael doled out daily tasks, and if no one else had anything else going on, she delegated. It wasn't like Wendy had chained us to her cartoon for the last three years. We all had other projects. Rachael was still performing as Aluminum Uvula and releasing seven-inch records with cover sleeves she designed herself. Mark Bread self-published his comic, *Asemix*, all abstract, which he released monthly give or take, starting in eighty-two; he was up to issue twenty-eight. He printed fifty copies of each issue and with a cover price of a dollar, he still always sold out a run. He never reprinted. Twenty years later they sell for over a thousand each on eBay. After the Christmas group show was over and his pictures were the only ones that sold, Justine Witlaw booked a solo for Mark, and in eighty-three, she framed and hung the best pages from *Asemix*. That was the last time Wendy saw Frank. Afraid that no one but comic book punks looking to mooch free booze would come to Mark's opening night party (probably a valid fear), Justine invited one of her blue-chip clients to organize a reading with her writer's group for the same night. So it turned out that Frank's wife and some other local writers read unpublished work in front of Mark's drawings. Justine's plan worked like a champ—that night a crowd of suburban blue-chippers hobnobbed with the Tenderloin's alcoholics and Oakland's crusty 'zine punks. The wealthy folks were enchanted by the credibility of the locals here to support Mark, impressed enough to regard his drawings with some degree of seriousness, and the five rows of chairs set out for the reading sedated this unruly side, too. Isn't it weird, Mark's show before yours? Justine said to Jonjay. He shrugged and said, Mark is the real deal, that's why. All that was left of what Mark had drunk was the plastic ringlets of the six-pack. He needed a refresher but was pinned to a wall by curious collectors. They asked about his influences and he replied: Kirby krackle, Kirby squiggle, Biz Aziz. The collectors mistook him and a rumour got around he was a foreigner living in town. Eskimo, one lady explained to her friend, from the Arctic tundra. Nothing Mark did, even slump down half-conscious in the corner, was interpreted as anything other than the delightful backward differences between our culture and his Canadian ways. The icy North resplendent with hundreds of words for snow was one intensely remote and unattainable thing for those who dressed in diamonds and pearls and lived in the tropical valleys south of the city.

Frank had yet to arrive and so Wendy was at a loss trying to guess which of these affluent people was his wife.

Is it her? Twyla pointed to someone about the right age.

Yoiks, don't point. Wendy swatted her hand down.

Must be her, said Rachael. Only the wealthiest could dress like a marm and still get noticed.

Oh my god, there she is, said Wendy.

She was in her mid-thirties, she used ounces of mousse to give rise to the tubular curls of her dark brown bangs, her hair was her best feature, hanging over dull pale skin, smooth and grey as a butter knife. Almost invisible red lips with no shape like the spine on a slim book of poetry. Not to say lovely, but plain in a utilitarian way that could be attractive. A long neck sprouting like a steel pole out of her black tunic, a gold charm hanging between her breasts on a gold necklace, slacks from the seventies. Although there were prettier women and better-dressed women and more interesting people to talk to at the gallery, she seemed to be the unofficial centre of attention, even though it was Mark's show. More of the guests knew this woman to say hello than recognized Justine. And she rolled and unrolled a literary journal in her hands. Yes, must be Sue Fleecen.

The story I'm going to read was published in *The Kenyon Review* this month and … thank you … it is about a man recovering from a fall, it's entitled *The Dean of Fine Arts*. Sue took a drink from a glass of water and smiled a nervous smile at the audience as she put the glass at her feet.

It opens with a quote from the *Rubaiyat* by Omar Khayyam, Sue said.
There was a door to which I found no key
There was a veil past which I could not see
Some little talk awhile of me and thee
There seemed—and then no more of thee and me.

Reginald Cudworth Jr.—whose closest friends called him Reggie even though he turned forty this year and held the position of dean of Fine Arts—was on his way to his office on the third floor of the John Dutton Building at the University of Southern California, Burbank, when he slipped and, in front of undergraduates, fell down eleven steps and broke his leg, his hip, and his pride …

Not a minute into Sue Fleecen's reading and a hand fell on Wendy's bare shoulder. A whisper in her ear: I knew I'd find you here.

Hush, Wendy said and flinched to get his hand off. She was standing at the back with us near the exit behind the rows of chairs where the audience was seated, and Sue's voice was barely audible.

When Sue told me the artist was one of your assistants, I had to come see, Frank said.

She turned and said under her breath, Frank, your *wife's* reading.

Ah, I heard this one about the dean before. He runs off with the wife of a music professor. Whereas I never get to see *you*, my number one client.

Hush. You should be in the front row where Justine and Jonjay are sitting instead of creeping in late. Where were you?

I thought she'd be last to read not first.

She *is* last to read.

When her reading was over and the audience applauded one last time before they stood up and began to shuffle out the door and onto the street, Frank said, Why don't I see you more often?

That's enough, Frank.

Another woman who had read interrupted them to tell Frank the others were going to meet at Fino's for a drink and he and Sue should come. He said they would. What are you doing now, Wendy? Want to come for a drink?

No, she said. There's an afterparty at The Farm, she said. Biz Aziz is performing *Hollywood Babylon*, adapted from Kenneth Anger's book, with songs spanning the decades.

Frank's shoulders fell. Come on. Can't we be friends? That *one* time ... *one* time. We've done so much good clean work together since then, we should be friends.

That is if you and I are capable of friendship.

Let's talk about this over dinner sometime.

Go congratulate your wife. And buy one of Mark's pictures while you're at it.

The evening was a success from Justine's perspective, even though she had to lock Mark Bread in the broom closet where he could pass out fetal with a roll of paper towel for a pillow or vomit into the mop bucket if need be, and the rest of the crowd could still line up to use her one lavatory in the back room. By the end of the evening there were little red dots on the wall next to most of his pictures. One woman left feeling very pleased with herself, saying that with all the panels on a single page it felt like she just bought six pictures for the price of one. A couple of reputable local collectors who had recently donated over a thousand nineteenth-century photographs of San Francisco to the museum came up to Justine before leaving and asked, Are you sure *that* one is sold?

Yes, it is, Justine said without hesitation.

Well, all right then, we'll buy the one next to it.

That was last year, and by eighty-four a rough thirteen minutes of the *Strays* summer Christmas special was complete.

Outside on Stoneman Street, Biz pointed skyward and said, Look now, before you all drive away and leave me here: the air's so crystal clear you can see goddamn bulldozers pulling veggies out of Bonnie's farm to put in a city park. Ain't that funny? Ironic shit. See that, Wendy? The Farm's being demolished. The barn is gone. That stage is gone. What kind of anti-hippie bullshit come-together-right-now garbage is that—gutting a *farm* to put in a *park*?

It's farcical, for sure, said Wendy. But Bonnie's promised to start another garden somewhere else, though, so. Meanwhile, you haven't said a word about this redo, she said and bounced her hair.

You looked better before the demolition, said Biz.

The night before, Wendy had started flapping her hands with butter-flies about the trip and around one in the morning acted on the urge to dye her hair a Madonna-inspired Marilyn Monroe blond, to match Jonjay's and the landscape for their tour of the desert. This morning she packed a skimpy sundress and flipflops in her purse for a change of clothes in case it was hotter than for what she was wearing, boat shoes, tight white cotton pants, and a blouse with a collar, carrying a leather jacket with her bag, and some prescription sunglasses. No other provisions were required since Frank Fleecen promised to supply lots of water, food, and other sundries.

A month ago, she had called him. You never call, he said from his office. Something's wrong.

No, but I got a favour to ask you on behalf of Jonjay, who doesn't know I'm calling … he needs your help for his art show with Justine Witlaw, Wendy said. He wants to go back to the desert. But I don't want him going alone. He might never come back.

Frank agreed right to arrange the trip. In fact, he could make it a business and pleasure trip and invite Piper Shepherd so the two could finally meet.

Bring your wife, too, said Wendy. I want to meet her. I didn't get a chance at Mark's opening last year.

My wife … ? said Frank, but she hung up.

You go on have fun in the sun, said Biz. When you get back this block will be sold and gutted, too—if *I don't* stay behind and guard No Manors you know those bulldozers down at The Farm will come flatten the manor hella fast, renovate, and swap in an all-new Evangelical family.

Biz fell onto Jonjay's back as he humped down the stairs overloaded with art supplies in an army surplus dufflebag trying to weigh him down to the point he couldn't move, but he was very strong.

Don't go. I hate this idea, letting *that snake* take you without my protection, she said.

No sweat, said Jonjay.

Don't you hate the bitch who stole your ideas? He's a class A exploiter. Watch your step.

Hate hates to hate hate, said Jonjay, enamoured with the wildflowers in bloom in the unkempt yard surrounding the manor; plucked a purple one. You can't steal the truth, he said and gave the flower to Biz. Ready to go, Wendy? Wendy? He looked for Wendy, who was not beside or inside the Gremlin. She was drawing a chalk hopscotch on the street for the Evangelical children next door (a fourth on the way). Wendy was forever trying to make up for the behaviour the Evangelicals had tolerated as neighbours of No Manors. But doing nice things for the children only made the parents more paranoid and unfriendly—the mother shouted for them to come indoors *right now*.

Biz shouted, See, look what you did, trying to be nice. She turned to Jonjay. What are you looking for in the desert you need so bad that you had to use Frank Fleecen?

What else? Eternity, as usual.

I thought you got that already.

Got it. Lost it. Got it again. Cat and mouse, cat and mouse. You can't sit back and live forever, you've got to keep chasing.

Whatever. I tell you better watch your step. America is a society of individuals bottom-dogging each other to death. Biz practically sang these words to us as she waved goodbye.

We flew down the interstate all the way to San Jose and Jonjay never put more than three fingers on the wheel as he screamed through commuters and no one said a word the whole time for fear he'd lose his concentration and blow us all up. An hour later we met Frank Fleecen outside of Hexen Diamond Mistral's corporate office in San Jose.

Frank took one look at the lime-green Gremlin and said, Let's take my car.

Where's Sue? Wendy wanted to know.

She'll meet us at the tarmac.

Fleecen drove one of those gleaming broad-shouldered European automobiles used in state funerals bearing national flags and blacked-out windows and blank licence plates, never going faster than a walking pace. But capable of rocket speeds, and you know it. Absolutely black exterior like a censor bar, bulletproof, the width of a semi-truck—that was Frank's car.

We got cozy on the blond calfskin and right away Mark fixed himself a Tanqueray on ice from the wetbar. Why not? Then we took off and trying to drink a beverage was a mistake that got us all covered in gin.

If televised state funerals happened at the speeds Frank liked to go, everyone on earth would be dead. His top speed seemed to be double Jonjay's, regardless of legal limit. He took *turns* at Jonjay's top speed. Jonjay didn't say a word. This automobile disobeyed the laws of physics, it was invisible to San Jose law authorities. At high speeds, Wendy's lime-green Gremlin liked to rattle and shake in a palsied way and sway from lane to lane. Fleecen's European absorbed all bumps and faults in the road. He pushed sixty, a hundred miles per hour, a hundred-fifty, two hundred—*lift off!*—everything became so calm and quiet. In fifth gear our ears popped and our stomachs levitated into our throats and we saw the trees and electrical poles at the side of the highway blur together into abstract tapestries of colour, and then, briefly, as Fleecen accelerated to yet a faster gear, sixth gear! the landscape couldn't decide if it wanted to pass us by or leap forward *ahead of us* the way tires of a car at high speed sometimes seem to spin in reverse, that was what the *landscape of California* was doing. Percussive waves of scenery.

Let's fucking showtime, Fleecen said with his neck craned up, and then, with a menacing smile into the rearview, he pushed the overdrive button on the steering wheel and we all grit our teeth to pieces the car was going so fast, silently hurtling at a meaner and meaner velocity down a pebbly two-lane macadam highway.

Unlike Jonjay's bat-in-the-belfry-style fingering of the steering wheel, Frank's hands were at the precise ten and two position on his woodgrain, as driving instructors advise. Jonjay maintained a casual demeanour at his top speed while Fleecen stayed professional from the moment he started the engine.

At this speed if I make even a fraction of a wrong move on the steering wheel we're all dead, Frank told everyone matter-of-factly as he gunned it.

Our eyelids were flapping like curtains and our lips were pulled back. Wendy was clutching the armrest as if it was an electrified fence. Riding shotgun, Jonjay watched with brute indifference, stunningly casual as the road ahead got sucked under the wheels at this hazardous clip. His arms were crossed over his chest, his bare feet up on the dashboard, and he seemed to be almost asleep.

Frank said, I love driving. Driving reminds me of my world of high finance, a never-ending marathon at a cheetah sprint with a hundred thousand competitors fighting to beat that arbitrary fraction of time it takes for everyone else on the market to act on information. Who is going to make the next green light and who is going to get left back at the red.

Rachael was pale as a sheet of paper. Dripping with sweat. She was ready to throw up. Mark looked ready to throttle someone. He put his head between his knees and massaged his face with his hands, crying.

Driving is not a race, Wendy said.

Yes it is, said Frank and Jonjay in unison.

Driving is how people get around, she said. You're not competing against innocent people, you're getting from point A to point B hoping not to get killed. You're the worst drivers I've ever known. Oh my god. Driving is not a *metaphor* for something. Driving is *driving*. You've got passengers. Quit wanking. Driving is a stupid way to get out your frustrations. No one wants to die because of your egos. Promise me next time you get behind the wheel you'll drive for the sake of driving and cut out the rebel artist and the Wall Street speed demon crap. Otherwise I'm going to boycott. That was ridiculous. I can't count how many corner gas stations you guys cut through in order to dodge a red light. As if you're bank robbers or something.

Browbeaten into silence, Fleecen punched in a code to open a fifteen-foot-high gate that took us onto a ferruled dirtpack road going up and down sweeping hills of grapes and berries and plain pine, then he finally made a reverse parkjob into a stainless steel carport that looked out onto a private airstrip and a small domed hangar. We got there around ten in the morning.

A personal jet the same colour as the car idled on the runway, rippling waves of engine heat. A pilot stood at the open doorhatch in a short-sleeved dress shirt. He tapped his captain's cap in a salute to us. Twin engines screamed at high pitch. The wheels were parked in the shallow mirage of the sky.

Look, I'm sorry I scared you, Frank said on the walk to the jet. I guess you're right. I was driving like it *was* the bonds market. I don't need to do that. But I thought I saw a car following us, so I wanted to ditch him.

Wendy said, Whatever, just quit the macho bullshit. She asked if there were any raw eggs on board. I've always want to fry an egg on a desert rock, she said.

Let's ask my chef. Frank guided her up the stairs onto his declassified Gulfstream IV, which, like his cellular phone, was a prototype.

Of all the perks of being the investment banker, this might be the first one I want, Wendy told him.

Wow-wee, said Mark and made his way straight for the wetbar. Best I ever get's tickets to the punk show I did a poster for.

Already inside the Gulfstream was Justine Witlaw, sipping from a martini and talking to a skinny red-headed man in a cotton suit in the chair across from her. Frank kissed Justine on both cheeks then coldly introduced the man to us as Quinn Kravis, the arb.

The what? said Wendy.

Kravis, this is the cartoonist Wendy Ashbubble and her assistants, Twyla and Mark, and this is the artist Jonjay. Kravis shook everyone's hands. Frank squinted at him, and without a smile, looked past him to his other guest, Piper Shepherd. However disinterested in him Frank was, it must still be noted Kravis was well dressed for a trip to the desert, matching hat, blue tie and blue deck shoes to match the sky, no socks. To match his hair his face was pink and savagely pitted by what must have been sebaceous acne throughout his teens. Even the rims of his ears were pitted—when he smiled even his gums were pitted. Kravis had thin arms and wrists, but wasn't exactly overweight in the middle, more keg chested than full barrelled. However, the impression was that if he ever stopped working out, his muscles would dissolve into buttery flab.

Kravis sounded ill when he laughed, a man retching. Ha ha. When you said on the phone where you were going, I couldn't help invite myself along. Ha ha *heh*. I wanted to see Death Valley since I was a kid. Perfect place to catch up. Out of the way of prying eyes, right? Ha ha *heh*.

Wendy, may I introduce you to Piper Shepherd, president of Shepherd Media.

Frank was interrupted by a gradeschool principal or a woman dressed as one, a brunette with bouncy mousse swoops in a bland blouse, who emerged from behind a door as we heard the flush of an airlock vacuum—sealed toilet. What could be so interesting about that plain and uneventful face, the sky-blue golf shirt under the palest imaginable pink cotton sweater, a pair of creased white polyester slacks cinched at the waist by a braided belt, and on her feet, leather flats? A woman for whom there was no sonnet. Sue Fleecen welcomed us aboard.

I saw your reading at Justine's, Wendy said sympathetically. Cool story about the dean.

Thanks. Ten revisions and six years to finish. Two years and seven rejections before I found a journal who would take it. A cheque for two hundred dollars. You can see why Frank thinks I'm crazy. We'll have lunch in the air but can I fix you something to drink first? Sue Fleecen showed us the inflight wetbar.

I'm still feeling kind of sinusy from the flight here, Wendy said and rubbed the bridge of her nose.

Flight? Oh, Frank's driving, Sue said. Yes, I know, it's like he thinks he's horseback hunting a woolly mammoth or something. I'm thrilled I got to come along for this, though. I never get to go on adventures. Frank won't let me.

This the first time in years I've let her out of the attic where I keep her chained, said Frank as he poured a finger of vodka into a glass and handed it to Kravis.

He likes to test me in public with literary trivia, said Sue, but the truth is, Frank hasn't read a novel since high school.

Hello, Sue, Jonjay said.

Hello, Jonjay, nice to see you again, Sue said and eyed his dufflebag. I see you brought your pencils. I'm thrilled to be involved in your art project.

A child with white hair and a wrinkly liverspotted face came through a door that led to the bustling galley, from the sounds of it.

That kishka is going to kill me, oh my god, the kid said in a gravelly voice, sucking on his thumb. He pushed his glasses up his nose. Have you tasted it yet?

Frank put a hand on the small of Wendy's back and said, Come, I want you to meet my close friend Piper Shepherd. Piper, allow me to introduce you to your top-selling cartoonist, the artist behind *Strays*, Wendy Ashbubble, and these are two of her assistants—

Wendy Ashbubble, wow, this meeting has been too long in the making, hasn't it? Piper embraced Wendy without waiting to learn our names. I've been meaning to schedule this face-to-face for years. Look at you. They said *lovely* but I didn't realize how lovely. Nothing like I imagined. Are you ready for this heat? Desert heat is unruly.

The middle-aged media baron had the mannerisms of a precocious boy. He was small like songwriter Paul Williams, no taller than any of the felted cast of *The Muppet Show*. He wore windshield-sized eyeglasses and his thinning white hair was combed over.

I love your strip, yes I do, said Piper. It's honest and straightforward and well conceived and funny. Funny most important of all.

Last but not least, Wendy said.

That's right. It's not technically perfect but in a good way. The mistakes are of the charming sort. Reminds me of *Krazy Kat*. Are you familiar with that old strip? Used to read it in the paper as a boy.

I pray to George Herriman every night.

Sipping a whisky, Piper said, Me, too, I *love* the funny pages. I grew up on strips. My favourite as a kid was *Dick Tracy*. Chester Gould, now there's real talent, not these journalists nowadays looking for the next Deep Throat. Dick Tracy took crime by the neck and wrung out the truth—those were true stories in black and white. The news is never black and white but I fear most reporters think it is, and none of them have Tracy's eye. Nobody remembers more than a handful of headlines in a paper. A newspaper's true legacy is in the comic strips it heralds. That's what people remember, that's why I started my own syndicate. Not just for the profits, but that, too, ha ha.

It's a great job, said Wendy. Being a cartoonist, it's what I wanted since I was a kid.

Now look at you, riding in private jets, Piper said. Ever been in one of these before?

No, I haven't.

They're actually a smooth ride for such a small aircraft. Frank is modest. I probably make half what he does and own my own Boeing 747, same class as Air Force One. Cost me more than I care to admit, ha ha ahem.

Wendy caught Kravis staring intently at the other two women not Frank's wife, and overheard him ask us for our numbers. Justine gave him the card for her gallery. *And what's your number?* he asked Rachael.

I'm a lesbian, Rachael told him.

Kravis clapped his hands. Sounds kinky, he said. Count me in.

The cabin was laid out as a rumpus room with varnished woodgrain and porthole windows. The Gulfstream's seats were long leather sofas and individual chairs that rotated all around and reclined flat as a single bed. Tables pulled up and dropped down for inflight conferences. A chef on board made us an extravagant lunch and two pilots in the cockpit waited for the thumbs-up to take off.

I love to pilot this beauty, Frank said.

No, please, no, cried Wendy and Sue at the same time.

But today I'll let my boys take the helm so I can sit back here with you and enjoy. The Gulfstream IV is the American eagle of business-class aviation, and fun as hell to fly, Frank told us. It's manufactured and built with the individual in mind. It's not a 747 but it flies like one. Like your own pair of wings. You could say that every Gulfstream IV has its own tarmac the way every eagle has its own aerie. They don't come cheap.

The flight to Death Valley took us all of forty-five minutes. In that short time we enjoyed a kosher lunch made by Frank's personal chef. Kravis was told not to touch the plump young blond flight attendants serving the food, whose English was adorably accented, here from Beersheba on a kind of reverse kibbutz to intern with Frank, their American relative via a distant half-cousin (the favours are endless, he whispered to Wendy at one point in the meal so that she all of a sudden felt guilty). On offer this afternoon was a plentiful selection of smoked lox and gravlax on bagels with capers, rye bread, and much too much smoked chicken farfalle and beef brisket, that we somehow managed to polish off anyway. Dill pickles galore. We stocked up the rest of the space on our silver trays with ripe-smelling bowls of gefilte and horseradish, a side of steaming matzo ball soup, not even feeling a drop of guilt about taking two links of beef and turkey kishka, bursting out of their tight skins, to go beside a plate of triple-marinated veal medallions in mushroom ragout, potato pavé and potato kugel, noodle pineapple kugel, and Frank insisted we try Chef Lowenstein's special amba, a wild spicy kind of ketchup.

Wendy pulled aside the chef and said, Hey by the way, if you happen to have a spare raw egg ...

In the middle of the meal Kravis stood to toast the to-be re-elected President Reagan, To the rubber ducky helping make us all rich fucks.

I'll drink to that, said Justine, waving her glass around, her eyes blinking out of unison this soon in the trip.

Cheers, said the rest of us. Even Jonjay said, He's a great father figure. Wendy coughed. You bet he is.

He better be our man, said Piper Shepherd, considering the sizable contributions I made to his campaign.

I'm hiring more lobbyists to help my lobbyist, Frank said between bites.

Shepherd dropped his utensils. Are you telling me you *don't* have more than one lobbyist?

Oh my god, there's dessert, said Wendy, her hands on her stomach.

Chef Lowenstein introduced us to an array of handmade chocolate mandelbrot, vanilla biscuits, lemoncakes, honeycakes, nunts, macaroons, fried bananas in caramel, and sugar doughnuts filled with blueberry slatko. Fruit picked that morning. Of course there was fresh-ground coffee percolating. And while we sat in our leather chairs eating all this fine food off all this polished silver, the blond interns from Israel poured us another glass of kosher wine. Then we sat back and watched the mountains of the Mojave Desert pass underneath the belly of the Gulfstream. We drew a breath.

Old movies are the junk bonds of television, Piper Shepherd said to Frank as we landed. Best thing I ever bought was the Looney Tunes catalogue.

Oh, wow, you own Looney Tunes? Wendy said. Don't you just want to watch them all day long?

Diabolical piffle, said Piper Shepherd, celebrating chaos, violence, vengeance, vandalism, and lawlessness. Corrupting those who have yet to be trained on even the basics of the toilet. That's what they said about Looney Tunes when I was a kid. But hell be damned they are funny and worth almost forty million to me in broadcast rights every fucking college semester. Can you count that? Forty, Frank. Forty. Imagine the money we would rake if I owned virtually *every* American movie made before nineteen sixty-fucking-nine because that's the kind of deal I'm sitting on here, Frank, the rights and reels to ninety-nine percent of movie classics.

What do you need? Frank said as he broke off some sugar-glazed nunt and ate it, speaking while chewing, seeing how much of this Kravis was hearing, which seemed to be nothing, since he was asking Wendy for her number.

Seven hundred million dollars, Piper whispered.

20

STRAYS

The trifling conversations that had taken up our time in the cabin of the Gulfstream evaporated in the heat. We were all alone in the baking desert with ourselves.

The landscape was so unlike the coast. Dry, dusty, and searing hot. There wasn't anything green in sight.

We seemed to have boarded some kind of kosher spaceship and in less than an hour hyperjumped to a farflung planet in another galaxy, with an atmosphere like our own but without any moisture in it. We stood in the crackling heat. The clay pebbles on the ground broke easily beneath our shoes into ash. The mountains around us looked like smouldering piles of coal in a giant firepit.

You got ten more minutes of two-lane blacktop, said the man who greeted us at the airport in Stovepipe Wells, pointing a long, sinewy finger due east. After the turnoff you're going down one lane of gravel for 'nother forty minutes, okay, but that road winds around the valley and takes you all the way to the playa.

We convoyed in two Jeeps Frank had rented ahead of time. Jonjay drove the Jeep in the lead, he said he knew where to go, and Wendy, trusting in him, followed behind and chewed her teeth. Off we went. To our right were the Funeral Mountains and the Kodachrome Basin State Park. To our left were the Cottonwood Mountains and the Racetrack Playa. It was hot in the shade. We had the air conditioning blowing. We took Scotty's Castle Road just like the man told us to, a single lane of gravel that bummed along through the flat wide valley of pale Martian borax and dolomite until the Cottonwoods mellowed out into soft, very high hills. The undulating rifts of the blond-white borax formed deep-riven troughs between bladethin peaks. The scrub shaded the Cottonwoods above these dunes. The rock was striped with rusty pink belts.

Our Jeeps passed alluvial fans spreading jewelled pebbles down the mountainsides. At Death Valley Junction, shade—taking as many pictures as we could of these eerie cones and tides of red-and-white rock, like sleeping dragons with swollen bellies covered in boiling-hot sand—the heavens granted us a penny-sized cloud.

From the overpoweringly conspicuous lavishness of Fleecen's private jet to the bedrock of this vaporous toaster, inhabitable only by coyotes, roadrunners, snakes, lizards, spiders, and other bloodsucking vermin immortalized in cartoons, we were glad our Jeeps sealed us in, cold and protected.

Driving about five miles an hour through narrow crevasses in the rock, we saw a gaunt hare with veined ears like lacrosse sticks do nimble sporting herd movements. The tiny haggard Joshua trees that populated the many nooks and shelves were like pencil sketches of biblical wisemen stooped over against the howling heat. And the chuckwalla lizard we saw was unreal, more like a medieval symbol not meant to be taken literally. Above us the enormous sun exploding over the mountains sent fuggy overripe heat down to our level.

Piper Shepherd asked if we were circling around and around a burning maze or if we would ever breach this crack. Death Valley, what sort of game are you playing here? he said.

Not me, Kravis said, rubbing his hands together. I love these tiny gaps we're skating through, this is my mien, these tight narrow margins.

Very outer space, said Mark Bread with his nose to the window.

Kravis sniffed him. Who the fuck is the source of that B.O. smell that's floating around? It's asphyxiating.

That's me, Mark said, and giggled. Justine asked me to bring some from the hamper. He enigmatically patted his pocket.

If *she's* in then so am I, said Kravis, slapping his own cheeks.

Frank's wife told Jonjay to stop the Jeep. She was getting out. She trotted off down the road to the second Jeep and Wendy stopped driving and leaned out the window and asked her what she could do for her.

Someone trade seats with me for a while, Sue said. I'm tired of hearing those men and their euphemisms. One of them claims he can do fifty pushups the other claims he only eats doughnuts. And the little one is a crab.

I'll go sit with the boys, said Justine, no problem. I can dish it out.

You don't want to do that. That man Kravis is an asshole, Sue said as she buckled on a seatbelt. I kind of wanted to strangle him.

Who *is* he? Wendy said. Why is he here?

This is the first time I've met him, Sue said. However, she'd heard Frank complain about him for years. Quinn Kravis was a pseudoclient of Frank's who raked in millions exploiting tiny fluctuations in the exchange rates of international currency. Say there's a spike in U.S. currency—he'd buy half a million British sterling and wait for the markets to back out and then sell the pounds at a tidy profit. Son of a laundromat owner, Kravis married rich—Hala Kravis was the daughter of Jamal Shahbandar, the Middle Eastern scientist who'd made his fortune selling chemical weapons like cyclosarin and VX to the Ba'ath regime in Iraq, before going into hiding in of all places Hoboken, New Jersey. Hala, an Iraqi-American glamour model in the pages of *Vogue Italia* at fifteen, met Kravis at a benefit for the Frick Collection when she was twenty-two, would bear him three children and call an eleven-bedroom estate in Westchester County home, with its mob neighbours and melancholy view of white sand and slate-grey Atlantic squalls. On their wedding night, Hala floated Kravis a million dollars of Shahbandar family money to start his private arbitrage equity firm, and after sex, instead of a cigarette, he started trading from the phone on the nightstand in their Beverly Hills honeymoon suite. Over six years as an arb scalping millions off the world financial market's minor discrepancies, Kravis had managed to rope Hala's entire inheritance into his investment stable—this family's billion, plus the investors Kravis persuaded to throw millions more at his feet before he rolled the dice, made his arbitrage office one of the biggest bullies of Wall Street.

A truly toxic personality, Sue said. Frank meets the worst sorts of men—great for my fiction, awful for real life. Socially, cretins. Even the Feds think Kravis is up to no good. He's in the paper quoted saying greedi- ness is next to godliness. He's a dracula. Bet you he's hitting on Justine as we speak.

What we saw when the mountains of Death Valley finally separated was this: Racetrack Playa's flat white surface shimmering with blue heatwaves for miles around, like a giant skating rink or a lake, an enormous mirror. We got out of the Jeeps and took our first tentative steps along the surface, cracked into plates of dried mud. The wind blew in our ears. Purgatory.

No one else around. Silence. Inside the bowl of time. Flat. Totally flat. For three miles in all directions. A frying pan. Surrounded on all sides by the rust-red Cottonwood Mountains shimmering in the heat. A blue dome over us. This intricate mosaic under our feet. The playa was cracked into hundreds of thousands of hexagonal tiles. A beautiful network of clay tiles made in extreme conditions. The air smelled of sand. The heat was an inescapable, dusty. Breathing burned. We did not adapt. Stunned, we spread out across the playa together and alone, toured the flatland from end to end, becoming dots to one another, to ourselves, our bodies becoming then vanishing, becoming again, then dots within our minds the longer we spent walking the Racetrack Playa.

What interested Jonjay about the playa was the sailing stones. These were practically the only other objects around to disturb the flat playa besides us, and we could see them coming from far away. There on the blank slate of the playa were inexplicably dozens of huge stones, and not only that, these stones had somehow, over time, *moved*, and left behind irregular swooping meandering paths in the dried mud, like drunk stones out for a stroll. Some of these stones had moved hundreds of feet across the basin.

Jonjay wanted to use large sheets of archival newsprint to do rubbings of the tracks, to record the movements of the stones as accurately as possible. Each stone might need fifty or more sheets of paper to get a complete rubbing of the entire path, which is what he wanted. The tracks behind the stones weren't elegant, these weren't tricks like the eerie mandalas found in crop circles. The stones indented the hardpacked snakeskin ground in aimless zigzags. No pattern at all. There were dozens of stones, hundreds of feet of paths to cover. This might take him more than an hour.

Hold on a minute, Rachael said. How many stones to you want to trace? Surely not all of them?

And how do you expect me to show these? My gallery isn't infinitely big. You waited years for *this*? You're never not infuriating.

Justine stood with her hands at her hips and watched as her artist got down on his hands and knees with a stack of paper and a box of charcoal and began to trace the long, chaotic lines. He wanted us to move methodically from the start of the stone and down along each long track, page after page, capturing as much of the detail as possible of the depressed mosaic floor of the playa.

Sue hugged herself and said, I would feel safer if I had on an astronaut's suit.

Frank got down on his hands and knees to help Jonjay. People push these around on a prank, right? he said. How else does a rock move?

That's what I say, too. People pushing. Justine turned her back to the wind so her hair flew in front of her face and she squeaked every time a pebble nipped at her calves. Eek! Beam me up, Scotty. I hope someone remembered to bring a bottle of something strong to this planet. She opened her purse and took out a forty of vodka. Ah, there we go. Mark, care for a swig?

She and Mark proceeded to get lit.

The temp was hovering in the hundred-and-one territory. It was October. The sky looked chlorinated.

Possibly pushing, Jonjay said and handed Frank a stack of paper. Plenty of theories flying around. But if you try pushing one now, it won't be easy to, and it won't leave behind the same kind of groove. And that's a lot of stones to push around—look, there's dozens of them out here. Who's going to do that? For hundreds of years? The pioneers who came through here wrote about it in their diaries.

Then what is it? Frank was doing as told, doing a charcoal rubbing of the trail next to Jonjay's.

Some say aliens. We're a few hours' drive from Area 51. But what kind of dunce alien communicates via dolomite in an uninhabitable desert? Special magnetic force field maybe. Except dolomite isn't magnetic.

Telekinetic spy training ground, said Mark.

Might be. I'm with those who say natural phenomena. Rain. Ice. Frost. Wind.

Of course, said Frank. Natural's all there is. And you're right. These trails are much too random for human intervention. Humans can't resist patterns.

Here are patterns, said Rachael of three parallel grooves, as if the stones were in a neck-and-neck race spanning centuries.

But no patterns over there, said Frank. And besides, these are hardly parallel just because they're all in a line. Yeah, wind could do this.

Except if *I* can't push one, how can wind? said Jonjay. Whatever it is, it's a drawing nature made. I've always wanted to come here.

The paths do give them personality, said Sue. There's some weird feelings I get from the stones, like they are alive, there's a presence to them. Don't you feel it? Maybe there is a sentient phenomenon going on here. I wonder if they're watching us from their lifespan of eons.

Torchlight blinding. Ears ringing with heat's tinnitus. Sweating under unmitigated solarity. Ultraviolet headaches. Heatstroking. The sun and heat didn't affect Jonjay the same way it burned us. He took breaks to drop off stacks of paper at the Jeeps, one stack per stone, labelled accordingly. Then he would wander the playa for a while, gazing here and there and studying the ground for stones with an especially interesting path. Meanwhile we took breaks back at the Jeeps and guzzled from icecold thermoses of water and ran the engine for a blast of air conditioning.

Kravis wasn't going to get down on his hands and knees, not for art. Not in his Gucci casuals. On a tour of the playa, he found an abandoned park ranger's shack made of clay and bleached wood beams warped by the scorching time under the sun, and, in the mood for some shade, he went in. We followed him in a short time later, not knowing he was inside. We found a charming black cookstove, a card table, two wicker chairs, and a cot upon which we caught Kravis asleep. It was cool indoors compared to the playa's frying pan, and the walls were covered in watercolours of haggard soldiers, sirens at the lagoon, dragon mountains, and other local Death Valley vistas spun into the floss of lonely fantasy. Not bad amateur art, we thought.

Hip studio, said Kravis as he sat up and yawned, put his sunglasses in his shirt pocket. Imagine this is your job, working out here, the kind of cosmonaut you'd become. Bet you anything there's a bottle stashed somewhere, probably under the mattress. Ah, there you have it. Wild Turkey—this man knew his business. Kravis found a tin mug hanging by a hook in the ceiling. And our lucky day, folks. Who wants to fight fire with fire?

He skulled the mug and licked his lips. Poured himself another shot before passing bottle and mug on to us.

Mark Bread proceeded to roll a two-paper joint for a hotbox.

We shouldn't be seen together, Kravis confessed. Not us—me and Frank, I mean. We're in cahoots, but you know, that's not kosher. Fuck it, I say. Who's looking? Idiots, that's who. He laughed. Give me back that bottle.

Dust the colour of coffee grinds swept across the ground in the wind, up into our faces where sweat dissolved the grains into lines of mud.

An hour later there were four of us walking together across the playa, Wendy and Sue in front, parallel like two stones. They had talked about what Wendy was up to, and what Sue was working on now, a short story about a renowned psychotherapist who leads a double life as a polyamorous drug addict.

I'm in psychotherapy for my teeth, Wendy told Sue. I have bruxism. Sue said the girl in her dormroom in college was like that, Sue could hear her teeth squeak and crack all night long. Wendy had tried a slew of doctors and treatments but none of them had cracked her code, she was wry and defensive and blind to herself as ever. She hoped for a consultation with the celebrated repressed-memory expert Dr. Lawrence Pazder, who was on tour of America.

I still brux, she said. I bruxy all night long. I call it bruxing, not grinding. I brux my teeth.

You must suspect something. What do you think is at the root?

I'm stuck between me and myself, Wendy said and turned her gaze towards Jonjay in the middle distance rubbing on his hands and knees. *That's* my problem. *I'm* what I'm biting down on.

Sue said, Maybe you and I are quite alike. I feel the same way sometimes, like I'm caught between the person I am and the one I want to be. Being married young, I guess my experimentation went into in my fiction. But my stories are getting more traditional, so ... I'm looking for more out of life these days.

It's like I experiment with people too much and end up drawing a traditional strip. Gee, why are we talking about these things, I'm sorry, I hardly know you.

I don't mind, said Sue. People fascinate me. Usually what's on our minds isn't what we talk about, we circle and circle but never get there. But I can tell you're an open person. You must be like this with everybody. You're not a private person, you're not shy to talk.

That's true, Wendy said. I can talk and draw.

Maybe it's not that you're trapped between your teeth. Maybe they grind because you're so open. After hearing so much from Frank about your success the past few years ... well, now I regret we didn't meet sooner. We could be fast friends.

Totally. Let's be. So, what's Frank say about me? I can't help but wonder.

Oh, you know. He says how talented he thinks you are, and how many deals you've helped him make, and I can tell he likes you personally. Now I see why he does, because you're smart and adorable and you draw all day. You've got the best life. I can see why with a personality like yours you're so close to someone so reclusive as Jonjay.

Jonjay-in-the-box? Look at him, harmless as a kitten, but get to know him and I promise he explodes in your face. But then you sit around and wait for the next time he pops up. The one that got away is my roommate, imagine that, Wendy said guilelessly. Jonjay is the real reason I grind. My life would be completely different without him.

Presently we joined up with Piper Shepherd, who stood beside the dolomite Grandstand regarding the landscape through slitted eyes, disillusioned with the desert or himself. He bared his teeth against the wind spitting shards of sand at his face. The Grandstand was a volcanic outcropping of batwing rocks, black and broiling hot, the only unflat thing in a three-mile span, it could be the remnants of a burnt-out alien craft. From its peak we could survey the entire surface of the playa shimmering in heatwaves. Sue climbed to its peak and stood beside us with a hand over her eyes and said, My god, this place is desolate, the embodiment of *goodbye*. Death Valley is like walking into that word, really getting a sense of its scale against the puniness and fragility of the human heart.

Then she got a pocket sketchbook from her handbag and a Pentel, and, with the cap in her mouth, began to write. Once in a while she took a deep breath and wiped her eyes and nose against the back of her hand as if she were quietly crying.

Wendy came around from the other side of the rocks to join Piper in the shadow they provided. The temp dropped a degree. Piper's face was hidden under the brim of a straw hat. He pulled a kerchief from the breast pocket of his white cotton blazer and mopped his neck.

Ice water? she said, holding out her thermos.

They sat down on a natural bench of dolomite and shared the water. Dust clouds pirouetted in front of them, then vanished.

It's hard to believe it's almost Christmastime, Wendy said.

Piper choked and laughed. Christmas is banned here, he said. Death

Valley is a Santa-free zone. Nobody opens presents in Death Valley. What the hell.

For the longest time now I've imagined if I ever made a *Strays* Christmas special it would take place in the middle of a hot hot summer. Maybe one of the animals hears what Christmas is all about and gets the date wrong. So all the animals plan a big Christmas celebration with gifts and dinner feast and songs and everything, only to learn it isn't Christmas for six more months.

But you *are* making it already, aren't you? That's the rumour, isn't it? Yes, I heard about this project, in fact, said Piper. He drank the last of the ice water. You mentioned it in an interview.

Are your TV channels looking for a cartoon special that could air in July and again in December?

If it's good, Wendy, perhaps. It *is* rather unorthodox to make it yourself, you know, and sell it to us finished. Normal way to go about this is—

Naw, I'm a control freak, said Wendy. This one is too important to me. I don't want to pass a script off to Hanna-Barbera or some know-it-all who rewrites my ideas. I'd rather make it on my own and risk it never gets seen. It's my money, after all.

Piper smiled. You're cut from the same cloth as your man over there, he said.

Who, Frank?

Ha! No, but yes, him, too. I meant your friend Jonjay. Single-minded.

Oh, yeah, me and those boys. Those two are nothing alike, but somehow I'm like both of them.

I get that sense, said Piper. And that's in addition to being your own person.

A few minutes later, as we climbed down from the top of the rockpile with Sue, we heard the two of them laugh.

Would you look at that, Wendy said, looking pleased with herself and frightened all at once as she pointed to the sailing stone at her feet. It was a flat slab of dolomite with a black top and on it there was an egg frying.

Sunnyside up and crispy on the edges, she said and peeled the egg off the rock and ate it.

Frank labelled his rubbings of the sailing stone's path in numbered order, put them into the dufflebag with the other packs. Justine hovered around the back hatch and seemed to be doing math in her head.

Kravis had enough of walking around in the pool of nothingness and came to watch Frank.

So is this kid the one moving all these stones around?

That's no kid, said Frank Fleecen.

Kravis pressed his hands to his hips and squinted. Know what I like most about it here in this dry emptiness? We are safe from Securities Exchange agents. We can say anything. Fucking liberating, isn't it? Nobody calling. Nobody watching. There's no one hiding around the corner.

Don't threaten me, Kravis. I don't care where we are. There's nothing left to talk about. Our business together is over.

I thought we were partners ... , said Kravis as if he was coo-cooing a baby.

Frank snorted. Partners, says the tapeworm.

All the work I've done for you. Don't turn your back on me now. I'm not blind. I see the deals you aren't cutting me in on.

I'm not colluding with you, Kravis. Find some other sucker to break the law for you.

Oh, so, then why do I still have a carbon copy of a cheque you wrote me, and an invoice for *services rendered*? I guess I forgot to destroy these.

Frank said, calmly, If you've come all this way to extort me, let me dash your hopes on these stones right now. I'm not afraid of you. You're a gnat sucking blood off the anus of Wall Street. I will crush you slowly.

You're funny, Frank. Extortion? Ha! You're not used to being the one in debt, are you? Kravis said contemptuously.

We walked alone through the quiescence. How fast was the pace of change in a place like this? Just the two of us assistants, Mark and Rachael, walking together, feeling once again like freeloaders along for a crazy joyride in a Gulfstream IV to this frying pan. There was nothing else to do but walk so we walked. Except make rubbings. So we rubbed more trails behind sailing stones for Jonjay. Our sense of time was in some ways heightened in the Racetrack Playa, where time did not matter, by our shadows stretching longer by the hour. Time was also the cacophony of our shoes in our ears compared to the vast silence of the motionless lifeless landscape. Mark finished off Justine's bottle of vodka and had to be carried most of the way back to the Jeeps.

Standing there at the Jeeps watching their shadows stretch were Wendy, Frank, Piper, and soon Justine Witlaw's long, bobbing shadow joined our group and minutes later she arrived and stood next to us. It was her idea to buckle Mark into a Jeep so he would be out of the sun. Jonjay had collected over a hundred pages in the dufflebag and that was enough rubbings, we thought. We were ready to go. Frank asked where the other two were, Jonjay and his wife, Sue.

Wendy checked her wrist for the time. But she didn't wear a watch.

We waited. Then we spread out a bit and started to call their names.

Jonjay?

Sue?

Sue?

Jonjay?

There was no way of telling how far our voices carried across the playa, but they didn't seem to carry at all. No matter how loud we shouted. Talking into the vacuum of the desert, or the portal of it, sometimes when we called out it sounded like we didn't say anything at all, and other times we heard voices from across the aural mirage of a great distance. We heard the wind say, Sue? Sue? Where are you, Sue? In Death Valley, the wind could roar in and make no impression on the bright blue jar of day glittering over us with sunspots. And the moon was up there too, it had gotten into position long before the sun gave up its time in the sky. The hard mattress of the Racetrack Playa was lunar and stretched for miles in every direction. Sue? And a thousand troughs in the rock led into scalding, dead-end canyons. Jonjay? The canyons opened into more canyons. Jonjay? The mountains cliffs stood shoulder to shoulder like Haight-Ashbury homes. Where could they be? A giant sand dune reclined in the nude, sunbathing her long, bare legs.

This can't be happening again, said Justine. He can't have. Oh balls.

Frank and Wendy didn't hear, as they searched face-first into the gale force of the wind coming out of the canyons.

It was late into the afternoon and the sun would set soon. We had to leave now if we wanted to make it back to the Gulfstream before dark. That narrow road was treacherous in broad daylight. We shouldn't stay on the playa any longer except they were gone. Exfoliating sandstorms and numbing drops in temp were known to rip through the playa at night. We wanted to call for help. It was not safe here. We had to find them. They were nowhere to be seen. We had to get out of Death Valley. Time was running out. Night would kill us all. We waited a little longer for them to return. We didn't all want to be stranded, though. We must go. Yes, we must. It was time to leave Death Valley. Call for help at the nearest phone.

I'm not leaving without them. They'll die out here. Wendy was close to tears.

The Motorola! said Frank and ran to the Jeep. His searched in his belongings for the cellular phone. He dialed. But he had no reception. Fuck, he said and threw the phone as far as he could into the playa. Frank said he would stay behind and hope to find them. He said, Leave me a Jeep. Then he went and dutifully picked up his broken phone.

Piper Shepherd stepped up and said he would stay with Frank and not leave the Racetrack until we returned with help. And because Wendy was staying, Rachael immediately said she would, too.

I don't care, Justine pouted, I'll drive. I can't stand to look at this place one more second. The first phone I see, she said, I'll tell them it's an emergency. She took the Jeep with all the traces Jonjay did from the playa. For all anyone knew, his last works.

Wendy said, Jonjay, he's pure pranks. But Sue is not going to let this last. They are bound to show up.

Even Kravis, who was not used to being silent, didn't say a word the entire way back to the airport. The reflected desert burned in his eyes. Justine drove with her chin over the steering wheel with an eye out for potholes and rocks. Mark half slept. At the Stovepipe airport we notified the authorities, then Frank's pilots flew us home while search and rescue considered what to do about Sue and Jonjay.

Piper suggested we split up into pairs and circle the playa in opposite directions and meet up on the other side to learn if any one had seen anything. We could take it from there. That sounded fine to all of us except that was a three-mile radius. It was almost dark. Let's just take the Jeep, said Wendy.

No, he's right, we should walk, said Frank. I don't want to miss any clues. We might find her notebook or a pen ... something.

So Rachael and Piper split off and went one direction, Frank and Wendy went south to look for a mark of the missing.

What we remember most about Death Valley was the relativity of things, the relativity of our size compared to the desert, and our weight, how incredibly heavy we felt, how our feet sucked to the ground, and how we shrank, shrank down to pea-sized, then to the size of a grain of sand, then smaller than that, to the size of the universe itself, one chiliocosm spinning among many. The heaviest, smallest things ever to exist, that's what the desert told us we human beings were. Like those stones on the floor of the Racetrack Playa, we were sailing across this dry seabed on the coracles of our imaginations, a mystery even to ourselves.

We didn't see anything, we told Frank and Wendy.

Neither did we, said Frank. But his face said he'd seen *something*.

21

According to Wendy, who told us later what happened, Frank kept saying strange, ominous things to her while they walked the edge of the playa. He was at first solemn and introspective, and so was she. The disappearance was aesthetic, that's what Wendy believed. It was a vanishing for art. But that didn't mean they would just as soon appear, it probably meant gone. Nothing moved except the wind. Blasting them with heat, the wind was like the door to the oven opening and shutting in their faces. They traced the perimeter of the playa where it met the slopes of the Cottonwood Mountains, looking to the ground for tracks, shoe prints, anything.

Frank was soaked in sweat. The webbing of his toupée stuck to his forehead. He wiped away the sweat rivering down his eyebrows onto his cheeks. His shirt clung to his chest.

Why would they vanish together? Wendy said. Maybe they climbed into the mountains and fell. In all these years, he never mentioned her name. Did they know each other?

I don't know, said Frank. I never introduced them. She knew his art because I bought those pictures ... and the formula ... so I mentioned him a few times over the years of course. Sue has an interest in art, for her writing. My wife's writing, my financial business—that part of our lives is separate from our marriage.

Sue doesn't seem like the kind of person to play along with a prank like this, Wendy said. Unlike Jonjay, she might understand how worried we'd be and care.

Frank's eyes were up at the peak of the mountain, where the shadows were darkest, forming caves in the rock that channelled deep. There's a lot I don't know about her, I guess, he said.

The North Star was out. The heavens were the colour of Delft. It was five in the afternoon.

Ever since I first laid eyes on you … , Frank began.

What do you mean? Wendy said. The more I think about it the more I'm sure they're alive, they've just run away. You drove them away or … I don't know what.

You don't believe that.

Why do you like me, Frank? I don't get it, we're so different.

We're both here, aren't we? He took her by the shoulders and pressed her to him, embraced her. She pulled away and asked what he thought he was doing. He mashed his chest against hers violently, as if trying to catch her, but she wasn't falling. She twisted her neck and he took her by the jaw and brought her mouth to his and kissed her. She kissed him back.

Then they remembered where they were—they could be seen, so they began walking again in silence. Frank stared at her the whole time as if on a cliff asking, What next?

We decided to rest for now inside the old clay hut Kravis found earlier in the day, when it was still hot out. There we would discuss what to do next. The last breath of daytime remained on the charcoal horizon. Frank pried open the door and we all went inside and made ourselves at home. Frank lit the gas light and Piper poured drinks and lit a cigar. Wendy regarded the paintings on the wall, then went and sat on the bed beside Rachael while Frank walked back and forth under the gas light hanging from a hook in the ceiling.

There's no use pacing, said Wendy. Nothing more to do for now, so sit down. She patted the empty space on the bed beside her. It broke Frank out of the spell and he sat down. All at once, his shoulders slouched forward and he began shivering. Wendy put her hand on his back and tried to warm him up. Rachael got up and went and sat next to Piper in a wicker chair at the little card table and lit a cigar for herself.

The park ranger arrived around seven o'clock. She was a handsome if dehydrated figure. Charismatic and tall, she had to bend to fit through the cavernous clay doorway. She pulled off her Tilley Endurables hat and shook out a mane of dusty blond hair, said, Make yourselves comfortable. Piper Shepherd's long pants were this ranger's short pants. Piper's short pants might fit as the ranger's panties. She was in her fifties, one of those women of the atomic age with doll's hair, a fuselage brassiere pressed tightly against her khaki shirt by a tight black belt cinched around her hourglass waist. Callused man-hands, selfless maternal Earth-loving cowgirl, born to dominate in any field. In this woman's case, that field was scorched earth.

You're welcome to smoke. Can I pour anyone a drink? All the art on the walls you see is by yours truly and for sale if you want to know a price. That's the maars of Ubehebe Crater. That one's of Zabriskie Point. I paint a lot of Dante's View.

Do you know our predicament? Piper asked her. We lost two.

Was over the Panamint Mountains taking care of a flat, otherwise I'd been here sooner. Got the call and came directly. It's too late for a search tonight. We'll go out sunup tomorrow. Glad I caught enough to feed everybody, she said and showed us the fat chuckwalla she'd trapped.

What happened? she asked as she set to work cleaning the animal.

Went missing this afternoon, Frank said. A couple, man and a woman. A blond man in sunglasses and shorts. My wife is brunette, wearing a white hat and sandals.

The ranger took a deep breath and wiped the dirt off her forehead. No, I never saw them.

In your experience, do people often go missing around here? Wendy asked.

I'll say this, it happens.

And then what? Do you eventually find most of them?

Sometimes … , the ranger said and then turned her back on us to face the cookstove, putting the rest of her conversational energies into a blow-by-blow of her prep and cooking of the chuckwalla, a red meat of sun-drenched anabolic flavour spiced with chili flakes to taste, and not unexpected or unpleasant in its chewiness. Aided by the Wild Turkey sauce and side shooter, the meal went down quickly. The chuckwalla's lizardskin was splayed on the floor, flattened out as the Racetrack Playa with all its octagonal scales, spread out to dry on top of some newspaper. We noted the pages had the comics, a repeat of *Pan* above last Monday's *Strays*.

The following morning a search-and-rescue team led by the ranger fanned out across the desert in helicopters and on foot to look for Sue and Jonjay. We waited at the playa.

Those were our last minutes in the desert before going. We would not come back here.

Did Jonjay know Sue? Wendy asked Frank again. He never talked about her.

I don't know. Friends? Not to my—.

Tell me if you know, Frank. Were they having an affair, did they run off together? What do you think, Frank? Answer me.

I don't know. I really don't.

Did you argue? Did she want to leave you?

I don't know, no, we didn't fight, said Frank. He looked ready to stay here and fry like an egg if Wendy told him to. You believe me, don't you, Wendy? I had nothing to do with this. I have no idea what's happened.

Do you think they're still alive? Wendy asked.

Yes, he said. I'm sure of it.

They must be in love.

I don't know, Frank said. I guess so.

Wendy collected her lime-green Gremlin from the parkade under Frank's building. She started the engine.

What are you doing now? he said.

What does it look like I'm doing? I'm going home. I'm going to go have a shower and bawl my eyes out. Jesus fuck, Frank. This whole trip was a disaster.

I know, I know. I can't even process ... what happened. My god.

And who was that guy, why was he with us? He was such an asshole. Seeing him should have been the first warning bell.

Yeah, fucking hell. I didn't want him there either, not a bit. Kravis and I should never be seen together, our lines of work are too enmeshed. The fool just invited himself. His inlaws own the Beverly Hills Hotel and he was there tanning, so he came all the way up from fucking L.A. to see me for no other reason than to turn the screws on me.

That's super fantastic. So this is your criminal sidekick or something. You really are being investigated by these agents. I gotta get out of here.

You have to trust me. I'll never let you down, Wendy, I promise. I love you, Frank said.

Don't say that.

But it's true. I do. Please don't go, Wendy. Stay with me.

The Gremlin's engine gave a startled howl and the vehicle chugged forward wearily and Frank had to leap away or get his arms torn off. She put the car in neutral again and held her foot down on the brake pedal. The street outside was all but empty.

He came back to the window. When will I see you next? I have to see you, soon.

I can't, she said.

Why not? We must, we're in this together.

In what together?

Don't you remember our ... kiss? Wendy, were you lying to me then?

You're coming on so strong, Frank.

No, I'm not. I know you feel the same way. I'm losing my mind, I know, I know. But please, you know it's true. I've loved you ever since I first met you that night with Gabby. I never dared to say this. It seems pointless. I know what you thought of me. I thought you knew I loved you. I thought that was why you avoided me all these years.

Maybe I was avoiding you. Maybe it is the reason, I don't know. But I'm not who you think I am, Wendy said. You don't know me. How can you love someone you don't know? Besides, I'm impossible to love.

Tell me you don't feel the same. I'll leave you alone. Just say those words.

I need time to think, Frank.

You'll think about me? he pleaded.

Don't ask me any more questions, she said.

Can I call you?

No, she said and drove away. Followed the entire time by a rust-coloured Datsun.

22

STRAYS

Wendy curled up on the couch and turned on a TV. We poured her chocolate cereal and fried her French toast and rolled her joints and flipped the channels for her. She lay there fetal as she took Biz through the events in Death Valley, recreating the crime scene as exhaustively as she could remember. We embellished when necessary. Had Sue and Jonjay died like pioneers, dehydrated, bursting into flames, sizzled, lost in the scorching dunes? Or had they run off together?

No doubt this was going to be in the papers, Biz said. After all, it's Frank Fleecen's wife. See if it was only Jonjay missing, some flake artist, nobody bats an eye, Biz said. But now Sue Fleecen with him, that's a scandal, that's gossip for your treadmill crowd. Rich lady like Sue, every society-page columnist is going to want a piece of this shit pie.

Wendy said, That's what makes it so confusing. Jonjay goes missing once a month. But Sue, Sue is a whole other ball of wax. If Jonjay goes missing it's because he wants to be missing. She pressed her hands flat against her eyes and let out a groan. I'm so tired my eyes feel two like loaves of bread soaked in iodine.

Does anybody want any more coffee? we asked.

You should be happy about the time he lived here, Wendy—it's almost like you married him. I never expected to see him last for that long in one place. But he likes living here. He needs a space like this, where everybody loves him enough to let him live rent-free.

What about Sue? Wendy said. What about Frank? Maybe Frank wanted them gone.

Or maybe the two of them got caught up in a passionate love affair lately and concocted a plan. What do you know about Sue?

Wendy got up and joined Biz at the longtable. I got the impression Sue is this beautiful ambient presence. We were walking and I started spilling the beans to her about my problems. I don't know why, I couldn't help myself. She's not eating off your plate, but her plate seems very available.

I slept all of an hour last night in that crazy cabin, Wendy said. I think Frank is in shock. His eyes were spinning in his head. His hair was on crooked. When we left him at his office, he smelled of sweat, a sort of oaky pine musk. He looked distraught. He might not recover.

And he kissed you? Biz said. You kissed him back?

Like I said, he was emotional. His emotions were all discombobulated.

Maybe you planned this together, said Biz. Ever consider that?

Yes, why not? said Wendy. I should have.

The roommates smoked joints for a while more and in the meantime drew things absent-mindedly while considering whether to call the police and see if there'd been any new information. Wendy stretched her arms across the longtable and lay flat her hands and Biz decided to paint each of her nails white with a little purple question mark on each. Then she did her own the same style but with an exclamation mark on every second nail. Searching through our memories for what might have happened to Jonjay and Sue Fleecen, we were lost in thought, our minds lay empty, arid, waiting for the arrival of an answer. Biz got up to make a round of herbal tea before going to bed for the rest of the afternoon.

I can't cancel rehearsal tonight with the girls, said Biz. Otherwise I'd hang out here and watch *Gilligan's Island* reruns with you. My Christmas bonanza this year is hella complex.

Wendy said, The thought of working on a project … And my skin is so dry. If I don't slide into a bubble bath soon I'm going to crumble.

The bell on the Easy-Bake Oven went off and Mark Bread opened the door and pulled out the tray of steaming, semisolid cupcakes. He tasted one and grinned, then Wendy ate two and drank some tea to dilute the sugar spasms.

Mark opened a window and left some cupcake on the sill for a seagull that flew by regularly and knew to check for his treats. He shouted, and the gull arrived moments later and devoured the sugary, mucilaginous bundle.

You breed the chelidrids and jaculi, Mark said to the seagull in a high-pitched voice, phareans and cenchriads, and even two-headed amphisbands, but live it up like Vanni Fucci. There ain't no tomorrow. You stumble upon that unknown, unlit unpath to fly again under the unstars. Past the broken gates and the unshriven. Zoom unzoom. Floating on your coracle blowing on your saxophone as you coast across serene or placid saccharine waters. Yippidy-doo-da-day. How speak you, transhumans? Pure experience or death.

Okay, Wendy said and scratched where it all of a sudden tingled at the tip of her nose and then slapped her knees. I waste too much time thinking about my problems. I can't believe Jonjay went missing. My brain can't handle that. I've got to get in that bath.

Over the days that followed, the search for the missing persons expanded. As news travels of the disappearance, volunteers have arrived at the Racetrack Playa from all over the tri-state area, including expert trackers and hunters with their bloodhounds and mystic horses, the desert survivalists and amateur sleuths in it for the cash, all of whom promise to find some*thing* if not someone, and bring closure to this terrible incident …

Change the channel, said Wendy, yawning long and silently with fear.

They fan out across the desert on foot and in helicopters looking for signs, any signs of the artist known as Jonjay, and Sue Fleecen, wife of the multimillionaire junk bond banker Frank Fleecen. It was his private jet they used to get to Death Valley. With them on board was Jonjay's art dealer, Justine Witlaw, Quinn Kravis, in charge of a large private equity firm, and Piper Shepherd, president of Shepherd Media, best known for buying up cable affiliates in half the states in America. They were on an expedition to see the Racetrack Playa, famed for its sailing stones, when calamity occurred—

I said change the channel, Wendy said.

I did, said Biz. It's on all the news. Only one going soft on the story is the Shepherd Media affiliate.

Stick around for a look at the brand-new technology dominating Wall Street: from IBM data systems, to customized Microsoft brokerage boxes, to digital Rolodexes and the Apple's mouse, we'll show you the latest gadgets powering your investments.

Police had questioned her twice, once at the airport in Death Valley and then again at the station on Mission Street. They'd asked her to come down that week and talk to them. The last time she was there it was to pick up Biz and Morphine Annie from the drunktank.

You don't remember anything else? said the lead detective with his notebook open and a pencil ready. His face seemed to be caving into the place where his moustache grew from, all his other features pointed to it, his downturned eyes, rosy cheeks, even his smile.

Let's go over the details of the afternoon one more time, he said.

Feels like I'm in an episode of *Dallas*, or at least the *Dallas* comic strip.

There's a *Dallas* comic strip?

There sure is, said Wendy.

He wrote this down. With J.R. in it?

Sure, the whole cast is in it, plus its own set of extras. I forget who draws it now, but Jim Lawrence, he writes it—he wrote the *James Bond* comic strip.

Was this trip the first time you met Sue Fleecen?

No, well, yes. I saw her once before at a reading she gave at Justine Witlaw's gallery ...

Was Jonjay there, at the reading? the detective inquired.

Yes, he was, Wendy said. She took a breath and said, ... Do you think they're alive?

I don't think anything, Miss Ashbubble.

Wendy passed right by the headlines in the national papers. She didn't want to read about the scandal or see her name. She didn't socialize with the drop-ins and drifters; instead she kept to herself, working from her seat in the kitchen nook. The phone rang off the hook with journalists whose demands she ignored. For a moment there, practically all the papers and news stations followed the story of Hexen's top financier's wife and another man—a mystery man, artist—missing in Death Valley. Mojave rangers and authorities of the desert said there wasn't much speculation among the searchers—the couple probably died of exposure. People vanished out there. It was history—the experts on TV, including the ranger Wendy and Frank spent the night with, warned that Death Valley was a miserably dangerous place to visit. It's the night that gets you, said a volunteer on horseback. On Wednesday, the newspapers quoted a hapless middle-aged pharmacist and her husband, a gas jockey, in Daly City, who swore they saw the lovers come through wanting to gas up their car and buy a prescription for birth control pills at their filling station/drug mart as they were heading out of San Francisco the day before in a nondescript vehicle packed with camping stuff.

Wendy's ears perked up. Nondescript, was it? Hmm-mm, that does sound suspiciously Sue-like.

Tabloids other than Shepherd Media speculated the couple were heading east. Thursday's financial reporters questioned if Fleecen's viselike grip of the derivatives market might weaken as a result of this personal loss. All the coverage twinkled with the language of *schadenfreude*, but sources close to Frank told reporters the loss had plunged the financier deeper into his work: Frank was busier than ever, brokering hundreds of new deals and selling record numbers of bonds, ending days with fifteen to twenty percent gains above market.

Friday's *New York Times* carried a profile of Frank that made him out as a career-focused math-brain workaholic who loved his wife and could not come to grips with his grief. The article dramatized the disappearance as a tragic accident. While Sue Fleecen wrote literary fiction for university-funded quarterlies that paid measly honorariums, the journalist pointed out that Frank preferred to make high-stakes multimillion-dollar deals on the free market that included his favourite comic strip, *Strays*, in the package. In the end, for Susan Fleecen at least, the news anchors intimated, money did not buy happiness.

Frank called that weekend to ask her how she was holding up.

On my back in bed if you must know, she said. I saw your profile in the *Times* yesterday. Makes you look nice. How'd that happen?

Oh, that's called the PR department at an investment bank going into code red. You have to get in front of a story like this, I'm told. Find an amenable reporter pronto. Goose him with free dinners, drinks, and loose women. Then feed him the story he's supposed to write. The coup for us was getting a *Times* guy to listen.

What are we supposed to do now? she said.

What else can we do but carry on.

How can you say that?

Because this is what I do. I work. There's no other option. The sun rises every damn day. The markets open and close no matter how I feel.

I heard that oysters can only reproduce under a full moon, she said apropos of nothing or everything.

Direct moonlight or a full moon? he asked.

A full moon. Maybe I should get going, you sound distracted, Wendy said.

Don't hang up, Frank said. I'm not at all distracted. My attention is always on you. I don't want things to go back to the way they were between us.

I didn't know there was a way between us.

That's what I mean. You deny your feelings. Yes, you are. You can't look at me. Can we see each other soon? Today?

No, I'm going shopping.

After a day driving around the Bay in her Gremlin browsing comic shops in the hopes she'd stop gnawing her molars, Wendy got back to the manor that evening to more bad news. Spending sixty cents here on a comic book and sixty cents there, eventually she amassed a large stack of new releases and back issues. The clerks in certain shops knew her. First they knew her as *that gal* coming in over the years buying what they referred to as kids' comics, which were kept in the shelves with the used books. Have you got any comics by Fontaine Fox? she would ask them. Who? And then once they put it together she was the creator of *Strays* the clerks began to refer to her purchases as *the work of syndicated strip artists*. The clerk pointed her in the direction of some of the latest greatest releases on the shelves. The latest greatest were never *Herman* and *Bloom County* treasuries, they were always superhero comics. Browsing the humour section and the children's section, she'd find ancient copies of *The Mischiefs* and *Popeye* to add to her pile. Then, noncommittally, her hands flipped through *X-Men* spinoffs, the clerks loved *X-Men* spinoffs, and the one about the blind man in a devil's costume, she had to buy that, too. Politely studying the panels. Her eyes barely registered the muscles let alone the storylines, if any, as her brain kept hitting the snooze button. To wake up would mean she had to deal with the thought of Jonjay and Sue. She walked out the door and saw in her hands issues of superhero comics she wasn't in the least bit interested in. Sometimes she even had books on hold at certain shops. *Your Fontaine Fox came in*, the clerk said. So you add to that pile of treasuries and kids' comics she did want, and two hundred dollars later, make that more like six hundred dollars later, more material than she was ever going to get around to reading. Not that it mattered. A lot she'd flip through once and pass on to us. Something might spark a conversation. It was all tax deductible, too. With the wagonload came a sense of relief. Working the rounds of the comic shops was a kind of trapline. She opened each trap to find out what was in store. Her collector's completist instinct was reassured by the gaps she'd filled in the manor's overflowing library, a library that was always going to feel a little bit incomplete. She bought mountains of comics to unburden her inner self. She bought comics because she could afford to, not because she wanted to read them. What solace, this wealth. This time she went shopping because she wanted to find out if she still cared about anything that used to matter to her before Death Valley. Driving around shopping, was it fun. The hunt for comics and comic shops, was it spoiled.

The same rust-brown Datsun followed her around all day, but again she didn't notice. She got home that night to find us stoned out of our faces, weeping and drawing clowns. Mimes, circus, rodeo, theatre, all types of clowns. That day as we continued the labour of painting the moving parts in a scene onto hundreds of sheets of celluloid, we got a call from Biz Aziz to let us know Vaughn Staedtler had collapsed at his home late the night before unable to breathe. He was in hospital.

Wendy took a joint out of our hands and sat down. She said, Look, I *just* bought one of Vaughn's earliest treasuries.

> *Dear Dr. Pazder,*
>
> *I shouldn't write you any more letters after this ... My situation has changed ... I've made changes ... I must give up on therapy as the answer and look elsewhere ...*

23

There was no more Farm under the freeway hairball to visit for lunch on the way to San Francisco General Hospital. We walked by a vacant lot instead, albeit a temporary one, while the city prepared to redesign what were vegetable, fruit, and flower gardens into sod with a small, shallow water feature the shape of a yin-yang. What was once a vacant wasteland of gravel surrounded by freeway overpasses had been turned into this thriving garden and a farm by local artist Bonnie Sherk, who tended its leaves for a decade. The Farm had provided food and a petting zoo to the community surrounding it, plus a stage for live performances. The stage would stay for now. The rest was too unruly for the parks board and needed to go.

The hospital had grown and adapted as well in the face of another kind of demolition, a much worse one that required urgent attention. It was no longer so quaint in there. Now it was clean and tidy and reeked of cleaning supplies, the halls hummed along at the urgent pace of an automobile factory going around the clock, and none of the clerical nurses had a minute to look half-asleep-on-the-job anymore. No longer were its

hallways decorated with the fingerpaintings of gradeschool kids; the walls were covered with health-wise posters featuring the latest facts surrounding the AIDS virus, which ended up being more than half-wrong. *You cannot get AIDS from a blood transfusion or mother's milk ... You cannot get AIDS from an organ transplant ... Condoms Save Lives ... You* can *get AIDS from unprotected sex.* We remember as we got off the elevator seeing a waiting room where five or six young men started to sob and wrapped their arms around each other, speechless. And shortly after that we saw four generations of a family suddenly come together in the same way as they wept, supporting one another. The intercom paged Dr. Dritz.

We met Biz Aziz outside the door to Vaughn's room, down a busy thoroughfare for doctors, nurses, and other staff hurrying to and fro with clipboards and equipment. That day Biz wore a pair of women's Jordaches with Converse All Stars, hair cut to a shadow across her scalp, and those finely plucked eyebrows. She didn't need lipstick or blush to be a goddess. She always was, on or off stage, in or out of drag. Or halfway in between, as she was today. She had her face in her hands, and when she lifted her head up and saw us coming, her eyes welled up again. Her face was red and her lips were swollen from crying.

He's asleep right now, she said. I just got back from the cafeteria.

How is he?

Doctors did some bloodwork and the first round came back pneumonia. Biz said the doctors thought he had AIDS so they tested *her*, too. She was waiting for those results. Chances seemed good they both had it.

No, not again, Wendy said. The group of us embraced there in the hallway. This terrible thing attacking the city, the country, and the world, that no one seemed to acknowledge, was winning a war against all of our bodies, regardless of our politics, predilections. The newspapers reported on a newborn baby with AIDS, so wake up! Blood transfusions or mother's milk or both, my god. We trembled in horror. This thing, this AIDS monster was everywhere, possibly on everything we touched. We realized right away our group hug completed a wave of grief that started with the men we'd seen in the waiting room by the elevators, followed by the family, and now us. This was why the hospital staff seemed to travel at a different speed from the patients and visitors, a much faster speed, faster than people walked in silent films, because they worked relative to the pace of incoming patients—for the staff, the clock ran according to one collective embrace a week, one group hug a day, or every minute. These days hospital-time was moving very very very fast for staff, while for patients and guests, hospital-time always took forever. And maybe these days it was slower than ever before. Every second brought you closer to the wall, that deadly question mark made of solid brick. For patients and their visitors every second on the clock of hospital-time was a struggle to heal or to succumb. Every breath was a performance for the audience of visitors, family and friends who came to watch you and your body fight. A visiting hour took an emotional toll on everyone that was all out of proportion to the duration. Until hospital-time was suddenly over. Head-first for the brick wall—either it evaporates like a hologram or it crushes you. One way or another, you always leave the hospital.

Vaughn awoke, and after he expectorated heaping dollops of yellow and green mucus from his chest, we all went in to visit him. He had a private room through his health care with a splendid view of the bay docks, a potted plant with long, striped leaves, along with the standard television plus cable, and an adjustable bed. It wasn't exactly plush, but last night he'd landed in a shared room with five teenagers who required almost twenty-four-hour care, surrounded by specialists and lovers, friends, family, and Vaughn was terribly afraid to hear any last words.

That's what I get for too much dancing, too much clowning around, Vaughn said from his bed, where an IV dripped saline into a vein in the underside of his wrist. He saw us staring at the feed. I told them not my *left* wrist, that's my painting wrist. Nurse says to me, how much painting you plan to do in here? and then she sticks me with it!

The colour was out of his cheeks. His eyes were dull. He still had to laugh.

People get sick. It's okay, said Wendy. You're a fighter. I'll bet you could still draw even *with* that thing in. Maybe this is a renovation. A restoration, like the Statue of Liberty or The Farm. Tomorrow you're a whole new man.

I feel like shit on a stick, Vaughn said and coughed up too much phlegm to swallow again, so he pulled a few Kleenexes and spat into them. I'm sorry, this stuff keeps collecting in me. Spitting's given me a splitting headache.

You want a chocolate bar or something? Biz asked. They got vending machines down the hall. Or coffee? Let me go.

Vaughn said the thought of eating or drinking anything made him feel sick.

Listen, Biz said, let me go get us all some snacks, anyway, feels too crowded in here. Then she ran from the room without waiting for a response. We saw her punch the wall hard enough to make a hole, and then she ran to the vending machines before anyone saw who'd made it.

She's the reason this old man's still alive inside, Vaughn said, oblivious to what Biz had just done. Best thing to happen to me in a long time.

Biz is amazing, said Wendy. She's never believed in me. I'm a fraud in her books.

Take it as a compliment, said Vaughn and reached for her hand. So long as you try, if you try, then fraudulence is at least a sign of ambition. Ambition is two-thirds of … something.

Maybe success, said Wendy.

I was never *me*, said Vaughn.

Sure, I know what you mean, Wendy said. Don't worry. None of us ever *are*, are we?

Biz came back in and left him a Snickers bar and kissed him one more time. I'll see you tomorrow, she said and smoothed his hair.

Vaughn didn't hear. He said, I never did my own work. I hired assistants. I'm lazy but I love life. I love life too much to work. I'm going to die a complete fraud.

What about your clowns? said Wendy.

Bullshit.

You get creator status, said Biz. You invented the first and only truly rock 'n' roll comic. *The Mischiefs* will be around after we're all gone.

I wish you could promise me that.

Those few patients who spent their last days in 5D where Hick Elmdales had died three years ago would have no idea that now their room seemed historical, intimate in its size, now that AIDS patients occupied the entire floor of the hospital, with dedicated doctors and nurses tending to as many as a hundred beds at a time, and as much equipment and resources as budgets allowed. Men were treated for drastic peritonitis, severe edema. Another man, worse off than most from lumbago, moon face, and a broken heart. Here was a mere child of a man suffering from severe hyperammonemia, megaloblast, common cancers and rare cancers and other forms of diseases only housecats ever got before. These dreadful cases represented today's youth, a satire, cruelly deteriorated under the plague of AIDS. Here were boys with handsome faces ravaged by invisible rats, here were dropouts of undergraduate degrees bedridden and frail as old poets, sicker than fallout victims, gasping for air, dying of it. The signs ranged from bleeding oozing rashes to hamburger eyeballs weeping melted cheese, skin pustules the size of red apples, the dry pukes, wet pukes, howling hemorrhoids, bleeding ulcers, shivers and shakes, runny nose, itchy eyes, anaphylactic shock. He was brittle and dry and ready to go. He was smoke. He was a pile of ice. He was shattered pottery. He was a tiny bird with broken wings.

277

Could a mosquito's proboscis inject you with the AIDS virus? Could a bedbug or a louse? Was AIDS on toilet seats and doorknobs? Was gay sex the cause of AIDS? Could a woman get AIDS from sex with a man with AIDS? Could your waiter give you AIDS, touching your plate? Was there AIDS in saliva? Why was there so much AIDS in New York, San Francisco, and Haiti?

The White House gave press conferences about the threat of nuclear annihilation. We were winning. Brezhnev was all of a sudden dead. Good for us. He was a bear if there ever was a bear. The nightly news reported on the many thousands of atomic warheads in the American arsenal, pointed at strategic locations throughout Eastern Europe and Asia. The movies showed us what a nuclear strike would look like. *Red Dawn* made it look bad. *The Day After* brought home it was hideous. And the latest, *Threads*, was the most hideous movie ever made—because *that* could happen. If someone dropped a bomb, how would our faces look afterwards? What would happen to the human body if exposed to massive doses of radiation and nuclear fallout? Special-effects artists showed us. Blisters and sores would form on the skin. Joints would break down. Organs would fail. Body parts would fall off. Blindness. Third-degree burns. Vomiting. Diarrhea. Cancer.

That night in his sleep Vaughn's lungs filled as if a faucet had opened in his system, and after retching for an hour he drowned this way. With drowning, there's no pain, said the doctor, whose face had android written all over it. Even as he continued to speak to us about the deceased, the doctor had clearly moved on.

The funeral was held in Santa Maria, the cemetery where Staedtler's parents were buried. Amid headstones and oak trees we stood at Vaughn's plot with the many hundreds of friends and admirers, the family, mostly dressed in black. The women wore black frocks. The men in black leather jackets. When it was our turn to shovel earth over his casket, we thought selfishly of ourselves and what our chances were of surviving the eighties. Vaughn's was not the only service being held in the cemetery that afternoon.

We followed the procession back to a funeral home in North Beach. The old folks Vaughn's age wore leather here, some men had ponytails, they chainsmoked, drank, and talked about drugs. The women were slant-eyed as soldiers. Thing was, when Vaughn Staedtler broke into the funnies in his youth with *The Mischiefs*, many papers were too afraid to subscribe because of the rebel image he portrayed on and off the page. Vaughn was the outlaw son of the Staedtler family of Southern California. Two years into drawing *The Mischiefs*, Vaughn's cousin ran away from home to be with him, then the SFPD arrested him in his studio and he did three months for kidnapping a fourteen-year-old and keeping her in a hotel in the North Beach. Comics fans like to point out his strip came a full two years before Elvis, and was a big success in the South, including in Memphis, where papers started carrying it in their classifieds section next to the automobiles for sale. Vaughn Staedtler was invited to appear on a parade float in Memphis with locals dressed up as the greaser characters from his strip. The older folks of Vaughn's generation told stories about how they preferred bourbon and pure horse to grass and LSD. Some of his litigious former assistants were present, looking beleaguered, insecure about paying respects to the man on the other side of a class-action lawsuit. Bill Blackbeard said a few words about Vaughn's significance to the world of comics, placing Staedtler alongside Walt Kelly and Al Capp as one of the great voices of irony, dissent, and bohemianism in the funny pages. Chester Gould stood with the help of an assistant and spoke of his friend-ship with Vaughn and the good work they did together on the board of directors of the National Cartoonists Society, despite, he said, Vaughn's famous cantankerousness. Art Spiegelman told us he arrived this morning from New York to pay his respects. We didn't know he'd moved.

Explains why you haven't seen me around the manor much, he said and laughed. Pardon me, I'm going outside for a smoke.

How did you know Vaughn? we asked a stranger seated at our table with a coffee and a plate of cheese in front of him. He was about our age, in his twenties, thick glasses, big hairdo, that's why we asked.

You know those clowns Vaughn's been painting? Yeah? Well, those are mine. I painted them. He paints his signature, that's all. He hired me to be his assistant. I didn't realize that meant he wanted me to paint everything. Every day he tell me to paint a clown, one with a hatbrim full of water and a cigar on fire in his mouth, or, paint a clown with a sad expression under smiling makeup, or just, *paint a clown*. Fucking clowns. Funny thing is, he owes me at least five thousand dollars. He hasn't paid me in almost a year. I've been borrowing from my sister's husband to get by. He promised me they would be bought by the Guggenheim.

You painted his fuckin' clowns? Biz said. Did you all hear that? Wait till I tell Wendy.

How did *you* know Vaughn?

I'm his *widow*, Biz answered.

I didn't know he was remarried, said the assistant.

Well goddamn, he sure kept secrets, didn't he?

And how did *you* know Vaughn? we asked another stranger who sat down at our table carrying a plate of Vaughn's sister's famous pot brownies (that he didn't seem to know were pot brownies, judging from how fast he ate them) while Wendy was in the ladies' room.

I knew him through King syndicate, the man said. He plucked brownie crumbs off his corduroy blazer and ate them. I worked as a travelling salesman. For nine years I sold *The Mischiefs* to newspaper editors all across California, Nevada, Utah, Arizona. Tough gig but it paid.

Wendy came back from the ladies' room with a tissue in her hand, wiped her nose and eyes and cheeks and sniffed back a final sob. Her mind's eye was still on the departed, now many, and she hardly noticed her company.

A former assistant got up to speak. She had long, white hair pulled back with a loose black ribbon. She wore a grey sweater over a black dress, and her name was Phyllis Glazier. From the silence that came over the room it was obvious Glazier was part of the lawsuit. However, as soon as she started to speak, she struck a kind of peace in the room with her softspoken, musical voice and graceful gestures of a choreographer. When Phyllis was a twenty-year-old with an art diploma from a correspondence school, Vaughn gave her her first job, inking *The Mischiefs*. And for eight years she painted the layouts of at least twenty different pencillers ghosting for Vaughn, including many infamous dipsomaniacs like Wally Wood and Frank Frazetta. That was her art school. She hadn't worked for Vaughn since the early sixties. She was going broke. He paid late if at all. She told us quitting was the best decision she ever made, but she never stopped missing Vaughn and his studio dungeon. She had loved working on *The Mischiefs*. Often Vaughn would arrive late in the afternoon to see what I'd accomplished, Glazier said, and he would point out places where I had made mistakes or could improve my line. I would set out to make the fixes and Vaughn would say, *No, no, no need to fix this one, fix the next one.* That was a time-saving lesson. He never touched a pen unless it was to impress a girl, but he never stopping thinking like an artist.

We respected Vaughn's privacy, his sister Esme said when it came time for a member of the family to speak at the lectern. When he came back from Korea I guess he changed. He turned into this wild artist. We all loved him—he was our big brother, the war hero with a comic strip about rebels, delinquents, reform school dropouts. He was a rock star before rock music, touring the country. I thought he was cooler than Elvis. I suppose we never got to see enough of the real Vaughn. All of the siblings lead such different lives. We never get to see any of each other except at these occasions, weddings and funerals. I guess the last time I saw Vaughn was ... years ago now, but I brought him some of those brownies, fresh from our farm. He ate too many and passed out on the roof of his house.

The guests all laughed knowingly. Then another person got up to speak.

They *are* delicious brownies, said the travelling salesman, also laughing.

Holy fuck, you scared me again. What are *you* doing here? Wendy gaped at this person seated next to her about to scarf down another brownie.

I'm sorry, I—I wanted say something, but the sister started speaking.

Say *what*?

Our case has moved up the ladder.

What case?

I'm now an assistant to Rudy Giuliani, U.S. attorney for New York.

You are no Jim Rockford, not even a Perry Mason. You're more like Columbo when he's scratching his head.

The SEC reports directly to the president.

The president. As in R. Reagan?

I am investigating a *crime*, Miss Ashbubble. It might be so-called white collar but it's still crime. A serious crime. Call that whatever TV show you want. My investigation is real.

Wendy was rubbing her chin with mild curiosity. I love crime shows. Solving mysteries. My favourite is probably *Rockford Files* but I love *Magnum* and *Remington Steele*, and *Miami Vice* is straight up my alley with its fashion and gunplay. Have you seen it yet?

Someone at the table next to us made a shush to quiet them, seeing as cartoonist Jeff MacNelly was at the lectern speaking. *Me and Dan O'Neill got so drunk one night ...*

Never mind what you're seeing on paper with your investments, the entire bonds market is a house of cards, Chris Quiltain whispered into Wendy's ear. Flooded with junk. Hexen is playing a Ponzi on the

S&Ls. *None* of the junk market is liquid. He bounces debts from account to account to hide from the IRS. We chase the money. It's an ongoing investigation.

Say no more.

I love that ring you're wearing. What is it, a honeybee made of glass?

She saw what was going on here. What's going on here? she asked and batted her lashes over her shoulder.

Can we find somewhere to talk, in private? Chris pleaded.

Of course, she murmured.

They went around the corner into the cloakroom.

You were there? Tell me. What do you know about his wife's disappearance?

I know it happened, said Wendy. That's all. One minute they're there, the next, gone.

Frank is trouble. He's dangerous, said Chris. Even Reagan is starting to see the truth.

You're dangerous, said Wendy.

Among the overcoats and jackets, he made his move without a second thought. Pressed himself against her, that elliptical mouth of his on hers, her back to the wall, the cage of his hands groping her ass, his mouth tasted of lip balm wax, his skin smelled of Ruthvah.

What are you doing? said Wendy. Stop for a second. What in the blazes—?

I'm sorry, Wendy. I don't know what got into me. I thought you were flirting with me.

Maybe I was. But only to find out what you're all about.

You're beautiful. I've been following you around, watching you. Reading your comic. I interviewed you, remember? Through the mail for *The Comics Journal*. I feel like I know you.

That was you? That *was* you. That was *you*. You sneak snake fucker.

283

You're the exact kind of corduroy reptile I modelled my snake Sam after.

You're so sexy. I want to take you out. I'd love to buy you a dinner. I think, listen to this, because it's true. I'm in love with you. You're the most amazing woman I've ever—. I'm a *good* guy. Get to know me, I am. We could—

Gimme a Kit Kat. Are you concussed? This just got gross. You follow me around. You're the shadow I didn't know I had. I don't know you. You're crazy. You're cute but you're crazy.

Am I? Do you find me attractive?

Look, buster, do you want to arrest me or date me?

Date you, arrest him, Chris said. Frank Fleecen's the one we want. You're the one *I* want.

Stop talking.

He's cooked, crooked, and triple crooked. I'm sure of it. You know it. You must. Tell me what you know. What has he told you?

Nothing. No more out of your mouth.

You're in business with a dangerous man. Frank's pulled you right into the middle of a massive swindle and you don't even know it.

Shut up and fuck me, you oblivious doll.

The screech of metal coat-hangers sliding in a bunch as someone parted the coats in front of them startled everybody. A pretty voice cried out, Mercy me! and an elderly stranger, no, it was not a stranger, and not so elderly, either, but a lively athletic middle-aged woman Wendy recognized right away. It was Jean Schulz and she was with her husband.

Charles Schulz and his wife apologized for interrupting.

Wendy said, *There's* my glasses! Right on my ... face. Well, thanks so much for your help, Chris. She took her glasses off and put them back on. I don't know *how* they got there.

Yes, wow, strange, said Chris. There they are. Sometimes it's the last place you think to look.

How do you do? said Charles Schulz. Meanwhile we're looking for our coats.

It was polite of Schulz not to recognize Wendy at this moment, but it still kind of stabbed her, since the last time they met—at Hick's wake—he had told her to call him Sparky. But now was not the time.

STRAYS

24

The hospital promised to run a few more tests and make sure, but the doctors told Biz that, on the surface of things, she did not have the AIDS virus. The relief was confounding. Biz went into shock. She couldn't be alone; she couldn't go up to her room. She didn't trust herself. In the week after Vaughn's death, Wendy doted on Biz completely. They would lie together on Wendy's mattress and Wendy rolled the joints, and one day she made a chocolate pecan pie, and she rented movies, an early John Waters, some rare shorts by Kenneth Anger, Cronenberg, Lynch, Alejandro Jodorowsky, Pasolini, Jesús Franco, as well Andy Warhol's *Dracula*. Wendy's bedroom had no draft, stifling hot, she kept the windows shut and the shades drawn and she'd warmed the air with incense. They half slept, half woke in the dim amber glow of the days and nights flickering by, eating cakes and pies and drinking coffee far too much, getting stoned on top of it. Sleeping all day, working all night, crying a lot. There was a decadence to grief and it was shameful, except shame made it harder to heal, and the cycle of pain prolonged the ordeal. The disorienting, cavernous feeling of abandonment played a number on their internal compass. Seven days passed before they awoke from this sorrow.

Biz turned to face her in the bed, and said, He gets it. I don't. He dies. I don't. I should have it. I *must* have it, unless he had it first. He never told me or nobody he hired that art school kid to paint those clowns he was so proud of. That's obscenity on top of an obscenity. What kind of man was I seeing? Floccinaucinihilipilification!

Those clowns *were* the worst, Wendy said and yawned.

The VCR on her dresser played the last scenes of *Mad Max 2: The Road Warrior*. Biz cracked open another cassette—*Prince: Purple Rain, Live.*

Biz yawned, too. I'm a wreck. Limp. No strength. Can't crawl out of bed. No appetite. Sapped of my will to live. Last person who meant something to me's dead, Wendy, dead. I should be, too. Shouldn't I be?

Eat some pie, said Wendy. Make sure to at least get some sugar in your system.

Yeah, I got to have sugar, said Biz with a fork poised over the pie Wendy had made.

Tell me if it's good.

It's good.

There's a whole bag of chocolate chips in the filling.

I said good. Biz ate through a piece with no lack of difficulty. You should be a pastry chef.

Anything other than a cartoonist?

That's right, said Biz between chews.

I don't think new options are open to me anymore. This is it. My one skill in life. If I can't do this, I'm doomed.

That's where you're wrong, said Biz. There's hella options always open to us. Look at me. I used to be loose, now I'm celibate. I used to be at war, now I'm at peace. I used to be in the closet, now I sing.

You're not like puny humans, Wendy groaned. I feel trapped by the choices my choices made. Meanwhile you fly free.

She was thinking about earlier that afternoon when Gabby had called to hear the entire story of what happened. Her editor said, And you saw the *Times* piece on Frank? Really powerful, sympathetic portrait of an American titan. Perfect timing. Your strip gets a little nod. I hate to say it but I'm going to use this to pin down the editor, strike while your name rings bells around those halls. See if I can't get you a subscription.

I'm going back to bed, Gabby. I'm losing my mind. I can't think about the *New York Times*.

Wait, before you go. You should call Frank, said Gabby. This one's not my business. He's got other bad news. Hexen's copyright lawyers sniffed out a company in Houston selling knockoff *Strays* toys and T-shirts to dollar stores, Texas all the way to Phoenix. Apparently they ignored cease-and-desist letters so now it's time to take them to court. Reason you might care is your contract says you agree to cover half of all legal fees with Hexen …

Well, shit.

Legal fees. She didn't want to call Frank. She thought about it, she even sat next to the phone. She did everything other than call Frank, including clean behind the toilets and write Dr. Pazder another letter. She wondered why, if Frank felt so strongly about her, and he was about to sue a bootlegger, he hadn't broken the rule and called *her*. She wondered why, if he was her business manager, she didn't tell *him* the New York District Attorney's Office was investigating him. A month had gone by since the trip to Death Valley and she hadn't said a word about her interactions with Chris Quiltain. All things known and familiar were falling away piece by piece, vanishing into light one after the other at a terrible rate.

Rachael concentrated on the cartoon and on her noise music and suffered from bouts of insomnia once a week. Mark became more absorbed by the effects of magic mushrooms and alcohol, and as a result, accomplished little.

Wendy remained determined, if shaken, to continue. What else. She managed to sketch ideas for fresh comic strips. These were about the perils of dating. She didn't see the connection to her recent adventures—she cited the parrots who flew past the Sutro Tower on the top of Bernal Hill. *They* made her think of the difference between mingling and monogamy. These birds who reputedly mated for life were nothing like her. Parrots were more suburban on that front, but the bright green plumage was right for San Francisco. So what about a single parrot? A bachelor parrot? She remembered seeing among the flock a single parrot with a blue head, without a mate like all the red-headed parrots, and Wendy got an image of a stubbornly individualistic parrot. A parrot with a purple head, a Prince parrot. She imagined this parrot might think all the other parrots were nuts for being so monogamous and paired up every living hour of the day. This one purple-headed parrot might even love to be single. This parrot wanted to love the world. Nicki, a proudly single San Franciscan parrot *playing the sky like a musical instrument.* She considered Nicki a kindred spirit to Biz or maybe Twyla, and then used a lot of her own life stories as fodder for the character. In the Prince spirit, Wendy kept Nicki's gender ambiguous.

That Motorola number on the kitchen wall nagged at her. She remembered the first time she ever called Frank, the day after Hick's death, and tried to count the times since then that he had called her on that phone about something to do with *Strays*.

I never call you, she said when he answered on the second ring.

On a good Saturday night I might sleep four or five hours, he said. These days I don't sleep at all.

Sometimes I feel like Jonjay and Sue were imaginary, like something you talk about but never do, she said. Biz thinks they *must* be alive. She's sure they took off somewhere. A torrid love affair. How likely is that?

I'm at the office ten, twelve hours a day, so, she could have a life I'm not aware of. I guess I might easily be the last to know. Did you ever suspect?

Never of this. Always of something. My gosh, sometimes *I* had to wake Jonjay up. He never did anything except when it was to get into trouble or draw a beautiful picture now and then. Problem with Jonjay, he can meditate all day in a lotus position and you're still suspicious of him. He can astral project.

When I'm alone at home, that's when it's the worst. There's no one there. But I am not used to being alone. All day long people scream in my ear. My home is empty. Silent. The halls. The kitchen. The living room. The bedroom. The rooms all echo. I keep the blinds shut. Because they wait at the corners day and night. Next to the stop signs.

Who does? Wendy asked.

With cameras. Stupid hacks. Ever since Bob Woodward and Deep Throat, the media are nothing but bloodsucking vampires sniffing around for toilet babies.

Gross.

Journalists *are* gross, Frank said. No cure for them, the slime. This phone is probably tapped.

How do you know it's reporters?

My life is public enough without having to see every private shit I take written about in the papers and covered on TV.

Did you talk to the police again? They asked me some questions.

A few more times. Detectives came here and asked to see my Rolodex of all things. And they visited my home. They treated me with less suspicion than the SEC agents. That reminds me, I saw your old friend Manila Convençion on television today. Did you see her?

You did? No way. On what?

The news. She was in town this morning, I guess. Hounded by hundreds or thousands of men as she walked down Market Street. All sorts of media. I know how she feels. Ever since we got back, I'm hounded by police, I'm hounded by press, I've got a phone in each ear, I'm yelling at arbs and runners and buyers, I'm tangled in a noose of pigtail rubber cord, listening to yammering voices all day in my ear go on about numbers. Numbers. When I try to sleep I hear the market tick. I lie down and close my eyes and the voices get louder than when I was on the phone. And when the voices finally fade, all I hear is this horrible auditory hallucination of a constant ticking like a metronome, tick-tock, that makes it impossible to fall asleep. I can hear it in my sleep. I dream in tick-tocks. Tick-tock! wakes me. I'm sweating from madness. The tick, the tock, the tick, the tock. Do you have that, Wendy?

Yes, but I know what the sound is—my teeth. I know why, because I had a childhood I've repressed. You need a *real* vacation, one where nobody goes missing.

That's what my brother says. Let's go for lunch and talk about it. Shouldn't we commiserate, isn't that the sensible thing to do? I care for you. Damnit, Wendy, you're the only one who understands me. I'm losing my mind here all alone like this.

She started to shake, she said it was too soon, and said goodbye and hung up and walked down the hill to the corner store on Precita Avenue, if only to be under that bright light in the sky.

Breaking news in the missing-persons case involving the wife of junk bond financier Frank Fleecen and another man. After what was supposed to be an afternoon trip in the company jet to Death Valley with a group of Frank Fleecen's friends and colleagues, the mysterious disappearance of Mrs. Fleecen has brought reports from all over. Our own Irwin Gerund went down to Visitacion Valley to speak with the owner of the All-Nature Pharmacy, Prente Abscondio.

The newscast cut to footage from an interview with Abscondio, whose name and occupation, pharmacist, were set below him on the screen. Could be her, Abscondio said. Sure look like it was her. I remember her face. She showed up in a same nice sports car wearing same nice sunglasses she did last week.

Last week you say? said Gerund.

That's right. She came in, asked for cough syrup. I did not say, *I see you before. I know who you are, Miss Fleecen.* I *did* put two and two together but she a customer. She pay me and I give her her change. Only later, then I decide I call you.

We asked Wendy if she just saw that and she was staring so hard at the Magnavox she didn't even hear us.

Cough syrup? What the fuck did they go there for? Wendy said. I'm going to go down and talk to this pharmacist. He sees Sue *twice* in the space of a week, that's crazy. Oh my golly. This *and* Manila's in town. Jonjay's not dead. He's hiding somewhere nearby. I'll bet Manila's a part of this. She always is.

That makes some sense, Biz said.

I'm going down to this All-Nature store.

Hold your horses, we said.

Well, by a strange turn of events we ended up downtown that afternoon when all of a sudden we saw Frank Fleecen coming towards us being chased down the street by four hundred or more young men, shoulder to shoulder running fast, hollering. We happened to be at the front of the crowd and quickly ducked into the nearest store for cover, beside Frank, to watch what he would do as male social groups collided on the sidewalks and street as a spontaneous mob. All the guys had the same notion in their head as we did: to get as close to one prime destination, one delicate location—a little white shop on Market.

She was about to make an appearance on this hairy bananas busy commercial strip cutting a long diagonal through downtown San Francisco, near the shopping malls, near the shady nightclub district, surrounded by budget pizza stops, Mexican takeout, independently owned convenience stores, gutted cinemas in the throes of renovation, old hotels with modernizing facelifts, new sneaker emporiums and

THE ROAD NARROWS AS YOU GO

casualwear outlets, Montblanc retailers, low-cost jewellers, and so on and so forth. At this one little white shop, that's where rumours said Manila was going to show up.

And so a swarm of guys descended upon this white shop on Market Street, driven by insatiable instinct to form this horrible, hormonal ochlocracy, dozens of saurian and simian buddies running headlong, friends protecting friends in tight circular clusters within the mob, departmental colleagues moving in single file in order of rank, the same brotherly blood coursing through all their veins and over all their eyeballs, everyone stuck together in their own groups while they congregated with everyone else into one big mob scene, every breed of guy represented, from the ones who beat you to the ones you so steadily beat, they were all here, a thousand men give or take, scrambling to gain a better view of the little white shop, hustling to overcome one another to get a better position in front of the store, howling, jostling, practically moshing, elbows up, and hungry-eyed, there was the stifling stink of locker rooms, basement suites, boardrooms, anabolics, and oil changes, enough guys were here en masse for SFPD cars to tail the crowd with sirens popping off amid hundreds of guys budging and shoving to get a better view, absolutely screaming at the top of their lungs, crying out loud for this woman, this *one young woman* who was not even anywhere to be seen yet, still coming, who was still supposedly coming, on her way, almost here, about to come, rumour had it, and all these guys waited for her around this intersection at Market and Valencia.

The SFPD officers used patrol wagons to clear a path to the curb and her white VW van was escorted through to a free parking spot in front of the little white shop and the crowd went berserk as she opened the driver's door and swung a long, thin leg out and put a stiletto heel on the asphalt. Flashbulbs exploded as her legs parted. Once fully out of the automobile and standing, she waved a bangled hand in the air and men flipped. She smiled and waved to us all, unafraid, not even surprised or delighted by the scene around her, but so used to it she seemed almost oblivious. Us men,

293

we wanted her, we wanted to devour her. A huge male bodyguard escorted her through the crowd to the front doors of the shop, and as the proprietor allowed in various arms of the media after her, we were already inside the space with Frank Fleecen, pretending to browse, just before the store's gate was locked, leaving hundreds of other less lucky men on the other side of the window to just gawk and stare and try to catch a word of what she said. Meanwhile, we stood about all of four feet from her and heard every word.

By eighty-four Manila was a well-known hinny. She carried the flag of freedom in the George Orwell–inspired Apple advertisement that aired during the SuperBowl. Posters of her sold in the toy section of Sears and Zellers. *Replicant Fitness*, her morning aerobics show, launched in the spring on Shepherd Media, was a runaway hit. It combined fog machines and MTV lighting with an aerobics routine inspired by Jane Fonda, androids and the music of Kraftwerk and Jean-Michel Jarre, performed on the sets from *Blade Runner* (bought on the cheap). Perhaps because Manila seemed to walk around made of no earthly substance and survived somehow without having to work for a living except stretching, making the scene in Manhattan, she made for easy prey for weakling journalists who had nothing to lose besmirching her fair image. We knew better. She was once our roommate and not so long ago. Manila Convençion could paint and draw, with a natural eye for colour, and a hero's confidence against the blank canvas or page. She read wildly and spoke a plethora of languages with the fluency of a local. Her body was unable to gain weight. Whatever she ate made her lighter. When she left the manor it was in a huff, but as soon as she arrived in NYC, she was beset by every kind of image-maker, from Steve Ditko to Keith Haring and Jean-Michel Basquiat, who introduced Manila to Tony Scherman, who took her out for Chinese food with Julian Schnabel, who painted his first portrait of a nude young woman who was simultaneously painting his portrait in the nude. Andy Warhol shot a stack of Polaroids of her and did a screen test of her on film, then made a silkscreen print etcetera and so on.

Since starring in her role as Apple's Macintosh, the athletic emancipator, she was more of a target than ever before. She had managers and accountants and owners and groomers wanting her attention, a team of obsessive-compulsive bulimic men in blue contact lenses who fastidiously combed and scratched her from top to bottom before she went anywhere. Her long, harrowingly thin, fishnetted legs were entirely exposed from the buttcheek down, and balanced at great expense on a pair of hand-cobbled Italian leather high heels designed by Kaisik Wong. She clopped along the white floor tiles, petting her fingers through aisles of 100% cotton, and all the men followed without hesitation or shame looking down her blueberry silk-sequin toga with a scooped neckline that plunged as low down as her navel without ever exposing the main attractions of her small, pert breasts. Her midriff and navel caught the male gaze like a diamond. Falling over her neck and tickling her shoulder blades, her great coiling, tousled mane of hair was the colour of white banana. She was tropically tanned from the top of her nut-shaped skull right down to the berries of her little painted toes. Her moisturized skin was as shiny caramel as latex house paint. On her skinny neck she wore a pearl-dotted choker. The toga also sloped straight down her back to the first dimpled cleft in her round haunches, so basically nearly nude.

The event was Manila shopping. That's all it was. We were close enough to her that our eyes watered. Provide us with shampoo samples, we could tell you which exact brand she used on that platinum blond mane she undid from a ponytail and shook out splendorously. In the course of her slouching, slinky, drugged movements picking through the racks of clothes, we saw the girl we used to know.

She didn't recognize us.

Frank didn't either. He came up to us in the melee and instead of asking us if we knew Manila he said, You, are you Irwin Gerund?

Frank moved on from us. He nudged this very pale, introverted man about half his age, prematurely greying hair, in a perpetual sweat, who craned his neck around and said, That's me for the time being, what's going on?

Could I ask you about a story you wrote yesterday?

Yesterday? Are you *blind* or crazy? Gerund said, not mopping the beads of sweat from the end of his nose and upper lip, but gesturing instead towards the young gorgeous woman, Manila, in front of us picking out lady things. Gerund shouldered his way to the front of the store near the cash register and with Frank beside us we followed close behind towards the main attraction.

As she lay down her purchases on the counter, two pairs of fishnet tights, an undershirt, some bathing bottoms.

I badly needed to find a place to buy tights, she said, shifting her weight to her other hip, profile to the cameras, nothing but her credit card for the staff ... Then I saw all these adorable men following me, she lisped. So sweet. Hi guys. She waved to the guys behind the iron trestle gate and a fresh surge of applause churned and crashed through all the men, the flesh-hungry men.

You'll sure draw a crowd if you dress like that, said the salmon-skinned constable of the SFPD unit, with his arms raised to hold at bay a pack of rowdy fans who had been able, like us, to squeeze their way in to get a closer look at her.

I dress like this wherever I go around the world. Well ... I don't dress like *this*, she said, pressing the palm of her hand to the big rip in her fishnets. The rip came right up the curve of her ass. She looked pretty easy with the insinuation a man could make over her circumstance. That's why I went racing out looking for a little white shop where I could buy some tights, she said. Right now I only ever wear this brand. They should name these after me I wear them so much. That's what's up.

To watch her hand slip over the coppery glow of her thigh brought the men outside to a mindstate approaching pure reptile, hissing and slapping their chins with their tongues. The jaggedy tear in the stocking's netting, which revealed nothing more of her body than was already on display, was nevertheless about as much as this crowd could handle. Guys howled. Men with ingenuity began to stack up dozens of chairs they stole from nearby coffee shops and restaurant terraces and climbed higher above the melee for a better view, in cunning preparation for when she returned to her vehicle. The police stationed outside kept having to whap people back with their batons, and a light skunky smell of pepper spray wafted in from afar, where looters down the block took advantage of the distraction to finger some stereo equipment. There were already a number of visible casualties closer by. Two men hung upside down from the awning of the little white shop and one man pressed against the gate was bleeding from the mouth.

What's the occasion? Gerund asked her with his notepad at the ready.

I'm nineteen today, she said proudly. I'm married. For the past year I've been into android aerobics. I get all my ideas because I can just *go* in a kind of trance. Like I'm in contact with the dead. Hendrix. Joplin. Holly. The lyrical ones. People like that. And I'm *so* excited to travel. I love to drive. I always want to include people in my reality from every angle.

What was it like in Seattle?

She looked Irwin Gerund in the eye as if he was a real unplayful prick for bringing up Seattle. His question was only meant to burst the bubble on her stunt here today, because it implied she was touring as part of a stunt and not somehow casually in the neighbourhood dropping by spontaneously and unannounced, unsponsored, unsaturated, underground, at midday on a Friday, to a little white store that features the same tights she wears on *Replicant Fitness*.

When I was in Seattle, I was with my *husband*, she gave as a curt, inadmissible reply.

Will you see friends while in town? Gerund asked her.

I hope so. She pouted. As she spoke, she wasn't forgetting to smile and blow kisses for the cameras everywhere in sight.

It was the exact same when she was in Seattle, Gerund turned and said to Frank so that he wasn't the only one who could hear.

The clerk behind the counter bagged her tights and passed them over to her.

Hola! she said, and swung the purchase in her hand and posed for a few more men.

Gerund and the rest of us were quickly swept up in a wave of men who chased after her to the curb where her van was still safely parked, untouched thanks to armed SFPD officers who had it surrounded.

No way her legs are worth all this attention, said Frank.

Next year it will be another girl, said Gerund.

Her proportions define our time, said a TV cameraman with sweat pooled around his eyes.

Manila waved her bangled hand in every direction before bending over one more time as she climbed into the VW van, shimmying across to the driver's side, starting the engine, and pulling out into the lane, tightly surrounded by protection. In an instant she was completely out of sight.

A tree trembled dizzily as a traffic helicopter rose straight up and skirted off to the south. The crowd dispersed. We were all alone again on the street under the sun. So we tailed Irwin Gerund and Frank Fleecen down the side street and listened to them talk.

You followed them? Wendy asked us.

We followed them, we said. Like spies, like Chris Quiltain, we followed Frank and the reporter. They seemed to know each other quite well already. But maybe only over the phone since Frank didn't know what Gerund looked like.

What did they say? Tell me.

Gerund said, What a showgirl. Want her? Gerund held up five fingers. Fifty thousand, he said.

That's something to say.

I'm serious, Gerund said. Everyone knows that's her game. It's a sham wedding to a homosexual. This big spectacle gets her some TV play, some column inches. She's up here to make a name for herself any way she can. Some chicks have no limits. Personally? I'm willing to give up two years' salary to taste that. What about you, you look like you could afford her. And I'll write about the whole sordid affair. Make us both famous.

I saw your piece about what happened out in Death Valley, said Frank. Tell me, what was your best lead?

Owner of the All-Nature Pharmacy said he saw a woman who fit her description, and a man waiting in a car outside while she walked in.

You didn't mention this in your article.

No. He's right down there in Visitacion Valley by the old hotels. I spoke with him, the owner. Said she was looking very tired and asked for a bottle of painkiller.

Where's this place?

Like I say, right down there in Visitacion Valley among the soup kitchens etcetera.

Is that why you didn't mention it? The neighbourhood?

No, because I don't know how much I could trust the source. The owner is probably out for the free advertising.

Frank said, Listen, can you do me a favour and run this story on the news again tonight?

Tonight? Ah, I don't know. This Manila Convençion appearance is all I got planned ... Why would I do that? There's nothing to the lead.

You must. Please. Tell the public one more time she was seen down at that pharmacy.

It's not as easy as that. To broadcast a rumour on the evening news. My producer won't run with speculation. Besides, I'm sorry to say, missing people get old fast. That was a week ago. The story hasn't got those kind of legs.

Give the story legs—this is important. Your stories reach a lot of people. This mystery, I'm sure it's something that'll get you ratings.

Gerund smiled, twitching his nose, but the bead of sweat, which was now a dry white bleb, stayed put. No offence, Frank, he said happily, but I don't see why I should go to the trouble.

Think of it as professional development. I doubt your producer supports your ambition, so perhaps in the meantime a viewer could help round up your salary.

Now Irwin Gerund saw Frank's play and broke out in hopeless laughter, clapped him on the shoulder and said, Tell me more about your career ideas.

That was the end of our story. We happened on Frank and Manila downtown this afternoon and that's what we heard. When Frank's exchange ended, the bribed TV journalist hailed a taxi, and Frank in turn took a taxi in the same direction. We came straight home to the manor.

Why would he do that?

Man's bat-shit crazy, said Biz, tapping out a cigarette and lighting a joint we'd just rolled. And Manila is here in town, on the evening news, but she won't place a call, that's bullshit. Listen up. You can dye your hair but you can't hide your roots. Don't come running to Mizz Biz Aziz when the party's over, she said to the absent friend.

Beside them on the coffee table was a partially inked Sunday *Strays* that Wendy admitted she was having a hard time finding the motivation to finish.

Because it's a lame picture, said Biz flatly.

Wendy looked at her work again after Biz's prognosis and nodded and nodded and nodded.

This Frank business doesn't make any sense. This whole situation is giving me teeth-chipping migraines. I can't believe he manipulated a news anchor.

25

The next day, Wendy drove her lime-green Gremlin down to Daly City to meet this pharmacist for herself.

There was a message on the answering machine for Wendy from Chris Quiltain in his clipped and formal tone, who left a phone number with a New York area code where he could be reached. We wrote his name and the number near Frank's on the kitchen wall and took the cassette out of the machine and replaced it with a different one, labelled it *Chris Quiltain's call*, and put the cassette in with the rest of Wendy's dubbed cassettes. You never know, we said to each other.

Our plan was to finish some more animation on the Macintosh. Ever since we saw the commercial with Manila in it, we wanted to try this new artist-friendly computer. Wendy bought us one. It cost five thousand dollars, it was worth more than her car. We fooled around for hours and learned how to draw with the mouse. The ability to *undo* instead of erase was a profound adjustment that allowed us to prevaricate over every line, right down to the pixel, and get even less accomplished. We had the idea to do a sequence of a few minutes of the animated Christmas special using

MacPaint illustrations we printed out onto celluloid and then photo-graphed. This would work for the cyborg dream Francis the rabbit has in the story, chased by *Centipede* video game–inspired versions of Sam the snake.

Around one in the morning or it might have been even later the phone rang and it was Wendy saying she wasn't coming home.

When she got to Daly City, she saw a filling station out front of the All-Nature Pharmacy, to the side of a parking lot. Before Wendy had a chance to decide what to do, a plump, dark-skinned young woman leaned her head in her passenger window and asked if she needed gas and Wendy thought she might as well let the girl fill the tank.

I saw your store on the news, Wendy said. Last week you saw those missing people?

The plump girl pushed the nozzle into Wendy's car, started fuelling, and said, My husband's got lot of ideas. A lot.

I guess he's famous now.

She rolled her eyes. Please don't ask for his autograph. I'm the one has to deal with him later.

Did he really see those missing people?

He sure hopes so. She was done filling Wendy's tank and told her that it would be six dollars.

Phew, prices go up.

What it is is Arabs price-fixing us, said the young wife, pretending to gouge a knife into her own stomach.

Pretty complicated stuff.

Not really.

All the same, I'll go inside and see what you got for sale, Wendy said after she paid the girl.

Never said you couldn't, the girl said.

Wendy parked and walked into the All-Nature Pharmacy, followed closely by the busty young wife. As she walked in the bell rang, and she saw Frank.

He was up at the cash register talking to the man she recognized right away as the pharmacist Prente Abscondio. When the pharmacist saw her come in, the conversation stopped and Frank looked at her. His eyebrows went halfway up his forehead and his mouth peeled open with a look of delight that was alien to his financier's face.

He straightened the knot of his tie. I wondered if anyone else might come down. I was asking the pharmacist some questions.

Oh, this I got to hear. The young wife veered up and lifted the countertop in order to get behind it and push her husband around. Compared to the pharmacist's pale complexion, his wife was a Tahitian or Hawaiian she was so dark from working the filling station side of the business.

I remember a pale brunette with an expensive gold watch asking for cough syrup, that's all I know, said the pharmacist. She looked the spitting image of the picture of the missing woman. Hairstyle and all.

No, what did *he* look like? Frank asked.

Handsome. Like a perfect specimen of California, Prente Abscondio said with his elbows up to block his wife's constant slaps. Leave me alone, woman! Stop beating on me!

Cheater! Malingerer! His wife threw an empty prescription dosette at him. It bounced off his face and hit the counter in a loud spin end over end.

My god, let's get out of here, Frank said and took Wendy by the arm and led her outside into the mild sun.

Hey listen, do you have your car? he asked. I took a cab.

Where's your Gulfstream?

The cursed thing.

What's going on, Frank? How long have you been here? This sham, why did you do this?

What sham?

My roommates, my assistants, they saw you today set this up, the whole kit and caboodle. You paid off a television journalist. Did you pay off the pharmacist and his wife, too? Who else? Jonjay and Sue? I want to know, Frank, is any of this real?

Fucking hell, let's get out of here, said Frank as he took her by the elbow, there's Quiltain.

The only other person in the vicinity was, sure enough, a man in corduroy reading a newspaper as he waited conspicuously at a bus stop.

You're lying to me, Wendy said. She drove over the speed limit down random side streets with Frank Fleecen beside her. His eyes checked the mirrors. Start acting normal, Frank.

I had to see you, okay? he said. I couldn't wait. I couldn't think of any other way. I knew you'd come here if you thought the pharmacist had information. Can't you see what lengths I go to? I did this to get your attention, Wendy. That's all. I know I'm a complete asshole. I don't care. I wanted to see you. You won't see me. Not even phone calls. I can't do this anymore. You're the one who's lying, not me. You deny you feel the same way. I needed to see you. So ... I got this plan in my mind.

You say things, Frank. You say these things now. What would you have done if Sue never vanished? Then what?

Frank clawed his cheeks as tears swam in his eyes. What I've done for years, I guess, pretended I felt nothing for you outside of our business together.

And what about Sue, you never loved her?

I loved her once, yes, and I thought I still did. God, we were together since I was in the tenth grade. Right up until the moment she vanished. Then it was like a whiteness before my eyes, as if the sun never went down for me that night in Death Valley. I was blinded, this fact that she was gone, of being without her. Everything was all of a sudden different.

My life, my idea of who I was. Even while we searched, I couldn't stop thinking of you.

At a stop light he leaned across the seat and kissed her. She let him. They were in Visitacion Valley but it was like Death Valley all over again. The kiss took a long moment before Frank let go. He pulled back to measure the effect.

She said, You are a selfish one. You even steal kisses. She thumbed the side of his mouth clean of her lipstick and was about to tousle his hair when he flinched.

Green light, he said.

I think we lost him, said Wendy with eyes on the rearview mirror. And oh yeah what's this about me paying half the legal fees so your high-priced corporate lawyers can chase down some lowbrow in Texas ripping off my characters? How much is this going to cost me? Thousands and thousands, right?

That's boilerplate stuff, Wendy. Most contracts split legal fees. We both stand to lose more money if we let the counterfeiter continue than we pay for lawyers to stop him.

Don't these knuckleheads just pop up again under a different name?

Been known to happen.

It's like they're in cahoots with lawyers.

Listen, come with me. Tonight I fly to New York, Frank told her. Why don't we talk more about this on the plane?

Are you serious? Another setup? Another trip in the Gulfstream? She squeezed the steering wheel in her hands. I'm supposed to go to NYC in like two days. You knew that. I'm booked into the Chelsea Hotel. My balloons are in the Macy's Parade, remember? You creep. You and Chris Quiltain, you're more alike than you think.

I have meetings with Piper Shepherd at Hexen's head office. I'll be in Lower Manhattan the entire time. I swear, this came up since we've been back. We're going over his purchase contracts for all the classic movies he's so hot on—this is worth billions. This is a big week in finance, anyway. Black Friday is a gladiatorial event for the stocks and bonds markets, blood will be shed, lives will be lost. Traders defenestrate. Traders and brokers plummet as fast as the market crashed. And guys like me make millions and millions. You should come and see, if you've never been on the floor of the Exchange—it's touched by a special madness. Hexen's office is a hundred years old. Looks like there's a pyramid on its top. Beautiful.

Fly all the way to New York in that Gulfstream? I might crack.

No, god, no, that's going back to GE for scrap—it's hexed. I'm borrowing Piper's Boeing 747 for the time being. Come, Wendy. Leave a few days early. Cancel your booking and stay with me. I'll work and work. You'll never see me anyway.

When I least expect it you say the perfect thing.

You can see the museums and bookshops and meet magazine and newspaper editors. We'll go see your balloons together.

My characters and your finagling afloat down Manhattan streets … maybe.

Yes, come with me to New York, Frank said.

Yes, she said. I'll go with you.

26

He dangled the jewel of New York in front of her eyes and she said yes. She planned to go later in the week anyway. What she said yes to was him. And not even to him, but to that part of herself that for years denied her any further attraction to him after that night in eighty-one. Wendy had never been to New York. She pictured Manhattan as drawn by the great cartoonist Winsor McCay, a city in microlines of astounding proportions, tall buildings forged of stone and glass and steel and stretched for miles into the air, and more like these buildings in all directions, three-sixty, whose populace walked and drove about on the canyon floors and worked their hearts out inside caves cut out of these manmade mountains, the towers of Manhattan's superdense skyline. She wanted the city to be like the dreams of Nemo. Sometimes buildings stood up out of their foundations and walked together like tall legs without a body. Other times the skyscrapers pointed down, out of the clouds towards the earth. That was the Manhattan she imagined.

They feigned a business relationship for Frank's nieces, on board again as his interns, so there was no privacy until they landed. The Zabriskie Hotel was right on museum mile, across the street from Central Park, and Frank had booked the penthouse suite. This was a sight more ostentatious than the room she'd booked at the Chelsea Hotel. The suite had more square footage than No Manors. He threw down his luggage, kissed her, she started to unbuckle his pants and he said he needed a shower first. So she wandered the living room, dining room, enormous bedroom with king-size four-poster bed, three full bathrooms. She could hear him in the shower. Wendy felt overwhelmed. She went out onto the limestone deck and caught her breath. She took in the panoramic view of Central Park, all the trees flickered in the lamplight with red and yellow leaves as the last fires of autumn awaited the snuff of winter.

The door to the bathroom was locked. Her mind instantly went to an image of a bald Frank naked under the water and the hairpiece resting on the lid of the toilet. She took off all her clothes and waited for him on the bed, looking up at the moon through a skylight.

Before there was time to pleasure him he fell upon her like a man suddenly so thirsty he was insane. So businesslike in life and in his eagerness to please her (she joked with us later in a phone call). He had to taste every last part of her body. There was a lot of fact-checking and number-crunching along the way. Meticulous and careful brokering. She was swept up in his negotiations. And the inevitable merger, when it happened, was all one-sided. The opposite of the foreplay. He thrusted, he held back. He bought and sold. It was all about him, the inevitable. And of course he wore the toupée the whole time.

That was … amazing, he said.

She dabbed him. Again?

Oh my god, my heart. I have to work in two hours, you know.

Again, she said and pounced on him. By tomorrow, I think we'll play very well together.

How does it feel to be in bed again with the so-called junk bond king?

It's the sex I was afraid to remember, afraid to forget, yes, I think this is better than … She was going to say better than Jonjay. She said, … Apart.

We were worried, we said when she'd called. Like, really worried.

I realize Frank's my type, she told us after she explained where she was and apologized, and yes, we were right: she should have called earlier using Frank's Motorola.

I want a man with no time for me so I can be alone with my thoughts and work, she told us. And now I have him. He's perfect. He's here but not here. I don't know why I resisted so long. Oh yeah, he's married.

She called us around noon in Manhattan, alone in the giant penthouse suite. She spotted a stack of bills inside a folded piece of paper with her name written on it resting on top of the thirty-six-inch television. Then her heart sank, it sank all the way to the year 1981 and she was back in a sleazy hotel in downtown San Francisco with a married man. She was afraid to read it, but this note said:

Have a breathtaking day in the Big Apple.
Here's some madmoney for souvenirs
—Miss your body & soul already—
Meet me @ Bemelmans @ 9:30PM
I'll reserve a table for 2
- XOX Love, FF

Not poetry but at least nothing about a return to regularly scheduled programming. *Love, FF*, this note said. A late dinner. They were on West Coast time anyway.

It was past two in the afternoon before she finally left the penthouse. She decided to carry all of it, a thousand dollars in twenties, because she liked the weight of it, like a small animal, a hamster's worth of money, almost living inside her purse. And she was also afraid of being mugged. Manhattan was famous for its muggers. She figured that if she was mugged, this much money might save her from being knifed to death. The mugger would let her go. You can't knife someone you steal that much from. You knife the person who comes up short and begs and begs. The mugger might even count up the bills and say, *Gee, lady, thanks for carrying so much dough around. Now I don't have to mug anybody else tonight. You saved a few lives tonight, not just your own.*

That first day out in Manhattan with her purse throbbing with what Frank considered madmoney, spending hours in the esoteric shops that lined every block, she found out how easily she could blow a thousand dollars in this city. She stopped at every comic shop and stationery store, art supplies, pen specialists, used bookstores. She roamed the display cases of an upscale pen store where she threw down three hundred dollars on a few boxes of nibs and two pens from Japan. The way she drew *Strays*, all she ever needed was a sign painter's marker, but like any cartoonist she could not resist buying a fancy stylo. You never knew when you might discover an even more perfect pen or nib. Sometimes pen shops had ink that no art supply stores sold and this ink would be more supple and genuine in its flow than the regular art store India inks, and a cartoonist would be driven to buy dozens and dozens of bottles to stockpile.

After the pen and stationery shops, she visited the Metropolitan Museum of Art. Room after room mesmerized her until she felt too drunk or stupefied to absorb any more. She turned her attention to the masses of tourists. Sometimes the room of a gallery would be full of dumbfounded families. She would sit down on a Mies van der Rohe chair and draw. The young kids on dates, the wives who stood in front of their husbands and said, *That is my style*, and the stiff way students moved from artwork to artwork seeing their own reflections in the centuries of creativity. In every room there stood a security guard in a boxy black suit and black shoes with thick soles so that when one of the visitors got the insatiable urge to put a finger to the paint on the bright blue background of a Mary Cassatt, or touch the marble skin of a Greek sculpture, someone was there to say, *Please don't touch the artwork, ma'am,* or *sir*. Wendy was not someone who touched artworks. The same desire to breach the divide was there but she knew better. *Washington Crossing the Delaware* made an impression for its almost cartoonlike composition and for the ostentatious room in which it was kept, as if this relic was all that remained of the kingdom of heaven. And so she sat in front of this painting for a few happy minutes surrounded by tourists and the guard. She sketched her own *Strays* version of the painting, with Francis the rabbit at the helm of the rickety woodslat pontoon spooning through a river of soft ice cream. She added a velvet rope. And Buck in a black suit stood guard beside the painting.

With a Pentel she made some more drawings of Buck as a security guard in an art gallery. As visitors studied the art, she sketched them interacting with her dog.

In the Met's gift shop she saw Munch's *Scream* on magnets. Pens and pencils swirling with van Gogh's *Starry Night*. Calendars of Klimt, notebooks with Picasso's whores on the cover, Goya's hungry Saturn on umbrellas. T-shirt prints of Pollock splatters. Warhol posters of Marilyn and Mao. She had a market in these same products, magnets, shirts, posters, notebooks. Her *Strays* stuff sold in Zellers, Kmart, Consumers Distributing, and corner pharmacies. According to Frank, *Strays* sold more calendars than Cézanne and more magnets than Monet and Manet combined. After all, this was one of Frank's specialties—that is, Frank was known to guide his clients by the teeth all the way through their debt obligations. Even from the sidelines, after years of dealings with the man now her lover, Wendy could see how Frank operated. Her ubiquity was no stroke of luck. Her animals were in every home in America because Frank's ambition constantly stroked her *Strays*. Stroked them for all they were worth.

It was six o'clock. Still three and a half more hours. Back out in the street, she ordered a hotdog from a vendor and watched people enter and exit Central Park.

Behind the treeline, a wall of stone and brick buildings visible through a haze of icy fog. She took in the whole vista. After a while it was dizzying, the grandeur.

She took a brisk walk through a few acres of the park and came out having settled the hotdog, so she went to see the Frick Collection and spent the next two hours in its rooms sketching more visitors. It was near impossible to focus on the people, though, when every room was so full of priceless antiquities. It was like a No Manors of rare Oriental porcelains, one-of-a-kind Fragonards, Rembrandt's masterpieces, Goya's cruellest portraits, and the seductresses of Whistler, Renoir, and Ingres. Here, in the middle of New York, beside Central Park and the grand hotels and museums, were palatial rooms filled with the world's rarities. Objects of unfathomable value, protected by security guards in double-breasted black suits. The guards didn't show any interest in what they guarded, or in their own dapperness. Again she sketched them. That was part of the job, to watch the visitors, not the art. But at least one of these guards might have gone to the museums as a child and dreamed of one day keeping fine art from harm's way.

If Wendy were an artist, she might pitch Justine Witlaw a show of oversized portraits of the art museums' security guards, twice or three times human scale. But she was a cartoonist and must be contented with two- or three-inch boxes.

*

Snow—she hadn't seen snow in years—fell over the Upper East Side's streets outside the window to the sound of the white and black keys of a grand piano plucking out a ragtime rhythm, a hand jumping up and down the neck of a standup bass, and the neurotic sound of a clarinet. Jazz flew into her ears from the side of the stage at Bemelmans she couldn't see from her leather bucket seat in a booth the size of Venus's halfshell. The glass pools of ice turned the sidewalks outside into mirrors, black as the top of the jazzband's grand piano reflecting the red and green holiday lights strung up along every awning. Outside, billboards and sandwich boards. Inside, a playful watercolour mural by the eponymous French artist ran across all the walls of Bemelmans Bar where she met Frank for dinner, promptly at nine thirty. Frank was already there when the stork of a hostess dropped Wendy at the table, and once she'd sat down he kissed her deeply and publicly.

Ravishing, Frank said of her dress.

It's a Nolan Miller, she said, this fuchsia thing with the sea-green batwing shoulder pads, gold satin appliqué patterning across the chest, and a bosom-enhancing collar. How's my hair? I didn't have much time.

Wendy, your hair's the sexiest. Black Friday's not for another four days so let's just sit back, drink expensive French wine, listen to celebrity ragtime, and deliberately try to enjoy ourselves.

His hand dropped two felt boxes on the table with the deftness of a magician. One was a pale silver, the other a dark navy blue. He told her to open the pale silver box first.

Inside the pale silver she found an elegant slender Rolex with a shimmering wristband so thin it looked spun from a thread of unbreakable spider silk, dotted with dewdrop diamonds, and a timepiece that showcased a single eye-shaped blue-tinged diamond at twelve o'clock. On the reverse of the watch was the engraving *With love, FF 11/84*.

She kissed him. It's so beautiful. I never wore a watch before. But this is one I always will, it's so sexy. Should I open the second box?

You should, but it's for me.

Wendy laughed. You bought yourself a gift?

Inside was another Rolex. His and hers Rolexes. His had a chunky wristband made from silver and gold bricks that interlocked in a nonre-peating mosaic pattern. On the reverse she read *Let time stop for me when with Wendy.*

You know that I love you, he said. Of that I am certain.

Once an awareness of their surroundings returned to their conscious vision, Frank handed Wendy a leather portfolio. He said, there's some mouth-watering hors d'oeuvres.

Her eyes tried to focus on the menu. As she scanned each page her concentration fell between the words. She went up, up, and down, down the pages trying to make sense of the options: Green Turtle Consommé au Xeres, Essence of Fowl, Boiled Ox Tongue, Roast Stuffed Capon in Giblet Sauce, Fried Scrapple, Calves Head Piquante, Rumaki of Chicken Livers, Hearts of Celery ... Eventually she realized something was on her mind.

I guess there's nothing else we can do, right? They either come back on their own, or they don't.

He shook his head side to side and tapped her new Rolex, said, We're all on borrowed time.

Bemelmans was on the main floor of the Carlyle Hotel, a mountain of elegantly carved limestone. And the almost carbonated Royal Sterling caviar Frank had her try did go well with the gin-gin mule she ordered. Whenever Wendy put her head back on the leather-upholstered seat to rest her mind a little, she saw a lovely dog with shaggy ears and a long snout painted on the wall next to her head with a fine-tipped brush in the inimitable style of Ludwig Bemelmans, creator of the *Madeline* books. The mural wrapped along the wall behind them and the other guests, and featured a park scene with rabbits at lunch and ballerinas dancing, teams of dogs, ducks and geese, not to mention the famous blue nuns and girls in yellow hats.

These murals are so beauti-ful, Wendy said with a burp. He draws the same animals as me with so much less *anxiety*. His lines are singing and dancing when my lines are crawling on their bellies. Can I have my own bar named after me, Frank?

Ashbubbles? Sounds great. Will you do a mural?

Oh yes, I would love to paint a mural, she said.

Back in the twenties, Hexen Diamond Mistral had financed the construction of this hotel.

You're so stupidly powerful, she said. You can do anything. Do you want to be president someday?

I'd much rather be me.

Power is your cartoon, she said.

And cartoons are your empire.

Frank, my feet are sore and I'm drunk. Take me home to the hotel and bathe me.

Not yet, said Frank. Let's stay a bit longer. I ordered you another drink. I might get something to eat. I'm hungry.

All I ate today was a hotdog.

You like it here in New York?

New York is a giant underwater cave. It's Atlantis. Under a spell. The fish-people hurry in schools down the streets, eat, and spawn. I keep waiting to come up for air but never do.

What about Central Park? Isn't it something?

Yes, it's beautifully manicured. It looks like a picture postcard from every angle. Where I'm from, there's wilderness—dangerous, imperilling wilderness. There's no hungry bears or cougars in Central Park.

Maybe we shouldn't go back to San Francisco, he suggested.

Yes, let's not. Let's stay in that bed in the penthouse forever.

The setlist scattered frisky versions of standard Christmas fare jazzed up alongside dance classics up to and including Cole Porter. The rickety band on stage knew every ragtime number ever pressed onto a shellac plate through the twenties and forties, and even though the middle-aged musicians did not look like the real thing, they ripped into hot jazz with a scrambling-eggs tempo. The tunes stirred the room into motion, whole tables leaped to their feet and multiple couples of upscale tourists shimmied out onto the hardwood dancefloor to cut loose. The house lights dropped and spotlights formed. Small neons and candles in coloured glass jars lit the various corners and tables. Wendy saw not a single candy cane or Santa Claus or other holiday trinket in Bemelmans that wasn't classed up and posh.

On the crash of a cymbal she spilled some of her drink.

Frank slid the Rolex onto her wrist and clasped his hand around hers and launched her onto the dancefloor.

27

She wanted in on his secret kink. What really got him cranked up? What turned him on? Tell. Tell all. What was that special thing his body needed? Some men did not know for themselves and she had to seek out that kink. Frank showed her his.

Once the two of them were naked and on or near the bed he slipped off his new Rolex and asked her to take off hers and take them and wrap them around his erection. That was his kink. He wanted her to keep the two Rolexes there dangling from his prick as she went down on him. Then came the idea of penetrating her while he wore the Rolexes, so that's how he fucked her the rest of the night.

It was two or three in the morning and she lay naked and awake in the king-size bed on top of the sheets staring at the moon's pitted face through a window. Watching her. She imagined Buck about to land his spacepod on its inhospitable surface. Beside her, Frank yawned and scratched under his chin where beads of sweat had hardened into salt.

Are you tired? she asked when his eyes opened.

319

He checked his Rolex, back on his wrist. I'll sleep for another hour. On average, all I need is two or three to function.

What if you could *not* function?

A lot of money in the American economy is riding on my ability to function.

A lot of *what* is riding on your ability?

Money. Loans. Investments. Debt obligations. Multimillion-dollar portfolios are at stake.

How much?

Hundreds of millions. Possibly billions are at stake.

Would the entire world economy collapse?

Possibly.

Wow, really? The entire world? The whole globe collapses?

Could.

Because I fucked you *all night*?

She pulled off his watch, swung his and her Rolexes in the air, and caught them one after the other in her mouth.

What was it about the Rolexes that turned him on? The extravagance, the beauty, the way they made his prick look like a prince? The sound of them ticking against his balls? Who cares, it was a kink.

She concluded that Frank would never take off the hairpiece, but especially during sex—the hairpiece's ultimate mission might in fact be for sex, *this exact sex*, and then secondly for his impression on others at work, and who knows what else.

Frank was long gone by the time she awoke, around noon, on his side of the mattress.

She got the gist of what kept him so busy. Frank was financing Shepherd Media's cascading series of leveraged buyouts for a dizzying amount of copyright ownerships, and a simultaneously escalating sequence of high-priced corporate takeovers. Shepherd Media's bid to buy outright the full rights and ownership to practically every classic American film produced before Robert Kennedy's assassination was still confidential, Frank said. Nobody can know. One day it dawned on the big Hollywood studios that they spent millions every year just to store their old, falling-apart film reels in giant warehouses and a lot of their titles were literally turning to dust under the poor conditions. When Piper heard this he immediately went around to all the executives to make a bid. He wanted to own them, all the films, and the copyrights to them, so he could rerun them on his TV stations at no additional cost, and then also license old movies to other TV stations he didn't own to add profit, sell permissions for repertory film screenings, and make subdeals to turn the whole catalogue into VHS tapes and LaserDiscs and so on.

After a light breakfast she ordered up from room service of black coffee, boiled eggs, and bagels with a side of salted cottage cheese and sliced bananas, she decided to suck it up and tell Gabby Scavalda she was in New York.

Wendy, there's letters pouring in from every city in the country about that last strip with your raccoon, Gabby said the moment she heard her voice on the other end of the line. You're pissing off the liberals. That's bad. Liberals stop at nothing. Do you know what you're doing?

I'm in New York.

I thought you got in tomorrow? Come down to the office and let me fete you. If I could strut you around the office for *one* hour, I know the sight of you would gnaw at everyone around here's petty little Ivy League egos for weeks and weeks. *Strays* is Shepherd Media Syndicate's most lucrative strip, Wendy. No other strip's got your popularity. I mean, come on, who has ever heard of *One Night at a Time*, about a family of vampires? Yeesh.

People love those crazy vampires, Gabby.

Okay. It's a success. But.

I just want to sight-see, you know, go shopping, find myself in

321

unexpected places. Be inspired by museums and galleries, sculptures and pictures, people-watching.

Let's meet for dinner tonight. I know the perfect place. You're going to love it.

After they made plans the phone rang and Frank purred in her ear, Do you miss me?

You love the *phone*, she said.

I do, he said. But I love you more.

She asked him how many phones were at his desk and he said, A thousand and one.

Staying right on museum mile of Fifth Avenue had its virtues. One was that after she got some doodling done she had the rest of the afternoon to see the many collections of priceless works of art right next door to her hotel. Along this glamorous and timeless stretch of the Upper East Side, every other building contained priceless works of art and time-worn relics from antiquity. The sidewalk was festooned with holiday frippery. Every lightpost was trimmed with wreaths, and strung all along the fences and in the trees were colourful blinking lights.

Another season without a *Strays* Christmas special. Thirteen minutes in four years. Another nine minutes to go. Now she noticed a poster on the side of a newspaper box of Buck, Hägar the Horrible, and Snoopy. Now she noticed her characters in the window displays of some Park Avenue toy shops. Now she noticed herself noticing. It was strange to be famous, she decided, if that's what this was. In a cartoonist's case, famous was the blend of a personal, private dream with the real world. The proliferation of one's daydreams among the general populace.

The streets were clear but there was snow in the trees and grass in Central Park. Soon her cat Murphy would make his appearance in balloon form above the heads of thousands of admiring New Yorkers. For someone so auspicious, Wendy felt out of place in the Upper East Side. She didn't dress like the women here. She didn't walk correctly either. She slouched. Her manners were all intuitive.

Before her dinner date, she visited Macy's on West 34th to see their holiday trimmings, a classic touristy thing to do. But especially apt, she thought, considering the winter parade in a few days. Take in the animatronic displays, awe at all the departments decked out, sparing no expense, ribbons and silver boas wrapped around the load-bearing pillars, no limit to garlands from ceiling to floor. Glitter, tinsel, and coloured balls. A leafy green wreath the circumference of a train tunnel hanging in the entrance, a red velvet bow pinned to it the size of elephant ears.

The map said the third floor was the toy section. She landed at the top of the escalator and saw how fully the makeover transformed the entire floor into a kingdom of seasonal dreams for wishful and wealthy children in this Christmassy wonderland. Famous from commercials, from the movies, Macy's was even featured in kids' books, with its long, lavish aisles of toys. Macy's was a pilgrimage Wendy never realized she had to make.

A twelve-foot fuzzy Francis stood at the entrance to the toy section dressed as a rabbit Santa, with his ears poking out the sides of his red jingle-bell toque, greeting kids with an upraised front paw. His eyes conformed exactly to the way she always drew them, three horizontal lines like the ones depicting heaven in the *I Ching*. And as she walked down the first aisle she saw all the toys there were of her characters. She stretched her hands out to both sides, over the heads of children who sat on the floor staring at the packages of the *Strays* board games and rubber dolls, and let her fingers ripple over the sea of *Strays* merchandise, plush stuffed animals, hard plastic, and cheap wood versions of Buck the dog and Murphy the cat, Francis the rabbit, Raquel the raccoon, Nicki the parrot, even Sam the snake.

Why can't I? said a toddler with a plush Sam coiled around her arm to a rakish white-haired downtown father with hollow cheeks and his hands stuffed into a snow-wetted peacoat. Too expensive, the father said distractedly.

Wendy's shoulders bunched up over her earlobes at the sound of a screechy beckoning from the end of the aisle: Thomas, dear, here they are, tup-tup, those Transformers toys are *over here*. A boy in blue overalls threw a plastic-packaged Buck automaton (batteries not included) onto the bottom rack of *Strays* merchandise and got off his knees and raced along the tiles to meet the mothering source of that crow.

Just when she thought no child loved *Strays* or wanted *Strays* merchandise, a mother and daughter in matching outfits walked up to Wendy and said, Do you know who *this* is, honey? This is Buck's *mother*! Isn't that right? Tell my daughter you're Buck's mother. She loves your strip, but Buck's motherlessness breaks her heart.

I'm Buck's mother, Wendy said. She pulled out a Rapidograph and drew the girl a quick doodle, *Love from Buck's mother*.

Browsing at a comic shop downtown near Washington Square, she found a copy of a recent issue of *Raw* magazine with a folio dedicated to Art Spiegelman's ongoing *Maus* when by coincidence she ran into the very author, who laughed when he saw what she had in her hands and showed her what he happened to be about to buy: *her* latest treasury—*The Mayor Wins by a Hare*—as well as issue nine of *The Mizadventurez of Mizz Biz Aziz*.

That's fantastic you're in town, Art said. I was just feeling nostalgic for the coast, about to buy these books. Gee, it's like you sprung straight out of my thoughts.

Have you read that yet? Wendy said of issue nine.

No, but I hear things. Been waiting to get a copy.

You're in it. Biz paints the wake like something straight out of a Hammer film.

I'm flattered. I'm scared.

Eating a big slab of Hick's corpse? How does that sound?

Don't spoil it for me!

But it's kind of mean-spirited, don't you think?

Wendy ... Art paused. Wendy, that's the *point*! Unleash shockzilla on an unsuspecting public. Used to be Crumb's territory, now it's Aziz's. Bless her heart, hope it never stops beating. Did you tell her you think it's mean-spirited?

Well, in a way.

Art said he missed San Francisco. He told her he had a meeting with his editors at Pantheon in ten minutes and must leave—, but he asked if he could take her out for dinner that night with his wife, Françoise Mouly, and to meet another friend, a local cartoonist Spiegelman thought Wendy would love. She told him she was meeting Gabby for dinner at Gabby's favourite Italian restaurant, Spaghettisburg.

We'll join you, how's that? said Art, pulling a cigarette out of a soft pack in his breast pocket as he spoke. I know the one. Great handmade noodles. First-gen Italians in the kitchen, can't speak a world of English. Let us tag along. I'm sure Gabby won't mind.

Their table at Spaghettisburg was so small, Art Spiegelman joked if it was any smaller they'd be having an orgy. Gabrielle was nonetheless very pleased to see the group—the more the merrier. In Manhattan, conversation was hardly idle, it was one of the core food groups that sustained life on the island, and Gabby was a connoisseur. She knew Art and Françoise well enough but not to invite for an intimate dinner. Richard McGuire was a familiar face from parties, a handsome man she had never had the chance to speak to. Art introduced them all to him—Wendy, this is one of the top three people in New York.

I'm a longtime fan of the funny pages, said McGuire. First I read *your* strip, then *Bloom County, Doonesbury*, and *Nancy* in that order.

Wowza, said Wendy.

I'm her editor, said Gabby, extending her hand to pet his. Delighted to meet you. We've seen each other at parties, I think.

Have we? said Richard McGuire and took his seat again.

All through dinner McGuire's knees kept brushing against Wendy's. Sometimes he slid a shin between her legs to rub up and down her calves. She felt compatible with him, that was the thing. She wasn't used to withholding. His scalp was neatly bald, his trenchcoat smartly post-punk, tight-fitting black sweater and black jeans. An asexual curiosity, McGuire reminded Wendy of Tintin, another forever young ectomorph rebel hero type, like Jonjay, and come to think of it, like practically all the boys Wendy went out with—except for Frank.

Spiegelman and Mouly's new project with Pantheon was to publish book-format comics based on pieces first anthologized in *Raw*. They intended to publish a collection of Mark Beyer's *Amy and Jordan*. They also hoped Richard McGuire would do something for them.

Richard is an *outstanding* artist, Françoise told Wendy. You'd *love* his comics. So brilliant.

Thanks, but there's not much to them yet, Richard said and spooned winter vegetable soup into his mouth.

Feeling the toe of McGuire's shoe climb up her left calf, she said, Shimminy doo-bop!

Maus is a masterpiece by the way, said Gabby.

Well, shucks, said Art. Unfortunately it's not done.

Gabby shook her head. You blew the ears off this century's greatest cartoon icon, Art. The mouse, Art, the mouse. The next century will not live in a cartoon world dominated by the story of a single mouse's face. You've dislodged the centre of the cartoon canon. Not a Bugs Bunny or Fred Flintstone has come close to budging Mickey. But history will show that with the publication of *Maus*, Mickey's been sidelined as the one and only mouse relevant to comics. *Maus* is the maturation of the soul that Mickey Mouse tries to deny.

Oh you think such a thing is possible in a mouse-theistic world? said Art in a jokey lisp.

Françoise cried out, Stop! Let's talk about anything else in the world besides Mickey Mouse! Pour Art a drink. Truth or dare. Truth or dare, Wendy. Which do you choose?

Truth, said Wendy and instantly regretted it.

Okay, said Françoise with an almost cross-eyed expression, casually turning her neck as if balancing an invisible egg on the tip of her nose with ease. Have you had sex in the last twenty-four hours?

Everyone laughed. Gabby covered her face with a napkin and said, What a question!

In San Francisco, Wendy explained, sex is a game of Russian roulette nowadays. AIDS has the whole city terrified of their own genitals. The gay James Bonds of the Bay Area are dying or celibate. It's a chilly time for sex.

Here in Manhattan, too—, McGuire put his hand over hers on the table, —and yet we stubbornly continue to fornicate conspicuously and promiscuously.

Good for you, said Wendy.

Françoise said, You see the obits for these young beautiful boys in the *New York Times* and must read between the lines when they mention cancer, illness of some kind, or no reason at all. It's sad.

It's hard to get people in San Francisco to acknowledge AIDS, too, said Wendy.

Art stamped out his cigarette and reached in his pocket for another one. He lit the cigarette off the candle on the table. For a few minutes all the friends did was eat.

This *is* delicious, said Wendy.

Told you, said Gabby. Guess who recommended this place to me ... Vaughn Staedtler. I'm sad I missed his funeral. I heard he died of pneumonia ... Oh.

Oh, said Art. His shoulders fell. The other shoe just dropped for me, too. Do you know, Wendy, did he really die of ... ?

As they waited in silence for a second or it must have been a third bottle of wine, McGuire hit the men's room. As soon as he was out of earshot, Art and Françoise leaned right over the table and said to Wendy, So? Isn't he great? He's something special, isn't he? And handsome, too. You two seem to be hitting it off. Don't you agree, Gabby? Oh, if only you lived in New York. We've been trying to find someone perfect for Richard but he's had a string of bad luck. One girl fled to do a master's at Anglia. Another chick dumped him for Steve Martin. Imagine that.

She told them Richard did seem cool. There was some discussion about their affinities as well as where their trajectories might contrast nicely. She was a strip creator and he was more of a conceptual illustrator. Apparently he lived in a loft space with access to a rooftop that had a beautiful view of the city. He was also in a funk band.

Hey, come on now, what about *me*? said Gabby, sincerely insulted. Aren't I available? What is my problem? Doesn't he like women his own age? Jesus, I live right here in town.

Richard McGuire returned to the table and Art said smoothly, Yeah ... you're right. Seems most artists I know aren't getting any of the trickle Reagan promised was going to come down from his tax breaks for the wealthiest, surprise surprise.

McGuire joined the conversation he thought was happening. Freelance rates haven't changed in ten years. But rent is through the roof.

People are leaving Manhattan, Art said. In droves. I moved here just when everybody decided to ditch the place. Can't find a studio space in SoHo for under seven hundred a month nowadays. People keep moving to the sticks.

Or L.A., McGuire said.

Even Boston, where prices are still reasonable, artists are moving out, Françoise said as she reached over into Art's breast pocket for his pack of cigarettes. She rolled her eyes. I only smoke when I socialize and drink. I'll regret this in the morning.

America, McGuire said, is leveraging itself to the hilt. All these highrises going up are being paid for on borrowed dime.

Junk bonds, said Art. At a twenty-two percent interest. Fuck. What's he like, Wendy, the kingpin of American finance, the titan of debt? You must know Frank Fleecen, right?

Wendy hardly talks to the man, Gabby said. I handle most of our dealings with Frank. Frank could sell water to a whale, she said. But you'd think he was a vampire ghoul the way the media goes on. He's no evil force. Unlike most of Wall Street, he's generous. He's just what Reagan wanted, someone to turn the economy around and pull us out of the decline the Vietnam War cost us.

The fine art of usury, said Françoise with her fork spinning up a bale of noodles.

What's the word? said Wendy.

Usury? Loans at high interest, said Françoise. A way to make money out of thin air.

Art said, Usury is all of our histories, our shared debt. What came first, money or debt? What once was a pound of flesh in Shakespeare's day is now a junk bond on Wall Street and might tomorrow be a synapse. Money. The big blueblooded banks claim Frank's bonds are diluting the market with risky debt.

She asked if they'd already heard that Frank's wife and Jonjay were missing.

Françoise said they read the newspapers.

Where might Jonjay be hiding? Art wondered.

Who knows? said Wendy. Maybe nowhere.

Do you really think he might be dead? Art asked. Cheez Whiz, I remember I was just a kid when I first met him. Hasn't aged a day, that guy. Freaky. I doubt he's dead. It's not in his character to be dead.

Wendy squinted as if with a sudden migraine. Hold your horses, you met him when you were a kid? The more I know about Jonjay, the less I understand. When I met him I thought *we* were the same age.

He was the kid who teased the hobos, he could steal you anything you wanted, you name it, even a girl's underwear. Then with the usual poof, he vanished, next I hear it's ten years later he's in California, publishing groundbreaking comics, living with Hick and Biz, programming computers or something in the Valley. He was so deep in the California scene, he was the unofficial mascot.

Some artists *are* the epitome, said Françoise and sipped healthily from her wine.

Art said, Lately my impression of immortality is that it's all a matter of who holds the copyright.

Meanwhile Richard McGuire was attempting to pull off Wendy's shoe with his foot.

This spaghetti is outrageous it's so good, Wendy said after a last pasta coil wiggled its way in between her puckered lips.

I love this place, said Gabby.

Marcel Duchamp used to eat here every night, said Richard. His studio apartment was down the block. It was called something else then.

A natural pause in the conversation felt nourishing, not awkward. Salvation Army bells rang out from across the street and snow dripped off the restaurant's awning as if to remind them of the approaching season. Wendy admitted to us that in this moment, she regretted how another year had passed without her Christmas special on television, and wanted to avoid the subject of the holiday.

Did you get a chance to read Biz's comic yet? Wendy asked Art, who motioned that he couldn't answer right away with his mouthful of noodles.

Françoise says, Art brings it home, he says look what I've got. I know what I have in my hands now. I might be in these pages. For the first time in a long time I'm afraid to open this comic, but when I do I feel transported. I mean her ink like blackened pools of blood, all these intense shapes framed so neatly and cleanly within panels. There is some special kind of horror here. I think Pantheon should publish the memoir at some point, don't you? She touched Art's wrist.

Art agreed wholeheartedly, yes. Gabby agreed. Richard agreed. He said he showed his copies of her comix to everyone he thought would appreciate them. He'd picked up a lot of funk thanks to the references in Biz's comix over the years.

Françoise said, This issue is the culmination of her talents, I think. I found the narrative horrifying and beautiful, extremely emotional and cruel but not satirical. I can't get over her artwork—the intuition at play is amazing.

It is satirical, Wendy said. Biz sees the world as one big satire.

Art continued now that he'd swallowed: I was glad to see your assistants make appearances, too, and not just published cartoonists. I expect your friends to go far. Lots of talent. What were the other two names again? Mark I remember because I buy *Asemix*. And we have Aluminum Uvula's seven seven-inches—mostly for her cover art, I admit. The audio is extreme. Has she put out any more?

Aluminum Uvula is your assistant? Richard said. That's amazing. And she's in issue nine? Wow. I'll have to read it again. I love her stuff. It's so brutal.

Rachael's got a lot of guitar pedals but no guitar, Wendy said. A lot of microphones but she doesn't sing. She records a couple hours of noise a week in her bedroom. I'm not sure how she decides when to put out another single. It all sounds like beautiful hell to me.

Then there's Mark's noise-based comix, said Art as he drank from his ice water, alternately chewing and spitting ice back into the glass. Kind of a gallery crossover, what he's doing, except if I remember correctly he's a bit of a Looney Toon. We put an *Asemix* page in the last *Raw*.

Yep. He's the same wise drunk Daffy Duck. And Patrick's got lots on his plate. Lots of work for me. Lots of freelance gigs. He was doing in-betweens for Hanna-Barbera, and he draws at least a dozen monsters a year as spot illos for Dungeons & Dragons modules. It's his stack of failed attempts to get a strip in the papers that breaks my heart. I had it lucky from the get-go thanks to Gabby here.

And the other gal. What's her name?

Twyla Noon. Twyla is my faithful *accomplish*—I mean, she accomplishes everything, while the rest of my assistants pitter-pat and I dilly-dally.

Your assistants *actually* ate Hick Elmdales? said Richard. I'm going to have to read that issue again. I thought those silhouettes were … I don't know, satirical … Mort Walker stereotypes.

No, that's us. I've had a long time to accept that Biz was eventually going to publish this issue. I watched her put the pages together over the last few years. I don't really know what she's trying to *prove* … Someone might think she's serious.

Biz is, Art said. Biz Aziz is always serious. He laughed and said, All I know is, when Jonjay handed me a piece of flesh on a paper plate of the drawing I'd done, and told me to *eat*, I could not help but take that moment seriously. Felt real to me.

Françoise stamped out her cigarette in the glass ashtray. I think with this issue, she said, Biz has claimed Hick's death as a pivotal moment for underground comix.

We *should* publish these nine issues in our Pantheon series, said Art. I mean, why wait?

Wendy thought of all the disagreements she'd had with Biz over the years and she regretted them all.

Absent-minded doodles scattered the table. Whenever one of them had finished doodling, Gabby supplied them with a fresh napkin so that by the time everyone was ready to go, no one had to pay for the dinner— the waitress told them their drawings covered the check.

The chef was a big *Strays* fan. He came out of the kitchen to personally shake her hand.

*

Under single petals of snow falling from on high to the sidewalk outside Spaghettisburg they embraced one another and said goodbye until next time. Spiegelman lit another cigarette and said he was going downtown to see John Zorn perform *Cobra* at White Columns. Françoise was tired and would share a cab with Gabby, since they were going the same direction. Gabby kissed Wendy on the lips. Ooh, I hate you, she said. Have fun tonight.

McGuire shuffled to and fro on his flirtatious feet watching Wendy decide what to do next.

Art Spiegelman said, Oh, I almost forgot. I brought this for you—, and passed Wendy a Kodak film canister. I thought you might get homesick.

She opened the lid and smelled the weed bud lodged inside. Yummy, thanks.

Sorry it's not got the Elmdales extra kick, Art shadowboxed, but it *should* do the trick.

Sweet of you, she said and kissed him on the cheek.

McGuire waved at the cab as it drove away. He turned to Wendy and said, Listen, I've got a rack of wine back at my studio, and rolling papers, if you want to go smoke that. I'm just around the corner. Spitting distance. I don't know. Night's young? Want to come by? I mean, feels like the conversation just got started. Don't really want to end things so soon.

Thank you, Richard, it sounds like tons of fun, but I can't.

You sure let me play friendly for a while. Gave me the impression you were into having some laughs.

I love laughs. I thought you were being funny. My whole life has been about laughs on top of laughs. I love meeting new people, and laughing with them, I really do.

Oh, that's it.

And I never had a regular boyfriend my whole life.

Never? But I heard you and Jonjay were an item—.

No. God, no. Everyone thinks that for some reason. Not since I was a teenager did I think he was my boyfriend. A relationship with Jonjay's more like signing up for a six-week aerobics class that meets once a week for an hour. After the class is over you instantly start getting fat again.

You don't think he loved you?

Oh, we loved each other, yes. Like best friends. Like incestuous siblings. But I had a lot of competition. He loved a lot of people. Lots loved him. I once caught Jonjay kissing his own reflection in the mirror. You understand? Jonjay loves everyone he meets for what they reveal to him about himself.

He's alive? McGuire asked.

Until they find his skeleton.

You really are beyond beautiful. Richard McGuire moved a sproing of hair off her forehead for a clear view of her eyes. So let's just go back to my studio and draw drunk. I love drawing drunk, don't you?

Sloppy weather, sloppy, sloppy, I do hope this blizzard's cleaned outta here before the parade on Friday. The doorman to the Zabriskie Hotel welcomed her in from the blowing snow. Grew up in it don't like it. Don't like the cold.

Oh gosh. She leaned on his shoulder. I must be so drunk. I didn't even notice how hard it's schnowing. Wonderful to shee you. Night-night, she said and without the money to palm him a tip she drunkenly kissed him.

When she asked the concierge if Frank had returned yet, the man said, No, ma'am, Mr. Fleecen had not, and, instead of any messages, offered her freshly steeped tea. This is my first trip to New York, she said, sipping orange pekoe from the mug he gave her. I think a very talented man hit on me tonight. What do you think of that?

The concierge pulled his long, bony hands out of the pockets of his black velvet vest and wiped the black curls of his black hair. He shrugged from ear to ear and said in a cordial tone that these men's come-ons might reassure her at the very least that Mr. Fleecen wasn't alone. She kissed him, too.

In the elevator, the elevator man blushed and grinned at his shoes as he took her to the penthouse. She leaned against the wall the whole time, blinking an eye, singing *I Feel Love*. According to his brass nametag his name was Baa.

Baa? she said.

Yes, ma'am?

Oh, nothing, thank you. She kissed him goodnight. Boy, was she drunk.

Could he smell the—she didn't ask, or did she?—the fact she was pissdrunk?

No, ma'am, said Baa.

In the penthouse she opened the film canister and took a whiff. Skunk. Went outside, rolled, and smoked a joint on the balcony under the one or two stars visible over Manhattan. A moment later she leaned away from the patio furniture and vomited excitedly into the pot of a trembling ficus.

The snow fell in countable numbers. She went back inside. Turned on the television. *Hostages in ...* Not that she was lonely.

His voice woke her up.

I'm a billionaire, he said and touched her shoulder. She'd fallen asleep on the sofa in the living room.

Gross. You smell like wall-to-wall carpet. Stale coffee. Hairspray. Cigar smoke. Cheap cologne. Sweet alcohol.

I'm stinking rich, he said.

Pee-yew. And no flowers? Some new boyfriend you are. Go take a shower and wash off some of your corporate swill.

What about you? *You* reek of nicotine. Did you smoke a pack of packs?

Frank carried her to bed and lay down beside her, ran his hands and face through her hair. Mm, wait a minute, did you *score*?

Pfft!

I mean weed, calm down. Gee, you *did* have a good night. You're all paranoid. When did you get home?

Hours ago. Or minutes. No idea. I already puked. I can't get the smell of Art's cigs out of my hair. I'm drunker than a sack of rocks.

I can tell.

They made love in a manner she later described as more physics than physical—he felt her up like an abacus, and she lay there under him and watched as he strummed all her beads back and forth, up and down across her body's rails, she was numbers adding up under his hands. Her math was so bad in grade four her teacher scolded her too many times to keep count because she never did the homework. He made love in sequences and patterns. Maybe this Euclidian approach was what she loved. Maybe she loved the new pace. She wasn't grinding her teeth. She realized this all of a sudden in the middle of an orgasm.

No more bruxing.

For her this was a true sign. This deserved a *Dear Dr. Pazder* ... She might actually be in love with this money manager. If she lay awake for a few more hours beside him in bed after a fuck like that, with a pen or pencil in her hand and a yellow legal pad in her lap, and doodled comic strip ideas while he snored, then that was her idea of early emerging domestic bliss.

He left another note on top of the TV. It was wedged in with a dozen longstemmed roses.

Wow, it's 6 AM. That's the best fucking sex & longest I've slept <u>in years</u>!
I don't know if you know the spell you've got me under.
You are the reason I am crushing Wall Street.
Meet me @ the Hexen offices today, OK?
I'll introduce you to the staff.
Strictly professional, my love, xo, FF

28

Wow. And, *Strictly professional, my love, xo.* Out on the deck, the snow was gone, and having melted off the streets, left Manhattan's skyline glimmering in a white and silver mist. The storm was sure to be a memory by the time of the Macy's Thanksgiving Day Parade two days from now. Thinking about *FF*, she put on a pink cashmere sweater with a low V-neck, jeans, and a pair of sneakers. The phone rang and she ran across the room to answer it with nobody in her mind but Frank as she fell across the sofa and kicked her Adidas up and said into the phone's ivory mouthpiece, Baby, baby, with the Rolex prick.

What the—, a growly man said, who the fuck are *you*?

Weh—ah, she said, bit down hard on her lip and squeaked.

Sue? Is that *you*? I *knew* something was up. Motherfuckers. I swear. You dirty cunts. Goddamn you *both*, you conniving, mendacious, double-crossing white-collar ... Is Frank there? Put him on. I try every fucking number I have for the guy and I'm down to the last of my disconnected when you pick up. Sue? Are you there? You listening? Now I know he's in New York. Don't lie to me, Sue. They won't let me in to see him.

Wendy's hand was at her throat.

The man on the other end of the line shouted. You know who this is. Tell him Kravis called.

She ran to the elevator and then ran through the lobby.

Hallo, she said as she hurried past the concierge. No tea or coffee for me this morning, thanks. Hallo, she said to the doorman as she hoofed it down the stairs, looks like you got your wishes, the snow's all melted.

Yeah, it's true, he said and waved a hand to the sky.

She ran around the block to burn off the call from Kravis and last night's drunk, and soon enough she was panting, so she went inside a stationery store she hadn't seen on previous walks. That was the end of running. For ten dollars she bought a brushpen imported from Japan and a pad of bristol board.

In the window of an upscale clothier's on Park Avenue, she saw a mannequin dressed in a black-and-white skintight dress and matching white turban, and, not normally taken with high fashion, realized she was wildly underdressed to be on her way to visit Frank at the Hexen office for the first time. A turban, she thought, she had always wanted to wear a turban.

A turban for women? Wendy asked the salesgirl as she stared at herself in the mirrors, and the girl assured her this turban was designed by Travilla. Travilla, Wendy said. Well, then. She bought the entire ensemble and wore it out the door.

The nearest diner had a neon sign outside that read *Chambers*. Inside it smelled heavily of tobacco and stale fry grease. A long counter facing the kitchen serviced men smoking cigarettes over plates of pasta and hamburgers, and two rows of booths along the window where men hunched over the Formica tables in conspiratorial powwows. She took a booth with a view of the neighbourhood.

Wendy looked up from sketching with her new Japanese pen and asked for a chocolate milkshake. She felt a bit overdressed in her turban. But she was used to that.

Does that say cranberry sauce? Wendy asked regarding options.

Holiday special. The waitress smacked her lips.

Sure okay, turkey sandwich with the cranberry sauce and stuffing and all that goodness, she said, then,—Shit fuck!

Chris Quiltain sat down opposite her in his chocolate brown corduroy suit and yellow shirt and ordered an open-faced Reuben and a Coca-Cola with lots of ice. He sat back in the pleather booth and smiled.

You look good, he said. Kind of glowing. Love the turban. Very chic. You must be excited about the Macy's Parade. That's why you're here, right?

Crap my pants, why don't you. You're the opposite of my friend Jonjay. He's never around and you're always.

I'm with the New York DA, Wendy—this is my second home now. He put his elbows on the Formica and formed a steeple with his fingers Tell us what you know, Wendy. Time is running out. Cut a deal with me and the DA and the whole enterprise collapses like a puff of smoke. Thanks to the one moral soul who cuts a deal with the good guys. That's *you*, by the way.

Shimminy doo-bop, and just like that it's all over? Good guys versus bad guys? She tore the end off the seal over her accordion straw and blew the paper prophylactic straight at Chris's face. He laughed. She asked, Does your snitch wear a wire and all that goodness?

For the person who wants to flip and save themselves a prison sentence, yes. But we don't have that person yet. We're hoping someone will cooperate. But Wall Street is a tight fraternity.

How often do you find a turncoat?

He drummed his fingertips against the Formica tabletop patterned with overlapping boomerangs.

Her Thanksgiving sandwich arrived and was delicious, who would have thought turkey dinner would work so well between toasted buns? She finished the sprig of parsley on her plate. That's how hungry she was.

I know a hotel around the corner, Chris all of a sudden suggested once his plate was nearly as cleared as hers. He took her hand and pet it top and bottom as though he did not want to wait a moment longer.

Stop that.

I could be good for you. I'm in a good position with this case to make a name. There's a chance I'll meet the president.

She ate the last of the french fries off his plate. The president, eh? That's not too shabby.

Chris said, I thought we had something.

We had my grief, Chris. Vaughn was a friend, a hero, a disillusionment. Grief is one of my favourite aphrodisiacs. You're handsome, interesting, more than slightly creepy. We tried to take advantage of mutual need, no thanks to Sparky.

You're fascinating, Wendy, how you walk through life being given everything you could ask for. You're so used to the feeling, you don't know what you want.

That's too bad for you, she said and desperately resisted scratching an itch under her cool new turban.

The waitress walked by and Wendy pulled at her apron and ordered two more Thanksgiving sandwiches with everything, plus another chocolate milkshake, all in a brown paper bag to go.

Chris slammed his palms on the table where his plate used to be. I want you to flip, Wendy. I want to take you to Rudy Giuliani and make you our star witness, our whistleblower. Our hero. I want you to be the brave one to crack open the vault of lies.

I'm just waiting for my takeout.

Don't you have an inkling? Fleecen, Shepherd Media, Lupercal, the junk bonds, the media, the plastics? Central America? Do you happen to know what Frank is up to while he's in New York?

Frank is in New York?

Chris squinted at her. Yes, we know that he is. Strange your being in the city while your *close personal associate* greenmails half Wall Street in the fastest shell game on the block. You know what he's up to? I mean, through all his allies? How you make your money?

By shaking the money tree? Look, doll, I'm here for the parade. This is all news to me.

He plans to crush Betamax out of existence, that's *one* ongoing example. Scoops up a majority of its shares this month through his secret allies, then he can hold the company for ransom to its own shareholders. All because his client Piper Shepherd has a deal in place with a competitive rival, the Victor company, the makers of the Video Home System tape cassette. Frank greenmailed the industry in an attempt to get rid of Betamax. Likely one of the greatest white-collar criminal masterminds the modern world has ever known. He's using the pensioners' fund and war veterans' fund and he's using homeowners' loans and rigging the bond market to advance his conspiracy. Evidence of insider trading all down the line, from the hedge funds, private equity firms, arbs, to the salesmen to the portfolio managers of the savings and loans. A big circle jerk. Are you listening?

I'm a cartoonist, not an informant.

I know why you won't turn. You're laundering money for him, aren't you? We've seen bank records. Listen, come clean. Help us nab Frank and we can help you.

I don't know one smidgen about Wall Street, or Law Avenue for that matter. Alls I know's doodles. Doodles Road. That's where I belong. I'm going to find a way to make a gag out of all this, *and you.*

Yet another beautiful man interrupted them. This one's hazelnut skin was covered in a satin sheen of perspiration, and he wore only a muscleshirt and jeans under his dirty white apron. Are you Wendy Ashbubble, by any chance?

She touched her turban. Why yes, yes, I am, she said generously. What can I draw for you? Buck or Murphy? You remind me of Buck.

Your takeout is ready, he said.

Help us ... Quiltain took the cuff of her jacket in his fist. Help us indict Frank Fleecen.

She must have given them her name. Beet red, she took the bag from the dishwasher and told the waitress to put the whole thing on Chris, then pulled out of his grip and ran out into the street.

Make sure nobody tails us, she told the taxi driver. When she checked the traffic behind them, his face was right up against the window. Heart beating wildly, she was losing her mind, overwhelmed by the smell of cranberry sauce and gravy on her sandwiches wafting up from inside the warm paper bag on her lap.

We had this idea for the opening shot of her Christmas animation. She was breathing heavily into the phone as she listened to us update her, her way of soothing her nerves after the latest encounter with the SEC agent. The idea we pitched her required we paint a panoramic background of the entire vacant lot where her characters lived and parts of the neighbourhood surrounding it, big enough to zoom in and out of without requiring a cut, and we would use the existing character animation over top of this new celluloid. The thing about animation is that every frame is an edit, so the trick is to make it look continuous. Our solution was to source a massive sheet of celluloid the size of the living room so the rostrum camera could sweep its way over the world of the characters in a kind of rolling dolly shot that zooms in to the character's level and zooms out again to a bird's-eye for full effect. We compared it to the effect of those long, unedited shots in Coppola's and Altman's films, and Orson Welles before them.

Timeout, Twyla. Did you say for the opening scene? Holy crackers, get Rachael on the line … Rachael, what in blazes is going on? Twyla gave me palpitations just now. My brains are quivering like jelly. I leave for two days and you all want to scrap the beginning and start all over? For a fancier background? We're halfway there. Thirteen minutes. *More* than halfway. No time to turn back.

Wendy was calling us from a payphone next to the elevators in the bustling marble lobby of Hexen Diamond Mistral's office on Wall Street. In a minute she would go up and see Frank, taking a surprise bag of seasonal takeout to share. The sauces were beginning to drip through the bottom of the paper bag.

Delicately, we went over the rationale for this ambitious new idea. The complexity would reveal itself in the final angle as the camera swoops up to follow Nicki the funky parrot over the vacant lot to see the world from a bird's-eye view, this painted landscape twisting and turning—the magic trick would click for audiences. Yes, challenges lay ahead. But the disorientation of the idea was the perfect way to set the mood for the rest of a story full of reversals. If we worked hard we would be done the painting by the time she got home—a lie we firmly believed. All we would need to do after that was reshoot the footage.

How *is* Biz? she said, changing the subject.

Once this week we slept through the night, and at breakfast we all realized it was because Biz had not woken us up screaming. She still slept in Wendy's room, but had started going upstairs to her own suite to make headdresses for her upcoming drag show, a loose adaptation of Rimbaud's *A Season in Hell.*

Biz is a New Orleans of one, Wendy said. Look, I gotta run, my sandwiches just spilled all over the marble floor.

Wendy heard the four o'clock bell ring on Wall Street and was taken back body and soul to elementary school. Amid the curses and howls and demands and pleas of the brokers and salesmen on the office floor, a sudden and total silence preceded the bell, as all the brokers' phones stopped ringing, and all the shouting matches paused, and at precisely four in the afternoon, a five-second fire alarm trilled through every room, cubicle, and hallway on each of Hexen Diamond Mistral's seven leased floors at the top of the Masonic Bankers Trust Company Building. The entire office of Hexen Diamond Mistral blew up into celebrations. Paper flew into the air as if typewriters had exploded. Whooping men celebrated their earnings, twisting and turning their secretaries in the air screaming, *Payload!* Spazzes. Some fellow at the far end of a row of cubicles in a blue shirt with a white collar and suspenders pushed his chair out from his desk, pulled off his tie, and started to run towards them down the aisle, screaming Hexen was up *twelve*—four points over the market. I'm a millionaire, he gagged and, after turning a lemony green, fainted straight off his feet. Five minutes later, as the festivities dissipated and the eye of the party's storm passed over the group, Frank whispered to Wendy, *I wish I could kiss you.*

Go for it, coward.

But at that moment Frank's cellphone began to chirp and he said, Hell—hello? *Not now.* And simultaneously businessmen of all stripes started to crowd around them and, buzzing with the queasy adrenaline of newfound riches, congratulated and thanked Frank and paid homage to the man with the Midas touch. Then another round of mentally deranged screams and howls interrupted them further when the Barrie-Teynte Index was announced. Bankers, cellphones, real phones, computers, and all the men started howling and barking again.

Arf arf! said Wendy. Aroo! Aroo!

Okay okay, I get the picture, Frank said. You think we're all greedy shitbags.

Aren't you going to answer your phone?

He answered the phone again. No, not now. Call me back tomorrow.

He said to Wendy, See? You're my focus. Now let me introduce you to some of my favourites among this crew of some two thousand pirates who made this one of the biggest days in Hexen's history and the biggest score of my career.

Frank studied a subordinate's computer screen. He said, According to the Barrie-Teynte Index, the high-yield bond market closed at a record high volume today.

Point five one, Frank told her, as if these numbers were the pride of a father. All thanks to the hurricane of my deal with Shepherd Media hitting ground on the market this afternoon.

Frank told the story of how a hundred years earlier, Hexen, Diamond, and Mistral were just three banking men with a polio-riddled scrivener in a single office on the ground floor of 14 Wall Street, investing and hypothecating money. But slowly, year by year, bond sale after bond sale, trade after trade, the bankers moved up from the literal ground floor until, a century later, here they were: Hexen Diamond Mistral leased the entire top seven floors of the Bankers Trust Building and employed over two thousand people. The Dow Jones, Frank told her, was at a hundred and five when the Bankers Trust was constructed, and now we're surrounded by skyscrapers to scale with today's Dow at *twelve hundred*. In effect, Hexen paid up front for these skyscrapers to be built, as the tallest of them were built on the largest loans. Right here. Right here in this office tower, the American boom was born. There's more money being made here, bought here, sold here, and cashed in here than anywhere else in the world. All the casinos in Vegas combined make a tenth of what's earned in this office. Whoever makes the market on Wall Street controls America's free market.

You haven't said if you like my turban. Wendy cocked her head.

You look beautiful, you do. I've never seen you in such an exotic outfit. You're sexy in that turban.

You like it? She tipped her hips and touched the weave on her head.

It suits you. You're not interested in my story, are you?

Of course I love your *origins*, Frank. Your *world* tour and story. That's why I wore *this*. To turban you on.

You do. You do, Frank said.

Who doesn't heart New York? she smiled and clicked her heels. She gave his arm a squeeze. I'm wanting less bonds and more sex.

He covered his heart with his hand and pinched his knees together. You just made me go hard.

I thought money made you hard.

This, right here where you are standing, Wendy, is the centre of the free market. Don't you think that's sexy?

Yeah, but can a free market have a centre?

And instead of pushing her towards some quiet place behind a Xerox machine or into an empty cubicle so he could ravish her top to bottom, Frank dutifully introduced her to this fatted, stained-tie-wearing inscrutable bonds salesman and that ulcerous, squawking belligerent cyclops, the day trader. This cursing yammering young portfolio manager, that hammer-fisted derivatives analyst concussing his own forehead over a bad play on a brokerage. Frank said, Don't worry, Karl, I'll cover you. Put a reassuring hand on the middleman's shoulder-padded suit and then moved Wendy along to another junk associate sucking on the tip of his tie. How are you, Rice? Frank waved a hand and the man shrunk away as though Frank was about to slap him.

Frank's a sheer genius, the men all agreed as they snapped their suspenders and scratched at the telephone sores on their chins.

It's gold at the price of graphite, another man told Wendy of the bonds business.

A thousand and one men in the choir: Frank is a financial genius. A genius. A genius. A radical. Rearranging the particles of American finance.

I'm serious, said an old hypothecator.

Ursurious? I'm serious! said Wendy, and it took the traders a moment to laugh. I just learned that word the other day.

Fenton and Outcault, two master gurus of the old school, Frank said. Outcault was black. Fenton was pale green.

These shitbags can sell an icecube to an Eskimo, Frank obsequied, sell sand to a camel.

Frank's the shitbag who can sweet-talk a songbird into flying straight down his throat, said Fenton or Outcault.

Shitbag? said Wendy.

Frank shrugged and said shitbag was a cultural thing, term of endearment in the offices on Wall Street.

That is us, two sclerotic old shitbag hypothecators, said Fenton, pushing back his chair and bowing from that seated position. He was the latter-cubicled of the gentlemen, and he pointed to Wendy with an orange finger covered in Cheetos dust, then waved her off just as soon as she approached him. Debt-nabbit, he said and squinted his glasses up the bridge of his nose, is this *really the* cartoonist we sell so much of? Well! Pardon my French, *well*. Be still, my bleeding pacemaker. You're *the* girl? Never remember to look at the section with the comics, sorry. Can't keep track of which one's Mutt and which one's Jeff.

Okay, now let me ask *you* a question, Wendy said to the two gentlemen. You both strike me like good-natured, well-raised, and intelligent men with loads of success and experience under your belts.

If by success and experience you mean bankruptcies and near suicides, then, yes.

So what makes Frank here so different from you two? I know he's super. But tell me why he gets all the attention.

Outcault said, You don't go around wondering why you aren't Frank. You go around praying he's on your side. Having Frank in the office is like being in possession of a dragon.

Fenton said, But listen, here's an example of Frank's work ethic. A lot of financing is billable by the hour, okay. So the more hours of work, the more you bill, the more money you pump from the client. Around here we're always competing to see who's racked up the most billable hours in a week, a month, a year. The more the better, right, okay. So Frank here, he is the man. Soon as he gets his hands on some client accounts, his hours are absurd. He's the Neil Armstrong of billable hours. Billing an average of ninety hours a week. *Average.* Frank always billed more hours to his clients than *anyone* in the office. *Anyone.* And it was no bullshit. He was here before anyone and he left after everyone. He had three shifts of secretaries—like doctor's interns—to keep up with his hours. So one day he billed a client thirty-seven hours in a twenty-four-hour day because he worked without a break through multiple time zones en route from a client's many homes and offices. Thirty-seven hours in a twenty-four-hour day. No one had ever billed thirty-seven hours in a twenty-four-hour day. No one had ever even thought of that, let alone had the bullballs to pull that.

Moving on from memory lane, said Frank. Enough flattery. And all this from the first man in the firm to crack a million in sales in a single day.

In eighteen ninety! Fenton said with a dismissive wave of his hand. In more recent times, I was the one that made us all a fortune holding on to all those oil stocks through the seventies.

Oh, wait, before you go, said one of these two. He picked up a contract from his desk and handed it to her. Miss Wendy, could you sign on this dotted line here and save me UPSing it all the way to Frisco and having you UPS it all the way back.

Wendy made a show as she adjusted her glasses to read the fine print. Okay, says here this is for Lupercal Incorporated and subsidiaries. Seven, eight, twelve, twenty-seven pages, gee-golly, Wendy said and shot Frank a glance. Should I read through this? I mean—can't just sign. What's this contract for?

Another bona fide deal with our lucrative friends over at the ever-expanding empire of Lupercal Incorporated, said the old man. This is another Central American one—says you agree to let Lupercal's brand-spanking-new factories in Colón, Panama—all set to flip the switch and start making all your future beach toys, keychains, wallets, hairbrushes, lunchpails, and—list goes on and on …

So she did sign.

I know kids high-five these days, said Fenton, but I've got osteoporosis in my hand.

Now with that all taken care of, said Frank in a singsong voice that placated the two wizened hypothecators, shall we move on from the ol' fogeys?

Seems like the more contracts I get the less work I need to do, she said.

There's always more work, said Frank. My father said, If work doesn't pile up on your to-do list then you obviously aren't working hard enough.

The cellular phone hanging from Frank's hip rang once, and he pressed a button and said, I'm not going to answer that.

Not? What's the point of a cellular phone you never answer?

You're here. I never answer a chirp when you're with me.

Then put down the walkie-talkie, why don't you? Toss the brick.

A pinstripe-suited man with a broken nose and long sideburns, constantly laughing and nodding as he cupped one chin over the receiver of his phone as he shook Wendy's hand. Men with skin like boiled lobster shell and a vascular approach to conversation that depended more on hand signals than a high vocabulary. Side bets, poker games, day trades, bond sales, calling each other shitbags, never walking or leaving one's desk except to piss, shit, windmilling their arms around like drowning men trying to save themselves from death with a telephone cord and a Rolodex, the habits of sorely neglected children, gambling circles formed as soon as the market closed, impromptu, around a deck of cards or handful of dice. A bonds executive who introduced himself as Glassman and wouldn't let her hand free of his two-clammy-fisted shake greeting her.

Is *this* the Replicant body I keep hearing about in magazines? Did I say that out loud? laughed Glassman. And the turban, nice touch. Gee, I hope I'm not embarrassing you.

Wendy sucked in a breath of Ruthvah.

We must be going, Glassman, but we'll catch up later, said Frank and ushered Wendy into another whole wing of desks starting behind a glass wall.

That guy is a tit-talker, she told Frank.

A what? Glassman? He's a top seller. Probably earns half a million a year.

Yeah? He told me I had a Bally's body. Are you jealous?

As soon as I find out what that means I'm going to knock the stripes off his shirt, said Frank and mashed a fist into his palm. Want me to fire him?

Forget Glassman. Forget them all. Let's ditch this male chauvinist palace for somewhere more horizontal, where things are more equal between the sexes. My hands all over your naked body. I'll give you head and vice versa.

Can't now, no, god, no time for— Don't torture me, said Frank, motioning for the wristwatch on the end of her slender arm. Time's a-ticking. This is a big celebration for us. We're making history today, Piper and Hexen and me and you.

She was affronted by Frank's rectitude, but let herself be led towards an onslaught of silver- and gold-pinstripe suits with astronautical shoulder pads, and the swearing, sweating men who wore them.

All these highstrung Manhattan businessmen chewing on their tongues and cuticles as Frank flirted with the idea of learning a few of the names of these minions, for the sake of illustration, as he toured Wendy through his vast empire. Suits in metallic colours, as if sewn with aluminum thread. Every fashionable shoulder pad on the market and ample widths of the wing-tipped yoke on the blazers. Invisible clouds of Ruthvah. They applauded the dealmaker, the rainmaker, paid homage to the grand wizard from the West Coast in the room. Frank. Men sold bonds for a scrap metal consortium because of Frank, men bought and sold bonds for a maker of vitamin C, sold plastic, sold hotels, sold milk, sold salt, sold sugar, sold maple syrup reserves, men in blue shirts with white collars and skinny ties, red pinstripes and white suspenders like clowns screaming *millions and millions!* to whoever was on the other end of the phone, phones galore, ringing, pulsing, thrumming, flashing, men hustling potato chips on the market, *Strays* merchandise, pork, mortgages—all the shitbags of capitalism, stock traders, bond salesmen, underwriters, clerks, and secretaries—all because of Frank. The market was closed but the workday was far from over. Computer screens and reams of paper and cursing shitbags was all she could see. A rack of telephones flashed like flight simulators on every desk with multiple conversations going as multiple others waited on hold as the men finger-punched more people for two-way, three-way, seven-way, nine-way conference calls. Hands-free headsets. The men dialed numbers they ferreted out of the plumage of giant Rolodexes that perched like birds on every man's desk. Rolodexes with the business cards of owls, vultures, hawks, eagles, Wall Street's predators and carrion hunters. Grey massage balls in the men's hands squeezed into merciless oblivion only to bounce back to original shape. Sell. Buy. Warner Brothers. Lupercal. LBO. IPO. TKO. Her mind kept flashing to the criminal conspiracies Chris Quiltain planted in her imagination. Chris's voice in Chambers restaurant: *Help us ... help us indict Frank Fleecen.*

Frank swept her into a bright boardroom the size of a tennis court. The room was full of executives standing around an enormous black mahogany table laid out with hors d'oeuvres. The name partners and the rest applauded her and Frank as they made their entrance to the private party. Waiters in penguin suits floated among them and made a genteel display of offering her wine spritzers in glass flutes and caviar in porcelain spoons.

Piper Shepherd was the first to greet her. She congratulated him. You look fine, Wendy, just fine. Belle of the ball, we used to say. But you know who you remind me of with that turban? That babe Victoria Principal on *Dallas*. Really.

But with tighter curls and a more outgoing nose? said Wendy.

Seriously. You know who I mean? Those uh … The reason I still watch *Dallas* ha ha. But really, my dear, what brings you to New York? said Piper, and kissed her once on the cheek. His breath unfortunately smelled of an unflushed toilet from the cock-sized cigar in his hand nearing its butt.

I'm here to watch my characters float past me in the Macy's Parade. But Frank heard I was in town and invited me to come celebrate your whopping big deal.

Oh, the parade, yes, of course. My granddaughter Coleco is so thrilled to carry one of your cat's tether ropes with me tomorrow morning. Sam?

Murphy.

Thinks she's the luckiest girl in the city. Are you holding a line, too? Will I see you bright and early at the rendezvous?

Oh, no, I couldn't. I'm too anxious, said Wendy. I just want to be among the fans and spectate.

My sentiments exactly. I demanded my stations show no closeups of me.

Did you say Coleco?

My granddaughter's father, this man who is my son-in-law, is the next Greenberg in line to inherit the Coleco fortune, its Cabbage Patch dolls, all its toy franchises, including his favourite, the Coleco system for video games. Tell you a secret, Wendy, I worked a lot of overtime to earn as much of a mattress as this. I don't know what my son-in-law did to deserve his.

I love a good mattress, said Wendy. I'm stuffing up one right now.

Come, drink up, drink up, and before the men start hounding you, let me show you the view. Piper guided her by the small of the back to the wall of windows overlooking a city of skyscrapers. He pointed with his cigar to the tallest, most modern glass buildings. All that money flows down from the tops of those expensive skyscrapers into the valley, much of it into Frank's pockets these days. Into the growth of my empire.

She watched Piper put his whole body into it. Frank's my favourite credit card. He's better than American Express or Visa or any of them. I just paid for the reels and the rights to virtually every movie made during the golden age of Hollywood. I bought my childhood at pennies on the dollar. Thanks to *that* man, the credit king, I am in possession of an uncountable fortune. All I can say is *fuck*. Possibly I'm crazy, but history's the judge, right? I'm here to bet the farm, Wendy.

Too bad, I love farms, Wendy said and toasted her flute to his.

You're right, Wendy. Farms are great. But a farm's just land. And land is hell. One life's all we get. Don't be tied to the earth, I've learned. Follow your heart and soar with eagles. What is a tragedy is what happened out *there*, Piper said, and Wendy nodded without being sure where *there* was yet. Ever since Sue and that fellow. Shakes. Insomnia. I sought therapeutic counselling. That's right. Not a cheap fellow either. But Freudian, so. I see what the loss did to Frank, too. Mind you. Everyone's different. He poured himself and all his sorrow into this godzilla deal. It's remarkable to see his stoicism first-hand. How are *you*? You seem okay about your boyfriend.

Not my boyfriend. A friend. More of a brother. Cain and Mabel kind of a thing.

A tall, lean version of Frank veered up behind Piper. Shitbag asshole.

Piper quaked at the seams. Don't do that, Lionel. Startled me.

Sorry. Hee hee. Didn't mean to.

How long have you been standing there, creep? Wendy, do you know Lionel? Frank's older, more inane, *bachelor* brother—a math whiz sequestered in a turretlike office back in San Jose where he socializes with no one but Frank and spends all day and night concocting financial instruments to better bend a buck, spend a buck, and possibly conceal a buck. Am I introducing you correctly, Lionel?

You are.

How do you do, Lionel? Nice to meet you. You're the slobbering image of your brother.

I am.

Is Piper telling the truth? Are you swindling great fortunes?

Yes and yes, Lionel said. But all above-board, of course. Thanks to superior math. Up-to-the-second computerized tests on the data. Results. More tests. Better results ... Gee, Wendy, you *do* look spectacular. Wow, that turban is something. Gosh, you look more gorgeous than Diane Keaton.

What's he mean by *that*? Piper winked at her.

You're more tanned than your brother, too, I must say. Does your turret face south?

Yes, but no. I swim outdoors, said Lionel and thumped his chest with the hand not holding a martini. My private pool. In my house. Retractable roof. Between the kitchen and living room. I can swim and watch TV while my girlfriend cooks dinner naked—

If he had a girlfriend, added Piper.

I love my pool, Lionel said.

Like most other Hexen employees, Lionel also smelled rankly of Ruthvah.

Wendy, meet Hexen the Third, said Frank as he swept eagerly in between her and his brother. And this is Diamond the Fifth, and Mistral the Second.

Mistral the First was a flock of white hair floating in midair over the collar of a suit and tie, and Mistral the Second was another elderly fellow with startlingly jaundiced skin and redshot eyes beaming out of a yellow brick face on top of a barrel chest leaning way forward over two spindly legs as he extended a long monkey arm off one of his two walking canes to shake her hand.

They love you, said Frank.

Lurv her, said Hexen the Third in an attempt at humour.

It is true, we *do*. We *love* you around here, said the eldest Mistral. This company would not be where it is today without your, I don't know what else to call it, special touch. Because I guess I don't read the funny pages, why I can't be more precise.

See how they all love you? said Frank as he pulled a bacon-free appetizer off a silver plate.

Who's got a spoon to gag me with? Wendy said in a courteous tone, and the partners enjoyed a laugh. On the house, she said.

You sound just like your comic strip, said old Mistral. That flock of hair looked like a shred of cotton batting pulled from a pillow, on top of a head so tiny as to be mistaken for absent.

And on the financial festivities went. And on. Far longer and so grindingly dull that the thought of gulping down another dyed cocktail and a vermin-sized foodlet off a silver platter while chatting politely with so many diabetic alcoholic mendacious old men nauseated her. The only woman in the room aside from the server girls, the only female allowed to drink, was Wendy. Men sucking on handrolled Dominican cigars that stank like ass to high heaven and deleted all the powers of the Ruthvah. The boardroom swayed with smells. More catering, more drinks, more cigars. After Diamond asked Wendy for an original drawing and she made one on the back of a spreadsheet of Francis the rabbit in his best pinstripe suit being chased by a calculator, all the other name partners wanted original drawings, too, to give to kids or, to keep things equal among the businessmen, themselves.

I like your bosses, said Wendy.

No, you don't.

They are more boring than plywood, she said, but I like them because they make *you* happy.

I make *them* happy, Frank said. A tenth, a hundredth of my salary's what each of them takes home.

A hundredth. I'm no good at math. Where does that leave *me*? Well off.

She said, All I want is to sit on your lap, but if you're going to make me stay here, you better tell that guy behind you with the platter of prawns to turn around and serve us some before they vanish—my stomach is growling, she said.

Frank pressed himself against Wendy's body. The door to the penthouse suite swung open.

Wendy was a bit too sloshed to be horny. But she went with it.

The penthouse lights were out. The room was dark. She sensed something different about the place. Absent was the fresh money smell she thought the hotel service must perfume the place with. A cologne of unfamiliar musk, not Ruthvah, permeated the room instead.

She pulled away from his tongue. Frank … ? Frank? she whispered, hesitating to make it a question.

Frank put his cellphone down on the table in the entranceway. Mm. You smell so good, he said as he engulfed his face in the loofah of her hair. Oh god, Wendy, I wanna fuck your pussy so hard right here and now, he said in a voice not quite his own.

She giggled. Oh, wow, *that word*.

I *knew* it! I fucking knew it!

Wendy screamed, high-kicking like a startled horse, and accidentally kneed Frank in the groin. Cross-eyed, tongue flicking out of his dry heaving mouth, Frank managed a reptilian squeak.

I *fucking* knew it, *you* fucking dogshit, a voice snarled in the darkness. You fucking two-faced *traitor*.

Wendy switched on the chandelier. The well-dressed man at the far corner of the living room slammed his hand down on the sidetable, shaking a Tiffany lamp, as he stood up from his chair. His movements, all lunging and pacing.

You're not Sue, you're … you're that—I already forget your fucking name—that—*cartoonist.*

She pointed to him. And you're …

K-Kravis, Frank spat.

You dick-hearted liar, piss-flavoured liar, you cheated me out of millions. You nearly cost me my reputation, my brokerage … Why haven't you returned a single one of my goddamn calls, you squiddy spineless bloodsucker?

How did you *get* in here?

I broke in, of course, said Kravis with a mean grin on his coinface and an American Express card flapping prominently between his fingers. I thought you *sold* this, you sticky fingered liar. Want to tell me why you still own a million-dollar penthouse in a city where you no longer live? Or, pardon me, but am I *looking* at the reason?

I've got half a mind to call the police, said Frank.

Go right ahead and get a full mind to, you no-good criminal fuck. I'd like to see you do that. Call the police. Hilarious. Pah!

What is it you think you're entitled to now, Kravis? You already spent your inlaws' fortune on bad bets. You're an addict with no impulse control.

Oh, I didn't mean to interrupt your *tryst*, Frank. How long has your wife been missing or dead for? But your private affairs are no business at all of *mine*, of that I'm fucking sure. Certainly not. You're here for deals, deals. Nothing but deals. You shut me out of that Shepherd Media deal, you conniving bald fuck.

Kravis had fixed himself a drink apparently, because he finished it now in a big overweening swig. The ice fell to the bottom of the glass like broken glass when he set it down on the coffee table. Well, I suppose then it's true what they say about tragedy plus time. I'm fucking sure you corporate backstabbers are opportunistic enough to waste no time laughing over a couple of dead loved ones.

357

Kravis, I never disclosed inside information on a deal to you. If that's been your impression in the past, you're wildly mistaken.

I do my part, Frank, I polish the financial shoes, I carry the market luggage, I do all your dirty work and heavy lifting, and in return you agreed to keep me going with a steady supply of very profitable inside fucking info. Very simple. Million-dollar debt transactions are revolutionary things, Frank. America's the place to pull a heist like yours. Hundred percent and higher interest rates. I've said it before, you're the Salvador Dalí of finance. But you can't do a job this size without help. You need me for your junk to work. And I did—I took that position for you.

Frank snapped. In a flash his dinner jacket was off and his Zegna tie unravelled from where it confined his neck, the top three buttons on his white French-cuff dress shirt undone, and he shouted, Get out of my home.

You forget I was wrestling champ at Princeton, Frank. I can still do fifty pushups a day.

Where I'm from boys play rugby, said Frank as he got into first position.

Wendy said, Grab him by the scruff, Frank, toss this pup out on his ear.

I remember. I remember Lupercal Plastics Infuckingcorporated—remember them, Frank? Nicaraguan plastic factories in need of some protection, Frank? I remember everything.

Where is it? Frank said.

Where's what? said Kravis, ducking back.

You're wired up, aren't you? Trying to entrap me, is it? You're conspiring, aren't you, coward. Come here and show me. You've been interrogated, haven't you?

Kravis slipped away from Frank's right fist, took a shot to his enemy's forehead, and that left him open for Frank to give him an unexpected blow below the belt.

Kravis let out a mulish Oof! and doubled over.

Frank seized him and both of them fell across the coffee table, sliding on the varnished finish, swathed in the comic books Wendy had bought earlier in the week.

Kravis tore his shirt open. Are you happy now? he barked as pearl buttons spat off, chest bare except for the occasional cottonball of shrivelled once-manly hair and a red scar like a zipper running up the centre of his ribcage. He flexed his muscles under a layer of pink flushed skin. I am not wearing a fucking wire but I am here to warn you it's getting like that. The DA and the SEC probed me *like aliens* today, full of questions I'd just as soon forget they asked.

You snitched *already*, didn't you? said Frank with disgust. What did you *say*? What *fabrications* did you spin to get out of this one? That's why you're on the *out*, Kravis, why no investment bank would have you—no loyalty. You're one inbred motherfucker, aren't you, Kravis? I've seen a thousand chuckleheads like you who grew up spitting distance from shit, and you come to the big city to make pay. You sold your vital wisdom at its low, and you bought in on Wall Street avarice at its high. Now you think you're in the opera box of life, with a fabulous wealthy wife and a mansion in Greenwich, but there's a can of dog food between your ears. I'm surprised you can *tell time* let alone arb the market.

You're public enemy number one on Wall Street right now, Frank, ask anyone. Goldman Sachs, Lehman—all their fortunes are shrunk, thanks to you. They hired Rudy Giuliani to lure you in, hook you, kill you, and fry you like catfish.

Now Frank opened the main door and said, Go home to your wife and your wife's castle and her family's money, Kravis. Go home and regret all this.

He slammed the door behind Kravis and locked the door. Spoiled-rotten, stinking drunk fool, Frank said and drove his fist into the door.

I heard that, Kravis shouted from the other side and slammed his own hand against the door.

She backed into the living room and stood under the chandelier thinking of the strong botanical hands and flowering face of Richard McGuire.

Don't say a *word*, Frank said and rushed into the room and put a hand under the nearest lampshade. Gotta sweep this whole damn place now. He could plant a microphone almost anywhere. Help me look. Damn him. Comes in here drunk and ranting about payback. Fuck him.

As she made an effort to inspect the lampshades and backsides of paintings, her mind wandered back to the sensation of McGuire's legs ambiently flirting with hers under the tiny table. Nodding at Art Spiegelman's fingers drawing in the air as he spoke. And Françoise snip-snipping at the noodles on her plate didn't seem to notice McGuire's moves in the least. Wendy began to wonder why she didn't take McGuire up on his offer. Continue the night fucking back at his little SoHo studio. Greenwich Village dinner. Noodles in tomato sauce. Was Richard the one, not Frank? She'd never know unless she let Richard show her.

She remembered asking McGuire, Can you tell me why there's so many hobos?

Out-of-work actors. All the best agents moved to Los Angeles.

Had she come to visit a month ago she probably would have followed up McGuire's under-the-table moves with some of her own. Instead she was here with Frank in this violated penthouse on Fifth Avenue.

After dropping a tumbler of ice and vodka into each of their palms, she went and opened the curtains so she could once again see the beautiful city lights over Central Park. Everything brightened up in the room. She sat down on the fur rug and pulled her legs up behind her, tucking her stockinged feet under her. Frank watched her the whole time, vibrating, she could see. She felt all of a sudden very fetching and lovely in her new role as Frank's mistress and took a long drink to show off her bare white throat.

So, she said. A life of crime, is it?

Kravis is an infant in the mental sense. I'm sorry we had an intruder. You don't seem frightened anymore.

Ah, I'm used to coming home to strangers. That's how it works at No Manors. Sorry I canned you.

Nothing permanent. Let's turn on the TV and have something to eat, then. I'll call the front desk and order us some chicken and rice.

So this isn't a hotel. You *own* this penthouse?

I didn't want to spoil the mood. I used to live here with Sue.

Really? Did she ever do this to you?

She scooted up onto her knees in front of him, gulped down the last of her vodka, and slipped off her Rolex, then his.

Those were some kung fu moves Kravis had. He wanted to clean your clock good.

Never. The man is one big Achilles heel.

Nevertheless, you gave him quite a low blow there.

Had to be done.

Just sit back and relax and drink your drink, Frank.

29

STRAYS

SORRY, SIR, BUT YOU'RE NOT ALLOWED TO TOUCH THE ARTWORK.

SERIOUSLY? YOU CALL THAT ART? IT'S A BIG MARSHMALLOW!

WELL, IN HERE IT'S ART. AND YOU CAN'T TOUCH ART!

THE PRICELESS K'ANG-HSI PERIOD CHINESE PORCELAIN VASES AT THE FRICK MUSEUM -- NOW THOSE I CAN UNDERSTAND... BUT A MARSHMALLOW IS NOT ART! BAH!

I STILL CAN'T LET YOU TOUCH IT!

LET ME HAVE JUST ONE BITE! PLEASE! A TINY NIBBLE! THAT'S ALL! C'MON!

THIS JOB IS SO WEIRD!

The Santa Claus balloon that led the parade began to drift south down Central Park West. Facing a mild if steady wind from the south, Santa danced limbo and the twist. The wind was not warm, the temperature on the ground remained a nudge below freezing. Icicles hung dripping from streetlamps and eavestroughs, and snow the colour of moon mud ran the curbsides. Standing arm in arm among the families and friends bundled up in woollies and scarves, children ages zero and up, grown adult children oohing and aahing, mature-faced babies in prams, crying, screaming, laughing, whining children, this was exactly how Wendy Ashbubble wanted to experience her first Macy's Thanksgiving Day Parade, her first balloons, just her and the man who loved her crowded in among the anonymous heartfelt families craning their necks at the spectacular floating dolls. The two of them freshly, secretly in love, walking on a cushion of air over the sidewalks of Manhattan, happy to be there to see her cartoon characters. She couldn't wait to see them, her creations, massive as clouds, overhead. Santa bobbed from side to side with the plump grace of his persona and the dream logic of love itself, generosity dripping from his red nose.

Then came a New Jersey fireman's marching band, chased by every borough's cheerleading squad under a three-storey thumbs-up Garfield balloon tethered to a dozen Nam veterans in wheelchairs waving meekly to the hale crowds; a Donatello from the Teenage Mutant Ninja Turtles over the Choctawhatchee High School cheerleaders all the way from Fort Walton Beach, Florida; Dennis the Menace danced in place like a boy holding his bladder over the Wyoming All-State Spelling Bee Champions; Chloe the Clown, patron saint of clowns, over the Mike Miller Dance Team (we watched the whole thing on television back at the manor); a Superman carried by Christopher Reeve and Joe Shuster, a six-storey-high Pink Panther in a U.S. lifeguard life preserver doughnut carried by Herbert Lom and Monica Vitti; a Ronald McDonald balloon carried by local football and basketball players with children's hospital children propped on their shoulders ...

Cameras swept overhead on cranes; at Times Square Miss Piggy and Pat Sajak were doing a live-feed colour commentary of the parade. Back home at the manor we waited to see what they had to say about the *Strays* balloons. We planned to celebrate getting toasted when the balloons appeared. At the moment an E.T. balloon carried by volunteers waving to the crowds, all wearing white hazmat outfits; next was a Mickey Mouse dressed as a sailor, nose-to-butt with a fancy new Spider-Man in a semifetal position about to ejaculate web from his wristband; a carrot-gnawing Bugs

Bunny; a float shaped like a fully cooked Thanksgiving turkey with gravy, mashed potatoes, and even giant pineapple rings on a towtruck under a six-storey Coca-Cola bottle; Underdog, then a Smurf balloon, all as big as ferryboats, coasting twenty to a hundred feet above the street and waving to the frightened and ecstatic children cowering in their shadows—; ... Wendy wondering, *Where the heck's my balloons?* as a Pinocchio bounced by with fully protruded nose; Kermit the Frog smiling over them now. Frosty the Snowman, the Pillsbury Doughboy, Cat in the Hat, a Mount Rushmore float driven by the schoolteachers' union, *Yeah, but where's Buck and Murphy?* Patience, patience, Frank said when the Nintendo brothers, Mario and Luigi, reared their heads. And the most applause yet for *another* version of Spider-Man triggering a spunk of webline from his carpal tunnel; a Cabbage Patch doll big enough to scare any sane adult, under the belly of which Wendy caught a glimpse of Art Spiegelman and Françoise Mouly moving towards her through the crowd.

What were they doing here? Had they seen her? Should she wave? What was about to happen? The last thing in the world she wanted, for some reason, was for them to see her. She gently nudged Frank and said she wanted to follow Charlie Brown for a few blocks. Moving invisibly through wave after wave of great hurrahs as the spectators saw the balloon in front of them, and for the NYPD tethering Charlie Brown about to throw a softball, she and Frank avoided a social encounter. Snoopy in Red Baron regalia, tethered to veterans of the First and Second World Wars. Then some more balloons. *Okay okay*, said Wendy, *but where's my guys, my goddamn li'l folks, my balloons for crikey!* The Michelin Man looking like a she-beast from out of the work of Edgar Rice Burroughs; Mr. Potato Head, a Care Bear, Kermit tethered to a contingent of bachelor surgeons—*My Kermy!* swooned Miss Piggy; a four-storey Big Bird, Scooby-Doo trailed by Raggedy-Ann; Bryant Gumble introducing Menudo live; an Uncle Sam float behind the Statue of Liberty, a Humpty-Dumpty balloon in front of another Superman. Then Fraggle Rock performed. *I'm getting dizzy enough to puke I'm so excited to see my guys, Frank,* on the street under the balloons many acrobats, baton twirlers, Shriners doing figure-eights in miniature cars, and ballerinas from the middle schools danced by, so did the rodeo clowns behind them, the sheepdogs moving flocks along, and the Broadway musical casts, but then finally, *finally* along came one of Wendy's creations—*Buck! Look, it's Buck! I'm right here, Buck!* she and Frank cheered and Wendy sobbed with joy when she saw her dog and his trademark flags for ears. Her all-yellow cat floated by in inflated form. *Murphy! Murphy! Murphy!* carried by what Frank said looked to be the heads of Shepherd Media and publishers at Dell.

He looks so great! Ah, I'm so proud of him. Murphy. From the skids to Broadway, gosh, what a stroke of luck I've had.

It's not luck, said Frank. It's pure talent and hard work. I always thought Murphy was a she.

He is a she, Wendy said.

Okay, but Buck is a boy?

Sure, she said.

Back at the manor on the Pacific coastline across time zones, we watched it live on TV. We saw at least sixty to ninety seconds of her balloons—we lost our minds. We *knew* these characters. Drawing them so much, they became some deep part of us, the way a nanny must feel about the children she tends as a parent. But we also drew the designs for these very balloons, and UPS'd them to the manufacturer nine months ago. This was sure some validation of our work as freeloading factotums and amateur animators. This was the material splendour of Manhattan—the Macy's Parade—and we were a part of it. But growing up in the modest to appalling conditions we had, and in ever-changing locales where we were given mediocre to no attention and no consistent lease on parental guardianship, our only role model the hard experience of self-reliance, seeing our work in a parade of this magnitude transformed us. We wept. A dog and a cat we devoted so many back-hunched hours to mastering, there on

TV. Roasted in colour commentary by Sajak and Miss Piggy, the Muppet in a cut-in video feed in the corner of the screen sniffling, *Oh, hey, look what we have here, a couple of my cutie-cute friends, Murphy and Buck from Strays, aren't they adorable, maybe a bit skinny—*

I like his little flag ears, said Sajak.

Cute, yes, but not compared to moi or moi's Kermy …

And then it was on to the next set of balloons, Pac-Man chased by his ghosts Blinky, Pinky, Inky, and Clyde.

Only because of our phone call with Wendy later on that day did we learn what happened off-camera. Our local Shepherd Media broadcast censored the footage. It started with a northerly wind that gusted strong and cold with calm temperate lulls in between. The gusts sucked at and pushed the balloons. Winds picked up force in the valley between the buildings on Seventh as they arrived in Times Square at the top of Broadway, straining the ends of the tethers.

Piper Shepherd and his preschool granddaughter, Coleco, heir to both the Shepherd and Greenberg fortunes, were at the reins of the Buck balloon.

Wendy told us how giddy she was to be there to witness this sight of the blown-up version of her own creations in the Macy's Parade, these little scribbles on paper turned giant-sized, incredible. A comic strip milestone. She kissed Frank over and over without even realizing. He wrapped his arms around her. The sky was a blue racetrack for a dozen clouds the shape of the Nike swoosh. Glittering snowflakes fell from trees and apartment ledges onto the crowd, or if compelled, snow traced the invisible pirouettes of the wind as it passed by in ferocious thrusts. All Wendy's misgivings of the past few months vanished that morning as she saw her characters alive, levitating over the children who knew their names.

A gust strong enough to bend the trees and pull hats off heads also made some of the balloons ahead of hers buck forward and back, and the Star Wars fans lost control of their giant R2D2. *Pa-pow!* its dome bopped

Buck square in the snout. The winds picked up a second time. The tethers tautened to their max, and Shepherd's little granddaughter was lifted up-up—up! Out of Piper's reach into the air screaming, *Grandaddeeeee!* As Coleco held on to the tether, the Buck balloon twisted higher and higher in the air, recoiling from the R2D2 balloon's blow in the bluster, and sent her swinging with a tiny Tarzan's grace through the air over the paraders. *Coleco, oh my, oh dear! Wa!* cried Piper Shepherd as he reached after her in vain. Either he could let go of his own tether and run to try to save her, or he could try to wrestle the balloon to the ground before it yanked him up into the air as well. The balloon tipped violently this-a-way, Wendy told us, and precariously that-a-way, swooping the four-year-old heiress in a wild circle over the screaming audience watching in horror from the sidewalks as she whipped past overhead, and letting go of the tether, by luck landing her into the arms of a Paul Newman lookalike in a white foxfur coat to match his wife's. Hallo, said Coleco.

Wendy almost fainted with relief to see the toddler safely back on the ground and in her joy made a blunder she will always regret. She gave out a cowboylike *wee-oop!* and pulled the brand-new snow-white Travilla turban off her head and sent it spinning up into the air—she was cheering for the little girl's return to solid earth *alive and unbroken* and didn't care one whit if she ever saw the silly couture impulse-buy ever again—but as the turban Frisbee'd upwards, up, up, the brooch slipped off the fabric and she watched in terror as the long pin speared Buck's stomach. A fling she told us she'd never forgive herself for, those few seconds aloft that she told us she would replay until the day she died, was all it took to ruin a perfect day. The brooch's pin took what felt like an eternity to pop Buck. And she lived in that eternity, her heart went to that moment over and over again so that when the brooch hit, it might not have popped her character, or it might have missed the balloon altogether. But it did, the pin struck clean. The belly let out a long shriek and almost as quickly the ears and head shrivelled up, wrinkled, palsied, the rest of the balloon collapsed as a suffocating blanket over Murphy's levitating feet. The Murphy balloon tipped forward under the weight of the raisin. The whole debacle loomed over right in front of Frank and Wendy. She saw Murphy was about to come down hard chin-first on a streetlamp. She screamed—no cowboy stuff this time, no phony *yeehaw*—she screamed, *Take cover!* like in war times. After another loud *POP!* and the Murphy balloon—a Lupercal product? she thought to herself—whipped back and forth whistling out air, thwacked the icicles hanging off the lamp. Spectators saw what was coming out of the sky like a Macy's Parade atomic bomb about to go off in their faces, screaming and shouting as families and friends dived for the nearest awnings or tree branches or all squirrelled up under their jackets and umbrellas for any kind of protection against the shards of glass from the streetlamp exploding came raining down among the icicle spears and chunks of snow falling like burst luggage off the telephone poles and window ledges. Glass and ice and balloons. Piper pulled at airpockets in the fabric as he searched for the source of his granddaughter's screaming. A nasty piece of glass broke right beside Wendy's feet but left her unscathed.

Dear Dr. Pazder,
You won't believe what happened to me … I was in New York
for the Macy's Parade and …

30

We didn't complete the massive landscape painting of the *Strays* environs on celluloid as soon as we had promised Wendy over the phone. That was in a brief moment of delusional optimism. Our excitement about *the new idea* cast a spell that made us think the painting would be a snap to finish. The tracking shot we envisioned proved more difficult than our enthusiasm had anticipated. The problem was using the original character animations, and it took us months to accept that we needed to redraw everything. But Wendy didn't fulfill her promise, either: she didn't come home right away, so she didn't have to watch us scrap finished work. Now it was her turn to vanish.

Rather than fly straight home to us from New York and observe our progress on the *Strays* Christmas special, Frank hired two ace pilots and the couple travelled to destinations in Central America where Lupercal LLC had factories and then jetted across the Atlantic to Europe and etcetera, whereabouts together they holidayed for a further three months into the new year. She wrote us with boasts of snorkelling under the blue plastic sky off the sugar-white beaches of the Cayman Islands pictured on the postcards. Sex in mosquito-infested resorts, on a private jet, in the ocean under stars. Industrial cities in Panama, Costa Rica, Honduras, and Guatemala. Stops in Belize, Antigua, and Barbuda, the Caymans, the Virgins, all to meet in private with bank managers, factory managers, and the like. She was taking advantage. He was here to espouse the profit-making beauty of the well-packaged high-yield bond, the power of the leverage buyout, and the future of trade between the nations. Capital must be fluid. Leverage empowers. Fucking nightly. She got over the popped balloons. Laugh it off. The parade seemed long ago when she was in Basel, her first time in Europe, where she visited art galleries full of paintings and sculptures by the dead while Frank met key managers of the Bank for International Settlements. Bombay, Hong Kong, and Taipei, havens for complex deposits. Hotels where she doodled and faxed. They jetted to Moscow.

This is all fine and dandy, said Wendy, but when do we go home and meet the president?

Soon, soon enough, just a few more stops, said Frank.

The coffee was so hot in Turkey it scorched all the glands in her throat. Turks and Caicos Islands, Nauru, Malta, Alderney, Andorra, and Zug. Liechtenstein. Turkey, Egypt, Israel, Czechoslovakia, Switzerland— he brokered deals to lend money at interest and deposited money in each. He passed on more and more business to Gabby for translations of *Strays* in foreign newspapers. He contracted the regional use of *Strays* to the underdogs in profitable industries like the ones he invested in back in America. She tried the coffee.

Somewhere in the skies over Europe, Frank explained his rationale for the trip. If and when America's economy loses energy, I need other markets to keep the debt-financing rolling. Same goes for *Strays*. You come close to saturating America, you need other nations to keep the dream afloat.

You're the richest man I ever met, said Wendy.

Me, too, said Frank.

Because of Jonjay's formula?

In part due to, yes, said Frank. You like to dwell on that. Why? What about my skills in this endeavour of ours, don't they matter?

What is it to you, all this money?

Money is my business. The material stuff can come and go. But wealth itself I like. And you see, every door on earth opens to the money.

You think money's the key to life?

No, but I happen to want a lot of it while I'm alive. I'm glad you seem to have gotten over what happened at the parade. It's a thing that happens.

Her hips did some bellydance moves. She said, I love how it feels to be naked in the aisles of an airplane.

Some of the strip gags she faxed us while away featured Buck and Murphy on a vacation, too. A remedy for what Murphy calls *the yips and yowls of too much city livin'*. Buck thinks a vacation *is the perfect way to empty our brains*. Instead of a vacation, they get lost, and the new and unfamiliar streets all of a sudden turn threatening when they consider the possibility of never seeing their friends at the vacant lot again. Panic sets in big-time for Murphy. Buck's in complete denial. They are together but they feel alone. The city seems to expand under their feet the more intently they search. This sequence went on for a harrowing six weeks. *Lost upon lost!* Buck slaps his paws over his eyes when he finally accepts the facts—there's no hope of ever finding their vacant lot in this superdense metropolis. Six weeks was an eternity in the life of a gradeschool reader of the funny pages, and this displacement was too much for young fans to bear. The letters to the editor were dominated by children imploring the newspapers to help the characters find their vacant lot. The strip was never so popular. A hundred new papers bought subscriptions as the story picked up steam. In fact we completed enough strips for the adventure to take seven weeks, but at the last moment, Gabby convinced her to cut a week from the storyline after she started hearing from numerous city editors who were fielding calls and letters from parents saying *Strays* wasn't funny anymore. When their kids open the papers in the morning to learn the cat and dog haven't found the vacant lot yet, it made them cry over breakfast and not want to go to school, rather stay home than risk getting lost. Crying kids convinced her.

She wired us five grand to buy a new Xerox machine—we blew the old one up—and two hundred dollars' worth of ink cartridges. With this we enlarged, shrank, and duplicated her characters and laid them on the lightbox to trace. All the details had to be imitated flawlessly or Gabby would call and complain, then send back strips for redraws. Tracing Xeroxes of her old strips was how we peanut-butter-and-jammed together a solution to meet her deadline of six strips a week including the double-sized Sunday colour.

Cartoonists stopped in to No Manors with the frequency of a bus stop during the first half of the eighties, and if they hadn't been there for it, they invariably asked us what we remembered from the weekend of Hick's wake. But not everyone had heard the rumour that Jonjay compelled us all to eat a part of the body, so we never knew how to reply. In eighty-five, though, all the cartoonists knew because of Biz's comic, and we even started to get phone calls from local editors and entrepreneurs. They didn't want to talk about *Strays*.

So? Is it true?

What *it*?

You know, *it*, they prodded. They got around to the reason for the call: Can you do us a spot illustration of *it* at the wake for an article we've commissioned? We've got a journalist to write about comics in San Francisco.

No can do, we would say. Too squeamish.

Pay is five hundred.

When's it due?

Can you create a cannibal-theme silkscreen poster for our Walpurgis Night Concert Festival? Budget's two hundred.

A hundred to do an illo of Hick Elmdales and Biz Aziz for the Arts section of the *Chronicle*?

When Gabby Scavalda called from Manhattan to settle a glitch in the strip, Patrick tried to pin her down. Tell me the straight dope, Gabby. What's my problem? All I get is weird slapdash freelance work. Why won't the big syndicates pick me up?

Patrick's dew-dapped dreams of his own successful newspaper strip had all but evaporated after years of harsh rejections. His latest foray— *White Collar*, about a polar bear employed as a middle-manager for a large corporation of penguins, had been turned down by every syndicate. He was ready to pack it in.

If there was anything Gabby liked more than permission to give the straight dope, we never saw it. She'd looked at some of Patrick's pitches over the years out of courtesy and had an idea what was going wrong.

Gabby told him, You'll never get in the papers if you give up. I can't speak for another editor but here's why I might pass if I was looking for a new strip and saw your work. First, it's very professional. You're a pro. You know what you're doing. So I look closely. You have excellent handling of your line weight. Thin lines spread out beautifully around bends and turns, and there's nice shadows. But so what? This is the funny pages. Your character designs are fundamentally flawed—there's nothing likable about how you draw them. They're derivative. And there's nothing fluid about your panels. The movement is all over the place. Editors get migraines from strips with bad flow. Everything looks stagnant or composed willy-nilly. Your own ideas aren't original, that's the biggest problem. The gags don't work. The humour is overweened. The funny is not funny. Your writing's not up to snuff. Your characters need depth. Here's the upshot, Patrick: you're better as an inker. You're an astounding inker. Maybe you should find a partner who can come up with the ideas and scripts and can pencil the panels for you to ink.

Dejected by the stumble, meanwhile Patrick took care of most of the buzzes at the door that were cartoonists and other types of artists looking to buy a dime or a quarter of the inspiring shit that we kept replenishing in the laundry hamper, which still reeked something special. Its properties remained untested no matter how many we turned on to it and now swore by it.

One time a syndicate called for Patrick. This was not one of the big five syndicates. Rather, this was Impetigo, based out of Milwaukee, whose business focused on the free weekly underground newspapers the other syndicates overlooked. Impetigo—with quote attributed to Wally Wood for a slogan: *Sex, Violence, and Horror*—had illustrators, sex columnists, saucy horoscopes, and the like to fill out the arts and entertainment listings—they syndicated underground comix full of twisted scenarios and frustrating anti-punchlines. The comix editor wanted to know if Patrick would be interested in doing a *Life in Hell*–style comic strip about cannibals and the devil. You know, the editor said, as a kind of wink to *issue nine*.

What a blow to learn industry as far down the ladder as the Impetigo Syndicate had heard about his rejections. Patrick agreed to prep a strip even though the money was worse than what Wendy paid.

That's to say, on top of the animated *Strays* summer Christmas special perpetually due, we agreed to do freelance on the side. It was all for editors and designers who wanted the same thing: Make sure *it's* in there. And if they didn't want a literal representation of that night, they wanted the mood. And they wanted the credibility of our names. Our ambition made us say yes to most everything (except Impetigo), even when we ended up working for free (Mark would say yes to anything, he was so dipso by then). Like Frank's plans overseas, we prepared for a potential future when we might not have the luxury of being assistants on *Strays* and freeloading at No Manors.

The more work that piled up, the more we divvied it up among the four of us. Twyla pencilled the comic strip. Mark pencilled client work. Patrick inked both. Rachael ran the show. When there was time for the summer Christmas cartoon, Mark pencilled keyframes and Twyla drew in-betweens. Patrick did most of the inking and painting onto the final sheets of celluloid. He and Twyla shot most of the stop-motion cinematography.

Our idea for the cartoon was to mix and match every animation technique in the book. Traditional cel animation interrupted by puppetry segments. Clay stop-motion animation. Mummenschanz-style mask theatre.

On an episode of *Entertainment Tonight* around this time, correspondent Leonard Maltin took viewers behind the scenes with Hollywood's most famous creature-makers, the special-effects guys who made the monsters. Creator of the creatures in *Sinbad* and *Clash of the Titans* and more, Ray Harryhausen showed Maltin how he used a basic stop-motion technique to bring to life his skeleton army, deathmatch dinosaurs, rampaging cyclopses, and royal snakemen. Harryhausen followed one rule: *If you want to draw a dog, first you have to be that dog.* He filmed himself acting as his monsters, then used a reel of his own mime as a frame-by-frame reference when he moved his models bit by bit in front of the stop-motion camera.

So that's what we did. We acted out every scene in the cartoon and filmed it. By eighty-four, not only did we have ten minutes of animation, we had a complete live action version we'd shot on a camcorder with us as actors.

So, while Wendy bounced from nation to nation on her sexful adventure with Frank Fleecen, our days got hairy bananas busy. There was no leisurely freeloading for us. The question was, how to get more work done? Sleep fewer hours. Sleep in shifts. Cycle through jobs. Eat more and darker chocolate. Skip showers and baths for days. Fuck it, let the hair grow on our faces and legs. Heat frozen fish, chicken, or whatever else goes nice with ketchup, guacamole. More coffee, more shrooms, more bud. Draw until our hands looked like pencils and our noses doubled for erasers. Coffee all night. Forget to put the garbage out or clean the toilets. Like in a horror movie, we decided to split up, divvying chores, more deadlines. Put the summer Christmas special on the backburner, *again*.

31

In February of eighty-five, Justine Witlaw went ahead with an exhibition of Jonjay's artwork.

I waited for half a fucking decade. I'm not waiting around forever. What else is there to do? she said. She promised to deposit his half of sales in a trust account to accrue interest during his absence. If he ever made a withdrawal from there, that was another matter.

Titled after a line Jonjay wrote on the back of a bristlecone pine study: *From a History of the Secret Origins of the Universe.* Justine showed ten of the most beautiful examples of Jonjay's rubbings of the sailing stones' trails, in large white wood frames and displayed in a snaking wave along one white wall of her gallery. On the wall perpendicular was a selection of his White Mountain series, watercolours of the cliffs and bristlecone pine trees. Across from the rubbings, she had her interns reproduce all the Death Valley traces at one one-hundredth of the actual size to fit them together onto a print (one of five, unsigned) to be studied for their shapes' strange similarity to the branches of the bristlecone pines. On another wall was a drawing on plaster of a pi-perfect circle

377

Jonjay had drawn freehand one night on the wall at Justine's apartment in Russian Hill. She had the piece of plaster cut out of her rental and carefully framed, then the room replastered (at a cost of well nigh five thousand). Next to the circle on plaster was photodocumentation of the inverted pentagram in the other circle he'd painted freehand, on the door to Wendy's lime-green Gremlin's carport, and of the pentagram's redo by the Evangelical boy next door.

A salon-style, loosely diamond-shaped cluster of small framed pictures completed the first of Justine Witlaw's two white cubes dedicated to Jonjay's doings. This salon was of ephemera. The coracles at sea Jonjay painted with a palette of rotting vegetables. All the absent-minded sketches he had made over the years while watching TV in between the bigger, more mysterious projects that delayed this show. His forays into comix. His sketches for the logo of Ruthvah - For Men.

In an adjoining cube, nine televisions and nine VCRs displayed late-night babble from Jonjay's library of ninety-nine VHS cassettes. Titled *Icing Sugar, 1981–82*, the setup showed Jonjay's curatorial of subliminally cheap late-night pawn shop commercials, hair-raising talkshow interviews, surreal newscast footage. At around the half-hour mark, all nine screens would show footage of the giant pile of mysterious white powder blocking traffic on the Golden Gate Bridge. Footage of the event, snippets of commentary, clips showing the mini-crash in the stock market as a result of the mysterious white powder, and his recordings of the public announcement of the scientific results. There was no mention of his—or our—involvement in the incident.

Another cassette contained a ninety-minute edit of his indoor mountain climb of No Manors, from the basement to the attic and down again, titled *No Mountain*.

In the centre of the gallery, a piece called *JNJY*—three arcade games flashed Jonjay's astounding high scores on Pong, Pac-Man, and Donkey-Kong, which visitors to the gallery were invited to try to beat.

Opening night, it was Mark Bread and Biz Aziz who got all the attention normally reserved for the artist. Justine guided her clients to us by saying that we had lived with the missing artist. Mark is my artist, Justine said, and you all know of Biz Aziz. Everyone did seem to know Biz, perhaps through her performances, and now also for the storyline of issue nine. Old Russian Hill retirees, the blue-chip collectors, they all wanted Mark to tell them—*what did* it *taste like?* Again, Mark ended the evening locked in the broom closet heaving red wine, beer, and cheese into a mop bucket. Justine pulled Biz Aziz aside and said, I don't know why it's taken me so long to ask, but could I show some of your artwork? I think I could do a lovely job presenting them here, that is, if you're willing to sell.

Don't curse me, Justine, said Biz through downcast eyes.

I won't.

You can't put some crazy hex on me.

No hex, Justine said. I promise. What kind of hex?

Don't ask. I'm impervious anyway. Got my own hex. Hex curses hex.

Justine pressed her hand to her heart. Justine assured her: The art work, the hard work, the work, that's what my gallery is about. Original works from your comics on the wall—, she spread her fingers out as she envisioned, —and mannequins on plinths wearing your costumes.

Irwin Gerund, covering Jonjay's exhibition for Shepherd Media's entertainment segment on the six o'clock news, said the show was the one *San Franciscans have been waiting years to see. And does not disappoint. Not only is the artist missing, adding mystery to these exquisite works, but the range of materials is breathtaking. Video, found art, watercolours, pencil, ink, and even graphite rubbings of the desert floor ...*

STRAYS

Every weekday morning while Wendy was away, we tuned in with millions of others to Shepherd Media's *Replicant Fitness* to watch host Manila Convençion do android aerobics. We called this inspiration.

Manila's body strained realism. Fairy-tale proportions. Instead of narrating her own moves, Manila silently followed the guidance of a disembodied, erotically husky female computer voice saying *And a-one, and a-two, and a-three …* Manila was backed up by three more superfit women also dressed as replicants: extreme makeup, skidpunk hairdos shaved and shorn in weird ways and dyed weird colours, fishscale sequins on top, fake-anaconda-skin bikinis, fishnet and spandex bodysuits, clear plastic jackets, all four replicants stretching in sync to Donna Summer's *I Feel Love*, Herbie Hancock's *Rockit*, George Clinton's *Atomic Dog*, *Planet Rock* by Afrika Bambaataa. The four replicants did erotic android aerobics reminiscent of both private dancers and break-dancers, juking on their backs, jerking on their stomachs, humping to the side, bumping to the back, stretching calf muscles, stretching thigh muscles, working those glutes, working those glutes some more, and back on their backs, glutes, thighs, glutes, abs—another hard workout on another foggy night in the middle of a busy street in NeoTokyo, surrounded by electronic geishas and courtesans, security robots, blackmarket crimelords, motley convicts, patrolled from above by flying police spinners. Sparing expense, Shepherd Media bought the shell of the muggy, nocturnal city street used in *Blade*

Runner for backdrop. Rain occasionally wetted their clothes. We didn't necessarily follow along with the routines.

When *Replicant Fitness* was over at noon, it actually felt dirty, as if we had all masturbated together. The steamrooms were out of the question now. So many people around us had died of AIDS, sex itself was becoming a turn-off. Aerobic eroticism was enough. We split up to double up: Twyla ground the coffee beans for Mark to brew a pot while Patrick and Rachael cycled downhill to the coffee shop without a name to collect any faxes from Wendy—it housed the unofficial *Strays* fax machine—and buy four more espressos to drink cold after lunch's coffee.

The coffee shop had no name, no signage, but was special at the time, for it had a massive iron roaster right on the premises, a huge thing imported on a train from Guatemala. We went there for the espresso. It was conveniently located right down the hill on Mission Street. When we wanted more than the coffee at home, this was where we went. Wendy had found the place. She liked to go there because there were lots of giant handmade wood tables, great for drawing on, and big enough to fit a group of seven. A longtable away from the longtable, she would say. Plus the unpredictable customers all made perfect subjects for sketches during the hyperactive upswing on the fierce caffeine. A lot of her ideas came from sketches done at that coffee shop without a name.

We were on our third pot of homemade coffee by the time the nightly news came on, when we heard President Reagan confess he never drank coffee at lunch. *I find it keeps me awake for the afternoon.* Old man.

Here at the manor there was no cut-off hour. Noon, midnight, what's the difference? Four A.M. was as good a time as P.M. to brew a pot. We drank cup after cup of sunlight. How many hundreds of pots did it take to animate the *Strays* Christmas special?

32

Wendy returned to the manor in the middle of April or May—perhaps as late as June of eighty-five. She carried with her three identical pieces of wine-coloured Louis Vuitton box luggage in small, medium, and large, inside of which were designer clothes, pounds of books and comics, and more work for us. Yes, Rachael, take a good look at the handwritten list of contracts she'd signed with businesses overseas in regional and foreign merchandise deals, reproductions, licences, and the one she was most proud of: to design the interior mural of the U.S.A. cultural pavilion at the eighty-eight Winter Olympics in Calgary, Canada.

We're going to need more freeloaders.

How's that Christmas special coming along? she asked us.

No thanks to you, said Twyla and turned her back and almost started to cry.

What's the matter?

We blamed Wendy for our failure on that front. Instead of hiring professionals, as sane people must have at some point advised her to do, she spent at least a hundred thousand dollars of her own money to let us dawdle over this dream of hers. The hours we clocked, the years gone by—compare that to what we'd accomplished—ten minutes?

We decided to show her what we had done.

Rachael set up the movie screen in the spare bedroom. Patrick massaged her feet. Mark rolled joints. The ambiance was set.

Out of the twenty-two minutes of screentime her script had to fit into, we now had about ten. We had lost six minutes trying to figure out how to include this massive celluloid background and then gained back three minutes in less than a month of work. We showed her the new beginning with the sweeping, three-minute tracking shot. Then we spooled in a few of the scenelets that would go in between the regular action. The cartoon opens with Buck walking alone, drawn in a style that's flatter than Disney but his movements have the same Disney smoothness. Before the first commercial break there's a pan across the lot to meet up with Murphy and all of a sudden the style switches rudely—as a joke—to Hanna-Barbera's low-budget corner-cutting roughness. That's what Murphy says when he pulls at his fur and comes up penniless—*time to start cutting corners*. When viewers return from commercials, they don't return to the same style at all. Instead they get a pixelated black-and-white MacPainted version of Francis the rabbit delivering a speech. It turns out to be the image on a television set. Clay next—for a dream sequence Nicki the parrot has we sculpted the entire cast and made a 3D set. Felt puppets and a set made of painted cardboard for another interruption. Us in costumes stop-motion. We even did that. There was always an excuse for these jumpcuts and unsmooth transitions. The transitions from technique to technique, though not seamless, didn't need to be to function, and we thought the whole thing had a rhythm that held it all together as a piece. Kids these days watched rock videos on MTV, we thought, and were savvy to our leapfrog from clay to paper, chalk to salt, wireframe models to computer animation. Or so we hoped.

Amazing. I love it. It's beyond weird so I'm in love. Wow. Keep going.

She seemed distracted.

I think you all deserve coconut Nanaimo bars, she said and opened the lid of a white pastry box in which a dozen of these confections lay in layered slabs waiting for us to eat.

More than two minutes a year, she said as she helped herself to one. That's *not bad* considering cartoons are *hard work*. And you taught yourselves the art. Can't rush goodness. What's happening is way insaner than I scripted. That tracking shot is worth the delay. But now we need to press on the gas. You've got all the pieces, friends. The backgrounds are ready. The character breakdowns. In-betweens is all that's needed here. Paint some colours on cells, away you go. It's wind behind you from here on out, pals.

We ate the coconut Nanaimo bars, and one by one, as the sugar high kicked in, sat down at the longtable to draw.

Meanwhile Wendy and Frank set about manipulating the minds of the Evangelicals who lived next door. Without explicitly saying so, the intention this time around was to persuade the family to part with their home, sell the only home the husband had ever lived in, it turned out, through casual smalltalk investigation—his name was Peter Jesus Bernal. Peter Jesus claimed his Bernal ancestors had staked this hill two hundred years or so ago in the Lord's name. He loved this hill no matter how much it's changed since.

It was Wendy's idea to approach Anton LaVey with a request. For the next week or so, LaVey and two of his mistresses lived in Twyla's room at the manor. Twyla slept in Wendy's bed and Wendy stayed all the way out in San Jose with Frank at his suburban home.

Whenever the family left the home, Anton LaVey and mistresses would present themselves conspicuously doing satanic things like wearing pagan symbols over black clothes and caressing each other publicly and so on.

Hail Satan, I'm your new neighbour, my name is Anton LaVey. I'm in the process of moving the Church of Satan into this building next door to you. I hope you and your children will attend some of our public sermons. I'll be sure to leave our literature in your mailslot. But in the meantime, it's wonderful to meet you. If there's anything the church can do to help, let me know. Hail Satan.

Frank came by one day and said he was scouting properties and lowballed them. The counteroffer Peter Jesus made was so meek and pitifully afraid Frank shook on it without doing more damage. He and Wendy took possession in September. Frank moved to the city. No Manors became her studio and she lived next door.

We still paid no rent. In a sense we were captives to her goodwill.

On a good day Wendy took us all out for lunch at the coffee shop without a name, where the specialty was to put the potato chips right into the sandwich. Also she wanted to sketch the handsome bean roaster, a neo-hippie of some sort with broad shoulders and a ropy white ponytail hanging down his back half the way to his narrow hips.

Where *is* the bean roaster? said Twyla, craning her neck. A trip to the unnamed coffee shop isn't the same without a sighting. But he's *so old* to think of as a sex object, she said as she peeled away the tomato that was sogging the potato chips in her sandwich. Aren't you turned *off* by the yicky white ponytail?

Totally turned off, Wendy said. Blair's ponytail's so yicky, the turn-off is what's such a turn-*on* about it.

Patrick said, The guy looks like Richard Dreyfuss on horse pills.

A longhaired Richard Dreyfuss crossed with Li'l Abner, said Biz Aziz.

Watch steam rise around Dick Dreyfuss as he stirs the cooling beans in the front vat, said Patrick.

He imports beans direct from a plantation in Guatemala, Wendy said. A floatplane flies sacks up here for him once a week. He told me so.

385

Did he? said Twyla.

Wendy wiped the side of her mouth and adjusted the Rolex on her wrist.

I thought Frank kidnapped you, said Mark Bread, who had been silent for almost three weeks up until that point.

He did, didn't he? said Biz Aziz. That's what I wrote in my diary.

You didn't, said Wendy.

Maybe blackmail or something, said Patrick.

Wendy, get real, *this won't last*, Twyla said. I *hate* to be the one to say so because pot calling the kettle black and no one *I* do sticks around but— but Frank's a corporate *raider*. You're a car*too*nist.

Wendy said, Frank and Sue lived separate lives. He told me the love that was there vanished a long time ago. Then I came along and threw a monkeywrench into his mindset.

A hella swindler's what I know about him. Biz Aziz wasn't one of those friends to mince words. I mean, don't you read the headlines? They call him a pirate in pinstripes.

Pishy-poshy, Biz, you're suckered by the press, she said. I've spent like ten months at his side, eating with him, talking with him, seeing him sad, bereft, and in pain, naked, and also laughing and joyful, seeing him work, seeing him at home, sleeping with him, fucking Frank. Fucking him. What am I going to learn in the papers I don't know better from fucking him?

Okay, Twyla said, then *at least* tell us what he's like in bed. Hairpiece on or off?

One of the espresso machines behind the counter roared into action and drowned out Wendy's reply as she twisted her wristwatch back and forth. The smell of espresso overcame our senses.

But where's that funky hippie? I *love* watching him work the roaster, said Wendy. He roasts the best, she sang. I love dark inky coffee, the spicy earthy smell of coffee, the golden revitalizing taste of coffee. Gold you can drink. Manic headrush, stomach boiling, gut racing. Dark warm liberation in a cup. Liquid midnight, river of insomnia. No offence, beer and wine, but if creativity has a flavour it must be coffee. The brainwave accelerator. Cheers.

Cheers, said all and polished off our cups. Mark went to the counter for another round.

I love the productive buzz I get on coffee, said Twyla. I can do strange feats of folly and profound firsts. I revamped those first minutes of character animation thanks to coffee. And some pot.

Smooth Patrick agreed. But you gotta make sure to pay attention to the mug you pick up. I've been known to swig back the water I'd been washing my brushes in.

I've done that, said Wendy. I thought a water glass swirling with pigment was the worst-tasting iced tea.

Let's play a game I just thought of, okay? Patrick said. Absences in comic strips. I'll start. The most obvious. *Peanuts*. Nobody taller than Charlie Brown appears inside those panels. The teachers and parents and barbers are always outside the panel. Even on TV, only the voices of adults are heard.

Wendy said, *Wa wa wa-wa*. We never see the red-headed girl Charlie Brown has a crush either, or the cat next door that Snoopy hates. Do those count?

Patrick raised his espresso cup to her. There you go.

The Great Pumpkin in *Peanuts*, said Wendy, and the Red Baron.

Twyla said the eyedots in *Little Orphan Annie*. She loved that a reader's imagination had to fill in the dots in the eyes, the souls of the character. And Annie is such a soulful character, she said.

Biz Aziz suggested the absence of an enemy in *Beetle Bailey*.

Mort Walker, said Rachael. Remember his strip *Sam and Silo*? What's missing from *Sam and Silo* is the fourth wall.

Wendy wagered, Well, how about George Herriman's *The Dingbat*

387

Family, better known as *The Family Upstairs* because the family upstairs is never seen?

Offissa Pupp's unrequited love for Krazy Kat, maybe? Patrick suggested.

Oh no, wait, wait, Wendy raised her hand, me me me, I know, I know: Krazy Kat's gender.

Mark said Nemo's father was absent from *Little Nemo in Slumberland*.

And the absent father figure of Phil Fumble in *Nancy*, said Twyla.

Reagan is conspicuously absent from *Doonesbury*—Trudeau uses that popped bubble to signify him, or the White House.

We knew Wendy was laughing at herself.

What's missing from *your* strip, Wendy? Biz Aziz asked playfully.

Home, obviously. Buck can't remember where his home is. Murphy wants the home he never had.

And the junkyard dog Buck is so afraid of is never seen, said Patrick.

Ah ha! So you *do* read *Strays*, said Wendy.

I read *all* my competition, said Patrick.

Rachael said, Why don't all sandwiches contain potato chips? Then she swallowed some coffee the wrong way, hid her mouth behind her hand, and said, There he *is*.

Oh my god, look at him, said Twyla.

The bean roaster came around a corner. He carried a sack of fresh coffee beans over each shoulder. He was wearing a sleeveless undershirt and his arms were flexed. He was oblivious to his audience as his work absorbed him. He made it look effortless to hump so many beansacks. Everyone at the table stopped talking for a moment and started drawing him as he got a knife and cut open the first sack. Then he poured the beans into the roaster and shut the lid on the roaster and using his whole body turned the lock, which was like an old submarine's lock, until the roaster was securely shut.

Inside his cage, he stood at attention, inspecting the roaster piece by piece. We watched, and drew sketches, as he lifted the lid and stirred the beans. A great plume of steam rose that he narrowly dodged.

Blair the coffee roaster. He turned the wheel, dialed the temperature, poured the beans into the galvanized steel funnel. Stirred the roasted beans, steaming in the cooling drum. Skin the colour of coffee. The smell of coffee. Brown as the bums who lived on the beach. Leatherskin beans. Offset by Blair's white undershirt. Dark spots on his dark shoulders, ancient acne. On his cheek there's a star-shaped imprint like an indent from a Phillips screwdriver.

Where's the *ponytail?* said Rachael. She was an amazing drawer when she wanted to be. Her drawing of the bean roaster that afternoon bore a satirical resemblance to the work of Hogarth, full of feeling.

In a bun, swooned Wendy. He's tied it in a bun.

Something about how Wendy's eyes burned twigged us.

Stop the clock. Tell *all*, said Twyla Noon. Did you fucking *sleep* with Mr. Blair the bean roaster or *not?*

Wendy laughed, tossed a balled-up napkin at her friend, and said, Shimminy boo-bop, you are a jerkface, Twyla. I did I did I fucked him okay I did. God. Okay okay. When was that, geez, a year or more, sixteen months ago. No, two years ago. Anyway. Same time this place opened, okay, I fucked him, once, in the freight elevator.

Twyla did a doubletake. Why didn't you ever tell us? He's *thrice* our age.

Plus, to make matters worse we got caught.

Of *course* you did, said Patrick.

Busted by the guy at the *cash* register when he went on a smoke break, found me with my legs up around the bean roaster.

That was when Blair stood to his full height and looked us all in the eyes.

Busted again, whispered Biz. He knows we're sketching him.

He bent back to stretch and untied the bun and let the white ponytail swing low enough to touch his sacrum, and then, after cracking his neck in two directions, proceeded to reach his arm between the iron bars of his cage and turn the handle on a door that was not locked and let himself out.

Now he was standing over our table, tall as a tree and musky with the attractive oily, earthy, living smell of coffee beans, half in shadow, the ceiling light bouncing over his gleaming shoulder so that we squinted and shrank from him without meaning to. A broad-shouldered, tall, narrow Richard Dreyfuss. The ponytail, the starch-white sleeveless undershirt. His jeans, new. Blue eyes shone through bean grease on his eyeglasses.

Blair Slobodchikoff, he said and in turn learned all our names. His attention to Wendy. Hello, Wendy, he said.

Hello, Blair.

Thought I'd introduce myself to your friends. Nice drawings. That supposed to be me, huh?

Twyla tried to show she'd drawn him as a mutant enemy of the X-Men—*The Insomnomaniac.*

We're your biggest fans, said Wendy and lifted her cup to him. Your sandwiches are a masterstroke, but we come for the shots. We love your coffee. Espresso is coffee with a genius IQ.

Thanks. You know, a goat-herding Coptic monk discovered coffee seventeen hundred years ago, said Blair Slobodchikoff, who looked like he could herd goats if need be. The so-called bitter invention of Satan. It *is* delicious. And good for your pulse.

… !, choked Wendy on her own tongue before being able to say, … And then some! You sure know your stuff, Blair.

The table broke out into laughter. We love coffee, said Twyla.

It's not just my fax machine that brings you back?

You on a break, Blair? Wendy asked. Want to join us for lunch?

Blair clapped his hands together in a washing motion. He pulled at his shirt to air out his chest. I'll be right back with a sandwich.

Don't lead him on, you're not single, said Twyla when he was out of earshot.

Oh, shush, said Wendy. It's merely lunch. I'm a monogtapus now.

After Blair ate a sandwich he invited us on a field trip to the shipyard docks down at the far east side of Chavez where he collected his coffee beans. I'm striving for the perfect roast, he said of his coffee. Then he turned to Rachael and said, I saw you open for Dead Kennedys at the Mab.

He fished in his glove compartment for the dubbed cassette he'd made of her singles that he listened to in his van.

I'll give you a copy of my new one about to come out, she said. Sounds the same as the others.

You want to go see her perform sometime? Blair asked Twyla.

She didn't catch what he said. She said, Me? Yeah, I've seen Aluminum Uvula play dozens of times, always a brainmelting experience.

Yeah, okay, said Blair.

The docks at the end of Chavez were restricted to the public, so Blair Slobodchikoff knew he was giving us a rare treat, a glimpse at the bay's inner harbour. A two-minute drive away from his coffee shop. He let us watch as Central American longshoremen silently unloaded his weekly shipment of five thousand pounds of coffee beans from Guatemala in sacks labelled Antigua and Huehue and delivered by a Panamanian float-plane. He said, They say that two thousand hours of work goes into every cup, from the time you germinate the seed to the time you brew it. Blair Slobodchikoff was not just the bean roaster, and expert in beans, he owned the coffee shop. Why no name? we asked. Who needs a name? said Blair. The docks around us pulsed with similar activity, anonymous bustling trade. Crates and barrels full of who knows what unloaded onto trucks and vans. Paperwork to be signed. The shadowy underworld of the docks was all we could think about, even if everything happened to be on the level.

Hell shit, everyone down here brags they know the pilot delivering the CIA coke, a secret plane that docks here every couple days with no paperwork, pilot with no ID. I could give two shits about what else happens down here on the docks, Blair said as he drove his twenty-five sacks of beans the short trip back to his coffee shop. Deliciousness is my primary concern.

Your coffee *is* delicious, said Twyla.

Coffee is as much an art as a science, he said. Maybe I could have your number. Maybe you like going to the movies? he said.

Twyla didn't know what to say. Movies? My number? She looked at Wendy.

Don't look at me, Wendy laughed.

I love movies, Twyla said.

I haven't seen a movie in the theatre in years, Blair said.

Twyla looked at Wendy again in that moment, her mind so focused on the chance that Blair Slobodchikoff might come to the rescue and save Wendy from Frank that she did not notice Blair was paying more attention to *her*.

My whole day just did a backflip, Blair Slobodchikoff, said Twyla when she got out of his van in front of No Manors.

33

Four A.M. Breakfast for Frank. Bedtime snack for Wendy. November of eighty-five. A year after Jonjay and Sue vanished. No sign of them, not a clue. Frank at the kitchen island, in the former home of the Evangelists next door, modernized top to bottom. Reading the *Youngstown Vindicator*, which subscribed to *Strays,* while Wendy toasted and buttered sides of a bagel. They each ate a half and listened to the rain against the skylights tapping along with the music on the radio. Frank was not in any hurry because the markets were closed for Thanksgiving. Such heavy weather meant it was dark as ink when his driver pulled up outside in the European to take him downtown. She refused to let Frank behind the wheel. Hexen's offices weren't in San Jose anymore—the twenty-minute commute took him north to the new offices leased in three storeys of the Transamerica Pyramid. Today he needed to spend a few hours strategizing with his brother and others—Frank's latest project was Washington, D.C., and influencing the policy wonks. To his mind, Reagan had not taken enough steps to free up credit in the financial sector. If banks are private businesses, then a regional savings and loans had to be able to borrow over thirty

393

times the amount of its deposits in order to do business in the new global village. It was time for Frank to wage a publicity war. The Baskin-Robbins argument was plan A—everyone wants more flavours. *Government isn't the solution to the problem, government is the problem*—weren't those Reagan's words? So Frank hired a team of lobbyists to push government through covert channels to form an independent financial quango to handle the deregulation of the bond market. Frank Fleecen would be placed in charge of this quango, and in this capacity, advise the president on the market's ins and outs. Once Frank was out the door, Wendy made a bowl of cereal and went back to bed and there read newspapers and planned to sketch.

She opened the morning papers and skipped past headlines—*Reagan's Credibility Shredded by Iran-Contra Link*; *Contra Plane in Nicaragua Reveals CIA Network*; *Ugly Face of Contras in Nicaragua's Secret War*; *Kravis, Arb, Latest Indictment for Insider Trading, a Coup for DA*—to the funny pages on F10, C9, D16. That's when she choked on her chocolate cereal.

Aw, crap, Wendy said, aw crap, this is good, this is *really* good. I'm in trouble now—gosh allmuggy. A shudder went up and down her spine and she clapped her cheeks twice hoping to wake up from a jealous dream.

She was not upset by the headlines, nor was she worried about her assistant Patrick Poedouce's debut in the funny pages with *Loch & Quay*. She'd known for months that was coming and was proud of him. *Loch & Quay* was a straight gag strip that poked fun at cryptids, henges, inquisitions, oneiromancy, secret societies, and other folklore. The debut was more of a ripoff of *Wizard of Id*, but soon the strip started to take on the absurdities of *The Far Side* but across three panels. A prison guard is commending the king on the latest increase in taxes, saying, *It all goes to health care.* The prisoner asks, *Oh, good, like what?* And the guard answers, *The important stuff: Hire more firing squads. Buy stronger nooses. Sharper guillotines.*

She would go next door and congratulate him in a moment.

But Patrick's strip was nothing compared to the other debut that day.

It was called *Calvin and Hobbes*. And it was a beauty. She felt her jaw lock and grit.

You're going to be okay, Wendy, take a deep breath, she said. Calm down. She tried to look away. She pushed everything off the bed, food, pen, and papers, and put her head under the pillows and pictured herself at five sitting on the hide-a-bed and her mother pointing to the host of *General Electric Theater* on television and saying, *Look, there's your dad.*

She walked across the lane to No Manors with her heart dragging behind her. Congratulations, Patrick, she said and lit a joint. There we were around the longtable attempting to celebrate for Patrick's sake the debut of *Loch & Quay*. But we had also read *Calvin and Hobbes* and so we drank to Patrick and talked about Bill Watterson. What else was there for us to do?

Calvin was on a whole other level of goodness. Who could deny the inking's perfect? Augh, sublime. Study those backgrounds. Everything is in motion, even the legs of tables. The linework was dramatic, calligraphic, full of heartfelt, speedy movements, hurried and yet totally confident, unerring, comfortable in itself and totally individual. A multitude of expressions in the dots of their eyes. Perfectly funny noses and memorable hair, effortless elbows, flawless hands. As soon as you saw *Calvin*, you wanted to draw like that. The dialogue was hysterical and smart, eloquent, artful—they all had distinct personalities, their jokes had nuance. No corny puns. No rimshots needed. The humour was punchy, anti-authoritarian, but relatable, the subjects drawn from life, and funnier than pretty much everyone else on the page, including *Strays*, even *Peanuts*. Everything that counted in cartooning was done perfectly here. Wendy was discouraged from day one by the superb layout, expert flow and pacing, and the meaningful storylines. It only got worse as the weeks went along and *Calvin and Hobbes* got better and better. When the Sunday strips arrived, that was the worst feeling. Wendy chipped a mental tooth every weekend. In a funk for days after reading yet another weekend

Calvin. Strays was not up to snuff now, she was sure of it—*Calvin* was so good, too good, she felt cowed. There were days when it sounded as if the inferiority complex *Calvin* gave her might abruptly cause her to quit. Out of total dejection. Give up. Retire. Move back to Canada.

I'm doomed, she said. She smoked another joint. In a year, *Calvin and Hobbes* toys are going to line the shelves of department stores. Every kid is going to want. I can see it now, there's two different Hobbes toys, one of the living imaginary Hobbes and one of the toy Hobbes. There's Calvin and all the Calvin accessories. This is a future of just Calvin and Hobbes toys—no more Buck, no Murphy, no Francis. This is the apocalypse. All my characters combined can't compete against this timeless kid. I'm going to go broke. I never should have donated all that money to charity this year. What was I thinking?

Calvin was on her editor's radar, too. Newspaper editors routinely sent copies of the best and worst letters from readers to the syndicate editors. Correspondence regarding *Strays* went to Gabrielle Scavalda, and she was greedily grateful for any tidbits that might help her bargain with upper brass or her artist.

Gabby would call to tell Wendy her elderly fans couldn't read her lettering. She'd call on behalf of those readers who found Wendy's sense of humour too bleak or unsavoury, who thought her drawings were illegible, unprofessional, bland. You make parents feel guilty, she told Wendy, kids beg to adopt lost pets. After Death Valley, Gabby began to take a more serious look at the complaints and dismiss the cutest of children's panegyrics. *Calvin and Hobbes* exacerbated the insecurity and vertigo of *Strays'* success. Success seemed temporary, fleeting, undeserved if compared to *Calvin*. More often Gabby found valid points in the disgruntled, defending total strangers before her own artist. She used to call them breakfast table critics and morning morality monkeys. Adults who write letters to the editor to complain about something in the funny pages should not be taken seriously, Gabby *used* to say. Now she called Wendy out on her clumsy mistakes and opaque, satirical jokes. Draw more Ping-Pong gags, Gabby would suggest. People love the Ping-Pong.

Come on, Wendy. Do it for the grampas. Slick up your look for the glaucomic who need magnifying glasses just to laugh at your comic. And by the way, around the office they're asking me what's the deal with your Christmas special? Is it happening?

It's coming. It's almost ready. Patience.

So you're really making it—this thing's been in the works for how long, four years?

Three. Okay, yes, four.

Coming up five. And how am I supposed to pitch how great it is if I haven't seen the thing? I need to see it. People are teasing me. If you're saying close to done I'll fly to San Francisco *tonight* to watch it if I *must*. You *know* me.

Come, then. You love San Francisco this time of year. Halfnaked tourists and bundled-up locals.

Why can't I have a *copy*?

I'm a protective mother, she said.

Did you see the New York DA's office indicted that guy who crashed our trip to Death Valley, whatshisname, Kravis? For insider trading? That's pretty far out, hey?

Yeah. Frank hates that goon. Hopes he goes to white-collar prison. What a trip. Two missing, and one criminal. Yeesh.

Cursed. Let's hope we remain unscathed.

Strays isn't going anywhere. I can push for a legacy strip from here. That's my dream. How many papers am I in now? It's got to be two thousand.

You're closing in on nineteen hundred.

Closing in on nineteen hundred papers for like a year. What's the stall?

I'm as ambitious as you are. But there's only so many papers in existence, Wendy. It's not *uncommon* for American comics to *plateau*. *Tiger* was once in nineteen hundred papers.

Once? Plateau? Did you say plateau? I don't live on a plateau. I live on a steep hill that's impossible to reach the top of. Stoneman Street, that's my style. You have to climb to get to me. You know what Biz Aziz calls this kind of talk? Floccinaucinihilipilification!

Wakaflockawhat? What's got into you, did you win a Nobel Prize and not tell me? Where's the aw, shucks, gee willikers young girl I first signed on back when the only paper who wanted your cartoon was the *San Jose Spectator*? Look, I told you this, if you want me to sell your strip to more papers, Wendy, you got to polish up your subject matter and characters.

It's too late to clean up my strip. This is its look, this is the sensibility.

Not true. Not at all. It's never too late. Look at *Garfield*. Look at old *Doonesbury*. Which do you prefer, old *Doonesbury* or today's polish?

The unpolished.

Come on.

You used to cheer for my self-taught punkish style back when you pitched me to the syndicate.

That was years ago. You were green. I didn't want to push you.

Now you want my Christmas cartoon to be a cheap commercial puffball and my strip to be one of those clockwork machines that plops out dependable cuckoo jokes—so it makes your job easier. I don't want my newspaper receipts to *plateau*, and you can't blame *me* if you and your travelling polygamists can't sell a winner. My job is to draw the comic. Merchandise sales outpace my newspapers. How do you explain that?

Listen—

Alls I'm saying is, if we don't do something double fast, Gabby, *Calvin and Hobbes* is going to stomp us out of a gig.

The comics are *shrinking*, not growing. In the thirties, you might have six comics on a funnies page. *Six.* Now it's ten strips minimum and some papers subscribe to seventeen.

That doesn't sound like shrinking. The comics are smaller but there's more of them. I'm not with the argument a smaller panel is a bad thing.

Okay, good, because a smaller panel means it has to be *easy to read.*

Get a sandwich board and a slogan, said Wendy. All I hear are doomsday excuses for why you can't break two thousand papers.

The option's there to fire Scavalda, said Frank that evening before bed with the television on to the top ten list of Manila Convençion positions on *Late Night with David Letterman.*

Number eight, *The flying wow-wa-wow-wa.*

Number seven, … *The Philip K. Dick* … ?

Divestment as an option had never occurred to Wendy before. The thought gave her shivers. Could she fire the editor who launched her career, without whom she would be nowhere? The opposite thought used to frighten her, that Gabby would ditch her and get a cartoonist more qualified to draw her strip. She revelled in the horror of imagining Gabby telling those travelling salesmen who ploughed the highways of America selling Shepherd Media strips to take *Strays* out of their jackets and focus on *Loch & Quay.*

The way to kill a strip—let it shed papers at its own pace until it vanished from the public without hassle.

She thought again of how much more polished and legible *Calvin and Hobbes* was, how universal, how true. Handmade and love-worn, like a favourite shirt.

Wendy drank a final snort of wine and set the glass on her bedside table next to a copy of Huysmans' *Là-bas*, and contemplated life as she watched Letterman count down, and Frank shave. Had she seen him without the hairpiece? Yes. She told him there was nothing wrong with his bald head the few times she'd interrupted him at the sink gluing it down. Did he sleep wearing it? Yes.

Number five, *My mother is* already *ashamed of me.*

She thought about shame and asked him, Didn't you and Sue want children? You were married for years and years.

Towel wrapped around his waist, hairpiece on, he stood in the doorway of their marble ensuite with a razor in his hand and half a beard frosted with cream. We didn't think about children. Problem was, Sue could not ovulate, or she got her period once a year. But no way of knowing when. Happened in her teens. She got ovarian cysts back when we first started dating. Freshman year of high school all but a few of her eggs were surgically removed.

Yikes. How sad. You guys were sad about that.

We were used to it. We were fourteen when it happened.

Sue must've been sad. Fourteen. Sheesh. Is it possible you mistook love for the span of time?

Maybe we weren't … , said Frank as he went back to the mirror to resume shaving. Or sometimes love is money in the bank and sometimes love is a bond of debt. We're in the bank. Sue and I, that was debt.

She rolled out of bed and tiptoed into the ensuite, dropped her silk kimono robe embroidered with Sam the snake chasing Francis across her back, and, naked, turned on the shower and tickled the water, testing its temp. She jumped in, then a moment after, jumped out again, belly-dancing in front of him. Kissing his smooth face, she simultaneously pulled his towel off. He laughed.

You're crazy.

We could make kiddies. Nothing stopping us.

Right now? He put the razor on the countertop and touched her wet skin. What a scary thought, being a dad on top of everything else.

Which came first, the chicken or the egg?

You calling me a chicken?

She hopped up on the marble countertop, and sitting there, brought him between her legs and kissed him. He let her run her fingers through his well-glued toupée. You know what I decided? she said.

What's that?

Even if I can fire her, I'm still not going to fire Gabby for giving me the straight dope. It's not her fault there's *Calvin and Hobbes*. I'm just going to proceed as per and ignore her. *Strays* is my creation, I draw it.

That's good thinking, baby, said Frank, already in a pink heat.

I control the strip's look, not the doubters. There's a reason I ran away from Canada's chilly conditions.

5

34

STRAYS

… go at throttle up …

   … go at throttle up …

No, not these words. Not yet.

Anyway we were done. The Christmas cartoon was complete. And it was Christmas of eighty-five. After a five-year struggle up all the hills, psychological, technical, creative, to say nothing of the hill under our shoes that led to No Manors—we climbed Stoneman Street enough times to put on muscle—it looked as though the bulk of the twenty-two minutes had been animated. Add it all up, there might be ninety seconds missing. Rachael phoned Wendy—who was travelling—to let her know all that remained for us to do was improve the pace in a few transitions, redraft the muzziest movements, and edit in establishing shots between a couple of the sequences in the *mise en scène*. Once that was done, we'd be ready to make a final cut with the soundtrack.

Wendy yelled into the phone: Rachael, I can hardly hear you. I'm on my stupid Motorola. I'm literally standing on a Christmas parade float covered in fake snow and there's life-sized mascot versions of my characters next to me waving to the families of Bethesda lined up on the street. It's cute. You should see me. I'm throwing candy canes at toddlers while Frank meets with senators and lobbyists. I gotta go. Just tell me this means I can pitch the cartoon to the networks to air next summer.

Yes! Rachael shouted.

Our thousands upon thousands of prelim drawings, cell paintings, and the rest of the prep work of the early eighties finally paid off. Now we had all these pieces of finished animation to pull from. If we needed Buck's head to do an owlspin in minute nineteen we could pull from the same action drawn for minute two. Rachael filed all the animation pieces, from paper sketch to trace paper to cells, in an enormous steel cabinet, in carefully labelled folders (*Murphy—left arm waving; Francis—ears twitching*). We had all sixteen phases in the standardized walking postures for each character, and perspective variations (running away from or towards the camera). Notes in each folder described the exact time signatures when these pieces had been used. Rachael's system let us make swift progress on the story after three years of work to get to minute twelve, and we completed the last ten minutes in a year.

Meanwhile, various pavilion sketches kept coming back rejected by one Olympics committee after another. The Americans didn't approve of watercolour (sloppy, too French) and vetoed so much detail (too expensive). The internationals found the composition uneven and ditto the proportions. The pavilion committee nixed Wendy's colour schemes, and the Canadian hosts thought the subject matter—animals doing Olympic events—might offend some audiences.

A curse on the Olympics and all their insane committees! Wendy shouted one night, and threw a balled-up poster-sized sheet of paper in the air, out an open window, and wanting to toss her editor and defenestrate the whole Shepherd Media Syndicate, too, while she was at it. She got desperate and began to throw all her pavilion sketches our way to see what would happen if we inked them. This was eighty-six now, and our teeth were fairly sharpened by the hours and hours we had sunk into drawing reams of storyboards, breakdowns, character shots, notan treatments, and finals for the Christmas special—and now she wanted us to put time into helping her with the Olympic pavilion.

Challenger, go at throttle up.
 Roger, go at throttle up.

. . .

 Challenger, go at throttle up.
 Roger, go at throttle up.

. . .

 Challenger, go at throttle up.
 Roger, go at throttle up.

Those words. Those words hang in our minds like wind chimes, they jingle at the slightest motion of our memories. That Tuesday in January tore the decade in half. We remember the year began with a choir of hope exploding and disintegrating over the Atlantic Ocean. America watched as the space shuttle *Challenger* left for outer space and all of a sudden burst into flames and became two then three trails of smoke falling slowly and inexorably back to Earth. It happened so fast the eye didn't have time to accept the horror. There was a schoolteacher on board and classrooms all across North America were watching live broadcasts on projection screens in gymnasiums. An astronaut to identify with was up there. We tuned in, too. Who didn't? *Challenger* vanished in the sky with its seven-member crew. You wanted to avert the eyes of the entire world from this sorrow plummeting out of thin blue air.

News of the disaster consumed our lives. We stopped doing anything else and read about the *Challenger* in all the papers and magazines and watched television coverage devoted to the disaster, and to the history of space travel, and saddening portraits of the astronauts on board who perished.

Nancy and I are pained to the core ... We've never lost an astronaut in flight. We've never had a tragedy like this, President Reagan said in his address to the nation.

One underlying purpose of every mission to space is to prepare for the safety of the next mission, said a former NASA aerospace engineer who had worked closely with Major Aloysius Murphy in Panama on safety systems and the first iterations of the shuttle cockpit. Talking in a panel about the history of disasters, the engineer said, Every astronaut knows you might not come home.

We wondered what an astronaut thinks of as the shuttle's cabin engulfs with flames. Strapped to your seat, you think, This is what I dreamed of doing all my life and I knew it was dangerous when I signed up and my mission will never be forgotten. *This* was my mission. Disaster was my mission.

At the time of the *Challenger* disaster, Frank was in D.C. wooing senators and congressmen over shrimp cocktails, martinis, etcetera in an attempt to shore up support for the financial quango, and Wendy was in Los Angeles for meetings with network execs to pitch her *Strays* summer Christmas special. She went as writer-producer and took Rachael as ipso facto director of the cartoon for silent support. The potential for failure seemed very much at hand—there it was, the VHS tape we made of the cartoon.

The first meet was with Brian Lynch, Head of Children's Programming at ABC.

If ABC buys now, the network could air it this coming July, Wendy said.

Brian Lynch took the cassette. He was honoured to be the first outsider to view the cartoon so many industry insiders were affectionately calling *Apocalypse, Strays*. Did the cartoon even exist or was it something Wendy said to sound mysterious? He kept looking back and forth between Wendy and Rachael waiting for us to confess there was no cartoon. Now Lynch knew for sure. A few minutes into the story, he was laughing. It's not what I expected at all but that's the point, right? I like the approach, or the lack of. It's fresh. Funny.

Then a secretary burst through the door in tears and switched off the VCR to turn on the live news. They never watched the rest of the Christmas special.

Let me think on it and get back to you, a teary-eyed Brian Lynch said as he led Wendy out of his office. Then he burst into a donkeysob, and covering his eyes with his arm, slammed the door of his office shut.

The noise outside Lynch's office reminded her of the time she had visited the Hexen Diamond Mistral offices in Manhattan. To get to the elevators we faced an entire floor of paroxysms—racing to react to the disaster, employees dug in like soldiers, telephones blasting at every desk. It was like the opening volley of a military action. Cries for help. Running from desk to desk delivering shorthand transcriptions of urgent phone interviews. No one on the floor noticed us walk by, least of all us. *Strays* was totally insignificant right now. The sky over America was still filled with rocket debris on its long arc to the ground. There were journalists in the room who had interviewed the astronauts.

35

She had booked three appointments over two sere days in Los Angeles, with Lynch at ABC the first day, and with CBS's president, Norman Zederbaum, and Peter Patterson at NBC on the second afternoon. The network offices were in entirely different suburbs, hours apart from each other, like feuding children with lines drawn between them. President Zederbaum was a hale old gentleman, broad shouldered, a veteran of two wars, the kind of man Wendy saluted on the street out of plain courtesy, a hello to age's inevitable provisions of wisdom, of which Zederbaum seemed to have accumulated more than his fair share. Once energetically handsome, if not tall, as a producer akin to Wendy's mother but on a grander scale, Zederbaum had been a relentless cowboy on the sound stage, rounding up the contract actors for cattlecalls and barking orders at unionized technicians. Much too old to do anything so physical for the network now, what luck he was president. Meetings were his milieu in advanced years—he took a few a week and golfed the rest. That wisdom from experience, mostly made up of backlot gossip good enough for blackmail, so long as his memory held out, that's what gave him influence. After that self-portrait, he asked Wendy to show him the cartoon.

When the Christmas special was over, Zederbaum turned to her and said, Dear, are you on drugs?

Zederbaum's underling was a man named Tom *TK* Watson. TK was another example of this same sort of unstoppable gentleman who had cut his teeth in the Golden Era of Television and could have retired when Ed Sullivan introduced the Beatles. But he kept on going out of a love of money. His eyes were black balls sunken in shadow. His deep, sombre voice came with its own echo, rattling around in the cave of his throat. The thin hair on top of TK Watson's head was the grey of lint. This was the Head of Children's Programming.

TK Watson spoke as if delivering a sermon over the grave of a child. You might not know it but I'm the biggest fan of *Strays*, have been since day one. Own all the treasuries. I do. More than you'll ever know … More than you'll ever know *I* wanted to be the one to bring *Strays* to TV. A summer Christmas special—this rumour made me laugh the first time I heard it, and I still laugh at it even after I've seen the—. The pitch is still funny.

TK Watson heaved himself forward in his chair, leaned his elbows on the table, and tapped his fingertips together in the air in front of him as he continued to speak. So, gee, what else to call it but a *masterpiece*. Deserves to be in a modern art museum, doesn't it? The masterpiece has arrived and we've *all* had a chance to take a look, and we are unfortunately going to have to pass. Yes.

To *pass*, she said. That's not your *final* decision? You want a few changes.

No, this is just too far out, Wendy. You made a cartoon for MTV, not CBS … We could air this at midnight, I guess.

This is not *art*, this is … nihilism, said the president of CBS. He spoke to her as if to scold an underling. He stomped around the office. Zederbaum could not sit down because this was not his office, not even his floor of the building, and so the president paced TK Watson's office like the ghost in *Hamlet*, speaking in a wet rasp made worse by his high collar and necktie pressing against his ancient Adam's apple. I'm not impressed, Wendy, I am not. This cartoon was not what I hoped for. You've compromised your good taste to please a failed generation. In an era of profound anxiety, children need cartoons with a calm, even tempo. Not this rampa-bam-bam, machine gun rock video editing you do here.

TK Watson took over from his apoplectic boss. You borrow from the history of animation in a willynilly spectacle that is more disorienting than our network is prepared for. Because I hope I *never* gave you the impression we wanted something like *Pee-wee Herman* or the old *Batman* show with Adam West, no, no, we always hoped this was a straightforward adaptation of your strip. This experiment is courageous, unforgettable.

Zederbaum nudged TK Watson out of his own office chair and sat down. From this new position he once more said, No. Too stimulating, said Zederbaum. You're a lovely girl, but this cartoon is downright indecent.

Times change, think about it, kids still love some zip, said Wendy. Maybe we should plug it into the VCR again and give it a second look?

The cartoon does *not fit* CBS at this time, TK Watson said more diplomatically.

You know what fits CBS? Wendy stood up to leave. *Third place*, she said.

Two hours on the freeway later she was in the lobby of NBC, drenched in sweat. The VHS copy of the Christmas special rejected by two networks was clutched in Rachael's white knuckles. Above our heads, a giant backlit vinyl version of the NBC peacock. Underneath it in polished copper letters was a quote attributed to Emily Dickinson: *I hope you love birds too. It is economical. It saves going to heaven.*

Already I like this network more. *Fuck* ABC. Fuck CBS in the nose. Those networks are a waste. Here's the one for me, goddamn it.

The receptionist recognized Wendy instantly and said he was a big *big* fan of *Strays*. He asked for an autograph and a drawing of Francis before he invited her to go up for her meeting on the eighth and penultimate floor, where Mr. Patterson was waiting for her.

And if you bump into anyone who tells you anything remotely *fishy*, the receptionist added, make sure to ask if they work for Letterman.

She took the elevator up to eight, where there was another receptionist.

Can you direct me to Mr. Patterson's office, please?

Mr. Patterson? Sorry, Mr. Patterson doesn't work here anymore. He was fired this morning.

… Do you work for Letterman?

Dah … uh … The guy leaped from the receptionist's chair and ran away down the hall.

Peter Patterson's office as Head of Children's Programming at NBC was twice the size of his colleague TK Watson's over at CBS, and Patterson was half the age of his colleague if not a third or fifth. He had a funny haircut, wore a wrinkly gingham shirt and stained khakis, and his collie slept under his desk.

Patterson told her, Listen, I want this cartoon for our network. A *summer* Christmas special? Oh my god, *perfect.* NBC is the home for this kind of craziness. My son is *nineteen*, he drapes himself in anything that's got *your comic* on it. Francis, right? He loves that feisty rabbit. Let me bring in Hank Lazarus, the prez, so he can put the final rubber stamp on this.

Patterson called in his boss. Wait until you see this.

Lazarus was a younger, plumper Patterson who positioned himself in the office in such a way that he took up the most amount of floor surface possible. He wore a Duran Duran concert T-shirt under a white blazer offset by a pattern of interlocking pink triangles. His creased white parachute pants were Gucci. His shoes fashioned from the skin of Komodo dragons.

No, said Lazarus. Show it to HBO. Are you like nuts or something? Didn't you see the *Challenger?* Oh my god. Not the fucking time. To be honest, I find the concept offensive. You can't mess with Christmas. Not this year. Absolutely not.

Patterson's eyebrow arched and he shrugged at Wendy behind his boss's back. There's no arguing with disaster.

We were sunk when word got back to us that the big three had passed on our Christmas cartoon. There was no way to talk about the rejection, so there was nothing to say. No Manors went silent. Patrick got out the newspapers and looked for a place to live on his own. Rachael hid in her room and recorded her eighth seven-inch single as Aluminum Uvula and booked a live show at the Broadway opening for Zetetic and Big Black (that ended in police and teargas). Mark, who was alcoholic so it didn't matter to him what happened, put every penny he got towards Old Milwaukee. And Twyla devised multiple strategies to save the Christmas special, including direct-to-video and other sensible and not so sensible options (bribes). Of all of us, Twyla was the least depressed by the rejection. It might have helped that Blair Slobodchikoff wanted her to move in with him, and that Marvel hired her on a get-to-know basis to pencil a *Fantastic Four* spinoff miniseries about the superhero Medusa at a hundred dollars a page, written by Roy Thomas, inked by Terry Austin.

Nothing for us to do but wait until Wendy made up her mind. She didn't need to say it for us to think it was *our fault* the cartoon wasn't suitable for the major networks. But Wendy had handed this project to us knowing full well we had no idea how to make a cartoon and weren't part of a Disney system that could control our impulses. It was her fault it was our fault the cartoon was a flop.

Obviously she approached Piper Shepherd after the first round of networks passed, to see if he would distribute. Shepherd Media wasn't in the business of new properties, Piper explained; his specialty was syndicated repeats of network shows for all his regional cable affiliates. *Replicant Fitness* was a success, true, but actually that was a Shepherd Productions property pitched to networks and bought by NBC, and rebroadcast on Shepherd Media's Bay Area affiliate. He promised Wendy he'd buy the repeat rights if she got a deal, but as a businessman, Piper didn't approve of the salaries and budgets it took to operate a network studio. He left the upfront risks to others.

In a way, Wendy, this is good for you, I mean to get into some fights, to do a bit of ducking and swinging to gain approval outside Shepherd Media.

Oh, I know from fights, said Wendy. I've been fighting to be me ever since I was born.

You could hear a pencil hit paper at No Manors. You could hear the pipes gurgle and drain when a bachelor in a room upstairs used the shared toilet, that's how quiet it was at No Manors.

One day Biz came down from her suite on the third floor with a surprise to cheer us up—a garbage bag filled with so much weed it was stretched out like a beach ball. She dropped it on the dining room's section of the longtable and stepped back to let us get in close and inspect.

Where did you get this? Patrick wanted to know of the astonishing amount as Mark set about rolling Phillies and Zig-Zags.

My Twomps hookup got a hella fresh hookup, was all Biz said and even that was too much. The news that week covered the funeral for South Oakland's drug kingpin, Felix the Cat, who caught a bullet in a roadside gunfight, leading to retaliations and a power vacuum.

How much do we owe you? Rachael asked.

Same as always, said Biz.

She stayed for one bowl and said she would come down later for more and do some drawing. Right now she was hanging out in her suite with the drag queens Lil Morphine Annie, Pelvis Restless, and Princess Strawberry DeAqueduct tailoring costumes and makeup for their next show at the Freight and Salvage—*La 628-E8*, based on the roadtrip memoir of Octave Mirbeau. We did notice the fact her face was made up in blazing theatricality but didn't see a need to ask why she had sequins and rhinestones decorating her cheeks and eyelids, purple and green streaks across her eyes, and cheekbones self-spray-painted in one of her vanity mirrors. But she was dressed casually in a Mickey Mouse tubetop and hot pants and thongs and had no wig on. After getting high she took the stairs back up to her room and left us to find a way to fit all this weed into Hick's laundry hamper.

It was perhaps only mere days after readers had finally digested the scandal of issue nine when Biz Aziz delivered another bombshell. In eighty-six, she published issue ten of her ongoing memoir, a thirty-two-page comic that combined diarylike narration captions with scenes from her relationship with the now deceased Vaughn Staedtler. No one outside their inner circle knew they were together in the last years of his life or that Vaughn's predilections ran the gamut (he was estranged from his three children). Over the years the occasional tabloid or letter to the editor mentioned his arrests in the fifties for two kidnappings, a female minor (his first cousin), and in the sixties for possession of drugs (an ounce of booger sugar) and a nineteen-year-old male catalogue model who had not called his parents for a month. The comic showed the progress of their relationship from friends to lovers to soulmates. There was a scene of Vaughn and Biz in the lowest reaches of a downtown steamroom seduced by Michel Foucault. A scene of them on the highway in one of Vaughn's sports cars, passing vineyards, going over a bridge, through a tunnel, to a remote and quiet beach for a picnic. Another scene in a two-seater with the top down, but this time chased by six high school jocks drunk in a pickup truck swinging baseball bats and yelling obscenities at them. Vaughn flipped them the finger—*Fuck you, squares!*—and squealed white-rim tires around a corner, parked in an alley, and waited for the truckful of jocks to pass them and disappear before they reversed out again. Here's where a speech bubble over Biz read, *Damnit, Vaughn.*

And in the next panel, over Vaughn, a speech bubble read, *I love you, too.*

Response came fast in letters and articles in fanzines and periodicals and ranged from straight homophobic to strangely misguided to reverential and laudatory. There was a comic critic on Berkeley college radio who didn't believe a word of it and praised Biz for her twisted satirical and fictional take on so-called memoir comix, a genre much in need of some bending. A writer for *The Komics Kwarterly* was convinced the relationship in issue ten must be a fiction, but was equally convinced that it was a fact when Jonjay cannibalized Hick Elmdales in issue nine. A much-quoted letter was originally published in *The Comics Journal* from an anonymous reader who claimed to know for a fact issues nine and ten were all true. The author claimed to have lived in the same building as Biz for four years and witnessed it all first-hand.

*

Since their spat on the phone the previous year, Wendy and Gabrielle Scavalda hadn't spoken much—coolly conducting business through Rachael, who fielded all calls to the manor and replied to messages on the machine. Gabby never dialed Wendy's private Motorola number. She used to revel in her role as Manhattan intermediary between her West Coast artist and the man in charge of licences and merchandising. But Frank and Wendy as a live-in couple put Gabby on the outside. She felt uncomfortable calling either one of them unless it was about something big. She quite naturally felt they were plotting against her. Instead of being the fulcrum between two poles, her role was more dissociated than ever from both the creative process and the business decisions. When we took her calls, her comments were abrupt, perfunctory, and retired from the task of influence.

In the week before Valentine's Day, Wendy took some cheques down to deposit at Solus First National and withdraw some cash while at it to spend on romantic trifles for Frank. She stood in line for the next available teller dreaming of a cheeseburger from Clown Alley across the street.

Wendy Ashbubble? the voice behind her almost pleaded.

Even before turning around she recognized SEC agent Chris Quiltain. Her teeth bit down on the image of his face that day in Chambers Diner in Manhattan, and in the coat-room at Vaughn's funeral. Today he looked the same but even more minionlike, if possible, as if someone had scribbled all over his features with a red correction pencil *no, no, no, no*. He still preferred corduroy suits. She was trapped. The only thing she could do was wait for a teller or run.

Can I speak with you?

How long have you been following me? she said. What's going on?

You come here often? To the bank?

Your pickup lines need some serious work.

So you haven't made a lot of deposits and wire transfers in the last two or three days?

You're spying again. I don't know what you're creeping me for. Now you have access to my bank account or something? I don't even know what a wire transfer is.

Just asking, he said. A big dip in the market, that's all. Lots of movement.

That's Frank's business. Ask *him*. Only market I know's the super. I don't follow the ups and downs. Besides, I thought you nabbed that guy Kravis.

The queue advanced a person or two.

We know you're in with Frank. This is your last chance, Wendy, to save yourself. You might be a willing accomplice or an ignorant dupe, I don't know. Either way we can cut a deal. Come work with me and the DA. Meet me. Let's talk it over. I'll lay out the evidence for you.

Did you stake out the bank or follow me here? What else? My phone? My home? My studio? This is very disturbing to me. I'm skittish on a good day. Fess up, Chris. If you can be on the level with me, I might trust you.

… I can't divulge— Just ask your teller for a complete transaction record for your account for the past month. Not the redacted version you get in the mail. Make sure you ask. Gotta go, he said and gave her his business card, scissored his legs over the velvet rope, and walked out of the bank in two more steps.

Next, said the teller.

I need to speak with Doug Chimney, she said.

A moment later the manager of Solus First National minced out onto the floor to meet her at the gate and led her back into his private office. Once they were alone she let loose.

What did you tell them?

Nothing, I—, nothing. Chimney guided her in and circled the desk to find his chair, which he stood half behind, as if to shield himself from her questions. He didn't offer a drink.

I thought we had something sweet going on, Doug, she said and instead of sitting in the usual chair she stepped round behind his desk to join him there.

We did. I mean, we do.

You're hooked, aren't you? They got you? When did Quiltain approach you? I mean, how recently?

He didn't, said Chimney, who was blushing and glistening with sweat. She was walking her fingers up the length of his necktie to the piggy flesh under his chin.

Why'd you go and do something so stupid? she asked.

You haven't been, you know … available lately, he trailed off.

Shit, Doug, I'm sorry. But you screwed us now.

When she brought up the substance of Quiltain's unsettling meeting with Frank, he didn't bat an eye. He said, Good ol' goddamn Quiltain will never stop, not until he's got us.

Super, just super, said Wendy, who didn't mention much about her follow-up with Doug except to say she suspected Quiltain had questioned him, too. Chimney completely lost his cool, she said.

Frank was silent. Silence was bad, she knew. His brain processed so many competing patterns so fast so regularly he scarcely ever needed to pause to consider his answer.

What did *I* do? she moaned.

Me. You did me. The SEC is on my case. You're collateral damage.

The accidental moll. Financial femme fatale.

Stop, you're turning me on. Problem is, once these SEC shitbugs get an idea, there's no way to rid yourself of them. I need to find a way to get to Chimney without Quiltain knowing. He's the kind who finds one bad apple in the cart and suspects a vast conspiracy in the produce aisles, the whole damn grocery store. Cost of doing business. SEC are an expense, like the press and lawyers. Not even a necessary evil, an inevitable one.

Regarding the transfers, he said, It's my job as your money manager to move your assets in and out of your various accounts as I roll pieces of your portfolio into my investment options with Hexen.

She stared at him long and hard and said, Kiss me.

Nevertheless, she remained on high alert for bugs and other unwanted surveillance, didn't know exactly who to believe, Chris or Frank. She took apart the phones and with Rachael's help looked for microphones.

Frank's attitude that everyone was intellectually beneath him had a way of numbing her fears and reassuring her that every anxiety-provoking problem in life could be plotted as part of a much grander pattern, one he was studying for profit. In fact we were all so hairy bananas busy putting the finishing touches and repairing last-hour disasters on the summer Christmas special that Wendy very soon forgot all about the close call with Quiltain at the bank. A day after Valentine's Day, Gabby Scavalda called Wendy on her Motorola to tell her she got the Reuben nomination. It's not an official list they publicize, said Gabby. But Dik just rang to whisper your name made the shortlist.

I just broke out in a flop sweat, said Wendy and sat down in her kitchen nook.

Five years. Five years of hard doodling. I think this is your year, Wendy, darling. Macy's under your belt. A strip worldwide. Three bestselling treasuries. Toys in every shop window. Cartoon special some smart network is going to debut. Victory. Celebrate. Go drunk yourself stupid. That's *my* plan.

You took the first risk on my dumb clumsy comic, Gabby. This is your doing.

I'm sorry I let the complaints get to me. I love the way you draw.

You're just doing your job. I need to hear honesty if I want to break two thousand papers.

All of her heroes in cartooning had received the Reuben Award. Schulz had won it twice. Even if the statue itself was a mockery of such trifling ambition—a turd-shaped pileup of cartoon characters designed by

Rube Goldberg as a grotesque joke on the winner—it was still the greatest honour in her field.

We pedalled bikes and pushed skateboards downtown to drink pitchers of beer at the White Horse and eat their free hotdogs and popcorn until we felt loaded. And then, slaphappy and boozed up, drifted deeper into downtown to more and more expensive bars, spending and spending. Same drinks more expensive. Celebrating.

You showed up and I put you to work, you never said no, I could trust you with my characters ... thank you, Wendy told us sometime that night. She got out a portfolio of original strips. Not hers, *other* cartoonists. A McManus daily, a Bushmiller, a Frazetta. Timeless strips. Dabs of Wite-Out here and there. Blueline pencils showing up under edges of the ink. We handled them with care. But we accepted her gifts. You got me through some dramatic times in my life when I couldn't focus on my comic strip let alone all the other work, she said. And now the cartoon is done, too, and the Reuben news ... , Wendy swallowed. I am grateful.

> *Dear Dr. Pazder,*
> *I know I haven't written in many months. However, upon receiving my nomination for the annual Reuben Award, I felt it was an opportune time to catch you up ... It's an honour few have ... Although I know my memory has repressed a bombshell, I'm certain of one thing: My father is a powerful man.*

Months in advance of the ceremony, we began to sketch concepts for our outfits the night of—like fashion designers. And then in the bathroom we got together to cut, dye, flatten, crimp, feather, frizz, mince, chop, extend, and highlight our hair in anticipation. This was razors, wax, glue, lotions, moisturizers, tweezers, mousse, spray, gel, clips, pins, barrettes, and bows. Instead of her income going exclusively to the high-fashion boutiques, Wendy shopped low first, then high, for possible clothes from any brand or brandless, without discretion or prejudice, daring herself to buy outlandish, fearless in the face of trends and gauches. And three belts was no unusual number for her to wrap around her waist. A break-dance T-shirt underneath an oversized submarine vest, gold dookie chain necklace and really, really long strands of pearls wrapped around and around her neck that still draped to her hips. Tight pink cotton pants under an ultramarine skirt.

Have I reached Wendy Ashbubble?

Yes. This is her assistant, Rachael. What can I do for you?

My name is Brian Lynch, I'm Head of Children's Programming at ABC. I think we met a meeting, the day of the disaster …

I remember. How are you, Mr. Lynch?

Sorry I never got back about the animation. I realized just today. Someone in the office told me they heard I passed. I told them I didn't pass—I flat forgot about it. The disaster …

What a day, said Rachael.

Yes, well, no doubt. Would you and Wendy like to come down again and look at a contract, meet the president, so we can get to work promoting this for our summer schedule?

Of course, certainly indeed we would, said Rachael, as professionally voiced as possible for someone jumping up and down and from room to room stretching out the intestinal rubber of the phone cord as she went.

Terrific. I adored that crazy cartoon. It's like a throwback to Looney Tunes and a leap forward for the art form all at the same time. And heart-felt, a sweet message at the end. Can't wait to foist this on an unsuspecting public. And listen—I heard through my sources about the Reuben nom for the strip and that's great news so make sure to congratulate Wendy for me when you talk to her?

Although we found no reason to suspect Frank managed to finagle her deal with ABC from afar, it is public knowledge that over the past

423

few years as Hexen's high-yield bond department grew to substantially outperform all the rest of the investment bank's operations combined, the profits came with more high-profile clients. Clients like ABC, who started to use Frank for mortgages and leases and then turned over their debt refinancing to him in eighty-six. By splitting up the payables on ABC's books, Frank managed to turn the outstanding backlist into junk bonds, sell off property and assets at auction, halve the staff, and leave the network with the cash it needed to develop new programming. Frank's influence was unavoidable.

Our own opinion of him at the time was decidedly mixed. Nervous awe set in when we saw him in person, and backstabbing envy took over in his absence. We were suspicious of him and we defended him. Wendy might love him but he didn't deserve her. He must be committing crimes on the bond market but he was also a genius who could get away with it. He had money but money was irrelevant, what counted was heart, and we had a hard time accepting he had Wendy's heart.

36

Then a message arrived special delivery, not regular post or UPS or another known courier. This deadserious fellow wore black and black aviator shades and carried his own 9 mm sidearm. Required Wendy show ID and sign for it in person. Inside a pretty box was an envelope with gilt lettering on the front, and an official U.S. government seal on the back.

WENDY ASHUBBLE

AND

FRANK FLEECEN

BY SPECIAL INVITATION FROM
THE PRESIDENT OF THE UNITED STATES OF AMERICA
AND HIS WIFE THE FIRST LADY

THE WHITE HOUSE IS PLEASED TO REQUEST
YOUR HONORED ATTENDANCE
AT THE STATE DINING HALL'S LUNCHEON

FOLLOWED BY
CONVERSATION WITH PRESIDENT RONALD REAGAN
IN THE OVAL OFFICE

Frank's shoulders flinched forward at the sight of the invitation he'd worked so hard for. He whistled through his nose and he stared. Holy shit, he said.

Lunch with the president. Isn't this *amay*-zing? Wendy said. She thought her knees would give out on her. Frank had to hold her up. All the colour went out of her skin. Her hair went brittle. She wondered aloud, Can I swallow food in front of the president? This is the best year of my life. I have you. My comic. I have my friends. My cartoon. A Reuben nomination. And now, about to meet the president. I might faint.

My good luck being *president* that when I invite my favourite Americans for lunch they all show up, Ronald Reagan said by way of an introduction before anyone sat down. That each of you has made a positive impact in this country is one reason I wanted to meet you, but you are also here because I have been touched personally by your endeavours. And some of you, by your talents—, tipping his paternal cheek to her and eyeing Wendy directly, —enrich my life *every day*. Welcome to the White House. Let's have lunch, shall we?

The twenty-five guests standing at their assigned places at the table in the State Dining Room applauded.

Don't worry, I'm old but I can sit down without help. Please.

All sat. At the table with her that noon hour on the solstice were the twenty-four others the president had invited. An astronaut. A former surgeon general. A car manufacturer. A microchip developer. A former Secret Service agent who took the bullet for Reagan. A television host. A war hero. An architect. A magician. A dinosaur expert. A children's show host. A televangelist. A bestselling author. A quarterback. An actor turned activist. A multiplatinum-selling singer turned humanitarian. An ex-mayor. A physiologist. A movie producer. Co-owners of an ice cream company. A plastics factory owner. A media empire mogul. A junk bond king. A comic strip creator.

What she wanted to ask Reagan would have to wait until after lunch. For the time being Wendy vibrated in a light-headed trance of anticipation as she rammed her crab salad into her mouth.

Frank had campaigned hard for these seats. She teased him that he was at the White House as *her* date, but his agenda was clear: he had to sell the president on the securities he trafficked in, high-yield bonds, and the urgent need to unshackle free enterprise from excessive government oversight and out-of-step regulatory agencies.

I know a vichyssoise when I see one, she said to the soup put in front of her by a butler.

All he needed was *five minutes*, Frank told Wendy, to convince this president why the press had him backwards. The facts backed Frank up: high-yield bonds were here to save America. In accordance with his principles, Frank ate each bite of his lunch deliberately.

Reagan's smile. How he ate his meal in feigned morsels, it charmed her. Reagan's apple-red cheeks. His bootblack pompadour. Years of camera makeup embedded in the skin gave the president's face the rubbery shine of a Halloween mask version of himself. Better jokes than half the comedians on *The Tonight Show*. Cold War hero. Leader of the Free World. The look but not the looks of Dean Martin. Nancy sat by her husband's side, stiff and scheming-faced.

It was Wendy's greatest desire in life. Without Dr. Pazder's therapeutic help she had made it here, to confront Ronald Reagan. And here she was in the room with him. Regardless of his imprecations, he had invited her after all, and he didn't show a trace of discomfort at seeing his illegitimate daughter in the dining room with him and the American luminaries.

Frank asked for a tall glass of Coke with no ice, and at an opportune moment, slipped his veal-stuffed chicken into the cola.

After a ninety-minute lunch spread out across six courses if you counted coffee-tea, the president met with each guest one-on-one in the Oval Office. This took the rest of the afternoon.

At one thirty, after the inventor of polyvinyl chloride was let out, an aide notified Frank it was his turn to see the president. He kissed Wendy and stroked her Rolex for good luck, and then strode into the Oval Office and greeted the president in an anxiously booming officious-sounding voice.

Then it was strange, because a different man came out of the Oval Office. His suit was two sizes too big. He kept shaking his head like there was water in his ears and hacking like an old man with a smoker's cough. Other guests tried not to appear as though they were staring. This Frank was frail and nerdy. His neck stuck out of his collar turtle-like and the hair on his head was comically fake.

What did he *say* to you? Wendy whispered to this cousin. She embraced him and then held his hands in hers, for she could feel him trembling.

Reagan said, *Time's up*.

Time's up? What does *that* mean?

He said, *You're a genius*. He said, I wanted to help, but I just got word the picture's changed. This business with the Contras, he said. Time to move on. Quit while you're ahead.

The president said that to *you*? Gee! That is terrible. Oh no. Wendy thought of her own meeting any moment now.

Frank looked dazed. He said, Reagan put a hand on my shoulder and said to remember this is not his first term. He said, This is my second term. And then he said, *God bless you*.

Frank shook off the horror, but it came right back, and he spoke in this very different voice from the voice she knew. I'm going. I must go.

Wait for me? Wendy tried to hold his hand. He cringed and pulled away.

I can't stay here another *second*. I might vomit on a flag.

Where should I meet you?

Motorola, he said and ran.

She took a long time in the ladies' room composing herself in front of the mirror, and then accepted a tour of the White House rose garden. The rose garden led fortuitously into the chocolate and candy shop. There she met up with the astronaut and the televangelist who had just bowled a few lanes together in the White House alleys. Wendy ate two of the president's chocolate bars and a few chocolate squares, drank the president's blend of chocolate milkshake, and finished it off with the president's preferred chocolate hoo-hoo cake. She felt better now.

As the sugar high kicked in, Wendy got lost in an image from her childhood, her mother asleep on the couch in the living room. Her mother never had a bedroom, just a pullout couch. Here in the opulent halls of the White House, the home of America's president, his wife, their grown children, and all their staff, Wendy saw the sadness of this memory. She saw the sadness with a clarity that seemed stupid of her to have ignored for so long. Crying in the presidential candy shop, she hid her face perusing a shelf of syrups.

An aide touched her gently on the shoulder and said she was next.

She wiped her eyes outside the Oval Office. Now the time had come to meet her father. Her heart was on fire, frozen, pumping madly, and stopped.

She went in.

The Oval Office smelled as though the president snuck in a second helping of the baked apple pie that came as one choice on the dessert menu at lunch, and as he strode across the carpet to greet her, arms open wide, he seemed to pause for a moment to swallow a last bite. They embraced. He smelled of baked apple pie. She swooned.

I guess you know why I invited you, he said as he went around the side of a sofa and then sat down on it. She followed him to the conference area of the oval and sat down on a sofa facing his.

Yes, she said.

These lunches are a treat for me. I've met many of my favourite Americans this way, he said, and learned a lot about how this country thinks. I want to thank you for bringing your humour and warmth and weirdness to the funny pages. Do you want a jelly bean?

Yes, please, said Wendy and scooped a handful from the glass bowl on the coffee table between them.

My candy chef makes my jelly beans for me right here in the Oval Office.

I tried a hoo-hoo, she said and blushed. My palate did a backflip.

Anyway. Your strip's my favourite and I'm not just saying that.

Oh no?

No, I used to say that my favourite was *Peanuts*.

Peanuts is my inspiration.

These days so many funnies are *mean*-spirited. I wish the guy who draws Opus would quit. Time's up, buddy. Too cynical. Charlie Brown gives you a laugh of compassion. That's eternal. More eternal than politics and parody, don't you think?

I love how he draws *Bloom County*. It's funnier than *Eek & Meek* or *Ziggy*.

No. Your lost pets, they spread love. Opus spreads fear. I read *Strays* first. Breaks my heart, busts my gut. Your hilarious pets get my day going. They *deserve* owners. Won't you ever give them to people to care for?

They scrape by with each other.

Those *are* good hoo-hoos, aren't they?

She nodded. She wanted to reach out and touch Reagan. Instead he leaned forward and touched her hands.

He laughed. His laugh laughed. Those apple cheeks. He was made of pie, that's how happy Reagan looked. So happy Wendy thought they might both start to cry.

I guess you know why I invited you, he repeated.

My mom never got over you, she said.

Reagan asked her if she was Christian.

Well, Wendy said, my *mother* was Jewish so …

What happened to her?

She passed away. Angina. Second act of *Inherit the Wind* community production.

Oh, how sad.

I was sixteen. Been on my own ever since.

And your father?

You're my father.

Reagan blinked. Of course, he said. Of course. I blanked for a moment. The president sat back in his sofa and brushed flat his suit pants. Well, I know it's hard. Some say life is a pickle we endeavour to turn back into a cucumber.

Mom never talked about anything other than showbiz. Always showbiz. To her, the stage was God.

An aide knocked, delicately opened the door. He pointed to his wristwatch and mouthed a few words.

Reagan nodded, and when father and daughter were alone again, father sighed and said this would probably be their one and only chance to meet.

So Wendy asked the president if he had any questions for her, and he laughed and said, Will that cat detective Tom Clues ever catch his culprit?

Yes, said Wendy. If you'll give me a kiss.

They flew home that night on Hexen's private 747—this long cylinder seemed very hollow, and they kept to separate areas. Frank didn't speak to her except politely to suggest she take a sleeping pill. He was poring through contracts with his interns looking for a solution in upcoming mergers and acquisitions. There was no way he could *quit*. The idea was appalling, that was the word he used. He *looked* appalled. Shaken to the core, eyes bloodshot, toupée aslant.

She didn't tell him about her meeting with Reagan; he didn't ask. Frank seemed to forget she'd even had a meeting. He was so absorbed in his strategies.

The attendant offered to thread a movie for her when she didn't go right to sleep, so Wendy spent the night slumped in a leather chair watching Hollywood action films alone with a sketchpad in her lap and a bowl of buttery popcorn.

To us it was astounding. She had done it, she'd met the president. And he claimed her as his daughter, denied nothing, and even felt something.

I feel for Frank, she told us when she got home. He's a mess. He went straight from the hangar to his office. I don't think he knows how to deal with bad news. I feel very peaceful, though. I met my father. It wasn't what I expected at all. It happened so quickly and yet it left such a lasting impression. I feel like I walked through a door in myself. It could have been a disaster like Frank and I wouldn't know until I was out the door. But when I came out of the Oval Office I felt light on my feet and calm. The calm didn't last but I feel more connected to myself having kissed him.

STRAYS

37

Frank never came out of panic mode after his one-on-one with the president. He was at his desk in the Transamerica Pyramid twenty hours a day in an attempt to do what the president could not, and use his weight in the bonds market, his financial acumen and salesman's smooth tongue, his lobbyists, his Hexen team and his half-formed financial quango, all to influence the politicians who wanted to see a curb to the credit market.

That whole month, ABC aired commercials every hour for the upcoming cartoon special, five times an hour primetime. The trailer flashed a montage of our animation with the theme music and a voiceover that promised viewers *Look out, Santa! What better way to find out the true meaning of Christmas than to try celebrating in the summer? That's what your favourite animals from* Strays *seek to find out.*

TV Guide put Wendy on the cover in between her characters and the headline *Are You Ready for Christmas this July?*

Then, two days before the National Cartoonists Society Awards, a letter from Solus First National arrived at No Manors to notify Wendy that the interest rate on her mortgage just spiked thirty percent. The same day a courier arrived and asked her to sign for an official letter from the United States Senate asking that she appear before a subcommittee in Washington, D.C., *tomorrow*.

Out came the Motorola. Her palms were soaked. Her jaw was gnashing. She never used the phone attached to the wall in the kitchen anymore. She walked in and out of No Manors using the cellular, distracted, in a blind panic. As soon as he picked up she said, Frank, I just got some *things* in the mail today I need you to explain.

I got one, too. A letter to appear before the subcommittee on blah blah blah.

What *is* this? D.C. is across the country.

A fishing expedition, Frank said. We have to go, though. I alerted the pilots to warm up the 747.

Okay so hold on, listen, before my aneurism. Second thing. Suddenly my mortgage on No Manors is up, and by up I mean *thirty percent* up—from last month. Any idea what's going on?

There was a pause on the line and she heard a truck's horn bleat. Then Frank told her, Wendy, listen, go cash out as many stocks and bonds at Solus as you can and cash out your chequing account. Whatever else. They're going belly up. The credit market is in a fast-freeze. Go talk to Chimney right now. Put the screws to him if he resists. Can you do that? Bring luggage to pack up the money. Put the money and copies of your cartoon special and whatever else you value in the bedroom safe. Right away.

Jesus. Who pulled the emergency bell?

Wendy, the economy is walking drunk along the ledge of a tall building right now.

Gee, make me grind my teeth again or *what*, Frank.

Once this dip is done dipping, all will be fine. Jonjay's formula predicted this, as always, and saved me. Can't move all the money out of the way of this but some. It sort of is hell. Meanwhile, caught up in the middle of a political witch-hunt. For becoming a powerful and formidable opponent to the old bluebloods running things in Manhattan, you and I must now go do penance, and act docile and incapable in front of this subcommittee of kangaroos. To wound me, they drag you into the fray. However, it's all for show.

We better be home in time to see my premiere, she said. I don't want to be stuck in a hotel room for it. I want to be at No Manors, drunk.

One day. In and out. We'll be home in twenty-four hours.

Frank, for once I need you to tell me the truth.

This is the truth.

No, I know something's going on. You ask for my trust, then I need to know the whole unvarnished truth. Otherwise I'm liable to be persuaded what this subcommittee claims to know about you.

Okay, said Frank. I'll tell you everything and you can decide for yourself.

What follows are the questions members wanted Wendy to answer at the hearing before the House Energy and Commerce Committee's Oversight and Investigations Subcommittee.

Rep. John Dingell, Michigan, Chairman: The Chair wants to emphasize that the subcommittee's proceedings today are neither civil nor are they criminal. The function of the subcommittee today is to make a series of inquiries. The Chair will observe that these are not criminal proceedings. The constitutional rights of the persons appearing before the committee will be very, very carefully protected with equal care and equal vigour. Our intentions today are legislative in nature and concern the adequacy and effectiveness of our laws. The Chair recognizes the honourable representative from Virginia, Thomas Bliley.

Rep. Thomas Bliley Jr., Virginia: Thank you, Mr. Chairman. The hearing today and the hearing scheduled for tomorrow are for the purpose of examining possible irregularities in the trading of high-yield bonds. Specifically with respect to transactions between an underwriter and affiliates of the underwriter. We are making this examination through a study of three particular cases involving the firm of Hexen Diamond Mistral. The high-yield bond market has exploded in the last few years as these securities are increasingly used for a variety of corporate purposes. Our objective is not to debate the value of high-yield bonds generally. Their economic importance, in my view, is indisputable.

John Dingell, Michigan, Chairman: Miss Ashbubble, are you aware of why you have been asked to appear today before the House Energy and Commerce Committee's Subcommittee for Oversight and Investigations?

Ron Wyden, Oregon: I'd like to start the questions by asking how long you have known the junk bond banker Frank Fleecen?

Dennis Eckart, Ohio: Where did you first meet Frank Fleecen?

Jim Slattery, Kansas: Are you, or have you ever been, a Satanist? Let me rephrase that. Are you, or have you ever been, in league with the devil? Just one more follow-up question. Have you ever signed any pacts with the devil or been part of any secret witches' covens?

Gerry Sikorski, Minnesota: Have you ever practised any of the following: sodomy, rape, incest, cannibalism, or murder? Think carefully before you answer.

Rich Boucher, Virginia: Have you ever buried a child alive, or been buried alive in a ritual sacrifice to Satan? Have you eaten human flesh? And how can you be so certain about that?

Jim Cooper, Tennessee: Have you ever met with Anton LaVey or any members of, or visited, the Church of Satan? What is the nature of your relationship to LaVey and the Church of Satan?

Thomas Luken, Ohio: What is the meaning of No Manors?

Doug Walgren, Pennsylvania: Did you or did you not partake in a ritualistic ceremony at Dystonia Manors in the spring of 1981?

Thomas Bliley Jr., Virginia: Were you, or were you not, at one point, invited to and accepted to eat the flesh of a man dead of AIDS?

Norman Lent, New York: When did you first sign a contract with Frank Fleecen?

Dan Coats, Indiana: What is your relationship to Frank Fleecen? I mean, bedroom-wise. Are you sleeping together? Have you ever?

Michael Oxley, Ohio: Did you ever take stock or bond tips from Frank Fleecen? Can you name your investments and holdings?

Michael Bilrakis, Florida: Did you reinvest in Lupercal Inc.? What reason did you have for buying stocks and bonds in Lupercal Inc.?

John Dingell, Michigan, Chairman: I have here before me a copy of a twenty-two-page comic book called *The Mizadventurez of Mizz Biz Aziz*, issue number nine ...

Jim Slattery, Kansas: I have here a sworn affidavit from a witness who testifies to an occasion in 1982 in which you forcibly compelled a small Christian child to paint a satanic symbolism on your garage door. Can you confirm the truth to this? Using black magic mind-control, did you force a god-fearing child to scrawl satanic imagery on your garage door? A simple yes or no answer will suffice, Miss Ashbubble.

Gerry Sikorski, Minnesota: How many times a month would you say you sleep as in sex with Frank Fleecen?

Rich Boucher, Virginia: Would you characterize Frank Fleecen as your business manager? Are you laundering profits for him through secret numbered accounts? As a follow-up I'm going to throw a few of Frank's clients' names at you and you tell me if you recognize any. Would you recall for the subcommittee the times you might have seen Frank Fleecen conversant with a bond salesman named Ralph Glassman, an arbitrageur named Quinn Kravis, or the fragrance entrepreneur Jon Jay?

Thomas Luken, Ohio: Do you make your investments at the advice of Frank Fleecen? When did you first start to buy and first start to sell bonds? If you're not making them, are you aware of trades going through your accounts at Locus Solus First National?

Doug Walgren, Pennsylvania: I have here before me a small glass phial, if you will, labelled *Ruthvah - scent of Crowley - for Men*—what do you know about this cologne, Miss Ashbubble?

Thomas Bliley Jr., Virginia: Frank Fleecen is more than your business manager, isn't he? What's that like?

Norman Lent, New York: I fear some of my other subcommittee members would like to paint you with the same brush as is being used on the child molesters in the McMartin preschool trial, the employees in the ongoing trial of their purportedly satanically abusive preschool in an affluent neighbourhood of Los Angeles. As a grandparent, I agree we must all be on guard to protect children from the influence of this modern age's cults, superstitions, feminisms, cynicism, and subjective liberalism, but I can't tolerate a witch-hunt. Once and for all, let me be the one to set the record straight—do you or do you not use your daily comic strip *Strays* as a satanic mind-control tool to turn our small children into devil's slaves?

Michael Bilirakis, Florida: This leads me to ask, are you, or were you not also secretly born and raised in Canada? And in the very same satanic Canadian city as Dr. Pazder's original patient, Michelle Smith?

Dan Schaefer, Colorado: Did you or did you not bury your mother in the same cemetery as where Michelle Smith remembers being buried alive by Satanists?

John Dingell, Michigan, Chairman: All right, we've each had the chance to ask questions. Let me just say on a personal note, Miss Ashbubble, that my entire family loves your comic strip, and knowing what I do about you now, I feel personally abused. You have exploited our trust in you for subversive motives and I can no longer read the funny pages confident they'll be a safe, wholesome place to laugh at a slice of life. Before we conclude, are there any other last questions from subcommittee members for the witness?

Rich Boucher, Virginia: Yes, I have one quick question I don't think any of us asked. Are you lying to us about anything you've said here today, Miss Ashbubble?

Norman Lent, New York: Okay, last chance, so let me repeat Rich's question, Miss Ashbubble. Are you lying to us?

38

The National Cartoonists Society Awards were held on the last Friday in June. Five days left. We remember the day of the awards because it was five days before the premiere of *The Strays Summer Christmas Special* and there must have been ten of us going to the ceremony in San Diego. Wendy got tickets for us and Frank, and we all flew in Hexen's company airliner. Piper and his wife would meet us there. Gabby Scavalda wouldn't miss this either. After months of debate, Wendy settled on a Kaisik Wong gown, Versace heels, and handmade handbag. Meanwhile, we were dressed in five dollars' worth of thrift store formalwear. Biz wore a tiara, a vintage silk Chanel dress from the Jazz Age the colour of champagne, fishnet stockings, and heels with buckles to match.

I want to thank the world who gave me life, Biz hissed as she walked through the crowds with us towards the bar, tickling the chins of strangers and talking to no one in particular. I'd like to thank the man who showed me what stupid is and what ain't. I absolutely got to say a thank you to Hick Elmdales wherever you are, you supported me when nobody else did. I must thank all my queens, alive or dead, wherever you are. Fuck AIDS, she said.

Biz downed two martinis in quick succession. Tipped the bartender and ordered another, turned about-face and walked between two stunned assistants for Tom Ryan's *Tumbleweeds* and made her way to our table.

Smooth Patrick was doing double duty tonight as a nominee's assistant and the creator of his own strip, *Loch & Quay*, nominated for best new strip. He was chuffed to say the least. Dressed in sunglasses and leather jacket to contrast the scotch white shirt and black tie. He carried a motorcycle helmet to the table. Smoothie also brought a date, she came on the back of his motorcycle. Her name was Clara, she was a talent manager for the Chula Vista rock band Murder, about to release their debut *Sham Sandwich* on an imprint of the record label SST. He wanted Clara to meet Rachael as soon as possible because it was only by telling her in the supermarket that he knew Aluminum Uvula that he got her to come with him on this blind date tonight.

Do you have a manager? said Clara as she wedged her chair in between Twyla and Rachael.

Patrick didn't take off the aviator sunglasses. Was my category around in your strip's first year in syndication, Wendy?

I don't know. Yes it was, I guess. Wendy turned her back as Bill Watterson walked right behind her through the mingling guests. She preferred to pretend not to see him over the anxiety of pre-awards hellos— her conscience could handle the antisocial deceit. His conscience chose the polite lie, too, apparently, or he was blind in his peripherals. She knew without having to be told, he must be nominated for cartoonist of the year as well. She imagined the same thought might have crossed Watterson's mind.

Oh, hi, Wendy, Bill said in his gentle Midwestern songbird's voice. Wow, it's been years …

All of a sudden she realized Bill Watterson's face was right there in front of hers. He looked like the exact kind of slope-shouldered librarian she invariably had a crush on when she was in her teens. His eyeglasses were the size of television screens and required almost nonstop attention to keep from slipping down the wide onion bulb of his nose.

Oh my god, Bill! I haven't seen you since *Calvin and Hobbes* launched— it is *so good* I can't stand it. You're the—I'm serious—(whispering so Charles Schulz, who was nearby, couldn't hear) the absolute *best* on the funny pages. I mean in my opinion of course. Sheesh, I'm excited every morning to read it. Makes me want to commit.

Aw, *she*-whiz, said Bill Watterson and ducked his head low, muttered a gracious *thanks*, and said how he'd almost given a strip after nearly twenty pitches when all of a sudden *Calvin* got picked up.

You should tell that to Patrick, he'd cheer up.

Hey, I can't wait to watch that special I've seen so many commercials for. It sounds really funny. What a terrific spin to have your characters discover Christmas but get the time of year wrong. And you made it yourself. That I like. Normally I think these things end up being big long commercials for stuff kids don't need. And the voices are all wrong.

Well, I hope you like it, Wendy said. *You* could have a cartoon so fast with your characters. Oh my.

Naw.

Naw? Yaw! Seriously. Where are all the Calvin toys? I want to buy them. Your characters are going to be stamped on everything. You'll be a bzillionaire, Bill. A monster money monger.

Maybe, but I kinda say no to all those offers.

No? As in, *Naw*? Really, to all? You accept none? said Wendy and took a drink from our hand and belted it back. But, but, but, nine-*tenths* of my income is toys and *stuff*.

Biz raised her martini to them and said, That's the only way I'd have a strip in the papers. No toys, no merch, no sponsors. Just the strip.

My syndicate hates me for it, believe me. The fights we get into are not cool. They remind me a lot of strips don't get asked for these deals. But when I think about it, I don't think Calvin would approve. Merchandise doesn't fit with his philosophy. To capitalize on his image like that would be antithetical to Calvin. He would tease me in my sleep if I sold him as toys, I know he would.

Boy oh boy. Maybe that's my problem. My characters are all about making money, said Wendy and massaged her jaw. They harass me nightly for not selling their godless images *enough*.

Watterson turtled his head into his shoulders, as if to apologize for sticking his neck out against what Wendy thought was inevitable in the trade. Good luck tonight, he said.

Yes … , she said. You as well.

Wendy fell on us and said, Oh god, I sounded like such an arrogant jerkoff, didn't I? Like I'm so much more experienced because I've been doing this for five years or whatever. He's older than me and I was practically mothering him.

There's punk-looking comics and then there's punk-acting comics, and that right there is both, said Biz Aziz, pointing a finger at Watterson as he got swarmed by admirers and friends.

Wendy stroked her chin and said, *He knows I'm nominated.* Now I'm afraid I'm *not* going to win and *he* will.

That's when Frank Fleecen sat down and kissed her on the cheek. How are you feeling? he asked. Excited?

All the names, but not all the names of cartooning, were here tonight. We saw Dik Browne hold court, Chester Gould take aim at the buffet table, and Gary Larson pick his nose. A dinner was about to be served that tasted about as good as biting into the seat of a taxicab. Five or six awards would be handed out interspersed with a lot of impromptu jokes and other vaudeville business to stretch the evening to three or four excruciating hours. The Reuben was handed out last, at around two in the morning.

Guess who I heard they invited to deliver the Reuben tonight, Frank said with a wink to Wendy.

Who? Ronald Reagan?

Manila Convençion.

Oh, her. Yes, well, said Wendy.

Frank's eyebrows went up. Bodes well for you and the Reuben, yes?

Oh god, you just made me so nervous.

You deserve this win, he said.

Can I veto a merchandise contract if I want to? she asked Frank.

Some product you don't like? That muffin mix is being recalled.

No, I love them all, even the worst ones. Just asking.

Frank blinked. Well, yes. *You* can veto. But not contractually. Cartoonists don't contractually *own* their comics. You are contracted to draw the comic you create for your syndicate.

Bill Watterson nixes all offers for toys and merch for *Calvin and Hobbes*—nothing but the strip. What do you think of that *zabaglione*? she said as she stabbed her chicken entree repeatedly with her fork and knife, not cutting through only wounding its surface.

What's the matter? Frank said.

What's the matter with you? she said.

I'm happy for you, he shouted. What else do you want? Fuck, my life is falling apart and you're nominated for an award? I'm happy. I'm happy.

You never said anything to me about your life falling apart. Wendy put a hand on his thigh and squeezed. Are you going to explain what you mean by that or just leave me to feel guilty for whatever? You know, Reagan told me he wished Berke Breathed would quit drawing *Bloom County*, think I should tell him? C'mon, Frank. Don't mope on my big night.

I'm happy for you, he said.

We sat nursing drinks and politely applauded for the other awards doled out that evening for best new strip, gag of the year, hall of fame, and the Popeye Award for outstanding service to comics—all in the lead-up to the award for artist of the year, the Reuben.

*

Manila chose to wear a man's black tuxedo that night, with a black silk cummerbund and a formal white shirt half unbuttoned, offsetting her tanned skin. Black patent leather high heels. Between her cherry-red lips was a fourteen-inch-long handrolled contraband Cuban cigar smoking along finely and reeking up the place. Her platinum blond hair, tied into a braid, she suddenly let loose with a wave and a flourish, and all the men gasped.

One last trick. She went down on her hands and toes and, smoking the cigar, counted out twenty-five one-handed pushups. The audience leaped to their feet around us and roared with the kind of applause normally saved for after the ceremony, at the strip club one block over and two blocks down.

The envelope containing the name of the winner of the Reuben Award was in her hands now. Spotlight on the infamous *Replicant Fitness* instructor. Manila opened the seal without fanfare.

The winner is, who else? My good friend and all-time favourite—Bill Watterson for *Calvin and Hobbes*, Manila said, and when he came up the three stairs, she handed him his trophy, kissed him on the mouth, and stood beside him while he delivered a speech that we don't remember any of except that it sounded more like a manifesto against consumerism than a list of thank yous.

Wendy sat and clenched her jaw behind a smile through his whole speech like a plaster clown it only takes one tiny tap to shatter.

Then she said she needed a minute in the ladies' room before we left the hotel ballroom. Light-headed, splash of water. Forty minutes later we followed her in to ask if she was okay. Not drunk, she said. Too lucid. Impaired by perfect sight. She groaned, What was I *thinking*?

She threw her torn-up acceptance speech in the toilet and flushed it away.

Our ride to the ABC party in the hills was in a rental car driven by an intern, and he wanted to get going, it was getting late (three in the morning), but now that Wendy had calmed down, Frank was missing.

I'll go find him, Wendy told us. I could use a walk to clear my head. She carried her heels in her hands and strolled barefoot through the banquet hall and the reception area, but all was empty.

The National Cartoonists Society Awards that year were held in the Beverly Hills Hotel, a sprawling and modern renovation, luxuries updated a year ago with all new fixtures, pool after pool, and views of the diamond-blue ocean and the golden beaches. The halls on the main floor had a whole mall's worth of shops that catered to well-financed whims. He was shopping in none of them.

She took a flight of carpeted stairs that spiralled up to the third floor, also reserved for banquet halls and conference rooms. She pulled open the door of a small waiting room, where three enormous windows were open, letting in air from the ocean, and the sound of the ocean, looking out onto the perfectly black night sky and the white sands of the beach. It was beautiful.

Oh, sorry, I didn't see you— ... There on a loveseat Wendy caught sight of a couple of men in suits, kissing and groping. She turned to leave. But then she realized one of the men was a woman, it was Manila in her sexy tux. And the man on top of her, with his hands in her hair and on her breast and ..., that was Frank Fleecen.

Wendy was already running.

She came running into the lobby. No tears in her eyes. We only wondered where Frank was. There we were, her four devoted assistants, waiting for her so we could go to yet another party in her honour—at four in the morning. Amid the last of the cartoonists to leave the Reubens party—Bushmiller, Johnston, Larson—three men wearing slate trenchcoats stood inconspicuously near the exit.

Wendy studied one of the men in a trenchcoat. Chris Quiltain, she said. What is it *this* time? Think you can get me when I'm down?

Then Frank ran into the lobby, in time to see her being led out the glass doors, and he called out: Wendy—

Frank Fleecen, you're under arrest, said one of the men in a slate trenchcoat and gently eased both Frank's hands behind his back and cuffed him.

Came in from NYC this morning to see this, Chris said from the front seat of the police cruiser taking Wendy to the nearest station. Had to watch, had to make sure it happened right.

Chris Quiltain, you devil, Wendy said. I wondered when you might show up with something kinky. I've never been to jail. What's it like?

Next day's papers ran front-page stories about Wendy's arrest as part of a sweeping round of indictments in New York District Attorney Rudy Giuliani's war on white-collar crime. She was described as *caught up* in Frank Fleecen's larger racket, and the charges laid against her alleged that she siphoned at least thirty thousand dollars *a month* of Frank's illegal profits through at least a dozen bank accounts at Solus First National and from there moved the money into numbered accounts in offshore banks. She was delivered to a women's corrections facility.

The indictments took out main players within the offices of Hexen Diamond Mistral and Frank's connections in the savings and loans. Police with handcuffs interrupted Doug Chimney on the phone in his office at Solus First National making an illegal sell; for the past three years he had allowed Frank Fleecen's bagman to deposit nine thousand dollars in cash every day into Wendy's accounts without her knowledge. The bagman, a flunky Hexen junk bond salesman with two alimonies and health problems, flipped on his boss for a deal to avoid time. These arrests followed that of Quinn Kravis, who agreed to cooperate with the DA for a reduced sentence. Kravis confessed to multiple counts of insider trading and accepting a bribe, and claimed Frank was not just part of an insider trading scheme but the ringleader who paid him and others to take up big positions, park stock, greenmail companies, and in return, receive tip-offs about deals ahead of public disclosure.

39

Freedom or riches? Jeans or khakis? These questions troubled Wendy's cellmate, Essa Mole Deattur.

She told Wendy to be glad for her view of the water tower. Not everyone had such a grand view. Most other cells got a clear sheet of uninterrupted hot blue sky, a purgatory you hoped to see a cloud in, a jetliner, any animate thing to obstruct that changeless picture of the atmosphere out of the eight-by-ten picture window. An eight-by-ten picture of everything and nothing. Or you had a view of fence. But the water tower's dimensions, its circumference, the cone of its rooftop, the concrete substance of it, the oblique angles, its shadows always changing—the water tower reminded Wendy of her life, of the purpose of drawing, to see the same thing forever differently. Days when the birds all took off at once from underneath its domed roof—she thought the little birdies must live there, nests must be under there, all of them a family, flying in formation like a powder. The tower took her away from this sanitized dungeon with nothing but the Home Shopping Network and back to someplace normal, full of choices. At a certain longitude, the water tower blocked out the sun and even cooled her cell. A temporary breeze amid the prison stifle. Time she spent meditating on the water tower passed at the pace of a soap opera, too quickly for nothing to have happened in the space of an hour.

Apart from the water tower, which constantly changed with the light, everything else in prison happened slower than dentistry.

She sat on the top bunk, or sometimes lay on her stomach, and looked at the water tower through the Plexiglas window, and she thought about her life and answered the questions posed by her cellmate. Both women were innocent, awaiting trial. Wendy's cellmate was arrested for shoplifting over ten thousand in Gap merchandise.

Night owl or morning person? Steal or starve? *Dallas* or *Dynasty*?

Another perk of being a nonviolent cartoonist she did not fully appreciate in the early days of her integration with the general population was that unlike most of the others imprisoned in the California Institution for Women outside the city of Chino, Wendy had only one cellmate, Essa. Some cells even had a fifth roommate sleeping on a foam mattress laid out over the remaining floor space. Essa Mole Deattur was more fidgety and unused to confinement than Wendy, and she'd been here much longer. She was maybe fifty pounds overweight and acted like it was all muscle. She had the laugh of a Disney villainess. Every morning, Wendy had to braid her hair or never hear the end of it. Ford or Dodge? Wendy's prison cell had a high ceiling, a window view, and a pregnant woman for a bunkmate.

She ought to be more creatively energized given the privacy, solitude, and being dislocated from bad habits. When she couldn't fall asleep she dreamed of Hick, of Jonjay, of Frank, of Biz Aziz. She dreamed of Twyla Noon and Sue Fleecen and The Farm and Aluminum Uvula. When her eyes wouldn't shut, she dreamed of herself elsewhere. She ought to channel her thoughts into drawings, she ought to draw if she wasn't going to sleep. In a blink, night to morning, and a buzzer to let her know it was time to get ready for breakfast.

Wasn't that what this was supposed to be all about, rehabilitate herself and become a productive member of society again? But she couldn't organize her thoughts. The atmosphere was not intuitive, it wasn't.

Hot tea or ice tea? Revenge or let bygones be bygones?

Definitely *Dallas*, said Wendy.

Yesterday my cellmate was Siobhan, she was sentenced to life but got out due to governor's clemency, Essa told Wendy. Got a terminal lung cancer from an asbestos factory she was at since a teenager. Said her it was her nerves what made her stalk her ex-husband and leave death threats on his message machine. Now she's got a couple months to live on a respirator. I hope your nerves are okay.

Wendy chewed her bottom teeth and said her nerves were pretty much shot at the moment.

There's others like you in here, Satanists, said Essa.

I'm not a—

There's the Manson family girls.

There is?

And there's a lady here from Martinsville for ritual abuse of baby children, like, molestation or something. Says she's innocent.

I'm not a Satanist, Wendy explained to her cellmate.

That's what she says, too. She's innocent.

I *am* innocent, said Wendy.

Yeah, said Essa. Me, too.

Essa Mole Deattur said she was a native of Baton Rouge who moved to California with a man who later got shot in the spine and died after messing with the wrong convenience store clerk in Carmel City trying to steal a bottle of rum, a stack of VHS movies, and a box of Tampax for Essa, who watched him twist, explode in blood, and fall. She was behind the wheel of the getaway and took off in squeals with the moon rising in her rearview mirror like a dead eye.

Essa was marking the beginning of her third trimester of a prison pregnancy.

Docs say I'm having a little girl, she said, caressing the cantaloupe-sized sphere stretching out her belly as she lay on the bottom bunk with extra pillows for lumbar support. The shock of her lover's shotgun death cured her of a life of crime, and when Essa settled into an apartment and took a minimum-wage job at the flagship Gap warehouse on the Hunters Point drydock, she promised herself she'd never look back. She was looking at eleven months for grand theft. Halfway through the remand hearing she realized her court-appointed lawyer was partially deaf. The judge was sold on high-tech video surveillance footage from the drydock that the prosecutor showed of a pregnant woman guiding two broad-shouldered men in black jackets to load half a dozen boxes of Gap khakis out of a delivery truck and into a Dodge minivan.

Wendy said she was innocent, too—at risk of serving up to three years on charges of perjury and insider trading or something. The police told her they'd caught her helping Frank launder money but she didn't know a thing about it. She still could not understand her own crime.

Cashews or almonds? Coffee Crisp or Crispy Crunch? Sade or Annie Lennox? Oil of Olay or Noxzema? Which do you like more, *Nancy* or *Cathy*?

Nancy, said Wendy. We used to play these kinds of games at my place.

I'm a *Cathy* person, said her cellmate. I used to tape her strips up all over my office walls at the warehouse. She's a Lucille Ball type of embarrassment to herself. She's late for everything. She's gaining weight and losing her hair. Mom nags. Work piles up. Men ditch her. That's life.

I met the creator of *Cathy*. Like, three days ago. Fuck. It feels like months.

Ruthvah or Old Spice?

Old Spice, said Wendy.

Interesting. Bra or burn? Burgers or hotdogs? Kmart or Zellers?

*

Six thousand six hundred and twenty women resided at the California women's corrections institution outside Chino, east of Los Angeles, in a gated, guarded complex built to room half that population. A thousand beds were saved for women like Wendy and Essa awaiting trial without bail. Across ten separate cellblocks, five thousand three hundred and seventy mothers were locked up, and two dozen pregnancies intermingled with the rest. Hundreds of women serving less than a month for nonviolent or drug-related crimes slept on day cots and army bunks in the recreational room, called the red light district. More than one young woman could not stop cutting herself and they kept rotating these waifs in and out of solitary confinement on suicide watch. Essa said there was a woman on death row here since Eisenhower. None of the inmates had seen the femme fatale's face since the sensational newspaper clippings but the guards said she'd kept her looks.

There was one guard for every three hundred women. Her guard's name was Rick and his booth in the centre of her cellblock's panopticon was scattered with empty fast food bags and candy wrappers and the greasy remnants of reread pro wrestling magazines, and Rick was the only guard who tuned the television to something other than the Home Shopping Network.

The buzzer for dinner sounded uncomfortably like the buzzer for No Manors amplified a hundred times. She lingered beside Rick's desk and watched the evening news. Footage of Frank leaving the courthouse and crawling into the backseat of a private car, flanked by lawyers, besieged by journalists and cameramen, appeared in a frame to the side of Dan Rather's head as he ran down the list of indictments against Frank, who was going to jail for years for racketeering and securities fraud.

Frank Fleecen was the image of American wealth in the eighties, Dan Rather said. Through risky hypothecations he turned a quiet investment banking firm into a seemingly unstoppable behemoth. Now it turns out his deals may have benefited him and his inner circle more than his clients.

THE ROAD NARROWS AS YOU GO

His genius, said Dan Rather, goes unquestioned among his acolytes but his critics say it was his greed, not his generosity, that helped extend America's line of credit. Thanks to years of Reaganomics, Fleecen has exploited the deregulated bond market to turn his chosen princes into captains of industry—ousting families from their own businesses in the process. Like a modern-day swashbuckler, chasing down companies in a series of hostile takeovers that have replaced seasoned managers and nepotism with trailblazers and inexperienced hotshots ...

Wendy listened to Dan Rather name off a half-dozen businesses, including Lupercal, Solus First National, and Shepherd Media ... And now, after a cat-and-mouse game New York District Attorney Rudy Giuliani says the Securities and Exchange Commission has been playing with Fleecen for almost a decade, the lion of Wall Street, the man they call the junk bond king, is finally brought to justice. Frank Fleecen has pled guilty to multiple counts of racketeering, insider trading, money laundering, and securities fraud and will serve up to *ten* years in a state prison in what is being called the largest criminal bust in Wall Street history. Fleecen specialized in a very obscure type of tender-offer securities swap pioneered in the nineteenth century by financiers like Cowperwood and Yerkes, who hypothecated loans nothing like the scale of today's magnate. Fleecen topped the *Forbes* list as the most highly paid financier in the world, clearing more than two point two billion in income from commissions on deals in the last six years, while alleged to earn an undisclosed additional income from personal investments. Prosecutors say it was the cartoonist Wendy Ashbubble, creator of the daily comic strip *Strays*, who helped Frank Fleecen funnel these secret profits through her bank accounts into a series of offshore dummy corporations. Even after he's released, it is certain Frank Fleecen will be one of the richest men in the world.

Rick the guard chewed distractedly on two Twizzler ropes. Incarcerated women shuffled by him in single file. Rick did not notice Wendy hanging back to hear Dan Rather ask an expert from the Securities and Exchange Commission, What effect is this whole scandal having on the rest of the savings and loans and the bond market?

The guest expert nodded and said, It's making lenders who were absolutely courageous in the boom, it's making them timid. In the boom, it was almost impossible *not* to get a loan. Now it's like pulling teeth.

Very difficult to get a loan, Dan Rather said. What does that say about where our economy is going?

Keep it movin', ladies, said Rick the guard as he waved at Wendy in particular with one hand. She got back in the line with the other women shuffling out of their cells past him single file down the narrow undecorated hallway of steel I-beams and reinforced concrete. *Time for lunch.*

… sweeping investigation that included the indictment of Fleecen and his top clients, including Quinn Kravis and the cartoonist Wendy Ashbubble, leading ABC to *cancel* her long-awaited *Strays* Christmas special set to air on July Fourth …

The prison was too big, a nightmare high school. The hallway's vanishing point was a bulletproof door far enough in the distance to be an indiscernible dot.

The messhall was a half mile from Wendy's cell, and the auditorium-sized eating area was too small to accommodate the whole prison body, so the cellblocks ate in half-hour shifts of two thousand inmates at a time. Collected your Melmac tray, waited to find out the bad news. Today the kitchen served brown gravy with lumps of unmixed powder poured over mucilaginous mashed potatoes and a kind of colourless, odourless, tasteless pea, and for a main course, ground beef, with ketchup packlets. Custard dessert. Homo milk to wash it all down.

After dinner Wendy sat in front of a television in one of the four corners of the rec room. It didn't matter where she sat, all the boxes were tuned to the Home Shopping Network. Hydrodouche, nineteen ninety-nine. Computerized golf coach, forty-nine ninety-nine. Fractional Reserve

Fiat System, twenty-nine ninety-nine, and if you order now, we'll throw in a second one *free*.

One woman sat by one of the television boxes with a flank of inmates acting as security guards, and no one was allowed to talk to her without a meeting. Her name was Carol.

You see anything you like? was the first thing Carol said to Wendy.

Yeah, I like the look of that blowtorch, Wendy said. The host on TV was selling a set of stainless steel mixing bowls for nine ninety-nine.

You're allowed a rice steamer in your cell. You should order one. You're that girl who draws for the comics, right? Everybody says like you're special. Are you special? Draw me something special, Carol said and gave Wendy a crayon pencil and opened to the blank last page of a paperback she was reading—*Tuf Voyaging*.

What do you want me to draw?

Anything.

Normally I get *paid* to draw. You going to pay me?

Really, huh? What do you want?

I'll draw you something *special* if we can change the channel.

What now, say that again? It looked like Carol's head was screwed on crooked, her neck pointed at Wendy.

Just for a change of pace. I want to get caught up. Pam woke up from a vivid dream spanning the entire previous season to find Bobby in the shower—*Good Morning*. Gotta see how that goes. Geraldo Rivera's got psychopaths. *Cosby Show*, *Family Ties*, *Golden Girls*. Lots of options out there.

Carol shifted over next to Wendy and watched her draw. How old are you?

Twenty-nine, Wendy lied accurately.

I was twenty-nine when I was a producer for the Home Shopping Network, Carol told her. Wendy drew her an inmate breaking out of the Tony Robbins book through a rip in the last page. You know, it's true what they say, every bad situation finds its scapegoat, Carol told her as she drew. Someone's got to take the blame. DA said their investigation found evidence I took bribes, embezzled merchandise, paid hush money, fired anyone I thought might snitch, and even washed money for the Hells Angels. But I'm just the damn scapegoat.

Bedtime, Rick the guard said. The guards were men to a fault, some were younger than Rick. Republicans, all Reagan's children. The guards unanimously praised the president, for he was the man who created their jobs. Until 1980 there was nine prisons for all of California, Rick the guard told Wendy. Thanks to Reagan, now there's eighteen. And they're packed, need more guards.

Wendy's lawyer told her the case was a matter of hysteria and would blow over. Her lawyer had not come from Frank's people—she didn't want Frank's lawyers involved at all—but her friends at the National Cartoonists Society recommended a good one. He lost the remand—she was deemed a flight risk, because prosecutors knew she was born in Canada—but he was prepared for the trial. His name was David Queensberry. He was a thin man in his mid-thirties with glasses, and he always brought her piping-hot coffee to drink.

He said, The country has temporarily lost its mind. Satanism is ... I don't know, a distraction. All this Iran-Contra business needs a scapegoat. I've seen court transcripts of these satanic abuse cases and they're all going to be thrown out on appeal. There's no substance.

Does that help prove I'm innocent?

No, why would it?

Give me something that helps me, said Wendy.

I'm working on it, the lawyer said.

In group therapy Essa said, I'm scared to get out. I don't know what I'll do. Productive member of what society? Who wants me? I been in and out of foster homes and youth centres and I'm done with the streets. I'm clean. I want to stay clean, pressed, pleated, tip-top, you know. I just want my life back.

Your whole life is ahead of you, Essa, the counsellor said, lots of time to prove yourself.

There were eleven women in group therapy and the counsellor sitting in a circle in green moulded plastic Eames chairs.

One lady said, Why'd they hide their bodies under my garage?

One young inmate, covered in self-administered tattoos, told the group she didn't want to talk and listed off on her fingers ten reasons why.

I'm the kind of addict who stole your TV and helped you go look for it, a nineteen-year-old named Rita Dominic told the group. But I got a headline for ya—prison ain't gone help cure a girl.

You can't trust anything with teeth, said an inmate who went by Virginia, recalling the disaster of her arrest. The doctor showed the toddlers from my preschool these anatomically correct dolls, and they would point to the genitals and ask the children, *Now tell us where Virginia touched you. Did Virginia touch you here? Or here? Did Virginia touch your bum?* Poor children. The children told the court they saw me flying around the room on a broomstick. They told the jury we hung them by their skin from the planter hooks in the ceiling. They said there was a torture chamber in a secret basement under the preschool where we filmed ourselves sodomizing them and burning their flesh with torches. Some of these children had never even attended our preschool, weren't registered. I'm not going to repent for a crime I didn't commit. How am I supposed to be rehabilitated for something imaginary? This punishment does one thing to me that I hate to even say aloud. It destroys my confidence in America.

We must all shoulder a lot of pain, said the counsellor.

I took a polygraph, Virginia said. I am innocent. I am innocent. Once they set my bail I'm out of here and never coming back.

Wendy, what about you? the prison counsellor asked. Do you think you'll ever accept *your* crime?

I'm innocent. Honestly? I still don't know what I'm going to trial for. I'm listening to Virginia and thinking the exact same thing. The charges sound so bizarre and unfamiliar to me and … I'm so afraid of years trapped in here.

Smirking and scrubbing her gloved hands together, the counsellor said she was used to hearing Wendy's kind of denial. Part of why we engage in group therapy is accepting what brought us here.

I should be retired right now, not in jail, said Virginia.

This place is a damage to my health, said Essa. I got a lot of diabetes.

Virginia looked at her across the circle, then returned to her knitting. She was knitting blue baby booties for her most recent grandchild. She told the counsellor, You don't understand me at all. I'm in here for two hundred and twenty-five years because a jury believed the prosecutor who said I'm a Satanist who molested children.

Wendy said, Denial of what?

The counsellor pushed on. To verbalize your guilt is the first step. To accept your trial and say to a group in public why you are here. Engaging with the system, to say aloud what brought you here. The counsellor cupped her hands together as if awaiting fresh water.

Wendy. Wake up. Wendy. She was buried alive in an underground crypt shaped like a panopticon, a womb. Wendy, wake up. Are you going to keep trying to fuck the one that got away? Wake up, girl.

No, no, no, I want Wendy with me, Essa screamed as guards lifted her onto a gurney.

Wendy woke to find her cell full of guards, more than just Rick, and her cellmate between contractions.

Rick the guard said, No way. Can't bring another inmate. Prohibited. Told you a million times. It's against the law.

All kinds of escape routes flew through her mind as she lay in her top bunk looking at the water tower. Then suddenly Rick the guard was in the door. Collect whatever of your belongings you want to keep, he said. You ain't staying here no more.

What do you mean? Where am I being taken?

As of this moment, you are officially a free woman.

Free, Wendy said. What about—?

You'll be the first I know of who wants to stay longer.

But how? My bail hasn't even been set yet.

Charges dropped, Rick said and shrugged. Collect whatever you need and follow me. Oh and by the way, your celly had a baby girl.

Wow. Well, she'll be out soon, too.

Not likely. She's still going to trial for murder.

Murder? She told me she stole some Gap stuff.

Rick chuckled. Yeah, that's for sure, a hundred grand in merch, before she unloaded a pistol into her boyfriend *point-blank.*

Well shit. What happens to her baby?

Rick scratched his standard issue. State law is clear on this one. The mother gets forty-eight hours of quality time with her newborn.

And then what?

Then either the baby goes to family, foster care, or you know, orphanage or whatever, I guess.

40

STRAYS

After almost five years living at No Manors, those interior walls, those bicycles on the ceiling, the shelves of books and comics, the roomfuls of tools and toys, this world within a world became interchangeable with our imaginations. One memory, four people. We lived along a single thread. The four of us, day after night producing all those drawings at the longtable, painting cell after cell of animation, loading up the frame to shoot each one … the years it took us to make that animated cartoon no one ever saw, the people we met and things we saw, it left an indelible mark on our memory.

Twenty years later and we still slept on the couches in the No Manors of our memory. No matter how much time passed between us and then, that view from the longtable remained close at hand. The present moment is in a relentless conversation with our memory of the past. Constantly changing under our feet like a sand made of temporally indivisible particles of language, memory is the landscape on which our future's journey is charted. Memory of the past formed the mountains and plains that opened the horizons or shut us in. We relived that San Francisco, the city our memory transformed into a mother who gave birth to our new selves. The future depended on our most extreme impressions of the past. The truth was whatever remained outside the blind spots. No Manors was home even after we left and went separate ways. We spent so much formative time in those halls and rooms on the peak of Bernal Heights. We were night owls with no self-esteem, but what inspired us to keep drawing was the talents of our friends and that view out the bay window of the city asleep under a cosmic scream shimmering light-headedly with stars. Night was the mouth we kept feeding and feeding. There at the beginning of who we would become, a memory of the night air blowing in the open windows and the door buzzer letting someone in. Behind a circle of fogs, that unforgettable view of the sun at dawn streaking across the rolling hills of San Francisco. We could doodle that view from memory. So many nights awake to see the sunrise pierce through volumes of cloud, as if to signal the fingers of god were about to descend and pinch chosen ones off the ground to take to heaven, or if not a godhand, alien crafts beaming unwitting civilians up off the hills of Divisadero and Fillmore into the arms of telekinetic ectomorphs with long probes. Our San Francisco was touched with a trembling energy left over from the acid swamps of life's protean beginnings, a fault line through the memory of the place that sent quakes of memory that penetrated our skin at the fingertips and changed flesh, then soul. Twenty years later we can still see the whole peninsula out the window of No Manors as clear in memory as any day, foggy with the spine-chills. Straight down the arrow of Valencia and Mission into the hills downtown, those steep lanes converging on the bridges, we draw on our mind's sketchpad. The present moment is defined by then. At No Manors we became the people we used to recognize only in the dreaming mirror of our inner eye—cartoonists, illustrators, freethinkers, artists, or—if not artists, doers.

As a result of Frank's conviction all licensing and merchandising rights to *Strays* reverted to Shepherd Media, and instead of shelving the strip, the syndicate continued to reap its profits. Not all papers cancelled, though most did, in outrage. Maybe a third stayed on to see what would happen. Hiring a new artist-writer to take over proved to be difficult and perhaps unwise, so Shepherd sold reprints at a cut rate to the willing newspapers. In a quick switcheroo, instead of new ones, the first *Strays* strips from eighty-one started to reappear the week after Wendy got out of prison. The syndicate renewed the contract with Lupercal so toys kept coming off the production line and going into stores that would stock them. If there was demand, they would handle it. As per her contract, Wendy still received a cut. Gabrielle Scavalda was demoted to travelling salesman. On the road up and down the Eastern Seaboard six days out of seven, five weeks out of six, Gabby took to driving with a bottle of Gatorade between her legs, cut in half with vodka, and wasted most of the nineties selling *Loch & Quay* and other gag-a-day strips to satellite papers.

We didn't hear from Wendy the day she was released from prison, and we didn't hear from her in the days after that either. She didn't try to contact us and we didn't know if she wanted us to look her up. We sensed she was ashamed. We thought she must be depressed since we were so very depressed. But we didn't know where she was. Visiting Frank, perhaps? Well, she could be anywhere. Then one foggy afternoon after a few months went by, she left a message on the answering machine when nobody was home that said she had to sell the manor and her house next door, and was sorry to say we'd have to leave. She said she missed us and wished us all well but she felt it was *better this way*. It was as if we were all in a relationship and she was breaking up with us over the phone. Either way, we didn't leave. We were after all freeloaders, and it was our habit to overstay our welcome. After this many years rent-free, we were ready to test Wendy's bluff.

Sooner than expected, a moving truck climbed Stoneman Street. It took the movers two days to pack everything into boxes, everything except for us and the forty-two-foot longtable. And the laundry hamper, which Patrick Poedouce kept.

Without further notice our time at No Manors was over. An advertisement went out in the classifieds for people interested in the lease on a five-bedroom quincunx-shaped main-floor suite in a dilapidated five-storey Edwardian in Bernal Heights.

Frank Fleecen and his insider trading racket, his conspiratorial hostile takeovers, greenmailing corporations, fake options and bogus instruments, his duplicitous mortgage hypothecations, his help balkanizing Central America, his responsibility for the collapse of the savings and loans—all that tainted Wendy, too, for she had opted to fall in love with this pariah.

But *her* story sold. We all cashed in. Our memories were not our own property. Memory was a hotel room we destroyed for entertainment purposes. If we felt strapped, memories of the manor were as good as a bank account. We told producers we had animated the never-aired *Strays* special. This cartoon was lore in the television industry of the nineties. Nobody came forward with a copy and ABC made the mistake of trashing theirs—that was the first thing that made the cartoon so valuable and legendary. We capitalized on that fact whenever we had to. And whatever details or memorabilia we could muster to sweeten the deal on our side were sure to increase our payment at the end. We sold Wendy's life story as if it was our own, piece by piece, and always with the same focus on the flesh, the crime, the drugs, sex, the cartoon.

Producers sought us out for our legitimately dirty eighties experiences, to transmute our memories into new entertainment. We were asked to look for inspiration no further than under our own fingernails. They all asked for the same thing: a wake, or at least a fresh take on urban cannibalism. They wanted the longtable. They wanted the laundry hamper. They just said, Give us some more of *issue nine*.

We lived at the manor at the time of Hick's death, took part in the wake, we were there when Jonjay disappeared, and we saw Wendy's success turn into a love affair that ended in headline news. Squatting at the manor all those years witnessing so much financed our futures. When things in life looked dire and as though all hope had come to an end for us, a new horizon opened up. This new world we entered into was eager for us to convert our life into fodder. We converted what we saw and did into latter-day careers. The flesh-eating, the deaths, the pounds upon pounds of dope, Death Valley's sailing stones, intimations of insider trading, and Wendy's downfall—this all became our bread and butter. If ever we were strapped, we could find work simply by mentioning to editors that we had lived at No Manors.

As the decades passed, comix readers traded gossip about the creation of the summer Christmas special that never got aired. The manor, the forty-two-foot longtable, who made what piece of art along the way, this had all become lore. The fans shared the legends and in doing so, circulated our names. Opinions on Rachael's musical adaptation of No Manors would appear in tributes to *Pan*. If you loved comics history then you hunted far and wide until you tracked down the rare copies of *The Mizadventurez of Mizz Biz Aziz*, and the rarest of all, number nine, where you could read all about Hick's wake. Number ten was almost as rare, and featured Jonjay's return to the manor and Biz's love affair with Vaughn Staedtler prior to his death.

Issue eleven also featured a one-page, nine-panel subplot of us slaving away on the *Strays* special. The only panel in the whole issue to show

Wendy was the frame in the centre of this page. She's surrounded by us and her own talk bubbles, asking questions and wanting updates, and then telling us she must go, her *business manager* is calling.

And Biz clearly showed time was not measured in minutes or days for us. We drank time in coffee cups. We smoked time. We drew out the years in reams. Counting up thousands upon thousands of drawings like a cult that had fallen under the sway of the most oblivious leader. The passion to please Wendy blinded us to any other audience. It was as though she had hired us back in eighty-one to mow her lawn, and we'd said okay, and taken her money, and without a plan, each of us had sat down at a different spot in her yard willynilly and got to work using nail scissors to cut each blade one at a time. Trying to make sure all the blades got cut to an even length. Frame by frame, drawing this animation, laying down a technique, only to find it didn't match up at all with what the others were doing. Everyone's approach was so different. We had no other choice but to mindmeld them all into something horrendous and hopefully beautiful.

Issue eleven of Biz's comix ends the series. The trials and tribs of producing/directing big-production drag shows on a dental-floss budget—coupled with backstage dramas, fan mayhem, post-Nam insomnia nightmares, daymares, regrets, guilt, anger, her friendship with Hick, her love affair with Vaughn—got to her. She published a four-hundred-page hardcover edition of the entire series with Art Spiegelman and Françoise Mouly's imprint at Pantheon in ninety-two with back-cover blurbs from Kathy Acker and Divine. She won a special citation from Pulitzer in ninety-three for *groundbreaking art and literature*. A twenty-city book tour across America made her a sensation, and she was the subject of a fifteen-thousand-word profile in the *New York Times Magazine*. After a disastrous panic attack at the San Diego Comic-Con, Biz once again removed herself from public view. The rumour was that Justine Witlaw found Biz Aziz in the Twomps, where she had gone to live with her son. A son conceived the week in seventy-one that Funkadelic released their album *Maggot Brain*, and now, fifteen years later, apparently her son aka Murder Dubz was heir to the throne of slain drug kingpin Felix the Cat, and if the stories were true, Biz had a room in his safehouse where she continued to draw but never published.

It was Patrick Poedouce who confirmed the rumour. When his apartment's front door was kicked off its hinges and his place ransacked, his eye blackened, and all that was taken was Hick's laundry hamper, rather than quail in fear in a corner, Patrick went out the next day to find who stole it. He didn't know where to start and his mind turned to Biz Aziz and this garret she was said to have in the house of a drug kingpin in South Oakland. When he finally found the place, a derelict Victorian in between two abandoned stucco postwar bungalows in a treeless neighbourhood, Biz Aziz said she wasn't surprised to see him. She introduced Patrick to her son and they happily returned Hick's laundry hamper to him. Then Biz showed Patrick what she'd been working on—a hundred and seventy pages long, it was called *Murder'z Diary* and depicted life in the Twomps from the point of view of her son, the extraordinarily ruthless crack dealer, amphetamine dealer, marijuana monopolist, and so on, using real quotes. Patrick persuaded her to let him show a copy around to publishers, and in 2001, Fantagraphics published *Murder'z Diary* with no promotional tour or interviews. Reviewers tended to praise the graphic novel for the same reasons they condemned the milieu from which the comic came, for the crack epidemic was dramatic and tragic and by this time deeply embedded in the American consciousness.

Collectors perennially traded *Strays* merchandise at San Diego Comic-Con and other conventions and through new & used comic stores. You knew it was a *Strays* original because it bore the Lupercal trademark imprinted on the bottom. That's around the time we started to consider what we had lying around that we could put up for sale to make a bit of extra money. The thing we knew had the most value was in those film canisters, our cartoon special. But after more than ten years, we didn't know who had the film. We hoped it was in Wendy's hands. But we didn't know. No one heard from her.

One night around three in the morning in the year 2002, surrounded by bottles of anti-retroviral medication, reams of paper, and drawing supplies, Mark Bread was lying in bed surfing eBay in the room he now rented on the third floor of No Manors for twenty dollars a week when he happened to see this:

Strays Summer Christmas Special—this is the real deal, folks. The complete 22-minute unreleased STRAYS animated cartoon ABC cancelled a DAY before the premiere. DVD, all regions. Excellent quality transfer off original VHS dub from reels. $30 per copy + Shipping.

The seller had original Peter Pan and Hook drawings signed by Hick Elmdales and other unheard-of *Pan* memorabilia posted for auction, as well as *Mizadventurez* issues, including issue one (only a hundred copies were printed) and issue nine. More dead giveaways, Mark thought, in the postings for *Strays* merch, *Medusa* issues, original art from *Loch & Quay*, not to mention *The Mischiefs* out-of-print books.

Whered u git this!? Mark e-mailed—right after he clicked to order a copy of the bootleg DVD.

It's me, Wendy, she wrote back a few minutes later.

OMG where r u fuck!?

Soon after the launch of YouTube in oh-five, *The Strays Summer Christmas Special* was posted in three segments. Within two days, a hundred and fifty thousand people had watched it. A million views within a year. Irwin Gerund saw a clip posted on a blog he pilfered jokes from and wrote a squib on his ShepherdMedia.com entertainment blog, and all the Shepherd Media papers picked up the post in print and online with links to YouTube. A million more watched.

41

Carrying Essa's baby girl blanketed and asleep in the same kind of cardboard box the California Institution for Women used to store her belongings, Wendy waited under a hot sun outside the gates for her taxi to arrive. This time she wouldn't be going back into Chino, the closest suburb, where she'd been sleeping in a fifties roadside motel while the paperwork settled guardianship. Blue sky above her, and the faintest quiffs of cloud over the peaks of the mountains along the distant horizon—the air across Wendy's face sparkled with desert dust. Now that all the paperwork was signed and baby Essa Mole Deattur Auer was in her hands, Wendy had half a mind to go back to the manor and start a new drawing, pick up right where she left off—really, she was that close to coming home. After all, it was only August; two months ago she thought she was going to win the Reuben and watch her cartoon premiere on network television.

Straight to LAX, she told the driver. The baby woke up in the cab and wept redfaced and shaking until Wendy figured out she was hungry for a bottle of formula. At the airport she bought a one-way ticket for a coach seat to Canada. The flight to Victoria was mired by turbulence and the customs official took a long time deciding. But once through, that little city she grew up in was still there on the foot of the big island off the west coast, yes, smack where she left the city six years before. All the same people, every house, the roofshingles, not a dog missing, not even very many new books on the shelves in the library.

Before Essa was captain of her high school's volleyball team, before she auditioned for an all-girls' college production of *Death of a Salesman*, even before she skinned her knees or learned to crawl, when she was still a baby with a round tummy and inexplicable needs, but so simple they seemed obvious and yet impossible to fathom, cyclical needs, and desperate: Was she hungry? Was she tired? Was she gassy? No? Then was she in need of a diaper change? Oh my god, maybe she *was* hungry? The rash, the wrinkles on her face, the diaper's elastic imprinted in the thighs, it exhausted Wendy with worry, thrust into motherhood. Baby Essa depended on the tenderness and affection Wendy supplied. Every squirm and squawk for love. Growing was her purpose. Wendy would rather harm come to her than the baby. Essa's babyface was more beautiful, soft, and better smelling than anything Wendy had ever seen or could imagine on this earth.

She took up lodgings in a top-floor apartment on Dallas Road, at the very bottom of the island, across from the beach overlooking the sea that separated her home in Canada and her real home, America. And because she was the single mother of an adopted child, Wendy had little time or energy to draw. She was lucky the cheques her syndicate sent twice a year were substantial. She improvised the rest of her income. Plus the added problem, she could not breastfeed. The baby Essa desperately wanted to breastfeed. She mouthed like a fish and swallowed air and scooped her arms through the air looking for Wendy's breasts and when she found one, aimed her head straight for it like a kamikaze pilot and latched there. If Wendy let her suck, the baby groaned and squealed and flailed her limbs, squeezing the milkless nipples between her gums until Wendy yelped and had to pry the girl off using the extra leverage of a foam swimming paddle. There was nothing pacifying about the baby's suck. She sucked for that one keen nourishment, breastmilk, and Wendy adored the baby for her perseverance. The baby could latch through a sweater, was how desperately she wanted breastmilk. Hang there from the breast, swinging from her latch like a piece of cave art. The more she wanted Wendy's breast, the less she took to her bottle of formula. And it agonized Wendy to see the baby resist formula. When she heard the baby cry, a place in her lower chest ached like an empty crib. One day she went through the whole operation of loading Essa into the carseat screaming and drove to the doctor's office. She told the pediatrician about the ache in her belly when the baby cried and they weighed the baby and saw right away she was not gaining weight. At six weeks old the baby must be *this* heavy, the doctor said and pointed to a chart, and she is only as heavy as *that*. I got no milk, Doc, Wendy said. She won't eat the formula.

You need milk, the doctor said and leaned over his lap and started to scribble on a prescription pad. Here, go to this address and pick up some breastmilk.

The British Columbia Breastmilk Cooperative was an adhoc sort of thing based out of a yellow brick bungalow in Victoria's valley neighbourhood of Fernwood, across the street from a physical rehabilitation clinic and another clinic for hearing loss and speech therapy. The park nearby had a baseball diamond and tennis courts.

On the drive there with baby Essa, Wendy passed by what looked like an old folks' home but that billed itself on a large sign as a Christian walk-in clinic for psychiatric care for the homeless, or something like that, and under that a name caught her eye: *Dr. L. Pazder.*

STRAYS

The Anawim House was a Siamese twin of Victorian homes conjoined on a double lot. If an apartment had shot up from the rooftop, the resemblance to No Manors would be more obvious. The Anawim was far better maintained. It was the combination of the oversized house and the residents she saw inside that did it: Addicts in rehab, psych-ward halfway patients. Shufflers incapable of so much as lifting their feet off the ground. Time's tragic freeloaders. Luggage under their eyes. Parched brows, cracked as the desert floor in Death Valley.

Here was where Dr. Lawrence Pazder first treated Michelle Smith for satanic ritual abuse repressed-memory syndrome, of which she was the first and only example, and where it appeared he ended up working again, almost a decade later, now in a self-imposed exile from the reputation he'd gained and lost for himself as the leading expert of a false psychiatric diagnosis. The doctor's return to Victoria came after a California journalist published an article in the *SF Bay Guardian* thoroughly debunking Pazder's theories of repressed-memory and satanic abuse. *Is Satanic Abuse a Hoax?* read the headline. The writer found no evidence of anything like what happened in his memoir *Michelle Remembers* ever happening in real life, none of the satanic assaults, the murders, the live burial. Michelle's own family refused to corroborate a single shred of what the memoir recounted. The mainstream news quickly jumped on the story and the career of Dr. Pazder fell apart in a matter of days.

When calls to appear as an expert witness for the prosecution in child sexual abuse trials came to a dead halt, home awaited Dr. Pazder. News programs ran stories on the reversal of court decisions, of children confessing it was all made up, that doctors and police seeded their questions with the answers they wanted to hear, and former teachers and daycare workers were being exonerated of charges they were satanic pedophiles, being freed from jail with apology, and the entire decade of satanic fears began to fade away.

At last after all these years, welcome, welcome to Anawim, come in. Of course I remember who you are, you're the one … from all your letters, said Dr. Lawrence Pazder, who seemed not at all perturbed by the fact he never replied and instead immediately made her feel special and scheduled. Pazder had a full head of snow-white hair parted to the right, and a clownish nose that made his smile seem more innocent than it probably was. It occurred to her that Punk Anderson in *Dallas* looked a lot like Dr. Pazder, and Punk was a duplicitous old school pawn in larger culture wars.

Wendy was to learn that Pazder spoke in one manner in the hallways of Anawim House and another way during sessions. When he spoke in public, you could see the Catholicism beaming out of his eyes and carrying his every word from his mouth with the spirit of forgiveness, openness, empathy, guileless gullibility, and absolute faith in the literal truth of magical realms. But once the door closed he went neutral and the professional psychiatrist came out. The godly glow faded to a sober, balanced, and empty aesthetic. A confidence took over that relied on systems of notebooks, charts, metrics, research. And also applied with this same objectivity, Pazder employed African spirit bobs, harmonic crystals, and rare earth magnets.

Their second session, Pazder told her after he blew his nose into a Kleenex that he wanted to put her under hypnosis. How exciting. He dimmed the lights. Brought out a beaded African charm. He put his hands on his lap and pressed the charm into the leg of his pants. The mind's a *mysterious* organ, Pazder said, sometimes our puppeteer sometimes our protector. Meat capable of keeping its own secrets. Denial, what a strangely human dilemma that animals live with and with no problem but which causes us shame, misery, and ruin. Our problem, we contain multitudes. Sometimes we experience things that are so powerful, so traumatic, the brain works for years to repress the memory. But the memories stay, just hidden. And the power of those repressed memories can still control the conscious self. The blind spot in our sense of our self is this repressed truth. That is the repressed memory of which I study. Hypnosis can disarm the patient, unlock the cellar door, and give you the safety to remember again what's under the stairs of yourself, and identify the pain that's causing the blind spot.

Let's do it, she said.

His pendulous African charm didn't do what she hoped it would swing by swing and put her into a weird cross-eyed zone of the unlit unconsciousness, dripping drool like Jonjay used to, and tapped into the deeper caves of herself. But it wasn't a general anaesthetic of the mind the way she expected it would be, with time missing. She remembered everything lucidly. When Pazder told her she was under, basically she pretended she was. *You are asleep. You are sinking. Sinking into deep. Deep memories. Deep memories. Memories. Memories of your childhood. Of your mom, Mom. Memories of a man. Man. Man. Do you see a Man in your deep memories, Wendy?*

Yes. Yes, I do.

What does he look like?

She told him the same stories she'd told herself all her life about a time her mother pointed to the man on the television introducing a story called *The Honest Man.* A deep memory of pressing her hands to the glass of the television. To Father. Cover his face with my hands. Maybe four years old. Listened to him speak with my ear against the screen. *There are times when the honest man is surrounded by dishonest men, and dishonest women, beautiful dishonest women. Now, how honest can an honest man be? That you shall soon see …*

And another deep memory, of a guided tour of a hydroelectric dam. A massive concrete facility not far from the city. Five years old. Maybe six. Four. Reagan gave her a box of chocolates. Image of Reagan pointing to a massive electric generator as she ate the chocolates. Sitting on his lap, definitely Reagan. Wendy provided the story in fragments over a period of a few weeks, to please Pazder's impression that she was hypnotized.

Essa was a dutiful baby and slept through most sessions. Sometimes she giggled at the nasal falsetto of Pazder's voice.

He had a trick, too. He told her that when he counted down to one and snapped his fingers she would wake up, no longer hypnotized, and remember everything of what they talked about. Ten. Nine. She would wake up feeling refreshed and alert. Eight. And when you wake up, Pazder said, you will remember *everything* you told me. Seven. You will remember all the memories you told me under hypnosis. Six. And the memories will not scare you … *One.*

The trick was that once the hypnosis session was in the past, then she had to question the feeling she had *during* the hypnosis that she *wasn't* under hypnosis, because the feeling might just be because Dr. Pazder *told* her to remember, meaning *maybe* he *did* draw out her deep memories, and what she said under hypnosis *was true* and Reagan *was* her father.

You say he *admitted* he was your father when you met him … ? said Dr. Pazder as he wrote his notes.

However much he placated his patient with questions that delved into memories of illegitimacy, she noticed he made sure to drop one or two questions every session that probed the story of Hick's death from AIDS and of the wake. Perhaps Dr. Pazder preferred to delve into more popular memories. She struggled under hypnosis not to remember.

He asked her to look closer at that *actual* zone of her repressed memory, the *recent* past. You *don't* remember. *Because* the times were intense, Wendy, Dr. Pazder said. Issue nine, Wendy, issue *nine*, Wendy, Dr. Pazder said in the drone he used. What happened? Do you remember? He wanted carnal truths. What Pazder called *those homosexual comics* featuring Wendy at the flesh-eating ceremony. *Issue nine.*

But unlike Michelle, who made up her demonic stories, Wendy flatly denied the events in issue nine.

Why are you here, Wendy? Dr. Pazder asked. What is it you hope to learn about yourself? After all these years begging for therapy, you refuse to open up.

Have you *read* issue nine? Wendy asked in her best attempt at staying hypnotized.

I … no, I haven't, said Pazder. I want you. To tell me. What you. Remember.

Wendy began to feel something awful happening between them. It was palpable how much they both wanted, doctor and patient, for therapy to somehow vindicate the reputations they each had built up in the eighties. It wasn't about Reagan anymore, it was about what this collabora- tion could do. Through the auspices of a revelatory memory, published as medical breakthrough, they both hoped the poles of public opinion would reverse. Problem was, they sought a different repressed memory. For as much as Wendy loved to believe in the unbelievable when it suited her, and deny the truth when it suited her, so did Pazder, who was attracted to the false promise of Wendy's scandal. Doubt, for the first time shedding light on denial. Doubt about her own self-myth—at last! A doctor had finally succeeded through incompetence in breaking her of the conviction that Reagan was her father. Face to face with her ideal therapist and seeing the complete denial of his desires, she all of a sudden felt embarrassed by hers. Doubt flooded in where her denial was strongest and suddenly she felt this intense pressure to get up and leave the doctor's office and never return. Pazder could not help but repeat his mistake and try to do for Wendy what he had done for Michelle's fantasies: use her to prove his faulty theories right.

Pazder should have asked her more questions about Jonjay. He should have asked her to remember everything about Jonjay, the artist who knew *The History of the Secret Origins of the Universe*, an art that, at least so far as we could figure, showed you how to dodge death.

42

STRAYS

Essa possessed a brassy, charismatic influence over Wendy from the start. Her love for the child was bone-deep and it was easy to convince herself she had been the one pregnant and in labour. It felt like it. She didn't know when the right time was to say something, so she never quite got around to telling Essa that her real mother was incarcerated in California. No more California—the baby was her world now. Now her world was brand new, softer than suede, with big brown eyes and light brown skin, ravenous and in charge.

Once she was weaned, Essa's diet consisted primarily of sweets. She loved treats and loathed real food. In a social situation she would throw a tantrum if anyone other than Wendy so much as spoke to her. Then in a remarkable adjustment she became a leader on the playground in gradeschool, a straight-A brown-noser, and obsessed with boys. Essa's big personality divided her classmates into friends and foes. Boys and girls vied for her attention or bullied her, there was no in-between.

Essa at four popped the lid off the maple syrup and gulped the bottle, ran naked around the house for hours and hours, and passed out into such a deep near-coma sleep Wendy called an ambulance.

Essa at five asked her mom, Does the actors get money for every time they're on TV?

Essa at nine wrote and directed her own play based on E.C. Segar's *Popeye* that she performed every recess for a week at her elementary school with an all-boy cast, except for herself in the role of Olive Oyl.

Essa at the age of eleven read all the *Brenda Ransom* novels in the bestselling series by the young adult author Susanna L. Massari. *Brenda Ransom Solves the Psycho Puzzle*, *Brenda Ransom Solves the Teen Cult Conspiracy*, and so on, hugely popular among her peers, the last generation of high school girls to not have e-mail addresses. Never occurred to Wendy to investigate the background of the reclusive author who had her daughter so obsessed. Brenda Ransom was an independently minded, blue-haired seventeen-year-old Californian who ran circles around her teachers, and stumbled into mystery after mystery. Essa began to model herself after the heroine: she dressed and acted like Brenda Ransom, repeating her credos—*Freedom has no shame! You snooze, you lose!* and so on—and set about turning her bedroom into an imaginary detective agency.

Essa was a sullen, introverted daughter who rarely spoke at home except to drolly mock her mother's absent-minded habits and neurotic attitudes, but at the same time she was an outgoing and vivacious friend or rival in the halls of high school and nearby shopping malls. Then one evening near the end of grade eleven, when the cherry blossoms were out and kites took to the sky, she asked her mother if Tom could come for dinner. Tom was her first serious boyfriend. The other eleven ex-boyfriends were secrets Wendy never knew about. So this was kind of a big deal to Essa. Asking if he could come for dinner was a signal she was *serious*. Or maybe even *in love*. Could her mother handle that? Wendy said a dinner guest was fine by her, and steeled herself. She was going to make mushroom risotto and eyeball this so-called boyfriend right down to the DNA. After all, this was the year 2001, and advancements in the art of diagnosing a faker had improved greatly since Wendy was her daughter's age.

In the mid-nineties, when Essa was old enough to entertain herself for hours at a stretch, Wendy had found time to draw comics again. A good thing, too, because around then the trickle of royalties she counted on to pay bills was down to a drip—sometimes a half-year cheque arrived for as little as three cents. It meant a mother-daughter roadtrip to the Bay was required so Wendy could crack the lock on her self-storage unit and begin the task of separating out the rarities from the bulk of stuff, deciding what to keep, what to protect, and what to sell. Tens of thousands of dollars' worth of original drawings, rare books, comics, toys, and other memorabilia. She estimated her haul would cover expenses for two or three years. Not knowing what to do with the six film canisters containing the 35 mm reels for the final cut to *The Strays Summer Christmas Special* made the thought of them stacked there in the icebox belted to the seat next to Essa distract her for the whole drive home. The film canisters sat on the floor of her bedroom closet for the rest of Essa's summer vacation, gleaming in the dark like the armour scales off a dragon. That fall, when eBay launched, Wendy saw her opportunity.

The self-storage unit proved to be worth a great deal more than she originally figured, largely thanks to Hick Elmdales's collection of near-priceless books. A decade later, she was still living off the shelves of No Manors.

It was Essa who convinced her to set up a website where she could post the comics she'd been drawing in her spare time. Pretty soon she was posting up to six strips a month, and in a matter of months she started to get hundreds of thousands of unique daily views, though she didn't know it. She was largely unaware of the extent of her readership or of the software that would count visits to her site. Her sense of her website's popularity came from the number of orders for *Orphans* merchandise (mugs, shirts, etcetera) she got through an online retailer she linked to, and that accounted for up to five thousand dollars a month, not bad. Everything about comics she used to do over the phone with Gabby and through contracts signed in septiplicate and original artwork shipped UPS was now done inside her home computer, with the help of her daughter in exchange for pocket cash. All the editing, printing, publishing was done in her drawing studio. She had no need for a travelling strip salesman to push her work on moribund newspapers, or an editor to plan her life, let alone a syndicate when she could lease a domain name for so cheap and design a page to present her comics exactly how she wanted them to look. Once in a while an editor at a syndicate would e-mail her with a friendly, *Hey, I'm a huge fan of Orphans—so funny! If you're ever interested in talking about the ins and outs and benefits of syndication, I'd love to tell you more. You're making one of my favourite online comics.*

Orphans didn't have a prescribed set of characters or concepts; instead it presented Wendy's most imaginative and unconnected short stories of no more than thirty pages, but more commonly three or four pages— weird, often disturbing comics with an autobiographical tinge. One early story depicts the inhabitants of the last land mass remaining on Earth after the big ice melt. The characters live in shanty homes on stilts to protect them from the tides that engulf most of their island every tide—it's not exactly funny material, but the characters are charming.

In another storyline, a gang of loitering teens behind a 7-Eleven pass the time playing games that are reminiscent of the ones we used to play at No Manors (comics that use wordplay for titles; Golden Era characters not in gloves; the result if two superheroes had children). There are moments of enlightened dialogue that make you laugh in admiration and poignant stories of heartfelt realism. There's an overarching sense of loneliness and guilt, or shame.

Not that the digital buzzer to Wendy's penthouse suite sounded in the least like the electric one at the front door of No Manors, but as soon as we arrived in the lobby, a wave of emotions rolled through us, transforming every sound, smell, and sight into vivid associations of our shared past. All of a sudden our reunion here in Victoria was conjuring powerful auditory hallucinations that were in effect like time travel, taking us from the year 2006 to the year 1981 when our identities were conceived.

We embraced, wept with nostalgia, and looked each other over. She blamed her grey hairs on a lack of sleep. If anything she'd lost weight. Her hips stuck out in the tight jeans and so did her breasts in the sweater, her arms were thin, and her legs tapered to tiny ankles, but maybe she was pretty and it was we who were expecting the girl who was always so attractive for going out of her way to make a clown of her fashion sense. Twenty years later and her neck craned out over her rolled shoulders, a returning-to-fetal posture that was the sure mark of a dedicated cartoonist. Permanent spinal deformation. She asked if we wanted anything to drink and brought us beer and homemade coconut Nanaimo bars (another flashback, almost as potent as flesh).

Wendy was sorry to learn Mark had been living with HIV after receiving a blood transfusion in the mid-nineties, and that Patrick was bankrupt and once again forced to live off the avails of the laundry hamper, and that she had missed Twyla's wedding to Blair Slobodchikoff in Golden Gate Park and she was just as sorry to hear about their divorce.

Discovering Blair was a compulsive philanderer ended the marriage after sixteen months, but Twyla remarried two years later. With this second guy she had a seven-year-old Sims video game prodigy named Jeff with whom they lived in Berkeley and she and her husband both worked as creative heads of businesses in the local animation industry surrounding Pixar.

We congratulated ourselves on the three point three (at last count) million views *The Strays Summer Christmas Special* had on YouTube, and remarked on the odd route it had taken to find its viewers. We told her about the offer we had to publish a kind of collective memoir of our experiences living at No Manors and that we hoped it would be a portrait of her especially, and, knowing us, she gave her approval. And she told us the story of her daughter, Essa.

After we were caught up on life, a silence fell upon us that seemed to beg a question. Although we didn't know the words to use to ask, they were hanging in the air. Wendy could sense it, she knew what we wanted to know and how to articulate the answer. She confessed something to us that afternoon. She said she was moved to tell us because we had come all this way to see her after almost twenty years, and she felt we deserved to know something of the truth after all this time.

I knew Frank wasn't on the level, she said. First time I met him at Coppola's restaurant with Gabby, I knew he was crooked. Just to see him. His face was all wrong. The toupée was nothing. His face was split down the middle, like a fault line running vertically down the middle of his face, so that one eye was squinted up a little higher than the other. In her memory, his nose looked broken to the left. The fault line split his smile in half to form more of a swaggery snarl. I was turned on just thinking about his secrets. When he asked me to open all those bank accounts at Solus, I played along. I played along when he took me on a trip to Central America to meet with factory managers and deposit large amounts of cash into offshore accounts. I played dumb. Because I loved him, I pretended not to notice. I was hooked. But I saw everything and I knew. His lie turned me on. What else could it be that drew me to him? I loved him. And I loved being so close to his secret. I could taste the briny deep of his secrets on his skin even after his shower. I knew his secrets better than he did. I really think he was in denial about his crimes. I wanted to see what would happen to us, if he was smart enough to get away with it. He never said a word to me about his choices but it didn't matter, I knew before I signed with him what he was. He was bad and I was so tired of chasing good. Then one day I forced him to admit it. I had to hear him say it. I don't know why. I guess because I kept having these dreams of what my life would be like if I went to Chris Quiltain and the DA and spat out everything I knew. I wanted to test Frank. And I remember, he said he would tell me, but he couldn't say over the phone, so he would write it down. We were on the plane to D.C. to appear before the fucking subcommittee, and he wrote it on a piece of paper from my sketchbook:

I paid off Kravis to buy some stock. That's it. One time.

Another lie. But she even found something sweet in the lie, it was a white lie, a token of the truth, like a pair of earrings for his lover, and Wendy could wear this lie with pride.

That's okay, she told him and kissed his forehead. I understand.

She told us that after she read the note, Frank took it back from her and instead of tearing it to pieces he stuffed it in his mouth, chewed and swallowed it. What was I supposed to do? she said. I just took a deep breath and put my hands on his face and kissed him. I knew he wouldn't tell me the truth. How could he? It would put us both in greater danger. And what did it matter? I loved the liar. But then I caught him making out with Manila Convención at the awards, and that was it, I'd had enough. I was shattered.

It's just you and your daughter here? we asked.

Someone else buzzed me a while ago, she said in an all-new tone of voice, drained of any apparent humour as she thought about it. Frank showed up at my old apartment unannounced five years ago, back in the summer of 2001. The same evening my daughter Essa had invited her boyfriend over for dinner.

Students of relativity: Time's slowest minute can be found in prison. Time served in California's minimum-security facility bore down on Frank Fleecen's physical wellbeing with not as much sheer force as on his mental health, which got a pounding. It didn't show but he suffered greatly from the deprivation. His mental health was doubled over sobbing. Meanwhile his external self was a goddamn Doric column showing only a few chips and cracks in the face of it. He was used to making his own schedule and living by his own routine, eating what he wanted to and when, with three or four phones on the go at all times and dozens of tasks to delegate. The part of him that needed his desk and a cellular phone on his hip, who needed to operate at a racehorse's pace for twelve-fifteen hours a day or go mad, that part of him repented with excruciatingly swift deliverance.

Then she told us the strange story of the day he buzzed from the lobby of her building unannounced. The Frank she opened her door to was pretty much the same except for one very significant change—he was bald. Ditched the toupée. She caught her jaw dropping. His dome was immaculate. The naked pate exposed more than skull: everything about his face changed. Without a comical distraction above, the bare scalp brought out the squareness in his jawline and the penetrating lustre in his almost black eyes. And yet he was the same Frank, hairpiece or no—brooding Frank, with all the energy she remembered falling in love with against her better judgment. That unwavering stare of his that drilled straight through your pupils, right through your brain and out the other side of your head, not even looking at you but seeing your *wants*—she liked that. How he would hold your eyes with his gaze and talk until you said yes. She remembered the once most powerful man on Wall Street. How could she forget? For years she would be listening to some innocuous radio program in the afternoon and the name Frank Fleecen would come up, and sometimes even her old name, in reference to some recent crime or boondoggle perpetrated upon an unsuspecting innocent public.

Now Frank wore a tailored jacket over a white turtleneck that looked to be made of fine silk. His pants fell properly. He wore braided leather sandals. This surprised her, too, and the pedicure. This was the man she used to remind to take showers. He seemed to be *literally* a cleaner businessman now. She wasn't sure what to make of him, whether he meant to present himself as a New Age guru in this new outfit, or a movie director, maybe a mobster, or a penitent.

Bad timing, she said. My daughter's boyfriend is coming for dinner. I'm making risotto.

I don't need to stay long.

The hair, she said.

Oh. Yes, I went *bald*.

She took him to her drawing studio where *Orphans* sketches were strewn around a Cintiq tablet she used to polish, colour, and sometimes draw. How was your vacation?

Worst twenty months of my life. Is that coffee?

Yes, she said and fixed him a cup in her studio's mini-espresso machine, and they sat down at the table with their mugs both steaming and a plate of sweet biscuits she bought at a health food store.

Coffee is the Mona Lisa of drinks, said Wendy in an effort to make a toast.

What have you done for money all this time?

She just laughed at the word coming out of his mouth already. Well, she said and rubbed her wrist back and forth. First thing I did, I sold the Rolex. That's right. Ten thousand dollars goes a long way.

Cost *me* fifty …

Yeah, well, I also sell *Strays* and *Biz Aziz* and *Pan* originals. I had a trove of colour sketches Hick made of Peter Pan and Captain Hook and all the others, now I'm down to two or three, that's it. All sorts of comics memorabilia. I used to post a list in the comic trade magazines, and later I switched to eBay. Lots of collectors in Japan. There was my record collection worth a mint, and rare toys and other original artworks, too. That's what I do. I sell stuff. Weren't you banned for life from banking?

Me? Yes, said Frank. I went straight into another prison. The doctor diagnosed me with a popular form of prostate cancer. I got hit with a nasty metastasized tumour. Instead of getting back even a shred of my previous life, I left prison and spent the next year and a half in and out of chemotherapy, round after round until my immune system was basically zapped to death.

I had no idea.

I saw scans of the tumour, Frank said. Like something from an H.P. Lovecraft story. Devastated me beyond words. Worse than prison. You'd think what could be more devastating than hearing a judge sentence you to five years. I was ruined by this cancer news. The idea of it growing inside me, just the idea almost killed me. My nerves were shot. My gut was in knots. My brain, fried. I couldn't count my own fingers. It was during this hell that I became acquainted with the best and worst of hospital beds, bedrooms, bedpans, and the true scope and scale of the American medical system and not to mention health care's influence over the economy. One revelation I had early on at Hexen was the sheer size of U.S. pension funds. And when I brought those pension funds into the high-yield market my leverage was outrageous. I was the unstoppable kingmaker. The only way to stop me was to ban me for life. So all of a sudden I saw how cancer research was the same. I'm taking experimental drugs and realizing cancer research is just like a hedge fund or private equity firm. I was terrified of being out of control of my own disease, of putting my investment in someone else's hands. I'm used to being the one in charge. It wasn't up to me if I succeeded in beating cancer, it was up to my doctors and the health care system. I saw that I was the unwitting customer of my own junk bonds, investing in cancer cures and rounds of treatments that I didn't get enough time to research. I wondered what I should do if I lived. I decided I wanted to invest in my own cure. Wendy, that's what I do now. I got cancer and I *beat* cancer and now I invest in medical research looking for the cure.

How did you beat cancer? Wendy asked.

Well, one thing I did outside the therapy was I changed my diet. I used to eat three hotdogs a day and two hamburgers. Now I eat a ninety percent Ayurvedic diet and exercise at least two hours daily. I eat no red meat. No saturated fats. No processed foods of any kind. No more candy. As little modified corn as possible. Lots of steamed broccoli. Fresh fish. Kale. I published a cookbook last year. *An Appetite for Life.* I'll give you a copy. The data on Ayurvedic scores high. See, now I use Jonjay's formula to find the cure for cancer.

His formula … , she had almost forgotten about Jonjay's secret. What was it called?

Cancer is a panicked guess, too, Frank said. Like an evil Pac-Man, cancer eats your health and energy trying to find ways to survive against the guards of the body's maze. I think this is what Jonjay had been using his formula for all along. When I was testing it against the market, he was using it as a cure for death.

He finished his coffee and remarked on what he described as the narcotic beauty of the view through the picture window that took up the entire south-facing wall of her studio and continued on into the living room. She sat across from this view on her drawing chair, and leaned on a stack of graphic novels. The ocean, the Olympic Peninsula on the horizon, the orange and white lights on the shores of Port Angeles, the waters changing colours, slate, cyan, blueberry, and the winds through the trees across the street, yes, you could say yes to this, too.

Ever see whales?

Oh sure, grey ones, humpbacks, orcas. And on July Fourth I watch the fireworks go off across the water.

I see that for your exile you chose paradise.

I didn't *choose* exile, she reminded him. And I was born here. The beauty is lost on me.

Mom? Are you home? Hey, Mom, can I borrow— Oh hi, who's *this*?

Frank stood and flattened his pants.

This is Frank, an old friend from San Francisco. Frank, this is my daughter, Essa.

They shook hands with genuine interest in each other, and then Essa stepped back and studied Frank with an ambivalence not typical of this teen with a generally unskeptical interest in men. But in this cute reticence, she showed she was maybe attracted to the latent father figure in his composure.

Frank was about to tell me why he's in Victoria, Wendy said. Do you want to stay and hear Frank's story?

Okay, said Essa with some uncertainty and sat on the free chair in the corner.

Frank happens to be a genius. You don't meet a genius every day, do you? Go ahead, Frank. Tell us what brought you here.

My health, he said. My good health.

He's going to cure cancer, said Wendy.

Really?

You know, Essa, you have your mother's eyes. You're a lucky girl to have such a talented mom.

When does your boyfriend get here? Wendy said.

His name is *Tom* and not for another half-hour, Essa said and then asked if she could borrow her mom's favourite Rolex to wear tonight and Wendy blushed hard at Frank and said yes, she could, and to take a sweet biscuit with her.

Essa muttered, Is *he* staying for dinner?

His name is *Frank* and yes.

Mom. Essa had her fingers in her mouth, her eyes were fiery slits.

I'd love to stay, I mean, if it's no trouble, said Frank to Essa.

No trouble at all, Wendy answered.

Mom. Oh my god. Essa stomped away growling and clawing the walls as she ran down the hall to her room.

After the bedroom door slammed shut, Wendy turned to Frank and said, I don't know what to do with her. She's at that age when everything I say in front of strangers blows her cool. But if she can have her *new boyfriend* over for dinner, I can very well have an *old* one.

Who is ... her father?

Nobody I know. I keep meaning to tell her I'm not her real mom, but she still doesn't know I adopted her.

Oh. But you two look so much alike ...

Every time I look at her I still see the sweet baby who slept on my chest and cried so much for the breastmilk my boobs couldn't deliver. When I adopted her the prison doctors called her a crack baby, but I never saw signs, except maybe clairvoyancy. She got more As in school than I ever did. Knows how to walk the tightrope. Can juggle. Card tricks, ballet, modern improvised dance choreographer. Volleyball. Loves to ski. Never had school ski trips in my day. Piano, guitar. Helps her friends make all their Halloween costumes. Ballet at least comes in handy later in life, I'm told.

Sounds like your daughter wants to join a circus.

More like the circus wants to join *her*. Writes and performs skits with friends. Memorizes lines from *Spin City*. Reads a magazine called *Beer Frame*. Knows all the songs on *The Simpsons*. She's a Broadway musical in the form of a twenty-first-century child. I can't keep up. She told me he's mature for his age.

Who?

Her *boyfriend*. A high school dropout apparently now of college age loafing around the city picking up sophomore chicks. Sounds real mature.

When Tom arrived an hour later, Essa ran to answer screaming *I'll get it!* Wendy's daughter and the boy then stood at the door for what felt to Wendy like many minutes too long talking and being quiet probably kissing before they presented themselves to her and Frank in the living room.

Mom, this is Tom, Essa said. This is …

Frank stood up and shook the young man's hand and introduced himself.

Hey, man, how's it going? said Tom in a bongwater drawl. He brushed his hair out of his eyes and turned to Wendy and said, Hiya, Miss Auer. Thanks for having me over. I'm a big fan of your eBay site. I was just saying to Essa I can't believe how much cool shit you've got.

Essa blushed and Wendy said she hoped he liked mushroom risotto because that's what they were having.

He said, Never heard of it but I bet I'll love it.

Tom was fair haired, strong boned, he had an imperial nose, full lips, a dimple on his chin, and whiskers that did not amount to a beard. Over one shoulder he carried a canvas pack loaded to the seams as though he'd just returned from distant travels. With his dark tan, he could pass for a bleach-blond Aladdin. Wendy thought it was cute Essa's boyfriend looked like the kind she used to crush on back when she was that age. A flavourful teen boy whose hair was all his own and whose eyes shone clear with innocent curiosity. Essa was safe with this boy; she had nothing to be afraid of from this darling adolescent, she thought. A respectably flaky youngster for her daughter to date, she decided.

Hi, Tom, Wendy said brightly. Nice to finally meet you. Essa raves.

Your daughter's the coolest girl, Tom said.

You don't have to say that, Tom.

Mom. Essa rolled her eyes. His name is *John.*

What? All this time I've been hearing *Tom.* Okay. Okay, sorry, John.

Hey, no worries. Thanks for having me over for dinner. I'm starving.

Essa asked if she and John could hang out in her room before dinner and Wendy said yes if they kept the door open.

Oh my god, said Essa on her way out. She did not keep the door open. The volume went up on her stereo to drown out their voices.

Frank commented that they made a cute couple, didn't they, and Wendy shed a tear that stuck to the side of her eye. What's the matter? Frank said.

Nothing. Just … I miss sex.

He seems androgynous enough.

He seems real fine.

Had no idea you raised a daughter. She's got an epic personality, just like you.

Just as Frank placed his hand on Wendy's face, Essa came back out to the living room and stood in front of them and announced that John was staying the night. He didn't have any place else to go.

No way, he isn't staying here, Wendy said and took a step away from Frank. You're fifteen. You can't have a boy sleep over.

Jesus, Mom. What do you think I am, a child?

Don't start with me, not right now. Let's have a nice dinner together. We can talk about this later.

Later? Like when? He needs a place to sleep. He'll sleep on the couch.

Go tell your friend Tom or John to wash his grubby hands and come to the table. We're eating soon.

I'm only eating if he stays the night, Essa said.

Fine then, dinner's cancelled.

You're just being mean for no reason. He has nowhere else to *go*.

You're my daughter and I'm telling you it's inappropriate.

I'm *not* your daughter! Essa screamed at Wendy. What do you think, I don't know how to use the Internet? Don't you think I'd ever wonder why my middle names are Mole and Deattur? My real mother is *in prison for life*.

Oh my god, Wendy said. Oh my god, I'm sorry. It's true. I wanted to tell you, but how, but when? I gave you those names so you would always know. I promise. Why else would I give you her whole name? So you'd know.

But how did you—? When did—? I don't—

Mother and daughter both let out sobs now, and then Essa turned and ran from the room groaning and locked the door to her bedroom, where Tom or John was waiting. Wendy followed but then after some time gave up her vigil and went back to her studio. She and Frank sat in awkward silence as they listened in vain to the mumbled voices in Essa's bedroom.

That wasn't how I expected it would happen, Wendy said.

I'm sorry, said Frank. I'm so sorry. This is my fault.

They sat and waited. Ten minutes later, when the chill seemed to have left the air, Wendy went back and gently knocked on the bedroom door. Essa? Do you want to come out for dinner and we can talk? Essa?

Wendy knocked. She knocked harder and still got no answer. Essa! Tom? Essa? Are you in there? Frank! Oh no, what's he done to her?

It took two blows, one good kick and a shoulder for Frank to break the door open. Her bed was unmade but no one was on it. The closet was empty. Behind the dresser? There was nowhere else to hide. They were gone.

Where could they be? Wendy searched the same places again and again.

Frank pointed to the open window, They can't have—

Wendy put her head out the window and peered down eight storeys to the empty street below. No, impossible.

Frank came over and stood beside Wendy facing the cool night breeze and the stars. By instinct she put a hand on the back of his bare scalp and squeezed when together they watched the sky as for a single fleeting moment two silhouettes flew in front of the moon.

She's gone, said Wendy. She's gone.